D1526032

QUEEN OF ASH AND IRON

A Novel of Boudica

MELANIE KARSAK

Clockpunk Press

❀ Created with Vellum

NOVEL DECRIPTION

Fᴀᴛᴇᴅ ᴛᴏ ʟᴇᴀᴅ ᴀ ʀᴇʙᴇʟʟɪᴏɴ ᴀɢᴀɪɴsᴛ Rᴏᴍᴇ.
Dᴇsᴛɪɴᴇᴅ ᴛᴏ ʙᴇᴄᴏᴍᴇ ᴀ ʟᴇɢᴇɴᴅ.

From New York Times bestseller Melanie Karsak, author of the Celtic Blood series, comes a gripping historical fantasy series of ancient Britain, Celtic gods, a fated romance, and the warrior queen who defied Rome.

Bʀɪᴛᴀɪɴ, A.D. 47

All at once, everything changes.

The rebellion of the Northern Iceni under King Caturix results in dire consequences for Boudica. Without Aulus Plautius's protection, Boudica must face the new, more severe Roman Governor Scapula. Struggling to make their way in a war-torn landscape, Boudica and Prasutagus persevere, but fate has a way of undoing our best intentions. Catastrophic events take place, undermining everything Boudica had worked so hard to achieve.

As the eagle betrays, the queen of ash and iron rises to protect all that she loves.

Continue the epic tale of the famous warrior queen in *Queen of Ash and Iron: A Novel of Boudica*, book 3 in the *Celtic Rebels* series by *New York Times* bestseller Melanie Karsak.

TW // Abuse, Assault, Sexual Assault

For those who fight for freedom…

NEW YORK TIMES BESTSELLING AUTHOR

✦ MELANIE KARSAK ✦

QUEEN

· OF ·

ASH and IRON

· A NOVEL OF BOUDICA ·

MAP OF THE CELTIC TRIBES A.D. 42

GLOSSARY

THE NORTHERN ICENI

OAK THRONE, SEAT OF THE NORTHERN ICENI

Aesunos, deceased king of the Northern Iceni
Albie, kitchen boy
Aterie, warrior of the Northern Iceni, husband of Finola
Aterie the younger, son of Finola and Aterie
Balfor, housecarl of Oak Throne
Bec, wife of Prince Bran
Belenus, deceased druid adviser of the king of the
Northern Iceni
Bellicus, son of Bran and Bec
Bran, second son of Aesunos
Brenna, first daughter of Aesunos
Cai, leader of Bran's warriors

Can, deceased brother of Saenuvax

Caturin, illegitimate son of Kennocha and Caturix

Children from Oak Throne: Eiwyn, Phelan, and Birgit

Cidna and Nini, cook in Oak Throne and her dog

Conneach, jewel crafter in Oak Throne

Davin, one of Bran's men

Damara, deceased wife of Aesunos

Ector, guard in Oak Throne

Ectorus, one of Bran's men

Egan, deceased father of Aesunos and Saenunos

Foster, Bran's horse

Kennocha, widow in Oak Throne

Mara, illegitimate daughter of Kennocha and Caturix

Moritasgus, stablemaster in Oak Throne

Riona, maid in Oak Throne

Riv, Brenna's horse

Saenuvax, deceased grandfather of Aesunos and
Saenunos

Tadhg, stableboy in Oak Throne

Ula, wisewoman of Oak Throne

Varris, warrior of Oak Throne

Ystradwel and Arddun, helpers to Cidna

FROG'S HOLLOW, VILLAGE IN THE TERRITORY OF THE
NORTHERN ICENI

Cien, sister of Lynet

Children from Frog's Hollow: Tristan, Henna, Aiden, Kenrick, Aife, Connel, Glyn, and Glenndyn

Gaheris, deceased son of Rolan and Lynet

Gwyn, deceased daughter of Rolan and Lynet

Lynet, chieftain of Frog's Hollow

Rolan, deceased husband of Lynet

Villagers from Frog's Hollow: Egan, Becan, Turi, Oran, Guennola, Kentigern

THE GROVE OF ANDRASTE

Dôn, high priestess of the Grove of Andraste

Tatha, priestesses of the Grove of Andraste

HOLK FORT

Arixus, arch druid of Seahenge

Condatis, patron god of Seahenge

Einion, druid of Holk Fort

Pellinor, messenger for King Caturix

Saenunos, deceased brother of Aesunos, chieftain at Holk Fort

Seahenge, holy site of the druids near Holk Fort

Fan and Finola, servants at Holk Fort

SEAHENGE

Becan, druid of the Coritani

Bede, druid of the Coritani

High Priestess Nimica of the Coritani

Ragnell, bard of the Catuvellauni

Uvain, druid of the Catuvellauni

Caturix, deceased king of the Northern Iceni

THE GREATER ICENI

Aden, saddle merchant in Venta

Aeddan, animal minder at the king's roundhouse

Ansgar, chief druid of the Greater Iceni

Antedios, deceased ancient king of the Greater Iceni, father of Prasutagus

Ardra, deceased novice druid of the Greater Iceni

Ariadne, midwife of Venta

Artur, son of Esu

Betha, Ronat, and Newt, kitchen staff in Venta

Boudica, queen of the Greater Iceni

Brita, Boudica's maid

Bruin, husband of Mara

Dice, Boudica's horse

Druda, Boudica's horse

Elidir, messenger of the Greater Iceni

Ember, Sorcha's horse

Enid, deceased mother of Prasutagus

Esu, deceased first wife of Prasutagus

Ewen, leader of Prasutagus's warriors

Galvyn, Prasutagus's housecarl

Ginerva, deceased mother of Esu

Uilleann, Olwen's horse

Isolde, stable hand in Venta

Jorah, guard at the king's roundhouse

Madogh and Broc, spies of King Prasutagus

Mordrat, Greater Iceni warrior

Nella, servant in the house of Prasutagus

Nightshade, Pix's horse

Olwen, second daughter of Boudica and Prasutagus

Pix, warrior companion of Boudica

Prasutagus, king of the Greater Iceni

Raven, Prasutagus's horse

Sorcha, first daughter of Boudica and Prasutagus

Vian, Boudica's secretary

ARMINGHALL HENGE, holy nemeton of the GREATER ICENI

KING'S WOOD, holy seat of the druids of ARMINGHALL HENGE

Tavish, head druid of the King's Wood
Melusine (Bergusia), widow of King Caturix

LONDINIUM HOLDINGS, PRASUTAGUS'S AND BOUDICA'S VILLA IN LONDINIUM

Briganna, maid in Londinium
Ede, cook in Londinium
Eudaf, housecarl in Londinium

RAVEN'S DELL

Brangaine, daughter of Chieftain Divin
Divin, chieftain of Raven's Dell

YARMOUTH, village and harbor in GREATER ICENI TERRITORY

THE ATREBATES

Cadell, messenger for Verica
Druce, messenger for Verica
Tiberius Claudius Cogidubnus, son of Verica
Verica, king of the Atrebates

THE BRIGANTES

Cartimandua, queen of the Brigantes

THE CANTIACI

Anarevitos, deceased king of the Cantiaci

THE CATUVELLAUNI

Adirix, chieftain of the Catuvellauni
Cait, priestess of the Catuvellauni
Caratacus, king of the Catuvellauni, brother of
Togodumnus

Cunobelinus, deceased king of Catuvellauni, and father of Caratacus, Togodumnus, and Imogen

Dagda, druid of the Catuvellauni

Dindraine, high priestess of the Catuvellauni

Epaticcus, deceased brother of Cunobelinus

Imogen, daughter of Cunobelinus, sister of Caratacus and Togodumnus

Phelan, messenger for Togodumnus and Caratacus

Rue, priestess of the Catuvellauni

Togodumnus, king of the Catuvellauni, brother of Caratacus

THE CORITANI

Ruled by three kings: Volisios, Dumnocoveros, and Dumnovellaunus

Fimbul, a chieftain in the lands under Dumnovellaunus

Finan, chieftain of the Coritani

Gwri, druid adviser to King Volisios

Varden, chief man to King Dumnovellaunus

THE DOBUNNI

Corinium Dobunnorum, seat of the Dobunni

Stokeleigh, fort near the Avon Gorge in Dobunni territory

Abandinus, king of the Dobunni

THE PARISII

Brough, seat of the Parisii

Cailleacha, queen of the Parisii
Ruith, king of the Parisii

THE REGNENSES

Noviomagus Reginorum, seat of the Regnenses

Urien, king of the Regnenses

THE TRINOVANTES

Camulodunum, seat of the Trinovantes

Aedd Mawr, exiled king of the Trinovantes
Brecan, chieftain of the Trinovantes
Camulos, patron god of the Trinovantes
Diras, grandson of Aedd Mawr
Flavia, attendant to Queen Lucia
Julia Vitellius, Roman mother of Diras
Lors, chieftain of the Trinovantes
Lucia, wife of King Diras

MAIDEN STONES, HOLY SHRINE TO THE TRIPLE GODDESS

Arian, Brigantia, Dynis, and Mirim, priestesses of
Maiden Stones

AVALLACH (AVALON)

Venetia, high priestess of Avallach

THE DRUIDS OF MONA

Caoilfhionn, arch druid of Mona
Luadine, leader of the Order of Bards
Rian, deceased arch druid of Mona, grandmother of
Caturix, Brenna, Bran, and Boudica
Selwyn, high priestess of Mona

THE ROMANS

Ampelius, secretary to Scapula
Atticus Julius Scato, officer of Rome
Aulus Didius Gallus, third governor of Britannia
Aulus Plautius, first governor of Britannia
Britannia, the Roman name for ancient Britain
Brutus, companion of Aulus Didius Gallus
Darius Volusus, Roman soldier
Decianus Catus, procurator under Governor Paulinus
Drusus Titus Flamininus, officer of Rome
Felix Arixis Isatis, legate of Rome
Felix Varus, Roman soldier in Oak Throne
Gaius Marcellus, praefectus of Londinium
Gaius Suetonius Paulinus, fifth governor of Britannia
Julia Agrippina, Agrippina the younger, mother of Nero
Marcellus Nipius Sorio, senator and adviser to King
Diras
Mithras, Roman god of war and obligation
Narcissus, secretary of Aulus Plautius
Nero Claudius Caesar Augustus Germanicus, fifth
emperor of Rome
Publius Ostorius Scapula, second governor of Britannia
Quintus Severan, soldier stationed at Oak Throne under
Governor Paulinus
Quintus Veranius, fourth governor of Britannia
Vitas, procurator under Governor Scapula

Ocean, the Roman name for the English Channel

Sai, mahout serving the Romans

Silvis Hispanus, Roman soldier

Tiberius Claudius Caesar Augustus Germanicus, fourth emperor of Rome

Titus Carassius, messenger for Aulus Plautius

Vespasian, Roman general in Britannia

Victory, Aulus Plautius's dog

CHAPTER 1

R*ise...*
Rise...
Rise...

Silver moonbeams reflected on the leaves of the oak trees as we raced down the woodland path from Venta toward Oak Throne. Druda was galloping so quickly that his hoofbeats sounded like a beating heart as they briefly touched the forest floor.

I tried to quiet the myriad of voices screaming in my head.

Caturix was dead.

Bran was in danger.

Aulus was gone.

And Scapula had sacked Stonea.

Everything that happened next—every word, every

step—had to be taken with precision, or the Northern Iceni were doomed. If I could get to Bran before the Romans, there was a chance. What I would do, what I would say, I didn't know. I only hoped the doubt Aulus had placed in Scapula's mind held some weight. If I could convince the new Roman governor that my eldest brother had acted alone, maybe, just maybe, I could save my people.

Prasutagus had listened to Melusine's story wide-eyed before turning to me.

"We must go. Scapula will raze Oak Throne if we don't stop him," he told me.

I shook my head. "*I* must go. You must stay in Venta and keep our daughters and the Greater Iceni safe. Because of Caturix, we are all in danger. But Aulus assured me he did what he could to ensure Scapula knew that you and I were with Rome. Now, I must hope Bran and I can do the same."

"But, Boudica," Prasutagus had protested. "What if something happens to you? What if these Romans do not believe you?"

"That's where I come in," Pix said as she sharpened her knife. "Ye don't need to worry, Strawberry King. No one will touch Boudica as long as I'm breathing."

Prasutagus frowned.

"I must go. And quickly. Stonea, Frog's Hollow, Holk

Fort, and all the others… I must stop the Romans before more damage is done."

Reluctantly, Prasutagus nodded and called at once for a party to ride with me.

"Galvyn," he told the housecarl, "sound an alarm across the city. Institute a curfew and rally the guard. Put Venta on alert. I want extra guards on the king's house."

"My king," Galvyn replied, then turned to attend to it.

Prasutagus came to me, gently stroking my hair. "Boudica… Ride safely. May Epona give Druda wings, and may Andraste guard you well."

"And you, Husband. May all the gods watch over you and our little ones," I told him, then headed out.

Mere hours later, after a hard ride, the torches burning on the walls of Oak Throne finally came into view.

The city was safe—for now.

But it was quiet.

Too quiet.

I could feel fear emanating from the place. Word must have reached them.

We rode hard, approaching the walled edifice. The gates were closed and manned. As we approached, I heard a call go through the city that riders had been seen.

Shortly after that, more men appeared.

Just above the gate, I spotted the figure of Bran.

"Greater Iceni," someone called. "It is the Greater Iceni!"

Slowing Druda to a trot, I approached the gate.

"Boudica," Bran called, spotting me. "Open the gates," he called.

Druda huffed hard, shifting his feet and trying to catch his breath as we waited. I patted the horse's neck. "You did well, old friend. You did well. You got us home."

The gates of Oak Throne swung open. Within, I saw that Bran had rallied the guard. Everywhere I looked, I saw swords.

"Boudica," Bran said, rushing to join me.

I dismounted Druda and went to my brother.

My brother pulled me into an embrace. "Do you know?" he whispered in my ear.

"Yes. Where are the Romans? Do you have scouts?"

Bran nodded. "They are marching toward Oak Throne."

I nodded. "Open the gates. Get the men to hang oak branches from the ramparts. And send a party to intercept the Romans."

"But, Boudica, Caturix..."

"Bran, your life and the future of our people depends

on what we do next. We must convince the governor that you had nothing to do with Caturix's rebellion. That it was all Caturix and the Coritani. You must show yourself defying Caturix and aligning with the Greater Iceni. It is the only way."

"Boudica, Volisios has sent word to me. He wants me to rally. Roman forces are already marching on the Coritani."

"Then they will soon become Rome, like the Trinovantes, Atrebates, and Catuvellauni. We must act now unless the rest of the Northern Iceni wants to suffer the same fate. Have you sent word to Holk Fort and the others?"

My brother nodded.

"Good. Now, summon a party. I will also send some of my people hoisting the Greater Iceni's colors. We will intercept the Roman governor and soften his anger."

"I don't understand," Bran said with a frown. "Governor Plautius never—"

"Aulus—Governor Plautius is gone. He returned to Rome. A new governor—Scapula—has come. We have been warned not to tempt his anger. Oh, Bran, Caturix has stuck your head in a noose. We must act quickly to get it out."

Bran nodded then gestured for me to come inside. "I'll rally the men now."

"Get your handsome boy," Pix told Bran. "I'll ride with the others to meet the Romans."

I turned to her. "Oh, Pix. Are you sure?"

She nodded.

"Do not start a war," I told her firmly.

"Nay, Strawberry Queen. I'll smile sweetly and show my mounds to soften the blow," she said, unlacing the top ties on her jerkin so her bosom heaved from the top.

"Pix," I said, shaking my head and laughing lightly. Leave it to her to find humor in disaster.

With that, we headed into the fort. People lingered in their doorways, their silhouettes framed by the light from their fires. Everyone whispered. I caught my name in their words. I paused as we passed the row that led to Kennocha's house.

"Bran, I must see to something," I said. "It will only take a moment. Will you see to my men?"

Bran followed my gaze. By now, my brother would have heard the rumors. He turned and looked at me, meeting my eyes. "Boudica, is it true about the widow and her children?"

I paused a moment. Caturix was dead. To tell Bran before would have betrayed my eldest brother's trust. Now, Kennocha would need Bran to protect her. If Bran knew her children were our blood, our niece and nephew...

I nodded. "Yes."

"Then we must look after her and her children."

How well I knew my brother. "Yes. I'll see you soon," I said, passing off Druda's reins, then made my way down the row.

Soon, I found myself standing outside Kennocha's small house. I knocked on the door. Kennocha appeared a moment later, clutching the shawl around her shoulders in one hand, a dagger in the other.

"Mama," a little voice called from behind her.

"Shh," Kennocha whispered over her shoulder, then looked out. "Boudica!" she said in surprise, then stepped back, gesturing for me to enter.

Within, I found little Mara standing not far from her mother, a worried expression on her face. When she saw me, however, she smiled.

"Didica," she said, then rushed to me and hugged my legs.

I bent and picked her up, kissing her cheek. "Hello, little nightbird. Why are you still awake?"

"The village is scary tonight," she told me.

I nodded slowly. Mara was my mother's granddaughter. Of course she could feel the changes in the air. "Yes, but you don't need to be scared. Ula is here. She will curse the Romans and change our enemies into toads."

At that, Mara laughed loudly, causing another little one to stir in their sleep. Sleeping in their bed was a dark-haired child about the same age as Olwen. Like Mara, the child had curly dark hair.

"There is a piskie in your bed," I told Mara.

She laughed. "That is no piskie. That's my brother, Caturin."

"Ah, Caturin," I said, my stomach swelling with grief that I had not yet let in. Caturix was dead. My eldest brother was dead at the hands of Rome. And there I stood, his child in my arms, another before me. I turned to Kennocha, smiling gently at her. "I am sorry I have not seen you these years, nor met Caturin. My own new little princesses have kept me busy."

She gave me a broken smile. "It's all right. Boudica..."

Kissing Mara on her head, I set her down, then went to the bed and sat beside the child, who stirred in his sleep, sighed heavily, then slept again. How sweet he was, with cheeks as white as milk, his long ebony lashes lying on his cheeks. Ah, dear boy, he would never know his father now...

"Boudica..." Kennocha said again, her voice wavering. "There were rumors in the village. Stonea... Boudica..."

I steeled my heart, then turned and met her gaze.

Kennocha read the look therein.

At once, her eyes grew watery. She set the dagger

down on the table and then sat, her shaking hands going to her mouth.

"Mama, what's wrong?" Mara asked.

Tears trailing down Kennocha's cheeks, she turned and looked back at me. "It is certain?" she asked in a whisper. "He's gone?"

I nodded slowly. "And Stonea with him. The Romans march on Oak Throne."

"Oh, Boudica," she said in a moan, tears rolling down her cheeks. "Should we flee this place? The children…"

"I am here to try to prevent anything more from happening. If I fail here, there is nowhere in Northern Iceni territory that will be safe, and soon, we'll all share Caturix's fate."

"Boudica," Kennocha said. "You should not have come. You risk yourself. The Romans do not want you. The Greater Iceni are allies still."

"Yes. And let's hope that shield is large enough to protect us all. And if not, well…" I smiled down at little Caturin. "Then I will be glad to see Gaheris again."

"Boudica…" Kennocha said sadly.

Bending down, I placed a kiss on Caturin's cheek. "May the gods protect you, my little nephew," I whispered to him, then pulled Mara close, hugging and kissing her. "Watch over your mother for me, little nightbird," I told her. "I must go attend to some work now."

"All right," Mara said, but she was unnerved.

I rose and went to Kennocha, who stood to meet me.

"Boudica," she said sadly.

I embraced her. "Bran will watch over you. He knows. We are all family now. But the children will be safer if no one else knows. Aye, Kennocha, they are our blood, and you are precious to us. We will do everything we can to protect you."

"May the Great Mother watch over you and give you strength," Kennocha told me.

"And you," I said, then let her go and departed.

The moment the door closed behind me, I heard Kennocha weeping.

I knew her pain.

Losing the one you loved, losing them forever, was unbearable.

Gaheris…

Leaving them, I walked in darkness back to the roundhouse.

The pinch of pain I felt over my brother's loss set in. Tears rolled down my cheeks. Caturix and I had rarely understood one another. But since our father's death, everything was different. I mourned the brother I'd grown to know and understand too late. The best way to honor his memory was to protect his children.

I only hoped that the gods were with me.

"Dark Lady Andraste," I whispered into the darkness. "Be with me in the days to come. Guide my words and my steps. Help me bring peace."

"No, Boudica.

"I will help you bring fire!"

CHAPTER 2

By the time I got to the roundhouse, Bran and Pix had assembled the party to intercept the Romans.

"Be sure to hoist both banners and an oak branch to signal your desire for peaceful talks," I told Cai. "Tell the Romans that Queen Boudica of the Greater Iceni is in residence at Oak Throne and desires a peaceful negotiation for her people. You may tell him that Prince Bran knew nothing of Caturix's rebellion. We are allies of Rome and wish to remain so."

"Do we?" Cai asked. My old friend searched my face. "Do we truly, Boudica?"

"Cai…" I said, then looked at the others, seeing the same question in the eyes of the other men of Oak Throne. "When you see the army, you will understand," I told them. "We ally now or die, as Caturix did. The

QUEEN OF ASH AND IRON

Northern Iceni will suffer for Caturix's choices, no matter what we do. The Fen folk…" I said, then paused. "Dead. Enslaved. Devastated. That is the fate that awaits Oak Throne unless we act now. I would see your families saved from the same horrible fate."

Cai nodded. "I understand," he said, then motioned for the others to prepare.

"He's not wrong to want to fight," Pix told me. "None of them are."

"It is noble to fight," I told her. "But we are fools if we think we can rid ourselves of these Romans so easily."

"Ye may eat those words in the end, Boudica."

I nodded. I already knew. Even as the words left my mouth, I doubted. With every move I made, I doubted. If all of our people rose up now, could we push the Romans back? Caratacus thought so. Was he right? Was I a fool for fighting for peace?

"May the gods protect me," I said simply, then stepped back. "Be careful," I told Pix.

"Ye cannot catch this sly fox," she told me, then nodded to Cai.

With that, their party departed.

The first sunlight trimmed the horizon. Rosy beams of sunlight were breaking on the horizon.

"Will this work?" Bran asked, a nervous tone in his voice.

13

"It will either work, or they will kill us all," I said as Pix and the others rode off. "At least now we have a chance. Not much of one, but a chance."

IT DIDN'T TAKE LONG for the Romans to arrive.

It started with a feeling.

The air seemed to shift, and then anticipation made the hair on the back of my neck rise. I had been sitting with Bran and Bec in the roundhouse when I was suddenly overcome with the feeling that something was...wrong.

I rose.

"What is it?" Bran asked.

I looked at Bec.

She nodded, having felt it too. "They've come."

I turned back to Riona, who was nervously wringing her hands. "As we discussed... Go now. Collect Kennocha and her children and take them and Bellicus to Ula."

In case the Romans did to us as they had done to Caturix, at least Ula could get the children out of the village and into the Mossy Wood where they would be safe. Although, I hoped it wouldn't come to that.

"Boudica…" Riona said uncertainly.

"It is just a precaution," I told her. "Don't let Ula boss you. Tell her I insist."

"She won't like that. May the gods guide you, Boudica," she told me, then went to Bellicus. "Come now, lad. We're going to play a game," she told my nephew.

"What kind of game?" Bellicus asked sweetly.

"A hiding game. Let's see if some other children would like to play," Riona said, then hurried to the back, taking Bellicus with her.

I heard Bec's breath catch as she steadied herself.

I looked at her and Bran. "Let's go."

Leaving the roundhouse, we made our way to the gate. As we went, a horn sounded from the ramparts.

But we already knew.

We'd already felt it.

We arrived just in time to see the Romans round the bend in the road and begin to make their way toward the gates of Oak Throne.

And they kept coming.

And coming.

And coming.

The sound of their boots, their feet marching in time, rang off the walls of Oak Throne. The sun broke over the horizon, glinting off their metal armor.

"Like pests in a wheat field," Bec hissed.

One of their commanders barked an order, and the army came to a halt, metal clacking as they did so.

Pix, Cai, and the others were at the front with the man I presumed to be the governor. I scanned the party, looking for Titus or any others I had met in Camulodunon but saw no one. Those men who had come to make treaties and alliances were gone.

These men had come for something different.

Aulus's warnings rang through my memory.

I inhaled deeply, then exhaled slowly.

Melusine told us they swept upon Stonea like a tide, a swell breaking over the fort in what felt like moments. The Fen folk had rallied and died, Caturix along with them as he protected a group of women and children trying to escape the fort. Some people had fled into the marsh, but the Romans had cut down all others—men, women, and children alike. Only a handful of Roman traders had lived, the Roman soldiers sparing them.

I steeled myself, trying not to think about it, trying not to envision my brother standing in the burning ruins, sword in his hand, fighting to save his people.

And dying.

The governor rode forward. "I arrive in Oak Throne to find the gates open and the banners of the Northern Iceni *and* Greater Iceni flying," he said, observing the gates. "You must be Boudica, wife of King Prasutagus," he said, directing his attention to me.

"I am Queen Boudica of the Greater Iceni, and daughter of the house of Aesunos of the Northern Iceni," I said in a loud, clear voice. "Do I have the privilege of addressing General Scapula?" I forced out, willing my lips not to curl in disgust at my words.

"You do," he replied boldly.

I eyed the Roman general. He was a burly man with a heavy black brow that grew in one line above his eyes, a long nose, and wavy black hair. He was beardless, his naked face betraying a scar on his chin. He narrowed his small, dark eyes as he looked me over.

"Governor Scapula, as a client queen of Rome, I welcome you to Oak Throne on behalf of myself and my brother, Prince Bran of the Northern Iceni. We invite you and your men to join us within, in peace, in hopes we may speak further with you regarding the unsupported, rash, and *independent* actions of our brother, King Caturix."

At that, Scapula smirked. He inclined his head to me and then motioned to his men. With that, the parties rode into Oak Throne.

"You have nerves of steel, Sister," Bran said as we moved to meet their party.

"Let's hope I can find the words to match them."

We made our way back to the roundhouse. There, the soldiers dismounted, the governor joining us.

"If you please, Governor," Bec said politely, gesturing to the roundhouse.

Balfor waited, holding the door.

"My men first," he said, gesturing for the soldiers to go inside to search the place.

Bec smiled tightly. "Of course, Governor."

Scapula laughed lightly, his eyes dancing across Bec's form. "Wife of Prince Bran or sister of Queen Boudica?" he asked her.

"I am Bec, lady of this house and wife to Prince Bran."

"Who are your people, Lady Bec?"

"I am a commoner, Governor."

"Unlike Queen Melusine. Hmm…" he mused, then turned to Bran. "They tell me you are more like your sister than your brother. Titus Carassius speaks well of you, Prince Bran. As did Aulus Plautius."

"I consider both my friends, Governor," Bran replied honestly.

Returning from within, one of the Roman soldiers said, "Clear, Governor. Just servants and dogs."

At that, Governor Scapula went inside, Bran and I hurrying after him.

"This way," Bran said, gesturing to the governor to go to our central meeting room.

Looking pale and nervous, Cidna appeared from the back.

"Wine and food for our guest," I told her.

Cidna nodded, then retreated.

"Please, Governor," Bec said, motioning for him to sit.

The governor's guards stood at the doors of the roundhouse, the main hall, one at the entrance to the kitchen, and at least two men were wandering the hallways.

"You will know of the events in Stonea and your brother's death," the governor said.

"Yes," I replied. "That is why we wasted no time trying to get word to you. Our brother Caturix allied with the Coritani against the will of the people of the Northern Iceni and against his agreements with myself, King Prasutagus, and Prince Bran."

"Wine, sir," Cidna said, appearing a moment later with a tray in her hands.

The goblets on the tray shook, the wine threatening to spill.

"Sir," he said with a laugh, then took a cup, Bran, Bec, and I doing the same.

I noted that he waited for us to drink before he took a sip.

"Aulus Plautius spoke of these disagreements *within* the Northern Iceni before he left," the governor said after a sip. "I did not believe it to be true. Many times, rulers will play these games to deceive. Yet, I arrive at

Oak Throne—which I am told is the true home of the Northern Iceni—to find the gates open and a warm welcome."

"My brother did not speak for us, Governor," I told Scapula. "He acted in allegiance with the Coritani, not with the rest of the Iceni."

Governor Scapula turned to Bran and said, "Now that he is dead, you don't mourn him? You don't wish to avenge him? No? Instead, you reach for his crown. That is very Roman of you, Prince Bran."

Bran stiffened, then said, "I seek only to protect my people. The people here are innocent, as are those of Holk Fort and other Northern Iceni holdings."

"But not the Fen folk," the governor said, plucking a slice of apple from the platter Cidna had set before us. "You cannot tell me they are innocent."

"No, Governor," I said. "My brother rallied the Fen folk and those Northern Iceni living on the western front to join him and the Coritani."

"Yes, the Coritani. We searched Stonea for Queen Melusine, daughter of King Volisios, but did not find her. Your brother Caturix was close with her father. Have you heard anything about the welfare of the queen?" he asked, then grabbed a handful of nuts.

"No, Governor. I assumed she was dead," I replied.

Governor Scapula nodded, then turned to Bran. "I know almost nothing about you other than the report you are a good dice player," he said with a laugh. "Given your brother's betrayal, Rome cannot accept you as a client king, Prince Bran. I would not see you rise as another Caratacus when my back is turned," the governor said, then rose, gesturing to his men that he was ready to leave.

"But, Governor—" Bran began in protest, but the governor cut him off.

"Your open gates and warm welcome are the only reason your fort is not burning, Prince Bran. I did not come to Britannia to fight Rome's allies. I was brought here for the fight in the west. Yet here I am all the same, and it is so very tiresome. At the end of the week, the Coritani will be Rome, and I will be back to hunting Caratacus."

Bran looked at me in desperation.

"The Coritani *have* openly rebelled," I told the governor, interceding where Bran was flailing. "But only a splintered faction of the Northern Iceni faltered in their agreement. Governor, there must be something that can be done. You say you want peace so you can fight in the west. We support you in that. You may know that Caratacus is the reason our father is dead. We will be just as happy as you to see him in irons. But the Northern Iceni… We are allies of Rome, sir. Our brother acted on his own."

"*Some* of the Northern Iceni are allies, Queen

Boudica. Not all. And the Northern Iceni must face the consequences of their actions."

"As the Fen folk should. But we are loyal, Governor. No one here wants to fight Rome," I said.

"You seem very intelligent for a woman, Queen Boudica, as Aulus Plautius told us. You must see why I cannot simply ride away and assume the Northern Iceni in this part of your province will do as commanded. There are consequences to actions. Prince Bran cannot rule your people. I will place a Roman—"

"We can crown Boudica queen of the Northern Iceni," Bran said hurriedly. "Rome knows her to be loyal —her and King Prasutagus. Boudica is a daughter of this house. My sister and I will ensure the Northern Iceni make good on their agreement with Rome. We both get what we want. You get a client queen you can trust so you can pursue Caratacus without worrying about the administration of Northern Iceni lands, and our people keep one of their own as ruler."

"Bran," I said, stunned. "But you—"

"But nothing, Sister. You have earned Rome's trust, and you are Northern Iceni."

His helmet tucked under his arm, Governor Scapula looked from Bran to me. I could see he was calculating. Finally, he said, "Agreed."

When Bran began to smile, Scapula turned to him. "It will not be so easy, young prince. Oak Throne is now a municipium of Rome. We will have men stationed here to ensure all transactions in this city benefit both of us—including an increase in taxes on your people to repay to Rome what was lost in this skirmish in Stonea. We both get what we want then, right?" he replied, smiling at Bran, but there was a harshness to his gaze.

The governor added, "And as of this day, the Northern Iceni must relinquish their arms. No man, woman, or even child can wield a blade. Call *your people* now, Queen Boudica. They will present their arms to Rome. The Northern Iceni—all of you—are now disarmed to show your peaceful intentions."

"You mean to confiscate our weapons?" Bran asked, aghast.

"You are a peaceful tribe, are you not? That is what you and your sister tell me. You have no need for weapons, and Rome has no need of a knife at its back while I root out the real threat to this realm," he said curtly.

"Governor," I said in disbelief. "Our weapons are no mere tools. They are the stories of our people... Our swords pass from parent to child. They are ancestor gifts, the stories of families. You are not asking for mere weapons, nor is this some symbolic gesture. In making this request, you ask for our identities."

"Then you must choose, Queen Boudica. What would you prefer to give up, your people's identities—

as you refer to your blades—or their lives? I only afforded you my patience due to the words spoken on your behalf by Aulus Plautius. From now on, I will take a measure of you myself. You say the Northern Iceni are loyal. Show your loyalty. If you decline, we will take the city and the heads of anyone against us. If you comply, you will prove your loyalty. Oak Throne will enjoy its status as a municipium of Rome, and you will be the queen of your people. I am asking for no symbolic gesture, Queen Boudica. The Northern Iceni must be punished for their actions against Rome. Be glad I chose this path when so many others were before me. I will summon my men to come into the city now and begin the collection. You may wish to apprise your people of the situation to prevent any... misunderstandings. Send riders, Queen Boudica. All Northern Iceni weapons will be confiscated by Rome. I will send soldiers to every village, farm, and temple to see it done." With that, Governor Scapula turned on his heel and exited the roundhouse.

"May the Morrigu protect us," Cidna whispered in a low voice.

Bran, Bec, and I hurried after the governor, who was already outside giving instructions to his men.

"Balfor, summon the people. Quickly," I told the housecarl.

He gestured to Albie, who went running off at a sprint to the center square where the bell hung.

"We will camp in your fields tonight," Governor Scapula told Bran, then turned to me. "And you, Queen Boudica, will tell me everything else there is to know about your lands."

CHAPTER 3

The terrified people of Oak Throne began to make their way to the tree at the square. Nearby, a contingent of soldiers began digging a vast ditch. Scapula's soldiers poured into the city, watching the villagers through the slats in their helmets.

Nervously, the people came one by one to the square where Bran, Bec, and I waited alongside the governor of Britannia.

As I stood under the shade of the great oak, I heard whispering from the tree.

Rebel…

Rebel…

Rebel…

I ignored the cries. Rebellion would see every man, woman, and child in front of me murdered. My gaze went to the little pack of children who always dogged my footsteps in Oak Throne. They were children no more. Eiwyn and Birgit were now young teens. Phelan had hair above his lip and a sword on his belt. My words and actions could see Phelan slaughtered and the girls defiled. I would not see what had happened to Caratacus's people done to my own.

But still, the insult of disarmament would be too great to bear.

The people were silent as the Roman soldiers dug and dug, their eyes wide with fear. No doubt, they imagined they would soon lay in the cold earth. I scanned the crowd, finding Ula there. She had pulled her hood up and watched from the back of the crowd.

In her gaze, I saw fury.

But I didn't see Ronat, Kennocha, or the children.

Ula may be angry, but she had hidden the children or sent them down the well ladder and out of the city.

"Oak Throne," Governor Scapula said, stepping forward. "I am Governor Publius Ostorius Scapula, the new governor of Britannia. I find the Northern Iceni in violation of their agreements with Rome. You have been found guilty of rebellion and of the deaths of my soldiers in Stonea. Your king has been executed for his crimes against Rome. As we speak, the Fen folk—as I am told they are called—are paying the price for your king's open rebellion and betrayal of his oaths sworn to the emperor," he said, then paused. He stared icily at the people, many openly weeping in fear. Then, he stood in silence. By not speaking, he let the people's fear rise.

It became nearly palpable.

"Oak Throne," he finally continued, "it is only through the negotiations of Queen Boudica and Prince Bran that you do not share the fate of those in Stonea. Rome knows Queen Boudica to be a friend. Therefore, as a daughter of the late King Aesunos, she will immediately ascend as queen of the Northern Iceni to ensure no further uprisings. Rome believes they will see no further rebellion under Queen Boudica's watch. Further, your taxes to Rome are doubled. A detachment of my men will remain in Oak Throne, now a municipium of Rome, to ensure taxes are paid and the peace is kept. And to further educate the Northern Iceni on the seriousness with which Rome takes promises, the Northern Iceni will be disarmed," he said, gesturing to the pit. "With your weapons buried, you will also bury your rebellious hearts."

That brought a cry of outrage from the crowd.

Aterie, Bran's warrior who had wed Vian's sister, stepped forward. "You cannot take our arms, Rome. They are ours! They belonged to our grandfathers' grandfather. We did not rebel *here*. Why should we be punished for what the Fen folk did? We will refuse!"

At that, the governor signaled to his men. Two Roman soldiers pushed through the crowd.

"Wait," Bran said, looking nervously from Aterie to the governor, but the man simply watched on.

"This is unfair!" Aterie shouted. "We will not comply."

"Aterie, be silent!" Bran called to him.

The other residents of Oak Throne looked on in horror as the Romans pushed through the crowd to the young warrior.

Beside him, a very pregnant Finola begged her husband to be silent.

"You can't do this. We won't comply!" Aterie continued.

When the soldier reached Aterie, they grabbed him roughly and then pulled him aside, closer to the pit.

The governor nodded to his men.

One of the soldiers slit Aterie's throat, silencing his protests, then dumped him in the pit.

There was a stunned gasp from the crowd.

Finola began weeping loudly. "No! No! What have you done? Aterie!"

"Rebellious hearts have no place in Northern Iceni territory," the governor shouted in a firm voice. "Those that are will cease to beat. Does anyone else care to protest?"

Something inside me grew hard. My hands shook.

From the tree above, the whispers continued…

Rebel…

Rebel…

Rebel…

Finola continued weeping loudly.

Grumbling at the others to get out of her way, Ula went to Finola and led her away from the crowd.

"Your swords, Northern Iceni," Governor Scapula said, gesturing to the pit. "Now. All of them. Those on you, those in your homes. All weapons. The Northern Iceni are henceforth disarmed."

Bran stepped forward.

He faced the others, looking across the crowd, meeting the eyes of the people, then he tossed his sword into the pit.

Some of the town elders, knowing full well what would happen if they did not do so, also complied.

The Northern Iceni began to disarm.

They came one by one, dropping their ancestral weapons in the pit where Aterie's broken body lay.

Some had tears in their eyes, kissing the hilts of their blades before throwing them in. Others stared at the governor and the soldiers with murderous rage.

Scapula wanted to quiet the Northern Iceni by disarming them.

His actions may have shaken the beehive instead.

Men, women, and children alike came forward and tossed in their weapons.

Ula was one of the last to come forward.

The crowd watched her in silence.

No, Ula. Don't tempt him. Don't tempt his wrath.

I held her gaze, begging her to be silent, but she smirked.

She stepped to the side of the pit and pulled her herb knife from her belt. She then took the blade, sliced her palm, and let the blood pool. As she did so, she muttered in a low tone under her breath. With fury in her eyes, she looked up at the governor.

"Let me give you this. In Oak Throne, Rome will eat, drink, and choke on fire. But for you, Publius Ostorius Scapula… You will die in shame, outcast by your people, unloved by your gods, your own hand ending your life," she told the governor, then tossed her knife and splattered her blood into the pit. The red droplets splashed on the swords lying therein.

Governor Scapula merely laughed. He turned to his men, gesturing to Ula in humor. "I collect the curses of old crones like fair maidens collect suitors."

The Romans laughed.

I quaked, thinking he would send his soldiers for Ula. If that happened… But the governor had given no weight to Ula's words. He thought her just another bitter old woman.

If he'd known better, he might have responded differently. Ula had placed a heavy blood curse on the Roman. One the old gods would surely answer.

But instead of going after Ula, the governor gestured to someone behind me.

Turning, I saw a soldier approaching with a spear in his hand—my spear.

The governor took it from the soldier and then handed it to me.

"Queen Boudica. I understand this is your weapon."

"It... It is."

He gestured to the pit. "You are queen now. Show your people how to act, as your brother has done."

And in the process, show them my subservience to Rome. That was what the governor wanted the people to see, that Rome had power over me. And if they had control over me, they had control over us all.

Clenching my jaw, I looked at the long shaft of wood. A thousand memories of Gaheris flooded to mind. And with each of them, I balked at the idea of letting the weapon go.

I met the governor's gaze.

He held it. The icy daggers behind his eyes were a warning.

I went to the side of the pit.

I hesitated momentarily, then looked at the people who watched me carefully.

"What does it mean to be Northern Iceni?" I asked the people, who were now openly weeping or burying a white-hot flame of rage. "What defines us? Are we our weapons, or are we our oaths? Are we our swords and spears, or are we the memories that we carry? Does our strength come from our arms or from ourselves? No sword, spear, dagger, or shield defines us. We are Northern Iceni in our blood. Our blood. That is what matters. That is what must carry on. That is what must *live*. Our hearts must continue to beat, even if there is no steel in our hands, even during trying times. Our courage is found in our hearts, not in the length of a sword. Remember that. No matter what you sacrifice, your heart is still Northern Iceni, and no one can take that from you," I said, then tossed the spear into the pit.

I stepped back, rejoining the governor who smiled and then motioned to his men, who began refilling the pit with dirt.

"Excellent, Northern Iceni. Now we can carry on as friends. Return to your homes. My men will be by to collect whatever weapons you have stored there. Until my army departs, I place a curfew on your city. Go home, people of Oak Throne. Think of the Fen folk in Stonea who lie at the bottom of their bog. You have chosen better. Your rulers have chosen better. Queen Boudica and Prince Bran chose your lives over their own ambitions.

"But know this," he said, his voice darkening with a warning. "If there is even a whisper of rebellion from your people, Rome will punish every man, woman, and child without distinction. Your farms, temples, and villages will burn."

The governor's words caused the air to chill.

But from the tree above, the greenwood was unfazed and continued to whisper...

Boudica...

Boudica...

Bring fire...

CHAPTER 4

S haken, the people of Oak Thone hurried back to their houses, except for Finola. Despite Ula's efforts to lure her away, she went to the side of the pit and dropped to her knees. Weeping loudly, she reached for Aterie.

"Oh, please give him to me, Rome. Please give him to me," she pleaded to the soldiers, but they didn't even look at her.

Bec went to her, Ula joining her.

I couldn't hear the women's words, but eventually, they got Finola up off the ground. Ula and Bec led the girl away, back to Ula's cottage.

I watched as the soldiers shoveled dirt onto the swords and Aterie's body.

The *schoop, schoop, schoop,* sound of their shovels

scooping up dirt rang in my ears, my body trembling with each shovelful of earth.

Had I chosen wrong?

Had I been walking the wrong path all this time?

I scanned the crowd for Pix, but she wasn't there.

I already knew what she would think, what she would say.

But it was the eyes of the Northern Iceni people that had awoken my doubts.

Fear, rage, and rebellion lingered in their gazes.

Schoop.

Schoop.

Schoop.

My head began to feel light. Dizziness washed over me.

Have I been wrong all this time?

Have I been wrong?

"Boudica," Bran said, shaking my arm. "Boudica?"

"Bran?"

"The governor," he said, gesturing with his chin.

Governor Scapula had rejoined his men. He was giving instructions, pointing in several different directions.

I nodded to Bran, then we joined Scapula.

I approached him cautiously, saying, "Governor…"

"Queen Boudica. My men need a building from which to work. What is available to us?"

"The guest house, there," I said, gesturing.

He nodded. "I assume you will eventually return to Venta, leaving your brother in charge here. We will begin building here in Oak Throne… A weigh station on the river, an administrative building for our men, an area for a barracks inside the walls of Oak Throne. You will instruct your brother to provide these things for our men."

"Of course."

"I understand Holk Fort, the second largest village of the Northern Iceni, is controlled by your holy people… these druids, correct?"

"Yes, Governor."

"Hmm," he mused. "We have had great difficulty with these druids in the west. They are very supportive of Caratacus and the people there. Will I have difficulty with the druids of Holk Fort?"

"No, Governor. The Northern Iceni are committed to peace."

"Not all of them, if we are to be honest," he said, giving me a knowing look.

"We *are* committed, Governor. As I said, my brother, Caturix, was manipulated by the Coritani kings—"

"Then your brother was a weak ruler."

I swallowed all the words that wanted to spill from my lips. Instead, I said, "Bran can accompany you to Holk Fort," I said, suddenly worried what may happen if Arixus's war god disagreed with the choices being made. "It may help ensure things remain calm."

The governor considered the offer. "Very well. Prince Bran may ride with my centurion. I will send my soldiers to your other villages for their weapons. Do you anticipate resistance anywhere else besides Holk Fort?"

While I had not said there would be resistance in Holk, the governor had read between the lines.

"No. But if we send our own people first to lay the groundwork, it would benefit us all."

"Or give your people time to hide their weapons. No, Queen Boudica, we won't be doing that. I have my own maps of the Northern Iceni territories. We will make our own way. Now, this Grove of Andraste. They are druids or…"

I felt like a rock had been dropped into the pit of my stomach. "No, Governor. They are much like the priestesses of Minerva I encountered in Camulodunum. Peaceful. They are holy women of our gods."

"I have heard no rumors of difficulties with your priestesses," he said. "Not like these druids. Very well. No need to visit them for disarmament, I presume."

"No, Governor. You would only find kitchen knives anyway," I said in something of a lie.

He huffed a laugh, then turned back to Bran. "Saddle your horse, Prince Bran, and prepare to ride out. My secretary, Ampelius, will return to the roundhouse with

Queen Boudica to identify where we may begin building."

"Of course, Governor. And I would be delighted if you would dine with me in the roundhouse tonight," I said, forcing the words through my lips.

The governor gave me a strained smile. "Very well."

Apparently, he was no more pleased about that idea than I. All the same, I had done right by offering and him by accepting.

With that, he nodded to me, then he and some of his men departed. A group of Roman soldiers and a small man I had not noticed before remained.

"Queen Boudica, I am Ampelius, secretary to the governor," he said, bowing to me.

"My housecarl, Balfor, will see you to the round-house. I will join you momentarily."

The man nodded and then departed, leaving Bran and me alone with the Romans as they refilled the pit.

I gestured for my brother to step aside.

We stood there for a long moment, unsure what to say.

Then, Bran whispered the words my own heart had spoken. "Have we made a mistake, Boudica? All this time, have we made a mistake? The Romans have all but taken over Oak Throne."

I looked back, watching as the last of the dirt covered Aterie. It did not pay to worry Bran with my own doubts. Already, he could feel them, even though I didn't speak them. If I was strong, Bran could be strong. So, I pushed my emotions aside. "The job of a ruler is to protect their people. Had Caturix not acted, none of this would have happened. We are paying the price for his choices, his actions."

"If we had allied with Caratacus from the start..." Bran whispered in a low voice. "All of us. If we had *all* pushed back then."

"There is nothing we can do about that now. Now, we must fix Caturix's mess. I loved my brother and will mourn him, but Caturix has done this to us, not the Romans."

Bran looked toward the pit. "Aterie..."

"He was foolish to speak out, but I am dearly sorry for his death."

Bran frowned. "I will get Foster and join the Romans. Arixus—"

"If he hasn't heard what happened at Stonea, tell him. He is quick. He will understand. And watch yourself, Bran. These men are unlike Aulus's people. But remember, it's not us they want. It's Caratacus. We must give them every reason to believe that we are no threat, that nothing further will happen here, and that they are free to leave us in peace."

"Yes. Yes, you're right. Be safe, Boudica."

"And you."

With that, Bran turned and went toward the stables.

I looked back toward the ditch once more. Dirt covered the swords therein—and my spear, made for me by Gaheris's hands. My hands shook, a feeling of rage washing over me. Calming it, I inhaled deeply, smoothed my skirts, and turned and headed to the roundhouse where I would pay the price of Caturix's choices and seek to undo the damage he had done.

A price we had already begun to pay in blood.

CHAPTER 5

Governor Scapula's secretary, Ampelius, was a man of business. At once, he asked for a map of the fort. He wanted to know where there were wells, who collected the taxes on behalf of Rome, where the treasury was kept, and all manner of issues that an outsider had no business knowing. My efforts to evade his questions were met with stony eyes. More than an hour into the conversation, my head was beginning to ache, and my patience was growing thin.

"What do you mean you will not share the location of the treasury, Queen Boudica?" Ampelius prodded me with annoyance.

"Secretary Ampelius, would you tell me where you keep your gold in your house? Rome is entitled to her share of taxes, nothing more."

The secretary held my gaze. "All monies coming to

the crown of the Northern Iceni will now be handled by Rome's auditors. After that, you may store your earnings in your treasury—wherever it is—as you see fit," he told me, then took down a note.

I opened my mouth to protest but then said nothing. This was the price we were forced to pay for Caturix's failed uprising.

Ampelius looked at the map once more. "This area," he said, gesturing to Ula's cottage. "There is a well marked here."

"It is dry."

"It is quite a big space for one hut."

"It is the home of the village midwife who grows healing herbs there. The space is needed for that use. Why not build here?" I said, gesturing to another spot in Oak Throne. "This area held the old market before it was outgrown. It is close to the gate and the river, and there is a well here. It is much closer to the commerce section of the fort."

"Yes. Very good. That is preferable," he said, taking another note. He stuffed his scrolls into his bag, scooped up my map, then told me, "That will be all for now, Queen Boudica." With that, he departed.

"Wretched little weasel. I hope you die of an infected toenail," I hissed in his wake.

Bec, who was just returning to the roundhouse, paused at the door, watching him go.

"I suppose he earned that curse."

"Ten-fold. Finola?"

"We've given her something to calm her. Her child is not due for a month, but Ula feared her misery might trigger the laboring early. She will stay with Ula for a time. Riona, Bellicus, Kennocha, and her children are still there."

"Ula must love having the company," I said wryly, then shook my head. "May the Great Mother be with Finola."

"With us all, Boudica."

"Have you seen Pix anywhere?"

"Not since you arrived."

I frowned.

"The people?" I asked. "How is it out there?"

"Silent. The Romans are going from door to door collecting weapons. The fort was not besieged, but it has been taken all the same. What do we do now?"

"Until the governor loses interest in us, we dance to their tune. Like our feet are on fire."

WATCHING the Romans work gave me insight into how the Romans fought. They were methodical, quick, and precise. But more than the physical changes underway at Oak Throne, I felt the shift in the air.

The greenwood quivered as it watched.

The old ones recoiled.

And with each hammer ring, I questioned myself and my choices.

Tap — Am I wrong?

Tap — Am I making a mistake?

Tap — Is peace now worth what comes later?

It was late evening when the governor arrived to join Bec and me for the evening meal. Along with him, he had brought half a dozen soldiers he had stationed around the roundhouse.

"Please, Governor," I said, inviting him to sit at the dining table.

"I was told to expect homey fare in your lands, Queen Boudica, but this is a fine feast you have set before me."

Cidna had unearthed every Roman treat she'd purchased in the last year, setting it on the table alongside roasted venison, pheasant, root vegetables, hand pies, and whatever else she had. Despite the bounty, I also noted much of it was overcooked or burnt, per usual.

"I hope it will be to your liking," Bec told him.

The governor gave Bec a warm smile. "If not, at least

the hand that serves it is luscious," he said, taking her hand and placing a kiss thereon.

Bec laughed lightly, then pulled her hand away as she smothered a look of disgust on her face.

"Are you from Rome, Governor? I know many of your people come from other provinces," I said, trying to turn the conversation—and the governor's attention —from Bec.

"I am Roman, blood to bone, Queen Boudica. I was, however, born in Egypt and spent some time there in my youth when my father was Prefect."

"Egypt... You must tell us of this country. We know nothing of it," I replied.

"It is a beautiful country. The Nile River flows through it, much like your Thames. Along the river is a green oasis. But beyond that are sandy deserts where date palms grow. And there are ancient temples in the shapes of pyramids taller than any building in your lands."

"And the people?" Bec asked.

"They are dark-haired, their skin touched by the sun. The women are beautiful, decorate their eyes with kohl, and wear gowns so thin that... Well, that is not proper to say before ladies. Like all peoples, they have their own gods. But many of their gods are peculiar creatures with the heads of birds, dogs, and even crocodiles."

I furrowed my brow. "Crocodiles?"

"Great serpents that live in the rivers. They have long mouths full of teeth. I have seen many a man devoured by such creatures."

"A whole man?" Bec asked.

"Does that frighten you, Lady Bec?" he asked teasingly.

"No. It is only... It is a wonder."

"It is. You told me you were born a commoner, Lady Bec."

"Yes," Bec replied. "I was a priestess before Bran and I wed."

"A priestess?" he asked, surprised. "In Egypt, the priestesses strip their clothing and paint themselves with gold. Do you do that here?" he asked, giving her a hungry look.

"It is far too cold for that in Britannia, Governor," she told him wryly.

At that, Governor Scapula laughed. "Yes, you are right. Although I do hear that to the north in the Caledonian Confederacy, as it is called—these lands north of the Brigantes—the men strip naked and paint themselves blue when they go into battle."

"There are fierce fighters in the wild, northern reaches of our island where the forests are ancient and the gods still walk," Bec told him.

"Is that so? It seems my men are not the only ones

who prescribe to superstition," the governor said, then chuckled.

Bec and I exchanged a glance but said nothing more.

To my surprise, the governor plowed through the meal, seemingly enjoying Cidna's food. He occasionally paused to examine this or that which was over or under-cooked but ate all the same. We kept the conversation light, asking him more about his time in Egypt as a boy. Had I not felt like I was dancing on a bed of embers, I would have found the whole thing fascinating. But as it was, I couldn't stop thinking about what was happening in the countryside throughout Northern Iceni lands as the Romans came knocking.

My worries were not for nothing. We had just finished the meal when a man arrived, asking to speak to the governor.

"Some reports of resistance so far, Governor. For the most part, it has been resolved. But in one village, a spark of contention. We have taken the chieftain into custody. She's demanded to speak to the queen."

"These people are in no position to demand anything. The sooner they realize that, the better. Where?" Governor Scapula asked, a disinterested tone in his voice.

"A village called Frog's Hollow."

Lynet.

I rose. "Chieftain Lynet. Excuse me, Governor, but I should go at once. I can… I will amend the situation."

"Resistance cannot be abided, Queen Boudica. Where it is found, it will be stamped out. Tell your people that," the governor told me, then looked to his man. "If they do not adhere to the queen's words, execute them."

"Governor," the soldier replied with a bow.

The governor sat forward in his chair and then poured himself more wine.

My hands shaking, I moved to go but paused, looking back at Bec.

Bec motioned for me to go on.

"I'll return shortly," I said, then hurried from the hall.

Gaheris, be with me.

Help me find the words to protect your family.

CHAPTER 6

By the time I arrived in Frog's Hollow,
everything was coming undone. I'd brought
my Greater Iceni guard, but Pix was still missing. When I saw the scene in Frog's Hollow, I suddenly
wished I had more men with me.

Half of the men of Frog's Hollow had been bound,
gagged, and were on their knees before the soldiers,
Lynet included. One of the small roundhouses was on
fire.

A sense of terror washed over me.

I scanned the crowd for Tristan and the others, mere
children when Gaheris and I were to be wed, but like
Birgit and Phelan, they were now teens.

Finally, I spotted Tristan with the other men, his
hands tied behind his back, his cheek bruised, lip
bleeding.

I dismounted Druda at once and went to the soldier in charge.

"What is the meaning of this?" I demanded.

The man eyed me up and down. "You know the order, Queen Boudica. These people defied the demands placed on them, so we took their weapons by force. They resisted," he said, gesturing to those tied up.

"Untie the chieftain," I said, motioning to Lynet. "Now."

"I don't take orders from the queen of the Iceni," the soldier told me stiffly.

"I am here to quell this problem on Rome's behalf. If you want to help, untie the chieftain, or I will tell the governor it was your fault I could not bring the people of this village into an accord."

Frowning, the soldier did what I asked.

"Boudica, what is the meaning of this?" Lynet asked me as the soldiers untied her gag and cut her ropes. The moment she was free, she jerked her hands away and moved to rise. When the soldier tried to help her up, she pushed him back. He came at her then, moving to strike her, but I stepped between them.

"Enough," I told them both.

I turned, seeing the other people of Frog's Hollow had gathered once more, lingering at the edges of the square. The firelight revealed the fear on their faces.

I looked from them to the mound on the hill.

Gaheris…

I cleared my throat then spoke. "People of Frog's Hollow. The Roman's words *are* true. Rome has come to collect your arms, as they do this night across Northern Iceni territory.

"But not in the Fens.

"In the Fens, Stonea burns. My brother, King Caturix, rebelled against Rome, leading the Fen folk to fight with him alongside the Coritani. Now, they are *all* dead. The western holdings are in flames, and Rome takes out her retribution upon the Fen folk for proving themselves to be false allies. Liars. Betrayers. Caturix broke his promises to Rome and committed crimes against our sworn partner. The cost of his betrayal has been the blood of the Northern Iceni.

"But not in Oak Throne.

"Not in Holk Fort.

"Nor does it have to end in fire and blood in Frog's Hollow.

"We do not have to pay for Caturix's misdeeds. Governor Scapula has agreed to my and Bran's pleas and has granted the Northern Iceni a chance at redemption. A single chance. It comes at a price. That price is your swords. Not your blood. Not your heads. Not your children, husbands, brothers, sisters, or wives. Steel is the price we must pay for Caturix's broken promises. The people of the Fens have not been so lucky. For them, there is only blood, the depths of the bogs, or the clapping of irons.

"I implore you… I—who would have once been one of you—I beg you, do what these soldiers ask. Please. Please."

Lynet eyed me closely and then nodded. "Very well. You have heard Boudica. You do not have to like it, but we must comply. Those of you who have resisted Rome's requests, do as they ask now," she said, gesturing to the wagon upon which was loaded other weapons—swords, spears, daggers, shields. "In King Bran's name."

"There is no King Bran," the soldier told her waspishly. "You stand before the new queen of the Northern Iceni, Chieftain."

Lynet looked at me, a confused expression on her face. But I could see her calculating. After a moment, she nodded. "Then come, as our queen has implored of us. Your weapons. Now."

There was some confusion amongst the villagers. They eyed the Romans and me with suspicion.

Then, with deep sorrow, they came forward, tossing their weapons into the wagon.

Tears pricked at the corners of my eyes as I watched, but I swallowed the agony and turned to the soldier.

"Cut these people loose," I told him, gesturing to those who had been bound.

Motioning to his men, he freed the people of Frog's Hollow, including Tristan.

I went to the boy, intending to look at the wounds on his wrists, but when I reached for him, he pulled back. He shook his head, gave me a hard look, then turned and stalked off into darkness.

My heart ached as I watched him go.

He felt betrayed—by me.

Many would feel the same.

Could they not see I was trying to save their lives?

Lynet joined me. "Boudica..." she whispered.

"Are you all right?" I asked her.

She nodded, rubbing her wrists. "They gave no explanation, simply came in demanding we disarm. Is it true? Your brother is dead?"

I nodded. "He sided with the Coritani...and lost."

"Aye, Boudica," she said, setting her hand on my shoulder. "Why are you queen and Bran is not king?"

"The Romans would not agree to it. Either Bran stepped aside and let me—already a client queen—take the crown, or Rome would take control of the province."

"By the gods..."

"But at least they will be alive," I said, gesturing to the people leaving their weapons. "Bran and I have given everything for that."

We watched as the people of Frog's Hollow delivered their weapons to the Romans. The soldiers then went from door to door, entering the roundhouses without care, searching for anyone hiding or any other weapons that had been hidden. They threw aside tables and bed covers, upended baskets and boxes, searching.

Some had attempted to hide their most precious blades, those that had been passed down for generations. There was screaming and crying in protest as they were taken from their hiding places and tossed upon the cart.

Throughout the village, I heard weeping.

But they were not bleeding.

They weren't dying.

In the darkness, Lynet reached for my hand.

When it was over, the people of Frog's Hollow stood bloody, tears on their cheeks, as the Romans tossed a tarp over their haul and began to move out.

"Queen Boudica," the soldier said to me, gesturing that the party was preparing to depart.

I turned and looked at Lynet. "Lynet… I am so sorry. You all are like family to me. I—"

"We are alive," she said, setting her hand on my cheek and smiling gently at me. "I do not envy you the choices you must make, Boudica. But we are alive and grateful to you for that."

I leaned in and embraced her.

Before leaving, I looked again to the mound where Gaheris was buried. For a brief moment, I saw the ghostly figure of the man I'd loved there. When he met my gaze, he set his hand on his heart, then faded.

Swallowing hard, I turned and left Frog's Hollow… at Rome's side.

BY THE TIME I returned to Oak Throne, it was nearly dawn. I couldn't remember the last time I had slept. My body ached, but my heart hurt worse. The Roman soldiers returned to the camp with their stolen goods. There, I saw many other wagons loaded with ill-gotten gains. My stomach ached when I thought about what would happen to the weapons.

Sold off at the market?

Melted to make Roman goods?

One option wasn't better than the other. The governor had not killed these people, but his play had been smart. He had broken their spirits and shown them the power of Rome. They were alive but defiled by Rome's hand. And that had been the purpose of the lesson.

The governor also didn't want a blade at his back when he went once more for Caratacus.

It was a strategic move.

Bran and I had done what little we could to counter it.

The people were alive, but their hearts...

I returned to the roundhouse to find an odd hush had fallen over the place.

The governor and his soldiers had gone, the house's regular guards in place once more. Within, the house was silent. Given the hour, surely Cidna and the others were asleep.

But still, something wasn't right.

The dinner platters had been cleared.

Everything looked as it should.

Then, I heard soft weeping.

I followed the sound to Bran's and Bec's bedchamber. Within, I heard Bec crying.

"Bec?" I called, knocking on the door before I pushed it open.

Within, I found Bec sitting on the floor. Her eyes were red from weeping. Her hair and clothing were disheveled.

"Bec, are you..." I said, reaching for her, but she pulled back.

The move had been instinctual but had been enough for me to understand. I looked my friend over, seeing the undone ties on the bodice of her dress and the tousled manner of her clothing.

Gasping, I dropped to my knees and wrapped my arms around her, pulling her close.

Bec wept and wept, wetting my shoulder with her tears.

As she did so, a white-hot flame began to grow within me.

"I will slip into his tent and slit his throat," I whispered. "This will not stand. I will go now before the soldiers wake," I said, then rose, but Bec gripped my arm hard.

"And undo the peace we have worked so hard to broker? The peace we have already sacrificed and bled for?"

"But, Bec—" I protested.

She shook her head. "It's nothing. It doesn't matter. I am Britannia, befouled by Rome, but my heart is still beating. If you do as you say, you may as well slit our throats too—and those of Bellicus, Mara, Caturin, Ula, Kennocha, Bran, and all the rest. There will be no holding them back."

"We cannot allow it to stand," I said, cupping her face as I gazed at her. "Sister," I said, feeling tears slide down my cheeks.

"We will bear it."

"I cannot. I cannot. This is my doing. How can I bear it?"

"It is Caturix's doing," Bec said angrily. "And if I can

bear it, so can you. You must say nothing to Bran. Do you understand me? You must say nothing to Bran. He will do something foolish. Promise me, Boudica. Promise me you will say nothing to your brother."

"Bec—"

"It is over. Nothing a bath and heady mead can't help me forget. But you will say nothing. Promise me, Boudica."

"Bec."

"Promise me!"

I nodded. "I promise," I said, then kissed her on the forehead. "Let me… Let me draw a bath for you."

"Yes… Yes, thank you."

I rose to go.

"Boudica," Bec called in a broken voice. "Bring the moon shadow tonic…just in case."

I knew the brew she mentioned. It would rid the body of unwanted pregnancy, but it was not without risk.

"Are you sure?" I whispered. "It can… You know there is danger."

"I will take that risk to ensure I walk away from this moment with nothing."

Nodding, I did as she asked.

My hands and feet moved, but within me, I had gone numb. I dared not let the feelings growing inside me take root. There was so much…rage.

Was this better than what Caratacus had done? The king had raised his people in rebellion. They bled and died fighting the Romans. But I had clapped my people in irons made of promises.

For peace, my people were disarmed.

For peace, Aterie was dead.

For peace, Bran had been robbed of the crown due to him.

For peace, our people would be taxed to poverty.

For peace, we would have to keep silent about what had happened to Bec, rather than exacting bloody vengeance.

For peace, I had enslaved my people with promises.

And underneath those chains made of words, I could feel it was just the beginning. One day, those chains would choke us.

CHAPTER 7

Bran returned around midday, mud-speckled and exhausted. He went first to the governor, giving his report, then returned to the round-house. Since that terrible night, the governor had not set foot again inside Oak Throne. I was glad. Because something told me that keeping my promise to Bec would not be easy. Perhaps the governor guessed as much. Or, perhaps not. Men such as him saw women as disposable. He likely cared very little about the impact of his actions. What he cared about was what he wanted.

It was Bec who suffered.

And for that, I would never be able to forgive myself.

Bran's return did provide an answer to one puzzle. Pix, who had been missing, returned along with Bran's party.

"Where have you been?" I asked her.

"Holk Fort," she said, picking across the dining table for something to eat. She lifted and put back several burned honey cakes, two that were still nearly raw, finally settling on one burned black on one side only.

"All this time?"

"Soon as I saw what the Romans were about, I set off. Good thing I did, too, because Arixus needed to hear what was coming for him."

"I... Thank you, Pix."

"Now, if ye will excuse me, I have my handsome boy to look after."

"Look after? Is Cai unwell?"

"Not that kind of look after," Pix told me with a wink, then departed.

Bran entered the hall looking weary. He plopped down into a chair at the table and then asked Albie to bring him an ale.

"Welcome back, Brother. How are things at Holk?"

"On the plus side, the fort is thriving. No mud. No mess. The people look well-fed and healthy. I would call our changes over the years a success there, except for the look on their faces when the Romans came for their blades. The people of Holk Fort have suffered from the bad decisions of their rulers. It felt like another slight on otherwise innocent people."

"What of Arixus?"

"Pix had apprised him of the situation before we got

there. He was…odd about it. He told the people to give up their weapons but assured them Condatis forged on their behalf. Druid prophecy, much to the annoyance of the Romans. They relinquished their arms all the same," he said, then looked around. "Where is Bec?"

"She's not feeling well. I gave her a tonic. She's resting."

"Should I…" Bran said, moving to rise.

I shook my head. "Let her sleep. The longer she sleeps, the better."

"Bellicus?" he asked more quietly.

"Still with Ula and the others."

"The governor's army seems to be preparing to break camp."

"Good. Let him go chase Caratacus. There is nothing for him here."

"He has already taken what he wanted," Bran said with a frown.

My heart broke at his words, but I stuffed my feelings away and said, "They are alive."

Bran nodded. "They are alive. We must address the people once the Romans go. They may not understand why I haven't taken the crown."

"Bran, you should not have offered—"

"Did you see any other way, Boudica? Had I not said anything, a Roman magistrate would sit here now. As it is, Oak Throne will be crawling with them. Our family has held the crown, but barely. Otherwise, we would be in no better shape than the Catuvellauni."

"I will name Bellicus heir of the Northern Iceni," I reassured Bran. "I promise you."

"It may not be up to you, Boudica. The shape of our world is changing. And thanks to Caturix, you may be the last ruler of the Northern Iceni."

"Don't say that. Don't give up hope. In time, this matter will quiet. Caratacus will give the Romans other things to worry about."

"Let's hope. They said there was resistance in Frog's Hollow."

"Yes," I said sadly. "But in the end, they complied once they learned what happened in the Fens."

"I can imagine it was like that everywhere last night. We will know in the coming days."

There was a heavy knock on the door of the roundhouse.

I heard Balfor speaking to one of the Romans. A moment later, Balfor reappeared with a Roman soldier at his side.

"Queen Boudica, Prince, the governor has departed. My men have been ordered to remain behind to complete the construction on the municipium buildings and establish a guard. I am to take charge here," the soldier said.

"Your name?" I asked.

"Felix Varus, Queen Boudica."

"Then we will work together to see that you complete your orders in a timely fashion in coordination with the prince, who will care for our people when I am absent."

"Yes, Queen Boudica. In fact, I needed to speak to someone about lumber. My men have identified a forest to your west with wide trees. We would begin cutting—"

"The Mossy Wood?" Bran declared, aghast. "Only if you wish to have every curse of our people and our gods upon you. No. I will show you where you can cut. That grove is sacred, Felix. Your men would be wise not to step foot there. Ever. Even our people go missing in that ancient place." Slugging back his ale, Bran rose. "I will go with you now."

"Very well," the man said, then turned to me. "Governor Scapula wishes you well, Queen Boudica. He says he will meet you and King Prasutagus in Venta as soon as possible."

And with that, the Roman turned and departed, Bran following.

I, too, left the roundhouse and went to the Greater Iceni men who had ridden with me. I found them at the stables, drinking ale and watching the Romans suspiciously.

When they spotted me, Jorah, the leader of this band, stepped forward. "Queen Boudica?"

"Once the Romans depart, someone must take a report to King Prasutagus. We must relay all that has transpired here."

"The Romans are pushing off, following the road south and turning west to follow the road back to Stonea. The Northern Iceni have been watching. I will send someone at once."

No doubt, they were on their way back to Catuvellauni territory.

"Good. And thank you, Jorah."

"Queen Boudica," Mordrat, another of the soldiers, began hesitantly. "Will the Romans come for our weapons?"

My heart hesitated a moment before I said, "No. As long as the Greater Iceni keep their promises to Rome, and Rome keeps her promises to us, we will be fine. This is the result of Caturix's actions. The Northern Iceni are lucky it is only their swords they have lost and not their lives."

"Many people will call those one in the same," Mordrat replied.

"Yes, but they will still have the breath to do so."

"The men who went to Holk Fort said they saw smoke across the Wash, coming from the lands of the Coritani," Jorah said.

I nodded. "There are no Coritani now. Now, they are Rome."

"May Great Epona protect us from such a fate," Jorah said.

"And the Morrigu stand beside us if she cannot," I replied.

When I left them, I made my way to Ula's cottage. Graymalkin, the cat, was sitting on the roof, watching me. The fluffy kitten had grown large in the years that had passed. He eyed me carefully, trying to decide if I was friend or foe.

"Don't you remember me, familiar?" I asked him.

The door opened. "I don't," Ula told me waspishly. *"Queen of the Iceni."*

I frowned at her. "They are departing."

"Won't you ride with them?"

"No. I will see Oak Throne settled."

"Occupied."

"Settled. And I will not argue with you in the middle of the street."

Frowning at me, Ula let me inside.

Within, I found Riona and Kennocha seated on the floor. They were playing a game with the children.

"Boudica," Kennocha said, rising.

"The governor is departing. You will be safe to return home now."

"Oh, Boudica, are you sure?" Riona asked, fear in her eyes.

"We will all live with the consequences of another's choices," I said sadly. "That cannot be helped now," I said then turned to Ula. "We have all done what we could to stem the loss of life."

"Half-shackled us to Rome, you have," she told me.

"And yet, you're still alive," I told her, irritated.

"It is a half-life if a person is not free," Ula replied.

There was some truth to her words, so I didn't argue. "Riona, Bec is unwell. She's resting. Will you continue to look after Bellicus?"

Riona nodded. "Of course," she told me then looked to Bellicus. "There will be time enough to bother your mum later. After you've had a bath and a nap," Riona told Bellicus then moved to depart. "I thank you, Ula. Thank you for sheltering us. Bellicus, thank Ula for letting you stay with her."

"Thank you, Ula," Bellicus told her politely, then the pair left.

I looked back at Kennocha who looked uncertain. "Boudica," she said then paused. "I think... I think maybe I should leave Oak Throne. There are too many here who whisper the truth. For their sake, perhaps I should not stay," she said, her gaze going to her children.

I looked from Mara to Caturin. The pain I felt at my

brother's death, which lingered under my fury at his choices, pricked my heart.

"You can come with me to Venta. Collect your things. We can arrange for your animals to be transported as well."

"Venta?" Mara said excitedly. "That very big city?"

Kennocha looked uncertain.

"I can see you comfortably settled there. No one will be the wiser, but you will be close to Prasutagus and me. It will be…safer," I said, glancing at Ula out of the corner of my eye. "I expect to depart for Venta soon."

"I… All right," Kennocha said. "Yes. We will come to Venta," she said then picked up Caturin. "Come, children. We have much to do. We are going to have an adventure."

"In Venta!" Mara said excitedly.

"Yes, in Venta," Kennocha replied then turned to Ula. "My thanks, Ula. From the bottom of my heart."

"Bah," Ula said, then waved her off.

With that, the trio departed, leaving Ula and me.

Ula turned and glared at me. "So, you will leave us here with Romans in our grain and not a sword to cut their throats with."

"I could have left you to die."

"You have all the same, you just don't see it. The canker has already attached. Now, it will fester."

"It is Caratacus they want. Not us. Soon, they will forget about us."

"And when they finally have him? You expect them to pack up and go home? You're smarter than that, Boudica."

"Every step I've made has been to keep our people safe. Every choice. Every move. Don't you see? This is Caturix's doing, not mine nor Bran's nor Prasutagus's."

Ula scowled then said, "One day, it will be one unjust action too many. One day, it will be one wrong too much. What then, Boudica? What will you do then? Will you lie down and tell yourself to be silent? The human heart has limits. Ask yourself what Caturix saw that you are missing. Perhaps he was not the one doing the betraying. Your Roman eagle has flown home. You are without a shield now, girl. Remember that in the days to come."

Not wanting to argue with her further, I turned to leave.

"Boudica," Ula called after me.

Agitated, I stopped and looked back at her.

"What good is it to be alive if you are not free?"

Annoyed, I turned and made my way to the roundhouse.

As much as I hated to admit it, Ula was right. But what other choice, really, did we have?

When I returned to the roundhouse, I found Balfor just outside.

"Balfor, please have a wagon readied and taken to the home of the widow Kennocha. She will return to Venta with me."

Balfor met my gaze and held it. "That is wise, Boudica. The rumors will not escape Roman ears. I would not see the children used as pawns."

"Nor I."

"Boudica, are they—"

"Yes."

He nodded. "I'll see to the wagon."

"Thank you, Balfor."

I turned and went inside, Ula's words still ringing in my ears.

Had Caturix seen something I had not?

My brother had always been level-headed. He was the most serious of all of us. And now, he was gone, lying in the bottom of the bog. The Northern Iceni had not been able to mourn their king, nor me my brother.

There was no time for that.

I needed to get Caturix's children safe. In Venta, Melusine also waited. She, too, would have to go somewhere to remain unseen. In Caturix's death, their worlds would collide. But it didn't matter anymore. Nothing mattered other than keeping them safe.

But even as the words rattled through my mind, Ula's voice haunted me once more.

"What good is it to be alive if you are not free?"

Curling my hands into fists, I made my way into the roundhouse and tried to ignore the whisper in my heart and answer to her question.

CHAPTER 8

That night, after the Roman governor and his army had departed, Balfor called the people of Oak Throne to the center square before the great tree. The pit that held the body of Aterie and the weapons of our people had been strewn with flowers.

At least twenty Roman soldiers remained behind. They gathered at the side to watch but did not interfere.

I could see on the faces of the people I knew well that the events that had taken place in Oak Throne had shaken them, as it had us all.

Bran was the first to speak.

"Tonight, we have called you all here to gather in remembrance. For my brother, King Caturix, for the people of the Fens, and for those loved ones who have died in the events that have unfolded in the preceding days. And for the path of the Northern Iceni people..."

"The Northern Iceni are people of their word. We are known throughout the tribes to be honorable. True. When the word of a Northern Iceni man or woman is spoken, it is a vow that is not broken. But we have broken our word. King Caturix broke his word to our Roman allies. I will be honest. We have all looked upon the return of Rome with skeptical eyes. We worry about their intentions. Yet, Rome did *nothing* to offend the Northern Iceni. They have been trading partners and allies. We did not rise against them when they first arrived. And for a good reason. You've heard the rumors that Caratacus and Togodumnus worked with our Uncle Saenunos to murder my father. Boudica and I know those whispers to be true."

At that, a murmur went through the crowd.

"Why would we ally with the Catuvellauni? What has Rome done since its return? Reseated King Verica and his heirs. Reseated Aedd Mawr's heirs. Togodumnus is dead. Rome pursues our common enemy, Caratacus.

"And what have we, the Northern Iceni, done?"

At that, a hush went over the crowd. In the darkness, all that could be heard was the flicker of torchlight.

"We all grieve the losses we have faced. The Romans will never understand what they take from us when they take our swords. They take our stories, our fathers, our grandfathers, memories of those we love," he said, glancing at me. "In their eyes, they have taken the dagger from a hand that has stabbed them in the back. That is all. And while we feel anger and shame, we must remember... Rome did not break its word to us.

"My people, the coming days will bring change. You will see our Roman allies here in the fort. And you will feel the consequences of the Fen folk's choices in an increase in your taxes and a change on your throne. I will never become king of the Northern Iceni. Boudica and I were presented with few options. Because of Caturix's rebellion, Rome would have taken control here. But the *Greater* Iceni have been true to their word, so the governor allowed us to carry on under a ruler Rome trusts, Boudica," he said, turning to me.

"It is not Rome's place to choose!" someone shouted.

"Who are they to decide?" another demanded.

The Roman soldiers shifted, but I motioned for them to be still.

"My friends," I called. "I know the Northern Iceni to be wise. You are not blind to the shape of our new world. If Bran and I had protested, we would have faced the full wrath of Rome for Caturix's betrayal. Right now, the Coritani burn, their kings have been pulled down, and their people suffer. That is the fate that awaited you.

"I am my father's daughter. I am Northern Iceni. I will stand between you and Rome to ensure the Northern Iceni do not suffer the same fate as the Coritani. That was the only offer we could make to protect our people. So, I stand here because you are precious to me. Bran will continue to lead Oak Throne. But in all other matters, I promise to keep you safe."

At that, the people grew silent as the truth behind the decision became clear.

Either I became queen, or they became Rome.

"Hail Queen Boudica," Ula shouted from the back of the crowd in a loud, gravelly voice.

The others looked at her.

"Hail Queen Boudica," Cai shouted.

"Hail Queen Boudica," others began to shout. "Hail Queen Boudica. Hail Queen Boudica, Hail Queen Boudica."

"And just like that, you have truly become Queen of the Iceni, the first in history," Bran said. "Hail Queen Boudica!"

I looked out at the crowd. Slowly, it dawned on me then that Bran and I had potentially walked into a trap. In setting a crown on my head, the governor had just made the Greater Iceni liable for any actions of their northern brothers and vice versa. One foot out of line, Rome could have us all, with only Prasutagus there to block the path. I hoped Aulus was right, that Prasutagus was the most respected of our kings, because something told me that in moving to protect my people, I may have given Rome the very thing it wanted—everything.

WITH THE ROMANS busy with their construction and Bec still in bed, I stayed a few days longer to help my brother deal with the shape of his new world and to comfort my friend.

"Why don't you go to Dôn for a time?" I whispered to Bec, who lay in the darkness of her chamber. I gently stroked her hair, feeling frustrated I could do little more to comfort her. I had given her tonics and herbs to help her mind feel free, but the wound she now wore was on her heart.

"Yes," she said sadly. "Yes, I think I will. Will you arrange it, Boudica?"

"Of course."

"Remember your promise. Say nothing to Bran. Only tell him it is a woman's ailment best handled by Dôn."

"Of course."

Bending, I kissed her on the head, then rose and went to the kitchens, where I found the servants and Pix.

"Pix, Bec must go to the Grove of Andraste for a time. Will you arrange for a party to escort her?"

"Ye will not ride with us?"

"No," I replied simply. The truth was, I didn't want

to go to the grove. But it wasn't Dôn I was avoiding. It was the whispers from the shrine of Andraste. Already, I felt a snag in my heart, a lump in my throat I could not clear. I didn't need a goddess from the Otherworld to chide me. I felt it. I couldn't help but feel it. The peace was unravelling. Ula was right. One day, it might be too much. What then?

Pix eyed me carefully, stuffed the hunk of cheese she'd been holding into her mouth then said, "I'll see to it now."

I nodded, then turned to Riona. "I will stay longer to help with Bellicus, but I must return to Venta soon. Will you be able to manage without Bec?"

"Of course. But, Boudica, whatever is the matter? She's been abed for days. She has no fever, but she's feeling so poorly. Should we have Ula come to check on her?"

"It is a woman's ailment, I believe. Dôn will be the best one to handle it."

"As you say."

Leaving the women, I went to find my brother, who was with the garrison of Roman men, helping them dig the foundations of their new building. The Romans laughed as they worked, Bran joining them.

I swallowed my emotions. With a smile, I joined them. "Gentlemen."

Bran waved to the men and then set his shovel aside.

"Boudica," he said with a light smile. "I thought to give a hand," he said, wiping the sweat from his brow. "They are good men, all in all, from all over the Empire. They had fascinating stories," he said, then took a swig from his water pouch. "It seemed to me a good idea to get to know them better—as men."

"Yes, you're right to do that."

"What is it?" Bran asked, reading my expression.

"I've arranged for Pix to ride with a small party to the Grove of Andraste. Bran, it's Bec. She's struggling with a woman's illness. It is nothing that cannot be remedied with time. I've convinced her to go and stay with Dôn for a while to get the help she needs."

At that, Bran pulled me aside. "She's been unwell since I returned. She told me not to worry, but tell me the truth, Boudica. Will she be all right? It's not like her to linger like this unless she is truly ill."

"She'll be okay," I told Bran, setting a hand on his shoulder. "But she needs a little time."

Bran nodded. "All right. Let me go speak to her. Care to take over?" he asked, gesturing to his shovel.

"Decidedly not. But send Cidna with ale for the men," I told him, gesturing back to the Romans. "It will serve as a bandage—for us all. As you said, they are just men. I'm sure they do not want to be where they are hated. If you can soften them to the people of Oak Throne…"

Bran nodded. "My thoughts exactly. I'll see to it," he said, then headed back to the roundhouse, slipping his tunic back on as he went.

Leaning against a fence, I watched the Romans as they worked for a time, then turned to go. When I did so, I found Birgit and Eiwyn waiting for me. I realized then that the girls had wanted to approach but had felt scared to get close to the Romans.

"Girls," I said with a smile.

"Boudica," Birgit said nervously.

Eiwyn, however, frowned hard at me.

I walked away from the Romans, gesturing for the girls to follow me. We headed back into the marketplace, stopping by the sheep pens.

"Sweet girls, are you both all right? Such terrible things... Are you well?"

"Boudica," Eiwyn said harshly. "How can you just stand there and smile with these Romans after what they have done?"

"You act as if nothing happened," Birgit chided me. "And everyone here is angry and afraid. They are saying many things. The elders are defending you, but many are angry."

"As they should be," Eiwyn said. "You stood there and did nothing when they killed Aterie!"

"If Bran and I had rebelled at that moment—and it

was a horrible moment—what would have happened?" I asked.

"We would have fought back against those Romans, and they wouldn't have taken our weapons," Eiwyn said.

"No?" I asked.

"No! They wouldn't have," Eiwyn barked angrily at me. "We would have fought them instead. Now, they're here digging away like it's normal for them to be here."

Birgit paused, not rushing to agree.

"Did you see the army encamped beyond the walls? And more, down the road in Durin's fields? And even beyond that?" I asked.

"We could have fought back," Eiwyn insisted. "Our people are strong."

"Yes, they are. If we were ever to come together as a great army, we would be a force to be reckoned with. But as we are, does Oak Throne have the strength to defy five thousand Roman soldiers?"

Birgit looked at me. "We would have been killed. All of us. That is why you said nothing."

I nodded to her. "I mourn Aterie. I mourn our losses. But in my silence, in the sacrifice of my pride, my honor, I saved more lives."

"Maybe it's better to die *with* honor," Eiwyn told me, then turned and ran away.

"Eiwyn!" Birgit called, but the girl was gone. Frowning, she looked back at me. "I'm sorry, Boudica. I understand why you did it. It just…"

"Hurts."

She nodded.

I pulled her close. "Yes. I know. It's a pain deep in the belly, so horrible you don't want to name it." I kissed her on the head.

"I will talk to Eiwyn. Finola and Aterie were her neighbors. She's just upset."

"We all are. I understand her grief and anger. But I'd rather have her hate me than see her dead."

Birgit nodded.

"I must attend to things now. I need to return to Venta soon."

Birgit wrapped her arms around my waist. "I love you, Boudica. Please be safe."

"You too. May the Maiden watch over you."

"And the Morrigu watch over us all."

CHAPTER 9

A few days later, I found myself in the saddle again as I prepared to return to Venta. Kennocha's belongings, including her goats, had been loaded into a wagon. Kennocha, Mara, and Caturin sat in the front seat, ready to set off. While I could see the nervousness in Kennocha's eyes, the children were excited.

But Kennocha wasn't the only one who had prepared to make the trip.

Finola, unable to stay in Oak Throne, where her husband lay dead under the earth, had agreed to come to Venta at Ula's urging.

"Ula thought it might be good for me to be with my sister," Finola told me. "If that is all right with you, Queen Boudica."

"Aye, Finola. I am heartsick about what has

happened. Anything I can do to help, I will. And you are most welcome in Venta. Vian will be glad to have you with her."

At that, she nodded then loaded her meager belongings into one of the wagons. One of my Greater Iceni guards helped her.

Another three families, including Eiwyn's, had also packed their belongings to relocate to Greater Iceni territory.

"Are you certain there will be a place for us?" Eiwyn's mother asked.

I nodded. "Yes. Prasutagus does nothing but build. In Venta or at Yarmouth, you will find a place. I will see to it."

The woman gave me a grateful smile.

It was the reason behind that smile that unnerved me. The families didn't feel safe in Oak Throne anymore. They were leaving family, friends, and a lifetime of all they had known to go to Greater Iceni territory, where they felt safer and were not subject to Rome's punishments.

I glanced at Eiwyn, who was saying goodbye to Birgit, Phelan, and the other children. When she saw me looking her way, she scowled and turned her back to me.

Bran joined me as I mounted Druda. "Be careful on the road," he told me. "The whole tribe is unnerved."

"As they should be."

"I will send regular correspondence. I'm sure Cai won't say no to paying a visit to Venta," he said, glancing toward Pix and Cai, who were locked in a passionate farewell kiss.

I huffed a laugh and then nodded. "If anything goes wrong, if you need me, send a rider. I will come at once. Otherwise, you are king here, Bran. I know it. The people know it. It doesn't matter what the Romans decided or what we agreed to. In our hearts, we all know the truth."

"Thank you, Sister."

"And Bec... If she needs me... Just send word."

"I will."

"Boudica!" Bellicus said, running toward Druda and me, his arms raised.

Druda eyed him warily, then snorted with annoyance.

Bran laughed, then picked the boy up so he could kiss my cheek with his cold, wet, and grubby lips.

"You're a mess, Bellicus."

"I was pulling worms," he said, showing me his hands blackened with soil.

"I see. Be good for your father. I'll see you again soon."

"Goodbye!"

With that, I rode to the front of our party and signaled for us to make ready to ride out.

As we made our way from Oak Throne, I spotted Ula sitting on the back of a wagon, Graymalkin in her lap.

She had not come to make amends, nor had I gone to her, but her support spoke her heart.

When I saw her, I set my hand on my heart and bowed in my saddle to her.

She waved her hand dismissively at me but gave a half-smile.

With that, everything was amended.

Turning, we made our way from Oak Throne, passing the busily-working Romans as we departed.

The sight of them, digging and building, like a fungus growing inside walls, filled me with a deep sense of uneasiness and sorrow.

Exhaling deeply, I turned and faced the road south once more.

My discomfort was the consequence of my choices.

Now, I had to live with it.

And with that, I rode from Oak Throne as Queen of the Iceni.

THE JOURNEY HOME seemed to take longer than ever before. To entertain Mara, I took the little girl and placed her on the saddle in front of me, as I often did with Sorcha. Olwen was too shy of animals to try it. Mara, excited to be on her big adventure, asked me about every stream, farm, and road we passed.

"I've never been beyond the crossroads before," she told me, referring to a marker just south of Oak Throne. "They say Venta is as big as ten Oak Thrones."

"Not quite, but it is larger. The most special part of Venta isn't the city, though. That would be the nemeton at Arminghall. The nemeton is a sacred place of the druids. It sits like a crown upon a line of power that runs across our land—of those roads of Elen of the Ways. There, we call the gods and give them thanks."

"Does it have great trees like the Grove of Andraste?"

I shook my head. "The nemeton is made of timbers, but none living. There is a single standing stone not far from it. It's called the King Stone and is a gateway between Venta and other menhirs."

Mara laughed. "You sound like a druid."

"And what's wrong with that?"

"Nothing, it's just… How does one become a druid, exactly? No, wait. Not a druid, a priestess."

At that, I smiled. One day, I could tell Mara her grandmother—my mother—had been a priestess. One day, but not yet. "That is a very sacred order. The gods themselves whisper to the women they wish to serve them. They will be drawn to the path, and from there, they will find their way."

Mara was silent for a time and then asked, "Are there places for priestesses in Greater Iceni lands?"

"No, but just across our border in Trinovantes territory is Maiden Stones, a holy place for women. Amongst the Durotriges, there are the maids of Avallach. We Northern Iceni have our grove. And far to the north, in the Caledonian lands, is the Isle of Mists, where women train to become great warriors. Lynet of Frog's Hollow is from that tribe and has a sister who is a priestess there. And there are many other sacred places, many I'm sure I've never heard of. Would you like to be a priestess?"

"Maybe."

"Why only maybe?"

"My mother has much work to do with her goats, and now…" she said, then trailed off.

"Now?"

"King Caturix looked after my mother, brother, and me. Now that he is gone…" she said, and I felt the heaviness in her heart. The child had not known Caturix was her father, but he had been a beloved friend and benefactor. "I will need to help with the work, especially now that we are going to Venta."

"Your family is dear to me, Mara. I will look after

you. I promise you that. You can always come to me for anything you need."

The child turned in the saddle and looked up at me. "Thank you, Queen Boudica," she said, giving me a soft smile.

Her resemblance to my brother was so strong that it evoked such a pinch of pain that I almost sobbed.

Swallowing it, I smiled and stroked her hair.

"Of course," I said.

When the child turned back, I covered my mouth with my hand and closed my eyes.

Caturix.

Oh, dear brother…

I promise you I will do everything I can to keep your little ones safe.

Caturix.

Brother.

I will miss you.

When we arrived in Venta, it was night. A horn sounded, alerting the roundhouse that we had returned. Everyone flooded out to greet us. When Vian spotted her sister, she looked confused momentarily, then hurried to join her.

Mara had fallen asleep against me as we'd ridden. I hadn't had the heart to move her.

Prasutagus joined me.

"You have a growth on you, my queen," he told me.

"A lovely one," I replied.

Prasutagus eyed over the party. "I got your messenger. You have come with a larger party than expected."

"These people want to relocate to Venta. I assured them we would help. Vian's sister has come too. Her husband was killed by the Romans. And there is one family in particular that needs special care," I said, looking down at Mara. How like my brother she looked in her sleep, her dark hair framing her face.

"I understand," he said, then called to Galvyn, the housecarl. "Please see to the Northern Iceni families. Let's have them housed inside the king's compound for the night. Tomorrow, we will find places for them in Yarmouth or Venta." Prasutagus then turned to the others. "You are welcome in Venta, my Northern Iceni friends. My people will see you to lodging tonight, and we will have food for your families. Be at ease. You are safe here."

At that, I saw many relieved smiles.

Prasutagus gently took Mara from me, holding the girl in his arms.

Kennocha joined us. "Thank you, King Prasutagus. I can take her now," she said, moving to take Mara while juggling a sleeping Caturin.

"Your hands are full already, dear lady. Let's have you in the guest house. Come. This way. My men will see to your belongings... and your audience," he said with a light chuckle, looking back at the goats peering at Kennocha from the wagon.

"They only care because I'm the one who feeds them."

Prasutagus laughed. "Nonsense. You're the one who tends to and loves them, and they know it. And they feel the same."

At that, Kennocha gave Prasutagus a grateful smile. "Thank you, King Prasutagus."

Leaving Kennocha's care to Prasutagus, I went to the wagons where Vian was helping Finola down.

The girl wept as she spoke to her sister, telling Vian all that had unfolded.

"Finola," I said, looking worriedly at her as she held her belly. "Are you well? There is a midwife in Venta who—"

"I'm just sick at heart and weary, Queen Boudica," she said sadly.

"Boudica, can she..." Vian said, a stunned expression on her face as she absorbed the news. Vian looked back toward the roundhouse.

"Give her Pix's bed. I'll relocate Pix for a time."

"Thank you," Vian said, then wrapped her arm around her sister and led the weeping girl inside.

Pix joined me, watching as they went.

"I told Vian to give Finola your bed."

"As ye say. I'll bunk with Ronat."

"Suppose she'll be open to that?"

Pix winked at me.

I shook my head. "You've been a bit quiet these days. I know you've been spending time with Cai, but... is all well?"

"I'm heartsick. Innocent people like that girl there," she said, pointing to Finola, "are paying the price for peace. I am sick with sorrow and anger over it. Still, there is nothing to be done. Now, let me go see how I can be of help," she said then went inside.

Feeling miserable, I joined Eiwyn and her family. Eiwyn was unloading two heavy bags from the wagon. Going to her, I took one from her hands and then helped her with the other.

"Got it?" I asked.

She nodded.

"Are you... Are you all right?" I asked her hesitantly.

"Tired," Eiwyn replied. After a moment, she looked up at me. "I'm sorry, Boudica. I'm sorry for what I said. I thought about what you told Birgit and me. I understand you're trying to keep us all safe. It's just… Do you ever get this feeling in your belly like something so bad will happen? You aren't sure what will happen, but you just know something will go terribly wrong? That's how I feel every time I look at those Romans. But that's not your fault. You're just trying to keep it from happening, right?"

I nodded. "Yes. No one has stated it quite so perfectly before. That is exactly what I'm doing."

Eiwyn set down her bag and then wrapped her arms around my waist. "I love you, Boudica."

"I love you too."

Eiwyn's mother smiled at us and then called to the girl. "Eiwyn, we must go with these men now."

"I will see you tomorrow," I told her, kissing her on the head.

Eiwyn took the other bag from me and then ran off, joining her family.

Turning, I went on a hunt of my own. My maid, Brita, appeared from within the roundhouse, Sorcha running in front of her, Olwen in her arms.

Sorcha ran to me. "Mother," she said, flinging her arms around me. "We were in the bath when you arrived. Can you believe that? What a time to be naked," she said with a laugh.

I lifted her and then planted a kiss on her cheek. "Well, you smell beautiful, inconvenience or not."

At that, she chuckled. "Brita told me I had carrots growing in my belly button."

I laughed, kissed her once more, then set her back down to take Olwen from my maid.

"Thank you for cleaning up my vegetable-ridden children," I said with a laugh, then kissed my sweet daughter, wrapping a curl of her straw-colored hair around my finger.

Olwen pointed to the families that had come, gesturing particularly at Kennocha and her children.

"They are Northern Iceni. They have moved from Oak Throne to Venta. We will help them."

Olwen furrowed up her brow and pointed at Kennocha again, this time more insistently.

"That is Kennocha and her children, Mara and Caturin."

Olwen nodded, then pointed to them again.

I leaned into her ear and whispered, "What you are asking me is a very big secret. You must tell no one. Those children are your cousins. They are the children of Caturix."

At that, Olwen smiled and nodded.

"What are you telling Olwen?" Sorcha demanded.

"Only that these families have come from Oak Throne. We will help them find places to live here in Venta."

"Why did they leave Oak Throne?" Sorcha asked.

"That's…complicated. Let's go inside. It's been a long ride, and I'm tired."

"What do you mean by complicated?" Sorcha needled me.

"Don't pester your mother with questions. Let's go make sure everyone has something to eat. Can you help in the kitchens, Sorcha? Betha and Ronat may need us. Or are you too tired?" Brita asked, distracting the girl by playing to her determination to do everything adults did.

"I'm not tired," Sorcha retorted indignantly. "I can help."

"Good. Let's go."

With that, we made our way back inside. We went to the kitchens, where we found Nella, Melusine, Betha, Ronat, and Newt working quickly to prepare food for the new arrivals.

"Boudica," Melusine said. Her eyes were bloodshot, and her hair was a mess. "I dared not come out in case I was recognized. What news?"

I motioned for Melusine to step away with me.

"All these people all at once," Nella grumbled. "And we're expected to feed them all?"

"No one expects you to feed anyone, Nella," Betha chided the grouchy old maid.

"Don't you want to feed hungry people?" Sorcha

asked Nella. Was she, even at this age, needling the woman? I wouldn't put it past Sorcha.

Nella mumbled something in reply but didn't complain again.

"Boudica," Melusine began nervously. "I saw Vian with a girl, a pregnant girl, who was weeping. And they said other Northern Iceni families have come," Melusine said, worry in her voice.

"That is Vian's sister, Finola. Finola's husband was killed by the Romans in a show of force."

"Oh, Boudica, what's happening?"

I relayed to Melusine all that had transpired at Oak Throne. As I spoke, Prasutagus joined us. The pair of them listened carefully as I shared all that had happened.

Olwen, still in my arms, simply laid her head on my shoulder and played with a curl in my hair.

"There was no other way to avoid the Romans taking over. It was Bran's idea that I take the crown—he put it forth to the governor. I hope I have not risked the Greater Iceni in the process."

Prasutagus nodded slowly. "The governor seems to be a tactician. He has a long game in mind," he said, then frowned.

"They asked about you, Melusine. I told them we had assumed you were dead."

"Then they are looking for me," she said nervously.

"I cannot stay here. I risk you both by being here," she said, wringing her hands.

"We will not leave you to the will of the winds," Prasutagus told her. "We will make a plan."

"What about my father?" Melusine asked. "What news of the Coritani?"

I paused, then said, "There was nothing definitive, but we could see the smoke from their fires even across the Wash."

"If he is not already, he will soon be dead, just like Caturix," Melusine said, tears slipping down her cheeks.

Olwen leaned forward, causing me to catch her before she fell, and wiped Melusine's tear from her cheek.

"Thank you, sweet girl," Melusine said, kissing her hand.

"The governor treated the Northern Iceni and Coritani revolt as a minor inconvenience to be squashed. He was anxious to return west to chase Caratacus," I said.

"Caratacus has taken the change in governors and the rebellion as an opportunity to raid with the Silures and Dobunni, pushing into Catuvellauni lands, burning and sacking Roman outposts as he goes," Prasutagus said.

"It was not opportunity. It was planned," Melusine told us. "The rebellion was meant to serve, in part, as a distraction so Caratacus could strike. I was not in the room when the plan was discussed, but the roundhouse at Stonea is small, the walls are thin, and I am curious by nature." Melusine shook her head. "Such small gains for so great a loss. It was an ill-conceived plan. I told Caturix as much. And now my husband is dead. My father is likely dead as well. And I am hunted."

"The Romans will forget you in time. They will be too busy with Caratacus," I said, trying to reassure her.

Melusine shook her head. "No, they won't. They will want to wipe out the royal families of the Coritani so there are no leaders left, no figureheads for anyone to rally around. That way, they can take complete control. I cannot stay here but have nowhere to go."

"There might be a way..." Prasutagus said as he considered. "You are safe here for tonight, Melusine. Just stay out of sight. We must attend to the Northern Iceni, let these fires settle, and I will think on this a bit more."

"Thank you, Prasutagus," Melusine said, giving him a grateful smile.

"All our fates are sealed," I told Melusine. "We will act together to keep one another safe. We will not abandon you, Melusine. You are with us now."

"From this life to the next, and the next, and the next," Prasutagus said, his voice ringing with the sound of prophecy.

CHAPTER 10

The days that followed became a whirlwind. Prasutagus had been extending Venta to the north. Some families had taken up tracts of land, but there was still space for the Northern Iceni families. Prasutagus and I found a section of land where they could reside together. It was still spring, so there was plenty of time to build. We moved the families, setting them up in tents and ensuring they had silver and manpower to build. Seeing to the families was easy, but what to do about Kennocha felt more challenging.

One morning, I walked outside the roundhouse to find Sorcha, Olwen, Caturin, and Mara running in circles after one another. Brita and Arthur watched over them, both chuckling at the sight of a very serious game underway.

"What's happening here?" I asked with a laugh.

"It is all Sorcha's doing," Artur told me. "They are silly goats, part of Lady Kennocha's little herd," he said, gesturing across the square to the animal pens where Kennocha was tending to her goats.

As I watched the children play, deciding the best way to help Kennocha became easy. Watching the four of them, I was watching Bran, Brenna, Caturix, and myself again. I had planned to place Kennocha and the children in a house in Venta, but at that moment, I made up my mind. Unlike Caturix, I wouldn't abandon them. They were my own blood. I couldn't stuff them away as Caturix had done. My brother was gone. His choices, good or ill, no longer mattered. Duty to our tribe had prevented Caturix from choosing the woman he loved. Duty to my blood compelled me to keep them close.

I turned to go back into the roundhouse to speak to Prasutagus on the matter when I found Melusine standing there. She was staring at Mara and Caturin, her eyes watching the children closely.

Finally, she looked up at me. "Who... Who are those children?"

While their marriage had been arranged, my brother had grown to love Melusine. He hadn't wanted to hurt or humiliate her. But now, somehow, the truth felt right.

"They are Mara and Caturin," I said.

"Mara and Caturin," Melusine repeated, staring.

I watched her gaze as she took it all in: the children's dark hair, Mara's heavy brow, and their names.

"Mara," Melusine finally said. "Like Damara, your mother."

"Yes."

"She's older than Sorcha."

"Yes, by a couple of years."

"And Caturin..." she said, then paused. After a long time, she added, "Like his father."

"Yes."

Melusine stood perfectly still for the longest time, watching the children. They had switched up their game. Now the little ones were chickens, and Mara was the fox. When the children scattered to hide from the fox, Caturin came to Melusine and hid behind her long skirts.

The children laughed as Mara chased after them. Finally spotting Caturin, Mara ran for her brother who dashed away laughing, his little belly poking out in front of him as he giggled and ran on his little legs.

Melusine laughed lightly, then shook her head, her eyes wet with unshed tears. "He didn't tell me."

"He didn't want to hurt you. He loved you."

Melusine looked across the king's compound toward the animal pens where Kennocha was tending to her goats.

"Our father wouldn't permit him to marry her," I

told Melusine. "She is a widow and a commoner. Caturix loved her, but it made no difference to my father. King Aesunos couldn't reject your father's offer for the tribe's sake, so Caturix gave them up. He wed you, not expecting to ever love you, but he did. He loved you."

"But he still loved her."

"Yes."

Melusine's lip quivered. "I didn't know I'd stolen another one's love, a child's father. Did my father know?"

"I don't know, but I don't think so. Aside from myself and my father, no one else in my family knew— at least then. Only later did the rumors begin."

"Of course they did," Melusine said with a light laugh. "They are doppelgängers of their father. Look how Mara scowls. She is a perfect reflection of Caturix." Melusine's gaze went back to Kennocha. "She must hate me."

"She's not the kind to hate."

Melusine watched the children for a long time, then said, "You must keep them here with you, Boudica. In the king's compound. The times are so uncertain. A woman on her own is not safe. Keep them here. I spoke to Prasutagus this morning. He suggested I go to the King's Wood, the place of your druids. I wasn't sure, but now… I must go so she and her children can be safe."

"Melusine…"

"I already stole from her. Let me give her something back. Let her children be safe here with you. And I will be close enough at hand in case anything goes wrong but far enough away from you not to raise suspicion. I will practice my trade amongst the druids and serve the holy brethren. Perhaps, in a few years, after everyone forgets my face, I can open a stall in the marketplace," she said with a light laugh.

"Melusine, are you sure?"

She nodded. "I will not put you and Prasutagus at risk…nor any of your family."

Melusine was leaving, in part, to protect Caturix's children.

"You don't have to do this," I whispered.

Melusine turned to me. "I loved him. He didn't tell me about them to spare my feelings. I know him well enough to know that. But I will not stay here and be a threat to his sister…or his children. I will give Prasutagus my answer."

Leaving her animals, Kennocha came to us with a tiny bundle in her hand. "Children, come see," she called to them. "Boudica, you too."

"Come on," I told Melusine.

"Boudica, no."

"I promise you, she isn't like that. Come," I said, taking Melusine's arm.

Following behind the children, we went to Kennocha. There, we found her with a baby goat in her arms. The pure white goat was resting gently.

"Oh, it's so cute!" Mara exclaimed. "We should name it Snow."

Kennocha laughed. "That is the perfect name."

"Oh, Snow, you are so sweet," Sorcha said, patting the little one.

The other children gathered around, doing the same.

When the kid grew tired of the patting, it struggled to be free. Kennocha set the creature down on its wobbly legs. It stood, looking at the children.

"It's a good omen," Brita told Kennocha.

"Agreed," Artur said. "There is new life for you and yours in Venta."

"I hope you're right," Kennocha said with a sad smile. Like Melusine, Kennocha was nursing the ache of the loss of the man she loved. Finally realizing Melusine was there—and who she was—Kennocha gave a light gasp.

Just then, the baby goat began to wander off, running on its little legs, making the funniest little scream as it went.

Laughing, the children followed it.

"It is a sweet creature," Melusine said. "May the gods and all the greenwood bless and protect all of your little ones, Lady Kennocha," she told her gently, holding Kennocha's gaze for a long moment.

"Thank you, Queen Melusine. And may the gods give you solace and protect you in this difficult time."

Melusine smiled gently at her, inclined her head, then turned and walked back into the roundhouse.

Aye, Caturix. In your death, the truth is revealed. May the gods keep you in peace in the Otherworld until you can all be together again.

CHAPTER 11

I t took some convincing to get Kennocha to agree
to stay with us in the king's compound.

"I cannot live here pretending to be some
lady," Kennocha objected. "And it could draw undue
attention to the children. And... it would not be right to
do so with Queen Melusine here."

"Melusine is leaving. The Romans are looking for
her. She must go into hiding," I told Kennocha honestly.

"Oh," Kennocha said. "But still..."

"Aeddan, our animal minder, would be very grateful
for your help," Prasutagus told her. "You are someone
who likes to work. I can see that. Help us. Keep your
animals in the king's compound, and help us tend the
livestock. We will see that you have your own place
here, part of our household but your own. There is a
small roundhouse that is available for you. This way,

you and the children are protected, but you are free to live your own life, free to come and go as you please."

Prasutagus was right to make the offer. Kennocha had lived on her own since her husband had died. And I could see the independent streak within her. She was no meek thing. That was, in part, why my brother had loved her.

"In Roman eyes, you would just be another servant. But you would be safe here," Prasutagus told her.

"We could help you establish yourself in the city if you prefer, but the children... How well they play together, Kennocha."

Kennocha considered for a long moment, then said, "I will earn my place here. No pandering. I will help see to the animals. It must be a fair exchange, not a handout. I will work for my place."

Prasutagus inclined his head to her. "Of course. We can speak with Aeddan today. Already, he has sung the praises of your goats. I am sure he will be happy to have you with us."

"And all of us glad to eat your cheese." I laughed. "I swear I craved it when I was pregnant."

At that, Kennocha laughed. "Very well. We are agreed."

With that, Prasutagus and Galvyn went with Kennocha to settle her housing and speak with Aeddan. I was relieved she had accepted. Venta was a peaceful city, but I didn't like the idea of Kennocha living alone with the children. Many traders and strangers came through Venta. There was always the chance something could go wrong.

In addition to Kennocha and her children, there was also Melusine to settle. Very early that same morning, Ansgar had ridden to the King's Wood to ask Tavish, who had taken Henwyn's place as lead druid of the King's Wood, to shelter the queen. Ansgar returned in the afternoon with the news that the druids had agreed.

"They understand the risks," Ansgar said. "Melusine will not be seen publicly. She will not attend the rites. But she may live amongst the holy people," he said, then turned to Melusine. "It will not be a comfortable life, Queen Melusine. There is hard work to be done. The tasks are shared by all who reside in the King's Wood."

"I understand. I am only grateful for their help," Melusine said.

"Then, if you will, we will make ready to take you there today," Ansgar said.

Melusine nodded. "Of course."

"I will ride with you," I told her, then looked back at Pix, who nodded.

Having come to Venta with nothing save the bloody tool in her hand and the clothes on her back, it didn't take long for Melusine to prepare to depart.

"Queen Melusine," Ansgar said, holding a bundle to her. It was the plain off-white robes of the druid's order, including a veil for the queen to drape over her head.

Melusine took the garments, stroking the fabric. "Thank you, Ansgar," she said, then paused. After a moment, she laughed. "My father always ensured I was dressed in the finest gowns. How he would chide me for getting them dirty when I worked on crafting, which he found too masculine. Caturix freed me from those binds, letting me do as I wished. But still, I was a queen, not an artisan. In these robes... The gods work in mysterious ways."

"The Gauls have a goddess named Bergusia," Ansgar told her. "She is a goddess of metalworking, worshipped by the people of Vercingetorix. Perhaps her gaze is upon you, Queen Melusine."

"Then I will honor her by taking her name. Melusine is no more. I leave this house as Bergusia."

"Don't look much like a Bergusia," Pix told her.

Melusine laughed. "Who knows. Perhaps I'll grow into it. But for now," she said, patting her clothes. "Let me go make ready."

When she had gone, I turned to Pix, handing her a pouch of silver. "Meet us at the gates of Venta. Go to the marketplace. See the metalsmith. Buy all manner of tools and some raw materials so Melu—*Bergusia* may continue practicing her craft."

"And a wee drink for Pix."

"And a wee drink for Pix."

"I will meet ye there, Strawberry Queen," she said, and with that, left the roundhouse.

I turned to Ansgar. "We are indebted to the druids."

"They are indebted to you, my queen. All around us, the world burns, but the Greater Iceni still stand. We are not blind to this fact."

I inclined my head to him and then went to make ready.

As I went, I remembered one summer when the fields outside the walls of Oak Throne caught fire. We had stood on the ramparts, watching it burn. The men went to put it out, carrying buckets from the river, working diligently to stamp out the blaze. We had just been children at the time. Caturix had gone with the villagers to help, but Bran, Brenna, and I had stood with Father and watched.

"The fire is on the other side of the river and very far away," Brenna had said. "Why must they work so hard to put it out?"

My father stared at the flames and then said, "Fire has its own nature, just like little girls," he said, lifting Brenna and kissing her cheek. "It wants to spread. It wants to burn. Unless we do something, the fire will take the field, and its embers will jump the river and consume us. Never underestimate the will of fire."

The will of fire…

I could feel the heat of it breathing down my neck.

WE ARRIVED in the King's Wood just before dark.

The small village was situated in a dense forest not far from Arminghall Henge. It sat along the River Tas. It was a secluded place with a large roundhouse at the center, animal pens, gardens, small outbuildings, a large center square with a fire, and a stream flowing from the countryside toward the river, making its way through the village.

Since Henwyn's death, Tavish, a younger druid I did not know well, had taken over as leader. Ansgar had described him as earnest, forthright, and much in tune with the forest lord Cernunnos.

Tavish was the first to meet us. He had been working in the square, banking up the fire. He was a tall, handsome man, near in age to Prasutagus, with shoulder-length curly blond hair and a muscular body that told of days of hard work. He wore a simple tunic and leather trousers. A boline knife and an herb pouch hung from his belt.

"I suddenly get the urge to visit the King's Wood

more often," Pix told Melusine, raising and lowering her eyebrows as she looked at Tavish.

I chuckled.

Behind her veil, Melusine was still.

Feeling her tension, I reached out for her hand and squeezed it.

"It will be all right. You'll be safe," I reassured her.

She merely nodded.

"Queen Boudica," Tavish said, joining us. "Wise One," he added, bowing to Ansgar.

He gave Pix a brief smile before turning to Melusine.

"I see you have brought our new acolyte," Tavish said with a smile.

"Bergusia," Ansgar said. "This is the druid, Tavish."

"Bergusia," Tavish repeated. "Lady of Metalsmiths. Are you so inclined, Bergusia?"

"I confess, I am."

"No need to confess it, lady," he said, giving her a soft smile. Tavish extended his hand to help Melusine from her horse.

She dismounted and then smoothed the skirts of her gown.

"You are amongst friends here, Bergusia. If there is a need for your veil, I'll warn you. Otherwise, there is nothing here to gaze upon you but the sun, the wind, and the greenwood."

Melusine nodded, then pushed her veil back.

Tavish stared at Melusine for a long moment, then added, "And me," in a low tone.

At that, Melusine's cheeks turned scarlet.

Realizing he'd become distracted, Tavish said, "I shall…shall I…I will see Bergusia to her quarters," he said, pointing to a small roundhouse deeper in the woods that I hadn't noticed before.

Behind me, Pix chuckled.

"We have her things," I said, then gestured for Pix to unload the goods she had purchased. I slipped from Druda and untied the satchels containing garments and other goods Brita and I had prepared for Melusine. Once we had everything, we followed Melusine and Tavish to the small roundhouse.

The house was situated in a nook in the forest where the land sloped. This protected the back of the house and made the roundhouse appear as if it were part of the natural landscape.

Tavish motioned for us to follow him inside.

Within, the roundhouse opened to a central firepit. Three small cots sat along the wall. There was a wooden table with benches near the door. The room was simple, perhaps stark, but comfortable enough.

"You will share this house with two sister druids. They are holding rites at the henge tonight but will return in the morning. This is your bed," he said, gesturing to one of the three small beds in the room. The space was hardly larger than the bedroom I'd once shared with Brenna. Melusine's world was changing, but for some reason, I didn't think she would mind. "And for your things," he said, gesturing to a trunk near her cot. "Let me give you a moment to settle in," he told her softly.

Bowing to me, Tavish departed.

"What is all this?" Melusine asked, gesturing to Pix's crates.

"Show her," I said.

Pix set the boxes on the cot, opening them to reveal the tools and other goods for metalworking. "A gift fit for Bergusia."

"There are raw materials in this chest," I said, gesturing to one of the chests, "including some finer things from Prasutagus's stores. It's not much, but I hope it's enough to get you started," I said, then pressed a coin pouch at her. "Do not hesitate to ask us if you need more. Our purse is your purse," I told her.

"Ye never say that to me," Pix chided.

"You will spend it all on drinks and daggers."

"Ye say that like it's a bad thing."

We all chuckled.

"Oh, Boudica," Melusine said, wrapping her arms around me. "Thank you."

"It is as the gods will. They saw fit to spare you, my friend. Now, make good on their gift. Caturix is gone, and we are all heartsick for it. But in the coming days, find the life you could never have before and live it. Live it with passion."

Weeping, Melusine nodded.

I kissed her on the cheek.

Leaving the roundhouse, we returned to the central fire where Tavish and Ansgar spoke.

Pix was right. The druid really did cut a fine figure.

I quickly glanced at Melusine, who seemed to be trying *not* to notice.

"Ah, Bergusia. How do you find everything?" Tavish asked.

"Very good. You have my eternal gratitude."

"I know it is not what you are used to, but will it be all right?"

"I am more than content. Thank you."

"Perhaps it would be wise to let Tavish help Bergusia get to know her new home. We should leave you now," Ansgar said.

"Yes," I agreed. "But you will let us know if you need anything. And Bergusia will be kept out of sight of visitors," I reminded Tavish.

"Yes, Queen Boudica. We will see to it. Always. You can count upon us."

"Thank you, Tavish," I told him, then hugged Melusine again. "You will not hesitate to ask for anything you need."

"Thank you, Boudica."

With that, I let her go and then mounted Druda once more.

"I will return within a fortnight," Ansgar told the young druid. "There is much to be done at the king's house."

"We will see you again then, wise one," Tavish said, then turned to me. "My queen," he added, bowing. He inclined his head to Pix.

With that, we turned to make our way from the King's Wood.

I turned in my saddle once more to wave goodbye to Melusine, but Tavish had already led her away from the square toward the stream.

I smiled.

Bergusia, watch over Melusine and fashion her a happy life.

CHAPTER 12

I stood on the shore of the Wash, watching the dark blue waters twist wildly. Overhead, a seabird called.

I scanned the water, my eyes desperately searching. *There!*

Bobbing on the waves, I saw a man clinging to a log. He bounced and weaved on the rough water. From what I could see, he was barely keeping his grip.

I jumped into the water. The cold water was a shock to my system. Fighting past the sensation, I swam hard toward the drowning man. I pushed through the water, gliding quickly as Gaheris had taught me. Moving fast, I swam toward the bobbing figure.

"I'm coming," I called. "I'm coming to help. Hold on!"

The man didn't answer.

I pushed further. The cold water felt like it was cutting my skin. How had the man survived in the water for so long?

Finally, I drew close.

"I'm here," I called. "I'm here. I'm coming."

The man clung to the log, resting his head on the wood, his dark hair plastered to his face.

"Hey," I said, swimming closer. "Come on. I've got you. Let me get you to shore."

Still, he didn't look up.

Great Epona, is he already dead?

Reaching out, I touched the man's hand. "Hey. Do you hear me? Hello."

Then, he looked up.

It was Arixus, the druid of Seahenge.

"Boudica," he whispered. "Come."

And with that, he let go of the log and sank under the waves.

GASPING, I sat up straight in my bed. My heart pounded in my chest. I could still feel the chill of the water on my fingers and toes. A dream. It had been a dream. But the sense of panic and terror had felt so real.

Arixus...

No, not a dream, a message.

The druid had summoned me.

I turned to find that Prasutagus was already gone.

In the weeks that had passed since the rebellion, my husband couldn't sleep. These days, he never went to bed before me and was rarely there when I woke. He did not speak much of his worries, but I felt them all. They were the same fears I shared.

Since Aulus had gone, the shape of Rome's presence in our lands had changed.

What had once been promoted as a partnership, a grand return of Verica, was beginning to feel a lot like what Caratacus had warned us of all along—an occupation.

The hand offered in friendship was slowly slipping toward our throats.

Bran sent news every couple of days with riders, sharing with me updates on the Roman construction underway in Oak Throne and the conditions of the situation. As I had hoped, Bran worked hard to smooth things over with the Roman soldiers and settle them into the village on friendlier terms.

It was working to some extent, but *only* to some extent.

Because they were there, a sense of unease had fallen over Oak Throne.

As well, the increased levies on trade were already taking their toll. Bran and I tried to make plans on how to improve the Northern Iceni's revenue to stem the bleeding.

But some wounds inflicted on the Northern Iceni had not healed.

Finola was due to deliver her baby any day now. The child would come into the world without a father, which was Rome's doing.

And Bec... Bec had returned to Oak Throne, but Bran said she was much changed. Bran was worried for her health. She'd lost weight and had become withdrawn. I had no place in between my brother and his wife. While part of me wished Bec would tell him the truth, I knew why she didn't. Bran's honor would not let it lie. He would try to kill the governor and die—and so would every man, woman, and child in Oak Throne, Bellicus included. I hated that she suffered. I hated the governor for what he had done. And I hated Rome for being here.

Sighing, I pulled on a robe and slipped on some lambskin slippers Brita had made. It was early morning a few weeks before Beltane. The night air still had a chill that lingered until morning. Forcing myself from my warm bed, I went in search of Prasutagus.

I caught the soft sound of his voice coming from the meeting room. Someone else was there with him. Smoothing down my hair, I pushed open the door to find Prasutagus and Ansgar inside. Prasutagus held a message in his hand. I could tell by the expression on his face that he was unnerved.

"Boudica," he said, looking me over, his brow crinkling with worry. "Everything all right?"

"I… I'm not sure. A dream," I said, then looked from him to Ansgar. "What's happened?" I asked them.

Prasutagus waved for me to join them.

"Queen Boudica," Ansgar said, inclining his head to me. "I apologize for the early hour."

"The King's Wood? All well there?" I asked, my heart suddenly worrying for Melusine.

"All is well with our people, Queen Boudica."

"It is what is happening in the west," Prasutagus told me.

Frowning, I took a seat beside my husband.

"Scapula is reorganizing his forces. Vespasian is still pushing southwest. He is deep into the lands of the Durotriges. Scapula has left behind a rough contingent of soldiers in Coritani lands. They are capturing and questioning those they deem important."

"For what purpose?"

"They are hunting Caratacus. He is raiding, burning, and killing. He lures the Romans into unfamiliar terrain and then slaughters them. Apparently, with Scapula distracted by the uprising, Caratacus has had some success pushing the Romans back."

"And now, the Romans are questioning the druids," Prasutagus said.

"The druids? Why?"

"It is their belief that the druids are helping Caratacus. The Romans sacked the shrine of Taranis in eastern Coritani lands and took prisoners. Some of the druids escaped by boat and made it to Yarmouth, where I met with them yesterday," Ansgar said. "They came disguised as fishermen to avoid Roman spies."

"Why are the Romans questioning the druids? Why do they believe the druids will know anything?"

"The truth is, the druids *are* helping Caratacus," Ansgar said. "Hiding his men, helping him move unseen."

"Why would they do that?"

"It is the order from Mona," Ansgar said.

"Mona?" My thoughts went at once to Brenna.

Ansgar and Prasutagus looked at one another.

"Boudica," Prasutagus said gently. "The news from the south is harrowing. The Roman alliance with the Dobunni has fallen. King Abandinus is dead, and their ancient seat has been taken by the Romans. Vespasian's men are pushing across the land. The Romans are being squeezed by their emperor to capture Caratacus using any means necessary, including capturing, questioning, and torturing our holy people for information. The holy order is behind

Caratacus and encourages us to push back before it is too late."

"Tell that to Caturix, the kings of the Coritani, and now, the Dobunni." I turned and stared at the fire burning in the brazier nearby.

All around us, our friends and allies were falling. Those who had aligned with Rome were either becoming Rome or going back on their alliances. "What of the north? Cartimandua?"

"It is said Queen Cartimandua is embroiled in local problems. Rome is supporting her, so she will continue to support them."

A map of our world played out in my mind. To the east, Rome held everything in its hand, either by alliance or dominion. But to the west, our world was on fire.

"There is more," Prasutagus said.

I turned back to him.

"Caratacus has asked for an audience with us."

A loud laugh escaped my lips, bubbling out unbidden. "And how does he plan to manage that?"

"He would meet us in Londinium. It would be easy for him to blend in there."

"Oh, yes. And no risk to us if we are caught speaking with him *in a Roman city*. And when does he propose this gathering?"

"As soon as possible."

I frowned hard. "The Northern Iceni have their

heads in the hangman's noose thanks to Caturix's and Caratacus's whispering. I will not kick the stool out from under their feet."

Prasutagus nodded.

"Caratacus aside, I must ride to Holk Fort," I told them both. "I dreamed of Arixus. Something is wrong. I must pay them a visit."

"I would ride with you, Queen Boudica," Ansgar said, "if you permit it. Arixus and his brotherhood should know what is happening with the order of druids. For too long, they have walked their path alone."

I turned to Prasutagus.

"You must go?" he asked.

I nodded.

"As your husband, I'd rather see you stay here. But I am not just your husband. You are the queen of all the Iceni now, my wife. If you must go, you must go. I could come with you."

"And leave Venta open?"

Frowning, Prasutagus nodded. More than anything, I wanted my husband with me, but we dared not leave Venta—and our children—alone.

"Rally a guard to ride with you. As many men as you need," Prasutagus told me.

"And one Pix."

He chuckled. "Ah, there is only one Pix."

CHAPTER 13

Later that morning, we prepared to ride out. I was surprised, however, when Prasutagus appeared with Artur alongside him. The boy was dressed to travel, with a bow on his back and a sword on his hip.

Reading my expression, Prasutagus said, "Pix's idea. And this one was only too happy to agree," he said, clapping the boy on his back.

My gaze went to Pix, who was tightening the saddle on her horse.

She winked at me.

I shook my head, then turned back to Prasutagus and Artur.

Since we'd wed, Artur had grown from a child into a young man. The whisper of hair on his chin and above his lip spoke to the man he was becoming. As I eyed his lanky but muscular frame, I remembered Gaheris looking the same. Pix was right to encourage him to begin seeing more of the world.

But still, I worried.

"The Northern Iceni are not settled," I told Prasutagus. "Many of the Fen folk are still displaced. The roads are not entirely safe."

"That's why I want to come," Artur told me. "Morfran and I will look after you," he said, stroking the bird who sat on his shoulder.

I laughed lightly. "Well, as long as Morfran is helping."

"Mother," Sorcha called, running from the house to join me. Mara hurried along behind her. "Here. Here," she called breathlessly. "Mara and I made this for you," she said, handing me something.

Mara and Sorcha had become fast friends in the weeks that had passed. Olwen was often not far behind the pair.

I opened my hand.

Within was a handmade necklace.

"A necklace," I said, lifting it. The girls had woven together feathers, shells, acorn caps, and a hagstone.

"It's a talisman," Mara told me. "To keep you safe on your journey." A flicker of emotion crossed the girl's features. For the first time, I saw something in Mara's eyes that hadn't been there before. She knew. She knew she was Caturix's daughter, which meant she also knew that I was her blood. Had Kennocha told her?

I put the talisman on, then leaned down and kissed Mara on the forehead. "Thank you, Mara. May the greenwood bless your hands."

"You're welcome, Queen Boudica," she said, smiling softly at me.

I hugged the girl once more, then turned to Sorcha. "And you, little firebrand. Many thanks," I said, kissing her cheek.

She giggled and then pulled away.

"Ye be in charge of keeping the king's house safe while we're gone," Pix told Sorcha. "Ye have yer weapon?"

Sorcha nodded, patting the wooden dagger on her hip.

"Good. Ye remember what I told ye?"

Grinning, Sorcha nodded once more. "Fingers in the eyes," she said, demonstrating the move. "And a stab to the belly."

Pix laughed. "Good."

Nella appeared a moment later, leading Olwen by the hand.

"Queen Boudica, this one woke from a nap anxious to get outside. It was all I could do to catch up with her."

"Thank you, Nella," I told the woman, then turned

to my daughter. "Wanted to see me off, did you?" I asked Olwen, scooping her up and kissing her cheek.

Olwen set her hands on my cheeks, squishing them, then kissed my nose.

I laughed and kissed her once more. "Sweet girl, I will be back soon," I told her, then handed Olwen to her father. Turning, I mounted Druda.

"I'll try to be back in time for the Beltane celebrations," I told Prasutagus.

"You'd better, my May Queen."

I leaned down and kissed my husband. When we finally let one another go, I sat up straight and clicked to Druda. The Greater and Northern Iceni banners hoisted, our party made our way from the city.

Turning in my saddle, I waved one last time to the others, giving the girls an extra wave, then we began our trek north.

It had been more than a month since the Roman skirmish in the Fens and the attack on Stonea. Yet, we still encountered displaced Fen folk on the road to Holk Fort. It was late afternoon when one small party waved us down.

"Boudica. Princess Boudica, please. Alms, Princess," one ancient man called. He was riding in the back of a cart pulled by a young boy and girl about Artur's age.

I pulled Druda to a stop alongside them.

"Grandfather, where have you come from?" I asked.

"The Fens… Ah, Princess, the Fens are burning."

"She's queen now, Grandfather," the young girl whispered to the old man.

"What did you say?" he asked the girl.

She merely shook her head and then turned to me. "Our farm south of Stonea was burned by the Romans, Queen Boudica. Menfolk, including our father, went off to fight with the king. We're the only ones who survived when the Romans came. We escaped with what you see on us, but just barely. A Roman knocked my brother so hard he can't hear out his left ear anymore, but we're alive. Better off than the rest. We've been trying to scratch a living out of the Fens, living in a tent on the moors, but it's no use. There's nothing to be had."

Mixed emotions of sadness and fury whipped through me. I could understand the Romans going after the warband, but people like this, simple villagers. What harm had they done? What threat were two children and an ancient man to the Romans?

I dipped into my bag of supplies, giving the people what food I carried. Artur joined me, doing the same.

"Go east to Frog's Hollow," I told them. "You will find welcome there."

"And the Romans?"

"They... They *are* about, so watch yourselves on the road."

With that, the girl nodded. "Thank you, Queen Boudica."

"Princess. Princess. What terrible times, Princess," the ancient man called sadly, then wept.

The trio left us then, continuing their trek.

We heard tales of burned farms, looted homes, and displaced villagers all along the road from Venta to Holk Fort. And stories of Romans.

"They took over our farm, Queen Boudica. Sent us all away. Killed my husband when he resisted," one tearful woman told me.

Like the first group, they, too, were from the Fens.

"Where are you going now?"

"Got a sister on the coast. Will stay with her and her family. Not all the Fen folk rose up, my queen. But the Romans treat us as one and the same."

I nodded. "Where was your farm seated?"

"Along the border with the Catuvellauni, over in Fern Glen."

"How long ago, good woman, were you pushed from your farm?" Ansgar asked.

"But two nights ago, Wise One."

Ansgar and I exchanged a glance.

"May the gods bring you safely to your sister's home. I promise we will attend to this matter," I told the woman.

"Thank you, my queen. Thank you. Ain't nothing been right since Saenunos killed your father, Queen. May he rest peacefully in the Otherworld."

"Thank you," I told her, giving her a warm smile, then watched as they rode off.

I turned to Ansgar. "They've emptied the Fens. Taken it. Not just punished, annexed."

Ansgar nodded. "So it would seem."

Clenching my jaw, I clicked to Druda and moved the horse forward.

Aulus had warned me. Until now, the Iceni had not felt the whip of Rome's lash as the other tribes had. And when we had transgressed, Aulus had intervened. I had not realized how much he had done so until now. Where I had seen Prasutagus and myself as a shield between Rome and the people, what I hadn't seen was that Aulus had been standing between Rome and me.

WHEN WE ARRIVED at Holk Fort, I was shocked to see the place teeming with people. Construction was underway in the fields around the fort as people built houses and animal pens. Everywhere I looked, I saw carts coming and going.

A horn sounded from the wall, alerting those within of our arrival.

We rode through the gates to find the city cramped. I had left Holk Fort in the hands of the druids, who had brought the place back to life without a chieftain. Now, the misery had returned. I could see it in everyone's eyes.

"Ye see," Pix said, reining in beside me. "In their eyes. The shadow of Rome."

"Yes," I said stiffly.

"Boudica," Artur said, joining me. "Who are all these people?"

"They are refugees from the Fens," I replied.

"But the Fens are Northern Iceni territory."

"They were," Pix replied. "Bran told ye nothing of this?"

I shook my head. "I'm not sure he realizes the extent of the problem."

When we reached the roundhouse, we found it guarded by half a dozen black-robed druids. While none of them wore arms—nor did anyone else in the fort—I had no doubt that these men had blades on them.

Arixus appeared from the roundhouse. "Queen Boudica," he said, bowing his lithe frame. Like the others, he wore his own dark robes. His long, black hair hung around his face. When he stood, he looked at Ansgar. "Brother," he said, inclining his head to the druid before turning back to me. "Please, come inside."

With that, I gestured for Pix, Artur, and Ansgar to join me while the others were seen to by Arixus's brothers.

I was surprised to find that the roundhouse had been stripped bare of the excessive finery that had graced every nook and cranny under Saenunos's watch. We adjourned to the meeting room. Fan appeared from the back, a tray in her hands.

"Queen Boudica," she said in surprise. "I am pleased to see you again."

"Well met, Fan."

"If you don't mind me asking, how is Finola? The news came from Oak Throne that she returned to Venta with you after that terrible tragedy."

"Her child is due any day now. A talented midwife is seeing to her, and Vian and I have done what we could to make her comfortable, all things considered."

"May the Great Mother be thanked," Fan said, then poured us all a drink. "Back again, you wild thing?" she asked Pix with a smile.

"I dog Boudica like a shadow."

Fan laughed lightly.

"I do not know your face, young man," Arixus told Artur.

"Arixus, this is Artur, son of Prasutagus and Esu...and me."

Arixus stared at Artur. He lifted a finger in the air and bobbed it gently as he studied the boy.

Artur turned and looked at me, uncertain.

"The gods know you," Arixus told Artur.

"Know me?" Artur asked.

Arixus nodded, then smiled. "Yes. A great fate has been woven for you. One day, you will wed a princess, and your bloodline will carry on and on and on, like a rock skipping on the surface of the water, all defenders of our faith."

"But, Wise One, I'm not *really* Prasutagus's son. My father was—"

"Do you suppose that matters to the gods?"

"I...well, no."

Arixus nodded to Artur and then turned to me. "So, you received my message."

"Yes."

"And did you see what I wanted to show you?"

I paused. Arixus had brought me north to show me what had happened to the Fen folk, and what was still happening, which was not what Rome had agreed.

Defeated, yes. Annexed? That was something quite different. "I think so."

"There is more. Be at ease this night. We will leave in the morning so I can show you the rest."

"And where are we going?"

"Seahenge."

CHAPTER 14

D espite Arixus's suggestion that I rest, I found myself awake and on the walls of Holk Fort. I wasn't alone for long. Pix soon joined me.

"Fen folk," she said, looking over the quiet camps in the fields below the fort.

"I am seeing echoes of the Trinovantes refugees."

"Nay, not an echo of the past, a warning of the future."

I turned and looked at her.

"Ye heard me."

I looked across the field. For the first time, I did not argue with her. The warning bells were ringing in my heart.

"Prasutagus and I are in neck-deep with the Romans now," I said. "And I still cannot get my heart to align with Caratacus."

"Then a hundred—nay, a thousand—Ateries will die, just as that poor boy did. Just as Caturix did. What if ye had stood behind yer brother?"

"Don't you think I've asked myself that same question?"

"Have ye? Have ye truly? All around ye are Rome's lies. Yer people's blood is on their hands."

"And what should I do? Rally the Iceni so we can meet the same fate as Caturix? I might as well slit my daughters' throats myself."

"Nay, not just the Iceni. The Trinovantes, the Cantiaci, the Catuvellauni, the Coritani, and anyone else you can get to listen. All of them, Boudica. Ye need to rally them all. Ye may not have any love for Caratacus, but if ye and he pinch the Romans in the middle..."

"They will send more soldiers. More, and more, and more. They will come like waves on the beach, and in the end, we will not be enough."

"Ye cannot tell me ye don't want to fight."

"Of course, I want to fight," I said, turning on her angrily. "My brother is dead. My people are disarmed. The Northern Iceni are in ruins. Of course, I want to fight. But at what cost? At what cost?"

Pix puckered up her lips and looked out at the encampment once more. "One day, ye will be sorry ye did not act sooner. Yer pretty Roman kept ye blind to what was happening."

"He did not—"

"Not on purpose. He loved ye and sought to protect ye."

I said nothing.

"But he's gone," Pix said, then turned to go. "And the eagle remains. What more will it take until ye see?"

WE RODE out the following day for Seahenge. Arixus and the members of his sect led the way. Pix and Artur followed behind Ansgar and me.

"It is an ancient place, Boudica," Ansgar told me. "And the brotherhood lets no one near without invitation. There has long been tension between the leadership on Mona and the brotherhood of Condatis over their secretive ways."

"Arixus has been nothing but helpful to me and my people," I told the druid. "I trust him."

Ansgar nodded slowly. "We shall see."

We rode from the fort toward the Wash. Both Druda and I could smell the scent of the sea breeze in the air. Druda snorted excitedly.

I patted his neck. "No racing today, I'm afraid."

"Racing?" Artur asked.

I chuckled. "When I was younger, I would take Druda to the beach, and we would race. It was the highlight of Druda's youth…and mine."

"And King Aesunos allowed it?" Artur asked.

"Not exactly," I said, skirting the conversation.

But Pix didn't let me slide. "What she will not tell ye is she was rebellious. She does not want ye to know."

Artur laughed. "Is that true, Boudica?"

"Which part?"

"All of it?"

"Maybe," I replied coyly.

We all chuckled.

Arixus and his brothers led us away from the road that would take us directly to the beach and began an inward trek down a narrow path through the marshy wetland. Large trees loomed overhead. We wound along a narrow trail. Dragonflies zipped on iridescent wings, and birds called. Tall grass growing on the flats shimmered golden in the sunlight. We wound down the narrow route until the land seemed to rise and grow dry once more. Then, I began to hear sounds.

Voices, animals, and hammers.

I turned in my saddle and looked back to Pix, who was grinning.

Soon, a small village came into sight. It sat like a crown in the middle of the swamps but was totally hidden by the surrounding forest and bogs.

MELANIE KARSAK

Arixus turned back and gestured at the surrounding wetlands. "Welcome, Queen Boudica, to the village of Seahenge. We are arriving just in time. The waters will come in at noon, making an island of this place. They will not recede until tomorrow morning, Condatis hiding the trail."

We rode into the village. It was arranged in two concentric circles, the outer buildings sitting on stilts, connected by hanging rope bridges. The bridges also led to the inner buildings on the raised land. A large, round firepit was at the center of the inner circle of what was essentially an island.

We rode to the center square and then dismounted. Arixus gestured to the brothers to see to the horses.

Many had stopped their work to see who had come.

I eyed them over, realizing at once what I was seeing.

Druids.

Priestesses.

Coritani.

Catuvellauni.

Fen folk.

And the sound of the hammers... Sitting just off the center square was a blacksmith's hut. There, five strong men had been working making swords. Beside them were bowers, leather crafters, and other craftsmen making spears, daggers, shields, bows, arrows, and more.

Seahenge had become a haven for our holy people whose activities were in open defiance against Rome's orders.

Arixus turned to me. "Queen Boudica, I give you your war chest."

At that, Pix laughed. "What will ye do now, Strawberry Queen?"

"I..."

"Come, I want you to speak to some people," Arixus said, gesturing for us to follow him to one of the houses.

Turning, we followed the druid. Behind me, I heard Artur ask Ansgar, "But I thought the Romans had disarmed the Northern Iceni."

"The Northern Iceni are cut from the same cloth as ourselves. If the Greater Iceni had been disarmed by Rome, do you think they would stay that way for long?"

"No," Artur replied.

Ducking low, we entered one of the houses to find three druids and one priestess seated at a round table. When we entered, they rose.

"Ansgar," one of the men said in surprise.

"Bede," Ansgar said, going to greet the man. The two men held one another's arms, gripping each other by the forearm, then embraced. "Ah, brother. I am glad to see you alive."

A fourth man entered behind Arixus. It was Einion, the druid of Stonea.

"Einion," I said in surprise. "May the Morrigu be thanked. You lived."

"Queen Boudica," he said, bowing to me. "I was away from Stonea at the time of the attack. Ah, my queen, I am sorry I was not at your brother's side as I should have been."

"I know Caturix would be glad to see you safe," I told him.

"Queen Boudica," Arixus said, gesturing around the room. "May I introduce High Priestess Nimica of the Coritani, the druids Bede and Becan, also of the Coritani, and Uvain and Ragnell of the Catuvellauni."

"Wise Ones," I said, bowing.

"Queen Boudica," the High Priestess Nimica said, inclining her head to me. The priestess was, perhaps, Prasutagus's age. She had long, brown hair and light hazel eyes. On her forehead was tattooed a symbol of the waxing and waning moon. She wore a leather jerkin, a sleeveless tunic underneath, revealing symbols of horses, moons, and stars inked on her arms. "I am Nimica, high priestess of the goddess Rigantona. My sisters and I come to you from the lands of King Dumnovellaunus. We thank you and Arixus for shelter. Condatis led us across the Wash to the safety of the brothers' arms."

"Hail Rigantona," I replied.

The druid Ansgar had identified as Bede stepped

forward. He bowed deeply to me. "I am the druid Bede, my queen. I was an adviser to King Dumnocoveros. When the Romans attacked, I was at the Vale of Anwynn with Becan. We, too, crossed the waters of the Wash, guided by a vision from Condatis."

"Queen Boudica," Becan said, bowing to me.

The Catuvellauni stepped forward next.

"Queen Boudica, I am the druid Uvain. My sister bard, Ragnell, and I come from the forest shrine of Druantia. We have lived in exile for many months, sheltering in Coritani lands until the Romans arrived."

As I looked around the room at my holy people, there was a sinking feeling in my stomach.

In hiding Melusine, Prasutagus and I had already committed our first act of betrayal. But this... this was an act of rebellion. If the Romans discovered I was forging swords and hiding those whom they deemed troublemakers... But they were not troublemakers. They were the holy people of our lands, children of stone and oak. Who was I, *what* had become of me, if I didn't protect them?

I could feel Ansgar, Pix, and Artur all staring at me.

I inhaled slowly, deeply. Holding my breath momentarily, I exhaled and said, "I welcome you all to Northern Iceni lands in the name of the Dark Lady Andraste and the Horse Mother Epona. May you find peace and shelter here."

CHAPTER 15

"Ale for our guests," Arixus called, gesturing for us all to join at the table.

"The druid Ansgar of the Greater Iceni, whom some of you know," I said, gesturing to Ansgar. "Pix, my guardian, and my son, Artur."

At that, some of the druids gave Artur a second glance. But I could see them calculating and recalling the boy as belonging to Prasutagus's first wife.

"Now, my friends," Arixus said, leaning forward, "tell Queen Boudica your stories."

The tales of bloodshed and misery that unfolded before me twisted my heart. From the moment Aulus Plautius sailed from Britannia, the leash keeping the Romans from harming the druids had been cut. The druids and priestesses had been met with the same treatment afforded to Dindraine and her priestesses. All

144

across the land, the sanctuaries of our holy people were falling to Rome.

"It is the same everywhere," Nimica told me. "Some of the ancient shrines have been destroyed, burned, and their followers killed. Our sects have gone into hiding, abandoning the holy places of our gods."

"Caratacus is hiding amongst the druids, using the holy places to rally people to his cause. The Romans have figured out his game and are acting to stop it. To the west, our most sacred places are bleeding," Ragnell said.

"Avallach?" I asked. "Has anyone heard if the holy isle has been discovered?"

Nimica shook her head. "The last I heard, the sacred sisterhood has remained hidden. May the Great Mother be thanked."

"Forgive me for asking, Wise Ones," Artur said hesitantly, "but won't the Romans place the blame on the druids of Mona?" Artur asked.

Arixus nodded to the boy. "If they are smart enough to understand how our order works, then yes."

"For all the trouble he has brought, Caratacus is the only thing standing between the Romans and Mona. The western tribes are pushing back against Rome," Ragnell said.

"And bleeding and dying for it," Bede said.

"Aren't we all?" Uvain said roughly.

"Not the Greater Iceni," Arixus said. "Not the tribes to the north, including the vast empire of the Brigantes."

"The children of Brigantia would rather fight one another," Nimica said.

The others nodded.

I stared into the small brazier at the center of the table, my mind humming as I endeavored to process all I had heard.

Every fear I had ever harbored was beginning to come true.

"Boudica," Einion said. "What have they told you of the fall of Stonea?"

"I know the village was burned and the people were killed or fled in the fighting."

Einion nodded. "And after?"

"After?"

"The Romans have taken Stonea. They put out the fires, rebuilt what they wanted, and are using the fort as a base of operations, a garrison for their troops. Boudica, the Romans have taken the Fens. The farms, the small villages, all of it. The people have fled. Whatever they told you about the Fens has been a lie. It was not a battle. It is an occupation."

I turned to Ansgar. "I must go to Stonea myself, speak to the Romans. That was not agreed upon."

The druid nodded. "You must go carefully, my

queen. Rome has finally begun to show herself to us. And she is not what she seemed," Ansgar said.

At that, the conversation turned to what the druids had witnessed in their travels. Burned and looted farms and villages. Bede spoke of the fall of the Coritani, having seen the death of his king, barely escaping with his life.

As I listened, my head spun, and a sick feeling washed over my stomach.

I rose. "If you'll… If you'll excuse me for just a moment," I said, then stepped outside.

I pressed my hand against my abdomen, trying to calm my rocking stomach and catch my breath. I leaned with one hand against the wall of the building and closed my eyes.

Andraste…

Andraste…

What must be done?

But the goddess was quiet. A few moments later, I heard someone approach me from behind.

"Queen Boudica?" Arixus asked. "Are you all right?"

"I… Yes. I'm sorry, it's just—"

"You do not need to explain," he said, giving me an understanding smile. "Come with me."

Arixus led me away from the village, exiting a different path than we'd entered. We followed a path down the bank to the water. There was a dock with several small boats.

"This side of the village stays wet. You can go deeper into the bog or row back to the Wash. There are many routes inland. One will take you by a stream that leads almost all the way to Holk Fort. Another path goes to another island, a farmstead hidden in the marsh. That is one of the many gifts of Condatis. Like Elen, he is a master of ways. But he is also a master of water. Condatis rules the rivers, streams, and marshes. You have lost your path, Queen Boudica. Come, let us see if Condatis can show you how to begin again," he said, gesturing to one of the boats.

I boarded the small rowboat with the druid, then set off in the darkness.

"The path we follow now is only available under the moon's light. The waters rise to reveal the way," he told me as he rowed.

I sat in silence, watching the marsh pass by as Arixus rowed. The woods were thick with alder trees, growing tall in the peat. Soon, I spotted what looked like a wall in the distance.

Arixus rowed toward it.

The shape of the structure ahead of me was confusing. As we drew closer, I realized the wall was circular. On closer inspection, I saw that it was a ring of timbers.

The wide oak timbers had been fitted tightly together, forming a circle into which you could not see.

Arixus rowed us to a rise in the land where rocks had been stacked to form a natural dock. He lashed the small boat to a pole, debarked, then reached for my hand to help me out.

We walked toward the structure. As we approached, I saw no way in. The trunks of the trees made a perfect circle with no entrance.

But Arixus walked with purpose up the path. Still, I saw no entrance.

Arixus looked back at me over his shoulder, giving me a sly smile, then stepped around a timber, disappearing.

I paused a moment.

"Are you coming, Queen Boudica?" the druid called.

Confused, I reached out to touch the timber. Stepping forward, I inspected it to find it was not flush with the other logs that formed the circular walls. Instead, it hid an entrance to the circle just behind it. Within the walls of the henge was an entrance that was low and just wide enough for a man to pass through. It had been entirely hidden by the false wall.

Ducking low, I stepped through it.

On the other side, I found myself within the sacred circle. While the outside of the nemeton looked like natural wood, inside, the bark had been removed from the trees, and their timbers had been polished to a shine. It glimmered silver under the moonlight. The timbers radiated the light of the moon. At the center of the shrine was an altar made from the overturned roots of a tree. The unruly roots twisted and turned upward. The altar had been polished to shine like the timbers.

Arixus went to the center of the circle and stood before the altar. He lifted his hands into the air.

"Condatis, father of water, ways, and war, I bring before you the first Queen of the Iceni people. Blood of the Northern Iceni. Queen of the horse people of the Greater Iceni. Daughter of the Grove of Andraste. Queen Boudica comes to you with an open heart but a clouded mind. Whisper to her what you will."

With that, the druid gestured for me to come forward. "Lie down," he told me.

When I paused a moment, Arixus held my gaze. "Do you trust me, Boudica?"

I nodded, then took his hand.

Moving carefully, I lay down on the altar.

When I looked up, I found myself staring at the crescent moon.

Soon, it would be Beltane.

"Father Condatis, I send Boudica to you now. May she find her way amongst the stars," Arixus said. He reached into his robes and pulled out a small vial. Wetting his fingers, he marked my forehead with some sort of oil. He then trailed his finger along the ridge of my nose, across my lips and chin, down to my chest, where he drew a symbol.

"Open your mouth," he whispered to me.

I did as he asked.

Arixus then poured drops of warm liquid therein.

With that, the druid leaned over me and smiled. "See you soon," he whispered.

I began to feel dizzy, as if the whole world around me had started to spin.

Overhead, the moon and stars began to whirl, spinning like a child's toy until they became one blur of silver.

Then everything went black.

I STOOD ON THE BEACH, the water lapping at my feet. Behind me, I heard Gaheris chatting with Druda and Mountain. His words were unclear, but the lilt of his voice told me he was happy. Of course he was happy. We were always happy when we came to the beach.

I paused a moment.

How had we gotten there?

I didn't remember riding from Oak Throne.

Something felt odd about the whole scene.

"Gaheris," I said, turning back, but Gaheris and the horses were gone.

Water lapped over my feet.

I looked down, gasping, when I saw the waves had turned scarlet.

But then, I remembered.

Gaheris was gone.

His death marked the beginning.

Overhead, a hawk called.

"Mavis?" I whispered, but the creature flew toward the sun, and I didn't see her again.

Somewhere in the far distance, I heard the bong of a bell.

It sounded one sorrowful note, clanging, resting, then clanging again.

I looked around, searching for the sound, but suddenly I felt like I was spinning. The beach became a blur, and a moment later, I found myself standing in Stonea. Around me, the village burned. Romans on horseback were thundering through the ancient fort. One soldier chased down a child no older than Sorcha, cutting the little boy down with a swipe of the sword.

"No," I whispered, horrified.

Still, the bell bonged.

Not far from me, I heard Caturix shout.

"Behind me. Go, go!" my brother screamed.

Turning, I raced toward the sound of my brother's voice.

"Caturix! Caturix?" I called.

Coming up on the king's roundhouse, I discovered a skirmish in the courtyard. My brother was there with his soldiers, fighting back the Romans, while others helped the villagers escape through a gap in the wall.

"Go! Go," Caturix yelled, gesturing for a woman and her children to get through while he raced to step between her and the Roman soldier pursuing her.

"King Caturix, come on!" Pellinor, one of my brother's messengers, called to him, gesturing for Caturix to fall back.

"Where is Melusine? Have you seen Melusine?" my brother shouted, a desperate look on his face.

"No, my king. We lost her in the fray."

A look of anguish crossed Caturix's face, yet he battled on, one eye behind him as the villagers escaped and another eye on the burning fort.

"Melusine!" Caturix called into the fort. "Melusine!"

A dozen heavily armored Roman soldiers pushed through the flames, their shields and helmets gleaming.

"There he is," one of the soldiers yelled, pointing toward my brother. "Take him!"

They swarmed over my brother like ants, and I saw Caturix no more.

"No," I whispered, reaching toward him. But when I did so, I began to fall forward.

Down, down, down.

Still, the bell gonged.

One lonely chime.

Over.

And over.

And over.

When I finally hit the ground, I kneeled beside the River Tas, not far from the nemeton. Here, the Tas and Yare met. My hands were shaking. When I looked down at them, they were covered in blood. I looked at the water's surface, finding a man staring back at me.

A man and not a man.

What looked back at me was a man with the narrow eyes of a serpent. He had a smooth, hairless head. His face and head were inked with the symbols of our people. His skin from the neck down was covered in the scales of a serpent.

He reached out from the water, grasping my neck. He had long black nails on his fingers, and his hands were covered in scales.

"Boudica," he said. "You stand on the crossroads. Listen. Listen. Listen to the land. You will know when it is time. Rise. Rise," he said, then pulled me under.

My mouth and throat filled with water. I struggled to breathe as I thrashed under the black waves. Condatis was gone, but I still felt stuck. Something held me in place under the water. I looked down, seeing hands, so many hands, gripping my legs. Beyond were faces of desperate men and women, all trying to keep me under. I looked up, seeing the surface of the water so close. On the other side of it, a fire burned.

Again, the bell gonged.

I pumped my arms hard, trying to swim upward.

I was so close.

So close.

But I could not break free.

Soon, I felt the last of my air leave me, and the weight of those hands pulled me down.

Andraste.

Andraste.

Help me.

Above me, a hand plunged into the murky deep.

I reached for it.

At once, it tugged on me, pulling me free of the water.

I broke the inky surface with a gasp.

Opening my eyes, I found myself sitting on the altar at the nemeton of Seahenge.

I looked around, finding Arixus leaning against the temple wall, smoking a pipe.

Rise.

Rise.

It was not the first time the gods had whispered that to me.

But now, I understood.

Now, I saw.

I stared at Arixus, then said, "We must rise."

He puffed on his pipe and exhaled, the smoke trailing into the night sky. He nodded. "The only question that remains is when."

I looked down at my clothes, realizing I was completely drenched, my hair wet. My gaze went to the moon once more.

"When doing so doesn't cause our world to burn."

"Boudica," Arixus said carefully. "Such a time does not exist. Everything is at risk now."

"We have invited the wolves amongst the sheep. We must find a way to get them out without risking the flock."

"An impossible task. May Condatis help us find the way."

CHAPTER 16

It was late in the night when Arixus and I returned
to the village. Everyone was asleep. The druid led
me to a chamber where Pix was already resting,
then bid me good night.

Unnerved, I pulled off my damp dress, slipped on a
clean dressing gown, then climbed into bed alongside
Pix.

But sleep did not come quickly.

I replayed the vision of Caturix's death over and
over in my mind.

If I had stood behind him, would Caturix still be
alive, or would I have condemned us all to death?

"Be still, would ye? And keep yer cold feet off me,"
Pix complained.

"Sorry."

"Where did ye go anyway?"

"To the Seahenge shrine."

"And what did ye see?"

"Water."

"Oh," Pix said. "Ye had a vision of water. Very helpful."

I pressed my cold foot against her leg.

"Hey," Pix complained.

I chuckled, then after a long moment, I said, "A piece of the truth. That is what I saw. Tomorrow, I will ride to Stonea and see what the Romans have done to my city."

"That may not be easy for ye."

"I will go all the same. If Rome is lying to me, I will see it with my own eyes."

"*If.* And after that?"

"After that, we shall see."

WHILE ARTUR MADE several convincing arguments about why he should come with me to Stonea, he eventually understood why I wanted him to stay behind.

"You and Ansgar are representatives of the *Greater* Iceni," I told him. "When you speak, you speak for your father. The conversations in Stonea may be difficult. We don't want them to have any additional reason to believe that I am speaking for *all* of the Iceni in these matters. Please, stay with Ansgar. I will meet you in Oak Throne in a couple of days. Arixus will give you and Ansgar a guard. But while you are here, however, be of help. Build, dig, plant, haul… show them what it means to be the son of the king of the Greater Iceni."

"Boudica, everyone knows I am not *really* yours and Prasutagus's son," Artur said softly.

"Do they?" I asked, arching an eyebrow at him. "Because you are not our blood? Is that the reason?"

"Well—" Artur said.

"Well, nothing. You are my son, so do as your mother asks and go dig a ditch," I told him with a wink.

Artur laughed lightly.

I patted the boy on the cheek then mounted Druda. Pix and the warriors of the Greater Iceni were fully armed and ready to ride out.

As we rode from Holk Fort, Arixus met us at the gate.

The druid bowed to me. "May Condatis guide the way there and home again."

I inclined my head to him, then made my way down the first of many paths…that would lead to rebellion.

THE RIDE to Stonea would take more than a day. We rode throughout the day, camping that night, then resumed on the path once more. The closer we got to the ancient fort, the quieter everything became. No one traveled on the roads through the moors. There were no sounds of farmers or fishermen carrying on the breeze. It was just still. Quiet.

Until Stonea came into view.

The morning was clear.

The mists that usually clung to the water, hiding the fort, were gone.

The sounds of loons and frogs were noticeably absent.

What we could hear were carrion birds.

Along the roadway leading to the fort, we found a grizzly sight. The bodies of Caturix's warriors had been strung from poles erected along the road. A month after their deaths, there was little left of them but bones, hair, and tattered clothing, but still, the vultures picked at the bodies, fighting one another as they hunted for one last morsel.

The sight unnerved my warriors, who had thus far been talking amongst themselves and laughing as we rode.

Now, they were silent.

"Boudica..." Pix said warningly.

I knew why she'd said it.

I knew why she was warning.

But as we rode, I examined every body closely.

Every. Single. One.

He wasn't there.

A horn sounded in the fort, followed by voices, and soon I saw a flurry of activity at the gate of Stonea. On the walls, Roman soldiers came to alert. Even from this angle, I could see that much of the fort had been burned and then rebuilt. Sections of the wall were new. Inside the fort, I saw the roofs of Roman-style buildings.

I clicked to Druda and rode ahead of the party, Pix behind me.

When I got to the gate, I found it barred.

I eyed the men on the ramparts, my eyes centering in on one who, from his dress, I knew to be the ranking officer.

"I am Boudica, Queen of the Iceni. This is the fort of Saenuvax, my grandfather, and is under Northern Iceni rule. Why does Rome block my passage?"

"Queen Boudica," the man replied. "Rome welcomes you to Stonea," he said, then gestured to the men. "Open the gate and clear the way!" he called.

With that, the men opened the gates, the soldiers stepping aside so we could enter.

Rome welcomes you.

Who is Rome to welcome me into my own house?

We rode into the city. Memories of Caturix's and

Melusine's wedding played in my mind. I recalled fleeting images of my father, Belenus, and Brenna. How Melusine, Brenna, and I had laughed about the wild marsh terrier puppies. Even now, I smiled when I thought about how angry my father had been with the housecarl for keeping pigs in the old roundhouse.

But now…

Whatever Stonea used to be, it wasn't that anymore.

The market was burned to nothing, Roman buildings were built in its place. Everywhere I looked, I saw no signs that Rome had simply fought a battle and left.

Rome had taken the city.

I dismounted, the others doing the same, then turned to face the soldier waiting for me. His dress was not the same as other Romans I had encountered, and he had a Gaulish look about him.

"Your name?" I snapped at him.

"I am Gaius Hiber—"

"You are a Gaul," I said, letting my temper get the better of me. "Do not tell me your name is Gaius whatever. What is your name?"

The man paused then said, "We… We are an auxiliary brought over from the mainland. I am Gaius—"

"All right, *Gaius*. Perhaps you can explain to me why Rome is occupying *my* fort."

"Queen Boudica, this fort was defeated in battle," he said, looking confused.

"In battle, yes, but this land is Northern Iceni all the same. Yet everywhere I look, I see only Rome. Roman soldiers. Roman buildings," I said, eyeing some construction underway in the distance. I spotted Iceni men chained at the ankle, working on yet another Roman structure. From the shape of it, I could tell it was going to be one of their temples. But then, I saw something more. In the shape of the stones in the archway, I swore I saw…

My hands shaking with rage, I turned away from the soldier and stormed across the fort toward the construction.

"Queen Boudica," Gaius called after me. "Queen Boudica, I must protest."

"Get yer filthy hands off me, Roman. I am a free woman of the Greater Iceni," I heard Pix curse at someone behind me.

I rushed to the site.

The Roman soldiers there paused, confused when they saw me.

I approached the building. My hands trembling, I reached out and touched the stone archway. The flecks of granite shimmered in the sunlight. At one corner, where they had carved the stone, I saw half—half!—of an ancient double disc symbol. The rest had been cut away.

They had taken the stones.

They had taken the menhir from the well of Uaine to build their temple.

I closed my eyes.

"Boudica…

"Protect the greenwood…

"Protect the stones…

"Protect the trees…"

"You have discovered our new construction. A temple to divine Claudius. We will honor our emperor here. The governor decreed that the temple be built to remember the great victory achieved here."

I looked at him over my shoulder. "You've taken the stones," I said, my voice filled with barely restrained fury. "You've taken the stones from the sacred well."

"I… The men said they took them from an ornamental display by the fort's natural well. We used them to—"

"Ornamental? May your ancestors curse you, *Gaius*. You know better!"

"Queen Boudica…" he began, but I didn't hear his words. As he spoke, I heard a muffled sound as my eyes took in the rest of the fort. All of the old buildings were gone, replaced, or burned. Some Romans were working beside the well of Uaine. They put stonework around the sacred well and constructed a pully system to collect the water. The roundhouse of my father's father was gone. Burned and cleared. Now, a Roman-style adminis-tration building stood in its place.

And all around me, hanging on poles, were bodies of the Iceni.

But in the square…

In the square before what had once been the round-house, one body hung alone.

Leaving the others, I began to walk slowly toward it.

"Boudica," Pix called in warning. "Boudica, no. Don't."

"Queen Boudica," Gaius also called after me.

There was little left but bones, clothes, and a tattered, decaying mass of raven-black hair. But I would know those locks anywhere. He had been stripped of the simple torc he wore and any other finery. Someone had even taken his boots.

But it was the hair…

The hair…

I stood at the foot of my brother's corpse, staring up at what was left of Caturix.

A hundred memories washed over me. Caturix, Bran, Brenna, and I laughing and playing as children. My brother frowning and scowling at us when he grew older. I'd always assumed Caturix had thought he was wiser than us. But later, I understood better. Our father forced Caturix to change. He laid a heavy cloak of responsibility on my brother's shoulders at too young an age and had taken too much from Caturix in the process. But it was one of my last memories of Caturix, with Mara on his shoulders, smiling and laughing with her and a pregnant Kennocha, that came clearest to my mind as I stood up staring at what was once my brother.

"Queen Boudica," Gaius said, stepping behind me.

I turned quickly, pulling my knife from my belt and pressing it to the Roman's throat in one quick, fluid movement.

The act had caught the other Romans off guard. They moved quickly to intervene.

"Cut him down," I seethed at the man. And while my anger gripped me, I realized that tears were also streaming down my cheeks. "Cut my brother down. Please."

The soldier signaled to his men to be at ease.

"I will," the Gaius told me, setting his fingers gently on my hand and pushing the knife away. "Cut the body down," he called to his men. "With honor," he added as he held my gaze. "We will prepare a pyre."

"And all the rest," I added. "All of them. You understand me, *Gaius*? All of them."

"I will see it done," he said, then held my gaze. After a moment, in a low tone, he added, "It was the governor's order."

"And just where might I find Scapula?"

"Verulamium."

"Then I will see my brother to rest and be on my way."

"Yes, Queen Boudica."

At that, I pulled my knife away and turned and looked at my brother once more.

I'm sorry, Caturix.

I'm sorry.

THE GAUL WAS true to his word. As promised, Caturix and the rest of the Northern Iceni had been removed from the poles and laid to rest on a pyre built in the marsh. The Greater Iceni warriors who'd ridden with me had been shaken at the sight. On edge, they worked to see the bodies laid to rest with as much dignity as could be mustered. But what dignity was there in rags and bones?

We had adorned the pyre with flowers and what grave goods we could scavenge or were given by the Gaul who had seen something in my eyes and had been moved.

That night, when the moon was high, we gathered before the pyres.

The Romans came to watch. And at my insistence, those they had enslaved had been brought forth to see.

I stood before the pyre with a torch in my hands.

"This night, we send these warriors on their journey to the Otherworld. Too long have they been delayed from joining their ancestors. Too long have they hung their heads in shame they did not deserve. They died warriors. Perhaps they died in the rebellion, but they died with swords in their hands, defending a cause they believed to be just. They died in the name of freedom. There is no dishonor in that.

"Now, this night, they will travel to the world beyond. And if the gods will it, they will return to us once more. But to these brave warriors, I say *stay*. *Stay* amongst the ancestors. *Stay* where you are loved. *Stay* in the Otherworld. Dusk has come to the lands of the Northern Iceni. There is no joy left behind the walls of Stonea, nor in Oak Throne, nor in Frog's Hollow, nor in any village, farm, grove, or shrine across this land. A bell knolls for our people. We are watching the closing of an age. Those of us who stand here in the gathering darkness feel it like a cold breath upon our necks."

Behind me, I heard weeping from the enslaved people as they watched on.

My fury at my inability to help them gripped me so hard I wanted to cut the throat of every Roman standing there. Instead, I continued on.

"*Stay*, warriors of the Northern Iceni. *Stay* with your ancestors. *Stay* with your mothers, fathers, grandfathers, and grandmothers. We will all see one another again. But stay. Stay. Great Mother, do not call these warriors again to fight. Lord Cernunnos, leave these hunters at rest.

"For darkness comes.

"Night has fallen upon the Northern Iceni.

"Terror walks in rows of glinting metal, breathing the name of friend.

"*Stay*.

"*Stay* in the light.

"There is nothing left but darkness here."

With that, I went to the bundle of bones that had once been my brother. I set my hand thereon. "Stay, Brother. Stay with Damara, Aesunos, and Belenus. Stay. I will take the sword from your hand now."

And with that, I set the pyre aflame, then stepped back, joining Pix.

"Now, it begins," she whispered in a low voice.

I nodded. "Now, it begins."

CHAPTER 17

We rode out the following day for Verulamium. I felt like a darkness had covered my heart. I saw endless signs of what Scapula's governorship meant everywhere I went. The Catuvellauni people were done. The tribe had been devastated. Those who had not run had either bled or found themselves in irons.

I cursed Caractacus, his brother, and his father for the infighting that had triggered Verica's and Aedd Mawr's flight to the Romans. I cursed Verica and Aedd Mawr for returning the Romans to these shores. I cursed Claudius and his ambition.

But most of all, I cursed myself for not seeing the truth.

Ula, Pix, the greenwood, Andraste—they had all warned me, but I'd been stubborn. I'd fought as hard as

I could to protect my people. I thought if we made an alliance with the Romans as Verica had, we would be safe.

But now…

The Trinovantes were ruled by a hapless Roman child. Which meant they were led by Rome.

The Atrebates were ruled by Verica's Romanized heirs.

The Coritani were conquered, as were the Catuvellauni, Cantiaci, and Dobunni.

And where did that leave the Iceni?

We would either have to become Rome, just like the others, or die.

Caturix had chosen the latter.

Prasutagus and I had charted a different course.

What had we already sacrificed without knowing it?

When we arrived at the ancient hillfort of the Catuvellauni, we found it heavily guarded. The place was a muddy mess, with soldiers coming and going everywhere. The lands surrounding the fort had been transformed into barracks. The old roundhouses had been pulled down and replaced with Roman-style buildings. Some soldiers were preparing to set out, presumably to Londinium, with hundreds of people in chains. As I eyed the men and women there, I realized they were a mix of Catuvellauni, Coritani, and Fen folk.

Upon seeing our party, one man cried out.

"Princess Boudica! Princess! The Romans have taken the Fen folk. Save us, Princess!"

A Roman rewarded the man with a sharp blow to the jaw.

I clenched my teeth and rode forward.

After some confusion, we arrived at the gate, where a soldier greeted us.

"Weapons," he said roughly.

"I am Queen Boudica of the Iceni. I am here to speak to the governor."

"Weapons," the man repeated.

My spear still lay in a pit in Oak Throne, but I handed over my dagger, my guard giving up their swords. With some reluctance, so did Pix. I was glad the Romans got only two of the ten weapons on her.

Without another word, the man took the weapons and departed.

It took a few moments for Scapula's secretary, Ampelius, to arrive.

"Queen Boudica," he said, giving me a short bow. "This way, please."

Taking two guards and Pix with me, I went inside. Ampelius led us to a small chamber.

"The governor is busy right now. He will see you as soon as possible. Please, help yourself to refreshments," he said, gesturing to a table upon which servants set ale, bread, and cheese.

With that, he closed the door and left us behind.

Pix sat down with a huff. "Not as warm a welcome as the last time ye were here," she said, looking over the paltry offerings.

"No," I replied, looking about the room. Had this been the servants' eating area?

"Nor should ye expect as warm a conversation, either."

"You'd best stop warning me, or I'm going to accuse you of being fond of Aulus Plautius."

At that, Pix laughed.

We waited, and waited, and waited. The ale grew warm. The cheese grew soft. And yet, we waited. It was near nightfall when Ampelius appeared once more. "The governor will see you now."

When we all moved to go, the secretary signaled to the others. "Just the queen."

"Ye little shite—" Pix began, but I waved for her to be still.

"I'll be fine," I told her, then followed the man.

As we wound down the hallways, I realized that the Catuvellauni decorations, which once trimmed the halls, were gone. When we reached the main council room, it was much the same. Roman goods, from wine decanters to silks to furniture, decorated the place. No more did I see any signs that this was an ancient fort of the Catuvellauni people.

Ampelius led me to a table at which the governor sat writing.

Leaving me there, the man departed.

I stood, waiting, as the governor worked, and worked, and worked.

Finally, he sat back and looked at me.

"Queen Boudica," he said, a look of mild annoyance on his face.

"Governor, I've come to speak to you about Stonea."

"Stonea," he repeated, nodding. "What of it?" he asked, setting the parchment on which he'd been writing aside and pulling out another.

"I…" I began, then watched as the governor started reading another dispatch.

When he realized I'd paused, he looked up at me briefly. "Yes?"

"Governor, when you squashed the rebellion of the Fen folk and disarmed my people, you made no mention of taking my ancient fort. There was no agreement between us that your men would occupy Stonea."

"It is a conquered city," Scapula said dismissively. "Therefore, it is Rome's."

"It is an Iceni city. Therefore, it is mine by my rights as client queen. I am a citizen of Rome, Governor. You cannot simply take what is mine."

At that, the Roman lowered his parchment and looked at me. "I am the fist of the emperor, Queen

Boudica. I dispense his justice. What the emperor gives, I can take back in his name. Your brother forfeited his capital during his short-lived rebellion. Now, it and all the Fens are Rome's," he said, returning to reading.

"This is not what we agreed upon when we spoke in Oak Throne."

He said nothing and merely continued looking over his dispatch.

"Governor," I protested.

At that, he lowered the parchment once more. "I don't know what you understood, Queen Boudica, so let me be clear this time. Your Fens are forfeit. Your fort is forfeit. Your Fen folk are forfeit. Your weapons are forfeit. And if you did not have the reputation you do, client queen, I would have taken everything else. But I agreed to your terms. You will keep your people quiet so I may pursue the real threat in this realm. And if you do not..." he said, then shrugged.

"Yes, you are very good at taking what is not yours," I said, giving him a steely gaze.

He returned my look with an equally severe expression. "Don't forget it," he replied sternly, then waved to his attendant. "See the Iceni queen and her people on their way."

With that, one of the servants approached. "Queen Boudica," the man said, gesturing I should depart.

I looked from him to the governor, who had returned to reading again.

With that, I turned and left the room, my heart pounding.

Rise.

Rise.

Rise.

CHAPTER 18

The road to Oak Throne felt longer than ever before. We arrived deep in the night, finding a mix of Roman soldiers and Northern Iceni at the gates when we arrived.

"Hold," a Roman soldier called.

"Hold yourself, Rome," I retorted in annoyance. "Open the gate for the Queen of the Iceni."

At that, the gate swung open, and we rode inside.

Not far from the gate, I spotted the new Roman encampment. A small group of Roman soldiers sat outside playing dice, drinking, and laughing.

Otherwise, the fort was quiet.

When I got to the roundhouse, I discovered everyone except for Bec was asleep.

"Boudica," she said in a weary tone. "It's so late. I will see to your men. Please, take your rest."

"Bec... Are you..."

"Couldn't sleep, that's all," she replied with a weak smile. "I'll return shortly," she told me, then waved for the men to follow her.

Pix and I went inside, Pix going directly to the kitchens. "I'll get us something to eat," she said. "And not molding Roman bread," she added with a frown.

Leaving her, I went to the family wing. Artur and Ansgar had departed Holk Fort after we'd gone, journeying to Oak Throne to meet us. I stopped to check on Artur. I slipped into the room quietly. Morfran opened one eye when I entered but didn't sound an alarm. Artur had kicked off his blanket in his sleep. I paused, covering the boy—who was no boy anymore, his feet nearly hanging off the end of the bed—then bent to kiss his head. Leaving him, I slipped from the room and cracked open the door to Bran's bedchamber.

My brother rolled in his sleep and spoke some nonsense words. With a heavy sigh, he relaxed once more and began snoring softly.

I closed the door and then paused there a moment.

There was no way to get word to Brenna safely. She would hear on the lips of travelers about what had befallen Caturix and the Northern Iceni. If the druids were supporting Caratacus and helping the rebellion in the west, my sister would understand what was happening. I was only sorry I wouldn't be there to grieve with her.

I rejoined Pix in the dining area, sitting down and eating what was left of the evening's meal: a simple stew made of venison and vegetables with far too much garlic and a round of undercooked bread.

Pix broke open her round of bread and studied the doughy center. "Still better than what Rome left us."

I stared into the brazier burning on the table.

"Boudica?" Pix asked.

"There is no way out," I said, looking up at her.

Pix set the bread down. "I will not chide ye. I understand why ye did what ye did. Ye had only one chance to unite, but the Romans sang a compelling song. And they sent the right songbird to ye, one ye would listen to and trust. Aside from that, your father's blood still wet Caratacus's hands. But yes, we are in the thick of it now."

I frowned.

Bec returned a few moments later.

When she entered, she met my gaze. At once, she read the expression thereon. She went to the nearby cupboard, pulled out a bottle of mead, and set out three cups. She filled each to the brim and then sat down beside me.

"To the Morrigu," she said, lifting her cup.

"To the Morrigu," I replied.

"May she guide ye on yer path," Pix added.

WE MADE ready to return to Venta the following day. Before we departed, Bran and I discussed my brief and terse conversation with the governor as I readied my saddle, the others also prepping their horses.

Bran, who had dark rings under his eyes, his hair a mess, shook his head. "So just like that, they have taken the Fens and Stonea as their own?"

I nodded. I hadn't told Bran about the bodies. I didn't want him to know what had become of our brother. I would carry that burden for us both.

"But you are a client queen, a Roman citizen in all but blood. What about your rights?"

"Forfeited because of the rebellion. The Fen folk were there in chains. I could do nothing to help them."

Bran ran his fingers through his hair. "That fort was our grandfather's. It has always belonged to our people, one of the most ancient settlements in Northern Iceni territory. And it has fallen under us."

Bran wasn't wrong. Long ago, Stonea had been the seat of the Northern Iceni. Now…

"Go to Holk Fort. Speak to Arixus. Ask him to show you," I said.

"Show me what?"

"Just…ask."

"Boudica," Bran said, worry in his voice. "What can we do?"

"I will return to Venta and speak to Prasutagus. We are tied, Bran. One move out of line, and Rome will swarm over us. But, perhaps, there are ways to move forward unseen. I don't know. But I know something must be done. For now, walk the line Rome has drawn for you, and keep their eyes and ears off Holk Fort. Our lives may depend on Arixus. We must protect him from Rome's gaze."

Bran's brow furrowed, then he nodded. He turned to Druda, placing his hand on the horse's neck and patting him. "Be safe, Boudica. Be careful."

"And you, Brother."

Bran embraced me.

Bec, who was saying goodbye to Pix, Artur, and Ansgar, Bellicus in her arms, joined me.

"Say goodbye to Boudica, you wiggly worm," Bec told her son, kissing the rambunctious child on his grubby cheek.

"Goodbye, Boudica," he said with a laugh.

I took Bellicus from Bec. Before the child could

squirm away, I grabbed him and planted a dozen kisses on his dirty cheeks.

"A banshee! A banshee has me!" he yelled, making the others laugh.

When I finally released him, he sprinted to the safety of Riona's skirts. "Save me," he told her.

Riona merely laughed.

I chuckled, then slipped onto Druda. My hands moved involuntarily to adjust my spear, which I always carried.

But it was gone.

It lay, buried like a dead thing, with all the other Northern Iceni weapons—and Aterie. I imagined his spirit standing guard over them.

Collecting myself, I turned to Bran and Bec. "I'll be back as soon as I can."

"Be well, Boudica," Bec told me.

"And you... All of you. May the gods keep and protect you," I said, then motioned to my party to ride out.

As we went, my gaze drifted toward Ula's hut.

I had gone early that morning to find her, but she wasn't there. Her fire was cold. Perhaps it was better that way. Already, I struggled under the weight of the truth. One cross word from Ula, and I might have broken. So, maybe it was for the best that she wasn't home.

I would speak with her next time.

Next time, I would be ready to hear the hard truths. But for now, my heart merely wept for my losses while something deep and dark within me began to rise.

CHAPTER 19

When we arrived in Venta, I was almost relieved to see the city was humming along normally. No show of Roman forces. No pale, drawn faces. No people in irons. Venta was growing, thriving, just as Rome had promised it would.

But now I saw that those agreements were written on the wind. All this time, we had been walking on ice. One wrong step, and we would be in no better condition than the Fen folk. Aulus had warned me, and he hadn't been wrong.

The peace of Venta was so much at odds with what was happening in Northern Iceni lands that it felt grotesque.

Pix reined her horse in beside mine. "I'm going to

ride to the King's Wood and check on *Bergusia*," she told me. "I'll find ye later."

"Why is it that I suspect you're going to check on Tavish?"

"Nay, Strawberry Queen. I saw that spark of the old magic between them," she said, referring to Melusine's and Tavish's instant attraction. It had been difficult to miss.

"Sure, you did. But when has that stopped you?" I asked her.

Pix winked at me, then clicked to her horse, turning away from the city.

As we made our way through the marketplace, Artur reined in beside me.

"Boudica," he began, then paused. "The Romans at Oak Throne... I could see in their eyes the people were afraid of them, even though Prince Bran was trying so hard to keep things friendly. Still, I saw fear. Could something like that happen here? In Venta?"

Artur had always been a sensitive child. Telling him a hard truth was like placing a weight on his heart. But I had promised to always be honest. "Yes," I told him. "It could. When Rome is our friend, she gives," I said, gesturing to the bustling marketplace filled with traders from all around, including Romans who'd come with rich and varied goods. "But when Rome takes..."

"But what happened to the Northern Iceni... That is

because King Caturix rebelled. That won't happen here as long as you and Prasutagus keep your oaths."

"If dealings between partners are fair and honest, you would be right. But what I saw in Stonea... Rome is a liar. We must move carefully, my son. So very carefully."

Artur looked ahead. He was silent for a long time, then said, "When we were in Oak Throne, I dreamed."

"Of your princess?"

Artur huffed a laugh. "No, Boudica. I am sorry to say, but the druid's vision was wrong."

"We shall see. If not a princess, what did you see?"

He turned and looked at me. "Fire. So much fire."

I reached out and took his hand, giving it a squeeze. "May the Morrigu protect us all."

WE ARRIVED at the king's house to a warm welcome. Prasutagus was there, Olwen on his shoulders, Sorcha and Mara trying to hide behind some barrels so they could jump out and surprise me. The men came for the horses. Artur, Ansgar, and I dismounted and joined Olwen and Prasutagus.

Morfran, on the other hand, went immediately to the

girl's hiding place. He perched in a nearby tree and cawed loudly, alerting us to their game.

"Not fair, Morfran," Sorcha chided the bird. "Now, Mara! Attack," Sorcha said, and they burst out, Sorcha hoisting a shield and her small wooden dagger.

Mara ran screaming—and laughing—behind her.

Sorcha ran for Artur. "I have you now," she said, rushing him. But Artur was deft, grabbing Sorcha by the waist and tossing her over his shoulder.

"Never. My raven and I have ended your spying. Into the water trough you go," he said, racing toward the trough in jest, Sorcha screaming to get down.

Mara slowed her onslaught and joined me, wrapping her arms around my waist. "I'm glad you're back," she told me.

"I am glad to be here. Where are your mother and Caturin? Everyone well?"

She nodded. "They went to the marketplace. Sorcha and I were with the tutor. I was making letters today!"

"Very good," I told her, kissing her forehead.

I went then to Olwen, who was reaching for me, whimpering and pointing to make her feelings known.

I took her from Prasutagus. Olwen wrapped her legs around my waist and her arms around my neck and squeezed me tight, pulling me close.

Confused, I looked at Prasutagus. "She hasn't slept

well for the last few days. She kept bringing your things to me. We told her you'd be home soon."

"Were you worried, little one?" I asked, stroking her fair hair. "I'm here," I told her, then turned to Prasutagus. "With a story to tell."

My husband, who had already read my expression, nodded. "Come inside," he told Ansgar and me. "Pix?"

"Went to the King's Wood."

Prasutagus nodded, then gestured for us to follow him.

I cast a glance back toward Sorcha and Artur, who were now in a deadly battle, Artur defending himself from Sorcha's dagger strikes.

"Careful, Sorcha," I called to her. "Even wooden daggers can hurt," I said, then looked down at Mara. "Would you like to join us?"

She shook her head. "I will go back with the tutor now."

I kissed the child on her head once more. The sunshine had warmed her curly black hair. "Very good. Study hard," I told her, then followed my husband inside.

Ansgar, Prasutagus, and I adjourned to the meeting room—Olwen in tow. The servants brought us refreshments, and I settled Olwen onto my lap. The child nestled against my chest and fell asleep almost at once.

"Tell me what has happened," Prasutagus said.

And then, Ansgar and I began. We shared what we had seen at Holk Fort, including Arixus's and the druids' part. And then, I shared with them what had transpired in Stonea and Verulamium. As I spoke, Prasutagus's gaze grew darker and darker. When I was done, we all sat silently for a very long time.

Finally, Prasutagus turned to Ansgar. "What is the message from Mona?"

"Mona is careful in how they approach the Greater Iceni, my king," Ansgar said. "They are guarded in what they share with us but not secretive. The druids in the west *are* hiding Caratacus on the order of the elders at Mona. The message they convey to us is to unite."

"Behind Caratacus?" Prasutagus asked.

Ansgar nodded. "They do not push on us as they push on others. For all the tribes of the west, the call is for rebellion. Action. From us, they ask for silent unification."

"Meaning?" I asked.

"Silver and information. As much as we can safely share."

I looked at Prasutagus.

He frowned.

"As your adviser, it is my duty to point out that you have choices," Ansgar said. "Help Caratacus and the rebellion or..."

"Or?" I asked.

"Tell Rome what you know in exchange for favor."

"I already tried that, and still, my brother hung from a pole."

"Had Aulus Plautius been here, the Northern Iceni would have faced a different outcome. I am sorry for your loss, Queen Boudica, but King Caturix openly rebelled."

I looked at my husband. "What do we do?"

Prasutagus looked thoughtful. "This news from Stonea is disturbing, and my heart aches for what happened to your brother. While you were gone, three Trinovantes chieftains came to see me. They are not blind to the fact that while Aedd Mawr's heir sits on the throne in Camulodunum, they are ruled by Rome. They are unhappy."

"As are those chieftains in Atrebates lands, even though Verica's line has returned," Ansgar said.

"Roman puppets," I said.

The men nodded.

I held Prasutagus's gaze. I could read his conflicted thoughts in his eyes. They were the same as I shared.

"Let us whisper," Ansgar said. "For to speak a thing tempts it to life, but it must be considered, and all consequences weighed. My king and queen, you could rally the people of the east. The people would be behind you. Working in tandem with Caratacus, you could pinch these Romans in the middle. You would need to reach out to the chieftains to raise a rebellion. It could work. And yet, I know you are not blind to the consequences if you fail."

My husband looked at me. "The pain of what you went through finding Caturix like that. If we fail…"

"Right now, Arixus acts in contempt of Roman order. If he is found out, the Northern Iceni are finished," I said.

"The governor was wily enough to know that by granting you the crown of the Northern Iceni, he has also placed the Greater Iceni into the trap. If the Northern Iceni fall, so do we. He has stacked the deck in Rome's favor," Ansgar said.

"Oh, Prasutagus," I said, my heart heavy with guilt.

My husband shook his head. "What choice did you have? If you and Bran did not get him to agree, the Northern Iceni would be Rome now, all those you love in chains. The governor played the game deftly."

"Then, may I suggest, it is time to start playing as well. Arixus should continue his work in secret. As for Caratacus," Ansgar said, then looked at me. "I know you fault him for your father's death, and you are not wrong. But…"

"Now, I begin to see what Caturix saw," I said with a heavy sigh.

"I honor your brother, but the plan was ill-conceived. The only way it could be done is as Ansgar said. The whole east must rally together. But I don't know if we dare risk it," Prasutagus said. "All the same, we can still help those in the west."

"Information and silver," Ansgar said with a nod.

Prasutagus looked at me.

I nodded.

My husband also nodded in agreement.

"Good," Prasutagus said. "Well, Wife. I think a trip to Londinium is in order. I would check on our people at the waystation, visit an old friend or two," he said, then turned to Ansgar. "Care to come along?"

Ansgar laughed lightly. "I am sorry to say, my king, that I don't think I have another such voyage left in me. Perhaps you should take the druid Tavish with you."

"Very well, my friend. We will make our plans. Today, however, let's drink," he said, rising to refill mine and Ansgar's cups, "and pray to the gods that those things whispered in this room never need to take shape."

CHAPTER 20

The following weeks passed in relative quiet. We waited as news came of Scapula's and Vespasian's penetration into the west and Caratacus's efforts to fight back. I was glad the governor had found something else to occupy his attention. While he still held Stonea and taxed the Northern Iceni obscenely, there was no further violence. The governor hadn't been lying when he said he didn't care about us —it was Caratacus he wanted.

The reason was plain.

Aulus had been recalled because he'd failed to catch the rebel king.

Scapula would be under enormous pressure to succeed where his predecessor had failed.

Prasutagus and I delayed our trip to Londinium

until the fall, planning to travel with the surplus shipments of grains and other goods.

"The men have reported that Rome has become increasingly difficult to deal with when it comes to payment," Prasutagus said sourly. "Let's see if they deal with the king of the Greater Iceni more fairly."

When the leaves turned shades of scarlet and sunflower yellow, and the fields had been harvested, we set out for Londinium. Deciding it best to leave the children behind, Prasutagus, Pix, Tavish, and I set sail with a guard. Three heavily laden ships sailed from Yarmouth to Londinium.

It had been years since I had last been to Londinium. My memory of the place was forever tarnished by finding Dindraine, Rue, and the other Catuvellauni priestesses being held captive. Now when I thought of Londinium, there was only sorrow. That shanty town had become the place where our people became slaves.

I slipped onto the bench beside Tavish, who stared at the sea in fascination.

"My queen," he said.

"Is this your first time aboard a ship?" I asked.

"Aside from the short ferry ride to Mona, yes. I confess, seeing our fair island from this angle is something," he said, gesturing to the land. "All one land, but a people so divided."

"Yes," I agreed sadly. Not wanting to dwell on sad things, I asked, "You must tell me. How is Bergusia?"

A smile lit up Tavish's face briefly before he mastered it. "She's doing very well, my queen. I think… I think she is happy in her prayers to the gods and practicing the art of her namesake. She is more talented than any jewel crafter I have ever seen," he said, then pulled out an amulet hidden under his tunic. On it was the head of a stag made of silver, the antlers inlaid, and the eyes adorned with green gems.

"Antler horn," Tavish said, touching the horns. "And agate from the river polished smooth."

I smiled at him. "It is a very fine gift."

"Well…" he demurred. "She is working on pieces for all of us, touchstones of our patron gods."

"It's lovely."

Tavish smiled at the amulet. "It is."

The journey was long, but we arrived in Londinium the following morning, sailing up the busy River Thames to reach the city. Much had changed since I'd been there last. The walls that we'd seen under construction were nearly complete. As well, men were working in the river. Flat barges had been anchored in the Thames where a bridge between the east and west banks was being constructed. Dozens of new piers awaited travelers. As we drew closer, I saw that Praefectus Gaius Marcellus had been true to his word. His massive basilica had been completed. I could see the red-tiled roof over the wall.

"The basilica?" I asked Prasutagus.

He nodded.

"And our house?" I asked.

"Our little villa, you mean?" Prasutagus replied with a laugh. Prasutagus had followed up on the praefectus's suggestion we build a house in the city. A two-story Roman-style house had been constructed for us in a district with many other homes for wealthy merchants.

"It has a good view of fires burning outside the temple of Mithras," Prasutagus said with a wink.

"I thank Mithras that we don't have to stay with the praefectus again."

"Let's hope. But I implore you on behalf of all the residents of Venta, no more peacocks."

"Agreed." My beautiful birds had become an adored annoyance. They reproduced rapidly enough to be of use, but the noise... We all suffered for my empathy for the creatures.

Our boats docked along one of the many new piers stretching into the Thames. The number of ships there had tripled since my last visit, as had the number of people. The place was crawling with Romans—soldiers, traders, and civilians. There were more Romans than there were our own people. Along with the Romans, I noted traders with unusual dress or looks coming from faraway lands.

Prasutagus and I stayed with the men. A wagon was brought for the first of the goods. The grains were loaded within.

"These go to the Romans. I will go with the men and ensure the Romans pay as agreed," Prasutagus told me.

"How can I be of help?"

"Beow will take the second wagon to the market-place. You can go with him and see the Greater Iceni market stall, but take a guard if you wish to look around. I can join you there when I have the matter of the grain settled."

"King Prasutagus," a sharp-looking Roman holding a stylus called, joining us.

"Now the robbery begins," Prasutagus whispered to me. He gestured for Tavish to join him, then the pair went with the man. They reviewed the contents of the wagon and the other ships, the Roman noting down the supplies being delivered.

I joined Beow. "This process is new," I said, gesturing to the Roman questioning Prasutagus about every barrel, bag, and crate.

He nodded. "Every time we come to Londinium, we pay a new tax to Rome. A tax to make port. A tax to sell. A tax on what is sold. A tax for the stall in the market-place. A tax on the house. And with each season, the price increases. Used to make a handsome stack of silver for our goods. By the time we're done paying Rome, it's hardly worth it."

"So much for the praefectus's promise that trade with Rome could make us rich. Are the Brigantes still selling?" I asked, eyeing over the ships.

Beow nodded. "And paying tax like the rest of us. The marketplace is different now. You'll see."

I watched as my husband handed the man a small sack of silver. Then, he and the druid rejoined us.

"I thought ye were here to make money," Pix told Prasutagus.

"*Someone* is here to make money," Prasutagus replied, then turned to Beow. "I'll see to the grain now. Tavish will join me. Boudica and Pix will go into the market. Please escort them back to the villa if there are any problems."

"What kind of problems ye be expecting?" Pix asked.

"None. But this is Londinium. There is no telling what can happen here," Prasutagus replied with a frown.

"Yes, my king," Beow replied.

"Boudica," Prasutagus called lightly as he turned to go. "No peacocks!"

We all chuckled, and Prasutagus departed with the wagon.

"Come, Queen Boudica, Pix," Beow said, gesturing for us to join the second party.

We boarded the second wagon, and then we set off through the city.

The Londinium I had seen when I was last here was no more. Now, it was as Roman as I imagined Rome itself. The perfectly aligned streets were paved with bricks. Square Roman houses sided every street. And everywhere we went, we saw Romans. Even those Trinovantes or Atrebates we spotted in the crowd dressed in Roman fashion. Many in the streets of Londinium were servants or slaves. Foreigners from Gaul and from the world beyond Rome hurried busily about.

"What is being built there?" I asked, pointing to construction by the river where a massive building was being erected.

"A villa for the governor," Beow replied.

"His own fort right on the river," Pix said with a frown.

"The biggest fort in Trinovantes lands," I added.

We rode past the old marketplace where I had purchased the peacocks. Construction was underway there as well. Workers were clearing the space and laying stones for a large building. Beow directed the wagon toward the massive basilica.

"The marketplace sits before the main building in the

open forum. There are stalls all around the square," Beow said, pointing. We approached the massive structure. Before, it was a vast green space where many market stalls had been erected. Rather than the organic flow of the old market, the new forum was arranged in neat rows.

Beow drove outside the forum, then pulled the wagon to a stop. "We are just in there," he said, pointing. "We will unload now."

Pix and I exited the wagon and went with the men into the forum. It was a busy trading hub. Everywhere we looked, we saw vendors hawking their wares. Anything a person could want was for sale in the forum, from fruit and vegetables to grains to leather to animals to fine goods. And everywhere I looked, I saw Romans —buying and selling.

A small group of Roman guards passed by, their quick gait revealing they were moving purposefully. They approached a vendor, Gaulish by his clothing, and began speaking roughly to him. We couldn't make out their words, but whatever the problem was, the man had protested. A moment later, the Romans grabbed him and pulled him from the stall, knocking over the vendor's goods in the process. The man resisted, throwing punches, but the Romans struck him on the head and he fell.

"It's a lie," the man yelled as they dragged him away. "It's a lie!"

Some of the other vendors laughed at the scene.

The moment the Roman soldiers had gone, a mob of children appeared, working quickly to pick the stall clean, stashing whatever they could into pockets and bags. As I watched, it quickly became clear that the children were Catuvellauni.

"Halt there," one of the market guards called with a yawn as he slowly walked across the square.

The children scattered.

Not long after, a group of Roman officials appeared with a flat cart, finishing the work the children had started.

"Thieves come in all sizes," Pix noted.

"I'm just glad the children got a share before the Romans turned up."

"You'll see them everywhere," Beow told me. "Watch your silver, Queen Boudica. They may pull on the strings of your heart, but they'll just as quickly pull on your purse strings."

Pix and I waited until the men had safely unloaded the goods. Then, with two guards in tow, we walked toward the main building of the basilica.

The structure was immense. There was a fountain just before the great temple. A statue of a woman wearing a helmet, an owl on her shoulder, poured water from an amphora into the basin. Outside, Roman men in togas and Roman ladies in their fine stolas hurried on their way.

"I've never been inside, though Prasutagus has gone a few times. I know our silver goes there and doesn't come back," Beow said with a laugh.

Leaving the basilica, Beow led away from the basilica and forum down the streets to the temple of Mithras.

When we passed a tavern, we saw a fight break out. Some travelers began shouting at one another in a language I did not recognize. Despite the barkeep's best efforts to calm those involved, the squabble broke into a full-on brawl, with everyone in the tavern throwing punches. We quickly sidestepped the place and contin-ued, finally arriving at the temple.

The building was large and made of dark-colored bricks. The temple doors were firmly closed behind bronze doors. Wide braziers burned on pedestals on both sides of the steps leading to the temple. Tall columns decorated the façade of the building. Deep blue banners embroidered with the image of a man with a cat's head and a snake wrapped around his body flut-tered in the breeze. The temple door opened for just a moment. Two robed men appeared, their drapes the same dark shade as the banners. Their hoods were up; their faces were hidden. They descended the stairs and began to make their way toward the basilica.

"Do they host any public displays to this god?" I asked Beow.

He shook his head. "No. They are very secretive. You never see their priests' faces. In the tavern, they say the shrine is actually underground. The building is mere formality."

"Have they built any other temples?" Pix asked, looking about.

Beow nodded. "In the marketplace, they have a small shrine for one of their goddesses they call Fortuna. And not far from the docks, there is a stone statue of their sea god. I understand they are building another temple in the old marketplace for a trio of goddesses they called Deae Matres. This place, however, is for their soldiers and important men," he said, gesturing back to the temple of Mithras.

I stared at the edifice, an uneasy feeling washing over me. I had always been at peace with the gods, but a sense of darkness and oppression emanated from the shrine of Mithras.

"I'm told this temple is nothing compared to the shrine they have built to their emperor in Camulo-dunum," Beow told me.

"To their emperor?" I asked.

He nodded. "Divine Claudius...built over the shrine to Camulos."

I clenched my jaw hard. All of my petitioning to

Aulus and his words to King Diras had come to nothing. In the end, Camulos had been tossed aside for a temple to a man who was honored by his people as a god and remembered by ours as a conqueror.

Beow led us down the winding streets until we reached a row of Roman-style houses. The houses were all two stories in design. Flowers and other niceties decorated the front of the buildings. Beow led us to one of the gates. There, the banner of the Greater Iceni fluttered in the breeze, and two of our people guarded the house.

"Queen Boudica," one of the guards said, bowing to me.

"Queen Boudica," the second added, doing the same.

One of the guards opened the gate, revealing a small courtyard. We crossed the distinctly Roman space, the garden paved with stones and adorned with two flowering trees, flowers, and a small fountain. We entered a house that rivaled our royal house in Venta in its style. It was nicely appointed, boasting Roman fabrics and furniture. Even the floor was decorated with small tiles to depict a flower basket. By Roman standards, I was sure it was considered sparse, but for me...

"Fey and foreign," Pix grumbled.

I nodded. Greater Iceni goods, mixed with Roman vases and artwork, decorated the place.

A moment later, Eudaf, Prasutagus's man, appeared.

Eudaf was a trusted adviser Prasutagus had assigned to keep his accounts and manage Greater Iceni affairs and finances in the city in our absence. An older gentleman with long, silver hair, Eudaf previously assisted Ansgar in managing King Antedios's financial affairs. I had met the man only a few times, since his business kept him in Londinium, and for the last couple of years, Olwen and Sorcha had kept me in Venta.

"Ah, Queen Boudica, I am delighted to welcome you for the first time to your villa—and counting house," he said with a light laugh. "The messenger came from the dock, letting us know you'd arrived. Aside from the standing guard, we are only three staff here, but we will do our best to see to your comfort, my queen."

"I need very little. Please, don't trouble yourself," I said, but already, I could smell meat and bread cooking in the back. My stomach growled hungrily.

"I would say speak for yerself, but yer stomach already gave ye away," Pix told me with a laugh.

"Let me show you the house, then," Eudaf said, then gave us a tour. A sense of growing unease washed over me as we looked around the Roman-style place. What had Prasutagus and I traded for all this wealth? Every Roman we'd met had promised us prosperity. That hadn't been a lie. The Greater Iceni had grown wealthy from trade. But at what price? Had we become Roman along with the Trinovantes and Atrebates? What were we now? The Northern Iceni were broken, subdued, and insulted. But what about us? What did the Greater Iceni appear to be to the others? Eudaf led us upstairs, giving us a tour of the richly decorated bedchambers. I reached out and touched the soft, red fabric that covered the bed. It was finer than any dress I owned.

"Modest by Roman standards," Eudaf said.

"And rich as a faerie king by our own," Pix replied, looking around with a frown.

"Yes," the man agreed. "We have done well in our trades with Rome."

If that is the case, why do I feel like I'd rather sleep on the ship?

But rather than saying so, I joined the others in the dining room below, where a feast made with the humble ingredients our people enjoyed had been laid out. There, I also met Ede, the cook, and Briganna, who attended to the general care of the house.

"I'm not a proper maid," Briganna told me with a laugh. "But if there is anything you need help with, I can assist you."

I inclined my head to her. "Thank you, Briganna."

Settling in with the guards and the household staff—who joined at my insistence—we enjoyed the fine meal. After it was done, I asked Beow to take Pix and me back to the marketplace.

How much the city had changed in a few scant years.

It had become so… Roman.

"Do they still sell slaves here?" I asked Beow.

He nodded sadly. "Yes, near the animal market. I don't go to that part of the market anymore, not after what we saw with the priestesses. But there is fat trade in slaves. Many come from Gaul to purchase them. Our people are good workers, and our women are beautiful."

My heart felt heavy.

Finally, we returned to the marketplace, where I spotted Prasutagus speaking with the Greater Iceni in our stall. Tavish stood beside him, looking about with a mix of disgust and wonder on his features. The rest of the market was busy, but there were no fights underway, so Pix and I decided to look around.

There were a wide variety of goods for sale there. We stopped by the stall of the Brigantes, who were selling silver jewelry, pelts, weapons, and other finely crafted items.

I picked up a small silver statuette.

"Brigantia," the man told me. "You are Greater Iceni, are you not? Do you know our patron goddess?"

"I do. This is a handsome model of her," I said, setting the piece back down and lifting another, a hag with a crow on her shoulder.

"And that is the symbol of our other goddess."

"The Morrigu?"

He shook his head. "The Cailleach."

"Ye worship the twin goddesses," Pix said.

"Brigantia rules the warm months. The Cailleach rules the winter."

"Then you worship much as the Caledonians do," I said.

The man nodded. "We have much in common with our northern neighbors."

"Save for a distaste for Rome," I told him with a wink. I lifted a dagger. "Your queen sends a fine selection of goods."

"Like the Greater Iceni, we have found good trade with Rome."

I set the dagger back down and then smiled at the man. "May Brigantia continue to bless you with good fortune."

The man bowed to me.

With that, we left him and continued on our way. Pix got waylaid at a stall where a man was selling blades from Hispania. Her interest piqued, she was already haggling when I moved to the next vendor who worked in embroidery. The woman there had many fine pieces. Blankets, scarves, bags, and even some lovely dresses, but it was the image of a red rose on an embroidered square that captured my attention. The rose was surrounded by a square of green- and-silver knotwork. Acorns and oak leaves trimmed the corners of the piece.

At the center was a bright red rose, the stem containing a single thorn.

"Almost the same shade as your hair," the old woman told me.

"On that account, I think I'll have it to match," I told her.

"Sewed it last Imbolc," she told me.

"You have a deft hand."

"Not that it's worth much to these Roman ladies. They find my works quaint. I used to make dresses for the queen of the Catuvellauni. Now, I sew pillows for Roman ladies' dogs."

"Well, this queen is glad of your gifts. It is a treasure," I told her, trading her silver for the square. "Thank you."

"Queen," she replied, bowing to me.

I slipped the item into my satchel and rejoined the others.

"Well?" I asked Pix.

"Got me two new daggers."

"Two?"

Pix nodded, showing me the daggers on her hip.

"How many daggers does a person need?"

"Have ye looked about you? All of them. I thank ye for them, though," she told me with a grin, handing me back my spare silver pouch I kept in the pocket of my jerkin. Confused, I patted the pocket to find it empty. Pix grinned at me. "Ye need to keep a better watch on yer silver."

I snatched it back from her with a laugh. "Pickpocketed by my own guard. A person isn't safe anywhere."

"How else do ye expect me to pay?"

Laughing, I handed it back to her, then we made our way back to the Greater Iceni stall. Our vendors sold an array of weapons, horse tack, raw pieces of amber, smithed silver, and more. We also had a vibrant trade of horses in the livestock market. And then there were those things not sold at market. Deliveries of mined tin, iron, and silver, which the Romans valued and we sold for a good price. As well, our grain fed the Roman soldiers.

Prasutagus and Tavish joined us.

"What do you think of your villa?" Prasutagus asked me.

"I suppose that's a matter of taste. It is finer than our roundhouse, and yet, I can't imagine wanting to stay there any longer than necessary."

Prasutagus laughed. "I feel the same. But it is good enough to host business guests when needed. For that purpose, it performs well."

"Even a latrine does its job as needed," Pix said.

"Quite right," Prasutagus replied with a laugh. "Shall we?" he said, gesturing to the path back. "We find

ourselves in luck, my queen. The praefectus is in Camulodunum. No forced dinners."

"For that, I thank all the gods."

"I will, however, meet with Madogh tonight. He has
something pressing he wanted to share with me," Prasutagus said with a worried frown.

"Do you know the nature of the matter?"

"No. I will learn more when I speak with him. If all
goes as planned, we can set sail early in the morning."

"Good," I told him. "I'll be glad to get away before
the praefectus can return."

Prasutagus laughed lightly. "What about you, my
wife? No peacocks today? Find anything else to please
you?"

"Nothing much to speak of, although Pix found two
daggers she paid for with my silver. Does that count?"

Prasutagus huffed a laugh.

"And you? Were the Romans more agreeable with
the king than his representatives?"

"The Romans have increased the duties on items
sold in Londinium."

"By how much?"

"Thirty percent."

I gasped. "At that rate, is it worth continuing to trade
here?"

Prasutagus considered for a moment, then said, "For

now, yes. But I can see a future where it will no longer be feasible."

"But they still desire our goods, do they not?"

"Now that Romans are taking over farms, cultivating our lands with our people as slaves, moving into villas in the colonia of Camulodunum, the shape of the demand is changing. Now, they can grow their own wheat. Rome can mine its own silver. Why pay us when they can make themselves richer?"

"Prasutagus…" I said worriedly.

"I know, Boudica. I know."

After the evening meal, Prasutagus disappeared to meet with Madogh. And despite Pix's best efforts to lead Tavish to bed, the druid resisted.

"I'm losing my charms," Pix lamented.

"I think the druid's heart belongs to another," I replied.

"Melusine *is* easy on the eyes. You in the mood to mess about?" she asked with a naughty grin.

"Go to bed."

Pix sighed heavily. "I *am* losing my charms."

"You are not. Just ask Cai."

"He can't be trusted for an honest answer."

"Why not?"

"He loves me."

"Poor you."

At that, Pix retired, and I also went to bed. But I

found myself sleepless, so I sat on the balcony of my Roman villa, watching the fires burn at the temple of Mithras. In the streets below, I saw a woman trade her body to a man for silver, the pair disappearing around a corner. The sounds of their exchange lingered on the night air. Later, another man paused outside the gate of our villa to piss on the flowers. The guard chased him off after a rough and rude exchange.

I left the balcony and went downstairs, finding Briganna in the kitchen.

"Queen Boudica?"

"Briganna, may I ask a favor?"

"Of course."

"A discreet favor, please? To be kept between you and me."

"You are my queen," she replied, as though the insinuation that she would be anything less than tactful was an insult.

"I have a parcel..." I said, hesitantly handing her a leather packet with my purchase from the marketplace stuffed carefully inside. "I would like it sent to Rome."

"To Rome. All right. I can do that. Ships are leaving every day."

I handed her a small slip of parchment. "I think this will be enough to locate the recipient. Please give it to the carrier."

"In case there is confusion, who do I say it's for?" she

asked, glancing at the parchment. I could see in her eyes that she could not read.

"I…" I began, pausing for a moment. "It is for Aulus Plautius, the former governor."

The girl nodded. "I understand. You can trust me to see to it, my queen."

"Thank you," I said, then turned and went back upstairs. I lay down in bed and looked out the window at the crescent moon hanging in the sky. From somewhere beyond my window, I heard a fight break out.

I closed my eyes. When I did so, I saw fields of vines, the air scented with the aroma of ripened grapes. I envisioned the sun on my face and the taste of olives and wine on my lips. I imagined soft fabrics, harp music, and the smell of perfumes.

Setting my fingers on my lips, I remembered the taste of a stolen kiss.

I let myself linger in the vision as long as I could until I couldn't ignore the sounds from the street below.

Opening my eyes, I lay still in my bed. I forced myself to listen to the sound of a man being beaten to death in the streets below by Roman soldiers as the eyes of Mithras watched.

It was very late in the night when Prasutagus woke me.

"Boudica," he said, gently shaking my shoulder. "Boudica. I'm sorry. Will you please wake and come with me?"

"Prasutagus?"

"We have a visitor. I need you to come now while it is still night. Just downstairs. Please."

I rose groggily.

My husband handed me a robe. "I'm sorry," he said. "I didn't know until the last moment."

"Know what?" I asked in a whisper.

Prasutagus frowned but didn't answer.

He led me downstairs, both of us going quietly so as not to wake the others. On the bottom floor of the villa, he led me to a small door that led underground. Taking a torch with him, he led me to the cellar. There, I saw jugs of wine, rounds of cheese, and drying beef. But then, I heard voices.

"Prasutagus?" I whispered, confused.

When I turned the corner, I entered a space with a small wooden table. There, I found Madogh, a Catuvellauni man I didn't recognize... and Caratacus.

"Caratacus," I said with a gasp.

"Forgive me, Boudica, for putting you and Prasutagus in—"

"In danger," I replied hotly. "For putting us in danger. What are you doing here?"

"I asked Prasutagus for an audience in the spring, but he declined, given the conditions the Northern Iceni faced in the wake of the rebellion. I hoped, however, you'd now be open to talking."

"Boudica," Prasutagus said gently. "Caratacus was already secretly in the city when we arrived. His man recognized and approached Madogh, asking again for a meeting. Given the message from Mona, I agreed."

I clenched my jaw hard, angry at everyone in the room.

"They crucified my brother," I seethed at Caratacus. "Hung him from a pole for carrion birds to pick clean. My brother is dead thanks to you..."

"While I am sorry for it, your brother is dead thanks to Rome," Caratacus said carefully. "I know why your heart is hard toward me. Caturix did not hold his tongue, accusing me of having a hand in your father's death. But those times and grievances are past us now. Now, we have a common enemy. I implore you to listen. There isn't much time. I must leave this place before the sun rises."

Prasutagus pulled out a chair for me, but I didn't sit.

"Speak," I told Caratacus.

"I risk everything to be here to beg you and Prasutagus for help," Caratacus said, gesturing widely, an honest expression on his face. "I implore you, rally the east. We must rise together: the tribes of the west, north, and east. It is all slipping away from us. Rome is taking over everything we love, and now they come for our holy people. Put the past aside and listen. Rally the east. The Trinovantes will join you, as well as those from the Coritani who have survived the fall. Together, we can press the Romans between us and send them from these shores."

"You spoke of the north," Prasutagus said. "You have won Cartimandua's agreement?"

"Not exactly," Caratacus replied cagily. "But I do have allies in the north."

"That is not an answer," I replied. "Once again, you would have us fight on your behalf—and die too, I suppose."

"It would not be like last time. We would rise up, all of us, together, one great army. If we can show the emperor it is too much trouble to stay in these lands, the Romans will retreat. But we must wound them severely. We must show them we are unified. The druids of Mona beg your help...as do I. Come on, dapple-grey," Caratacus said, giving me a soft smile. "I know your spirit. You are a rebel. Join me."

I crossed my arms on my chest. What he said made sense, but my fury with Caratacus for forcing himself on us, married with my grief over Caturix's death, made my thoughts unclear. I wanted to rise up. I wanted to rid this land of Rome forever. I wanted to avenge my people and my brother. But alongside Caratacus? That gave my heart pause.

"You have made your plea," Prasutagus said. "Now, you will give us time to consider."

"I will need your answer soon, Prasutagus. The Romans will make their plans. So should we. In the meantime, I will fight the war everyone else is too afraid to wage," Caratacus replied, an annoyed tone in his voice.

"You forget yourself," I told the Catuvellauni king with a sneer. "Were it not for your father and the actions of you and your brother, Verica and Aedd Mawr wouldn't have left this island. They never would have gone to Rome for help. *You* are the reason Rome is here. *No one* forgets *that*. Nor will I ever forget that you reached for my father's crown. My brother's and my father's blood are on your hands. Leave this place. Now."

Caratacus looked to Prasutagus, who nodded in agreement with me.

My husband gestured to Madogh. "Same way you brought him in."

"King Caratacus," Madogh said, motioning to a servant stairwell at the back of the cellar.

Caratacus rose but paused a moment and looked at Prasutagus.

"Prasutagus... I understand you spread silver in Rome in an effort to find my sister. I..." he said, then paused, struggling for words as he swallowed the emotions that filled his eyes with unshed tears. "I appreciate that more than I can say. Has there been any word?"

Prasutagus shook his head. "I'm sorry. No."

Caratacus nodded sadly, then turned to me. "Boudica, I know what I have done. I know what faults are mine. But please, consider my words. We *must* rise now while we still have a chance. I implore you to leave the past behind," he said, then turned and walked away.

Prasutagus and I stood in the dark, dank space, listening as the others retreated.

Soon, it became silent once more.

Prasutagus turned to me. "I'm sorry."

"Say nothing. It is done and over."

After a long moment, Prasutagus said, "He isn't wrong. As much as you despise him—which he has earned—he isn't wrong."

"No."

"Vespasian is torturing and interrogating druids. The holy orders in the west have gone into hiding. Caratacus has been with the Silures. They have formed a massive army. If they get the north to fight—"

"If. He was very vague about his negotiations with the north."

Prasutagus nodded. "The Catuvellauni king has been sending messengers north. Broc has gone to discover the nature of the negotiations."

"He is trying to win Cartimandua."

"Perhaps."

"If she rallies the Brigantes..." I didn't finish the sentence, but Rome could be crushed if Cartimandua rallied the Brigantes.

Prasutagus met my gaze and nodded. "We will endeavor to learn more. Boudica, I *am* sorry. I did not expect to find him here but thought it the gods' will."

"As I said, speak on it no more."

For a long time, Prasutagus was silent, then he said, "I fear the future, Boudica. I fear Rome's lies."

"Yes. Me too."

"Londinium is a preview of what this land will become. I fear we have sold our children's future to Rome," he said, then took my hand. "Boudica, we may have to rise so we do not die."

He spoke the horrible truth I was coming to believe as well. I pulled my husband toward me, wrapping my arms around him. In that dark place, we finally saw the horror of the world we had helped create.

In our quest for peace, we had doomed ourselves.

CHAPTER 21

The end of harvest season quickly slipped into winter, and with the snow and cold, things grew quiet. But it was not the quiet of peace. We were standing on the edge of a knife. Waiting. Just waiting. To see what the Romans would do. To see if Caratacus could get the alliances he needed. To see if Scapula would turn on the Iceni. To see which way the wind would blow in this disaster that was slowly unfolding. It was the same way for the next three years.

The seasons passed quietly in the east, where Rome had nearly forgotten us. While they did not forget to take their levies, otherwise, they left us alone. The Romans encamped in Oak Throne grew bored and complacent, two of them taking wives of the Northern Iceni women. They played dice with Bran, Cai, and the others on quiet evenings. Otherwise, Rome forgot us.

The news from the west, however, was far worse. Skirmishes occurred between Caratacus's Silures and Cornovii allies and the Romans. Caratacus and his companions attacked Roman parties on the roads and burned Roman outposts. He was waging a war of shadows...and winning. Scapula pursued him to no effect. But every time Caratacus eluded the governor, retribution was taken on the people. Burned villages. Enslaved people. Druids on the run.

Yet, Caratacus persisted. Word came that Caratacus was silently building an alliance west and south. Chieftains, deposed kings, and all those who had suffered the lash of Rome were eager to unite.

Which left the east.

Thus far, however, Caratacus had not won the assurances we needed.

"I am waiting," Prasutagus explained to Ansgar. "I have not yet heard what I want to hear."

"For what do you wait?" Ansgar asked. Those three winters had been hard on the druid. His body grew frail. Though his mind remained sharp, I saw the shadow of the Crone about him.

"A reason to believe he will succeed. Old wounds have not yet healed. The Trinovantes chieftains have yet to come to terms with the scars of the past. They hate Caratacus. Until Caratacus can prove he has the men or gets an alliance in the north, they will not rise. No Trinovantes will risk their lives for Caratacus. And without the Trinovantes, the Greater Iceni cannot succeed. So, for now, we will listen," he said, turning to me. "But we will not act."

I nodded in agreement.

So, we waited and listened.

By the spring of 50, however, the whispers of the Crone grew loudest. A late winter fever swept through Venta. While almost all of us came down with fever or developed a rattling cough, it passed quickly through the young and healthy, but for Ansgar and Nella, it meant the end.

I sat at the bedside of the maid who had given me so much grief in the early years, patting her head with cool cloths, trying to ease her passage.

"Boudica," she whispered softly. "Water? Please?"

I poured her a cup and supported her weight so she could drink. She had grown so thin and frail in the wake of the ailment. When she was done, I lowered her onto her bed once more.

"My mind is awake but dreaming. I remember my mother."

"That is a good memory. Did you grow up in Venta?"

"No, at a farm south of here. Prasutagus's mother brought me to Venta..." she said, taking my hand. "Boudica, I am sorry for the past. You have been a good mother to Artur, a good wife to Prasutagus, and a good queen."

"Say nothing of it," I told her gently. "It is already forgotten."

"I expected you to be a spoiled princess, but you are a mother bear," she said, then laughed. "Just like me. No wonder I hated you."

At that, we both chuckled.

"I will rest now," she told me. "But... if you will send Artur to me."

"Of course," I told her, then rose and left the room. Artur was waiting just down the hall. "She would see you," I told him.

He nodded, then paused. "Boudica..." he said gently. "Prasutagus just came. Ansgar is dead."

I sighed heavily, then embraced my son, holding him tight for a moment, then let him go.

Artur went into Nella's chamber. When he closed the door, I leaned against the wall and closed my eyes. Our world was changing shape again. Somehow, the druid's death marked a beginning...or an end.

As I suspected, Nella saved her last goodbye for Artur. When he exited her chamber, she was gone.

One dreary spring evening, a light mist falling, the Greater Iceni met at Arminghall to bid farewell to the dead. Along with Ansgar and Nella, more than two dozen others had fallen victim to the fever. Pyres had been prepared for the rites, which Tavish and Prasutagus led.

Melusine did not come, deeming it not yet safe.

As we gathered in the drizzling rain, watching the fires transport those who had passed to the Otherworld, I felt terrible dread.

"I remembered something," Pix whispered to me. "When I was a girl, the elders used to say that the old ones would always pass before dark times, times of change. They said their spirits knew not to linger more so they wouldn't die in darkness."

I turned and looked at Pix. "You remembered when you were a girl?"

"Just a little…" Pix said, looking toward the burning fires. "Did see it in the flames and recalled the message."

I looked at the burning bodies and the weeping families. All those who had died of fever were of advanced age. "Perhaps they were right."

"Aye," Pix agreed.

The sickness that swept across Venta was mirrored by the spreading sickness that was Rome. The disease gripping our land, which we had seen in Londinium, spread outside the city. Roman greed increased until it became grotesque. Their demand for taxes grew, not just on us and our trade, but on our people who were expected to pay annual dues. The Greater Iceni were expected to pay unreasonable fees for the privilege of being client citizens.

There were always disputes when the publicans came to collect, but in the spring of 50, the Romans unexpectedly doubled their taxes. The people were unprepared to pay a fee they hadn't known was coming. Reports of Romans ransacking houses, looting, and taking *people* in payment spread across the land. It was even happening in Atrebates and Trinovantes territories.

When the Romans arrived in Venta to collect their dues, a brawl broke out in the marketplace. Prasutagus raised the guard to help quell the violence and then went with our household guard to intervene.

"Shall I come?" Artur asked. My adopted son was no child anymore. With a lean, muscular frame and a trim, black beard, he was a fully grown man and an excellent warrior.

Prasutagus shook his head. "Stay here with Pix and your mother and sisters. We will close the gates to the king's house. You are in charge of the guard."

Artur nodded. "Yes, Father."

I smiled, proud of the young man Artur had become. He'd always been a serious boy. He was the same now that he was grown. More than anything, he wanted to prove himself useful to Prasutagus.

Esu, I hope you see. Look at the man he has become.

When Prasutagus slipped on his horse, I went to him.

"Be careful," I told him.

"And you. Stay inside the king's compound. There have been disputes across the city. I will do what I can. Tell Vian to double-check our payment and prepare to double it. They will rob the people first, then come for us."

I nodded, then stepped back, watching as he rode off.

"When I am older, I will go with my father and cut down every Roman harassing our people," Sorcha said waspishly, her hand on the hilt of the short sword Pix had bought for her.

"I like yer spirit. But, today, ye best get yer frustrations out. Come on, we'll go have a bout," Pix told her, gesturing for my daughter—and Pix's designated protegee—to follow her to the sparring area.

Olwen came to me. Taking my hand, she gestured to Mara.

Mara stood staring at Prasutagus's wake, chewing on her lip and squeezing her fingers.

I nodded to Olwen, stroking her honey-colored hair. My sweet daughter had never spoken, but she saw and often communicated more than others, having a keen sense for feeling others' moods. She felt the fear coming from Mara, whose father had died at Roman hands.

"Come, girls," I told Olwen and Mara, reaching for Mara's hand. "There are pies to bake and preparations to be made for the Imbolc festival. We need not concern ourselves with the Romans. Soon, Cernunnos will take out his bow for the first spring hunt while the maiden dances in the full moonlight, new flowers growing under her feet as she prances. Let the Romans choke on their coins. We will make pies."

I flicked a gaze toward Artur, who nodded to me and then smiled at Olwen and Mara. "You can go with Boudica, or, if you want, you can come with me to check on my ravens."

Mara laughed. "They are too noisy."

"I agree. And pies are much more rewarding," I said.

Artur chuckled. "Perhaps, but the birds are coming along well. Already, I have trained a pair to fly to Yarmouth and back with messages. Morfran can even fly from Venta to Oak Throne. I will send messages now to the others to let them know the Romans are coming. Soon, I will have the birds flying to every city."

"It is true," Mara said. "My mother was just saying how good Artur is with his birds."

I smiled at Mara. "She would know. Your mother is an expert in animals. I applaud your work, Artur, but alas, no bird training for us. Nevertheless, I promise to save the first pie out of the fire for you."

"Agreed," Artur said, then we went our separate ways.

I took the girls to the kitchens, where Betha got the girls to work making dough. Afterward, I went to the formal meeting chamber, where I found Vian working. Her fingers were covered in ink, and she concentrated hard on something she was sketching. She hardly noticed me as I approached.

"Oh, Boudica," she finally said, looking up. "Can I help you with anything?"

"The Romans have come for their taxes. They are in the city now, but they will reach us eventually. Prasutagus asked that you double-check our payment."

Vian nodded, then rose. "Of course."

"And, Vian… Double of what we paid last time."

"Double?" Vian exclaimed.

I nodded.

"Robbery."

"We invited the foxes into the henhouse and told them to make themselves at home. Now, we pay the price."

Vian frowned. "I'll see to it," she told me then began her work.

I was eternally grateful Vian had decided to stay with us. Finola returned to Holk Fort to be with her mother after her child was born. I worried Vian would go with her sister, but she stayed. Now that Ansgar was gone, we increasingly relied upon Vian, but her quick wit was up to the task. While Ansgar had the wisdom of a druid, Vian was shrewd in other ways. The Romans were quick to tax all we made. Vian found ways for us to produce more to outpace Rome's reach.

"Thank you, Vian," I told her. "I'll be with the girls in the kitchens if you need me."

Already distracted, Vian merely nodded.

I rejoined Betha and Ronat, who had already plied Mara and Olwen with treats as the girls worked the dough for the pies. Brita, my maid, also joined us. Soon, we all had our hands in the dough. Despite my best effort to turn the girls' attention to something pleasant, I couldn't help but feel the tension in the city.

My eyes constantly strayed to the door as I waited for a call from the gate.

It came a couple of hours later.

"The king! The king and Rome," I heard one of the guards shout.

Mara paused a moment, her hands on the dough.

"No bother of ours," Ronat said lightly. "Keep mixing, Mara. Your ingredients are still raw," she said, then met my gaze, giving me a wink.

I bent and kissed both girls on the head, pulled off my flour-covered apron, then went to greet my *guests*.

Prasutagus rode at the front of a party. The Greater Iceni guard followed. And then came the Roman soldiers. There were more. Every time they came, there were more. And through the open edifice of the gate, I saw even more soldiers in the streets of Venta, which were unusually quiet. An entire city had been silenced by their presence.

I clenched my jaw and waited.

Vian, Artur, and Pix also arrived. I scanned the yard for Sorcha, but she was nowhere to be seen.

"Our firebrand?" I asked Pix.

"Waiting in the stables with a dagger in case they try to steal our horses. Isolde has an eye on her."

I shook my head. "If it were up to Sorcha, we would begin a rebellion tomorrow. Her disdain for the Romans comes from somewhere deep within her."

"An old wound," Pix had said. "Perhaps she fought with ye and me when Caesar came. I know that firebrand's spirit, even though the gods do not whisper her name to me. Who is to say?"

I suspected she was right.

Prasutagus rode to the roundhouse alongside three Romans, including Procurator Vitas, who had arrived at the side of Scapula and was the man in charge of fleecing the tribes.

He was a wiry man with curly silver hair, a large nose, and a mean gaze. He dismounted and then gestured to his soldiers, motioning for them to inspect the house.

"Procurator," I said stiffly, stepping before the men and raising my hand to stop them. "This is the king's home, and the king's family is within. You are a welcome guest in the house of King Prasutagus and myself, client king and queen of Rome. I will not be subjected to an inspection."

At that, the man looked me over. His expression told me he thought little of me. Instead, he turned to Prasutagus and lifted an eyebrow at him.

"My wife is right. As Emperor Claudius said, we are all Romans now. Why don't we go have a drink, Procurator," Prasutagus said, then stepped toward me.

We were supposed to be allies. An inspection of Oak Throne was one thing. Caturix had been in open rebellion. But the notion that the Roman guards would search the home of the king of the Greater Iceni showed a shift in attitude. The home was sacred to our gods and theirs. They would not invade a friend's house at the risk of offending their gods. But they had not looked at us in the light, which told me everything about Rome's shifting opinion.

"Very well," the procurator said, motioning for a small guard to follow.

Galvyn met us inside and led us to the meeting chamber where Vian waited, the Roman coins already accounted for and placed in a chest. Betha and Ronat were in the back of the room setting out refreshments.

Little Newt, who used to assist them, was not so little anymore and was now part of the king's guard.

"Procurator," I said, gesturing to the man to take a seat as I poured him a glass of wine.

With an exasperated huff, he slumped into the chair, slapping his stylus on the table.

Ignoring his tantrum, I handed him the cup. "Sir."

"Queen Boudica," he said absently in thanks, then drank, exhaling deeply after he'd drained the cup.

I poured him another as Prasutagus took a seat beside the procurator.

"I say, Prasutagus, that was quite a dust-up today in Venta. There have never been reports of such open contempt from your people."

"My people have not been asked to pay double the annual fee before," Prasutagus said stiffly. "We are not rich people, Procurator. The amount you asked today was half a family's annual income."

"Well, roads are not built cheaply," the man replied, motioning in annoyance for Betha to hurry with serving him a plate. "And they were warned."

Scowling, Betha brought him a plate, the vessel clattering when she practically dropped it in front of him.

I sucked in my lips so I wouldn't laugh.

"No, Procurator, they were not. Rumor only, but no messenger from you nor the governor."

"Well, we are very busy," the man replied, then began eating.

I cast a glance behind me. Roman soldiers waited at the door. Two outside, two inside. Pix and Artur had joined us in the chamber. Outside, I spotted Ewan and Newt.

"You need not worry," the procurator said, then paused between chews. "Those we have taken into custody for failure to pay will be returned to their families after a year's labor."

"If they are still alive," I replied waspishly. "And in the meantime, their families will struggle to raise the sum for the next tax without their menfolk to work."

"I cannot be held accountable for laziness and lack of ingenuity. You made promises to the emperor. I am only here to collect upon them."

"How many men have you taken?" I asked. "And what is the cost of their debt?"

I looked to Prasutagus, who nodded.

"Yes, as my wife asked, how many and the amount of their debt?" Prasutagus followed, guessing my meaning.

The man paused, then looked from Prasutagus to me. "You would ransom these layabouts? Those who would dare raise a fist against Rome?"

"Rather than see them in chains? Gladly," I replied tartly.

"In the future, we will all be better prepared for increases in taxation with forewarning," Prasutagus told the procurator with a stern gaze. "Perhaps some leniency is due this year due to the unannounced nature of the increased taxation," he said, then his voice turned darker. "I know you need men, Procurator. But you do not need Greater Iceni men."

Prasutagus held the procurator's gaze, and I felt a shift in the air. My husband rarely evoked the magic within him aside from holy days or in prayer, but I sensed it now. He was using his skills as a druid to press his will on the Roman.

The procurator stared at Prasutagus for a moment, then dipped into his satchel and pulled out a scroll. He unfurled it, looked over the notes thereon, then set it before my husband. Grabbing a stick of charcoal from his bag, he scratched out a price.

It was a fortune.

"I will not give you those who have bloodied my soldiers, but if you want to pay for the rest, that is my price."

Prasutagus looked from the scroll to me.

I nodded.

"Agreed," Prasutagus said, then shifted the scroll so Vian could see. "Will you see to it?"

Vian's eyebrows shot up in alarm, but she nodded and left.

"Your daughter?" the procurator asked.

"No. Vian is our secretary."

"A woman secretary?" he replied with a laugh. "I say, you people do things very backward. So, I assume you have your own payment prepared."

Prasutagus nodded, then went and collected the chest, setting it before the man. "The Greater Iceni's payment."

The man's brow flexed in confusion. "And that of the Northern Iceni? You are the queen of both, are you not, Queen Boudica."

"Yes, but my brother Bran—"

"Chieftain Bran will pay his own taxes for Oak Throne. I already have men on the road to the fort. They ride under heavy guard since the Northern Iceni are prone to rebellion, but I suppose Scapula pulled your teeth. All the same, Oak Throne will pay revenue on its own lively trade. But as for the Northern Iceni as a whole, you are missing a chest, Queen Boudica," the man told me with a smirk, then reached for the wine decanter, filling his cup once more.

"I..." I said, looking at Prasutagus.

"This was not agreed, Procurator," Prasutagus said stiffly.

"A misunderstanding, it seems. Best ask your female secretary to dig a little deeper," he said with a chuckle, then went back to eating.

Tension filled the space as I struggled to know what to do, what to say—and not say.

After a moment, Prasutagus turned to me. "Will you see to it, Boudica? Vian can assist you."

My hands shaking, rage filling me, I turned to leave.

"The new rate, of course," the procurator called behind me.

I clenched my fists and did not turn back.

Behind me, I heard Prasutagus turn the conversation. "I heard they are building something called a coliseum in Camulodunum, Procurator."

"Ah, indeed. Are you familiar…"

Not wanting to hear more, I left the room and went to my bedchamber. There, I found Vian struggling to move the bed.

"I was just about to get Galvyn to help," she told me. "I was trying to channel my anger to help move it."

"This may help… We need silver to pay taxes for the Northern Iceni as well. Those monies Bran prepared to pay will be for Oak Throne only. We need to give the Romans payment for the whole tribe."

"All the Northern Iceni?"

"Yes. At the new rate."

"By Andraste's toe!" Vian seethed. "I hope he chokes on a chicken bone and dies."

"Yes," I replied simply.

Working together, we slid the bed aside and carefully

entered the hidden vault. Once inside, Vian began counting the tax for the Northern Iceni, her counting device in her hand. At the same time, I collected coins to liberate the people of Venta the Romans had taken.

Midway through, Vian paused.

"If they triple, quadruple, or more the tax next time…" she said, then looked around the room.

Already, the Greater Iceni treasure had been much depleted.

"May all the gods be thanked that Prasutagus did not spend all the Roman gold the emperor gave as a gift," Vian continued. "And what he did spend has paid for itself five times over. But all the same, you and Prasutagus must increase the quarterly taxes on the Greater Iceni to be ready to pay your own share."

As I looked around the room, the future played before me. I watched as the gold dwindled and dwindled, the chamber growing darker until there was nothing left but torchlight. Vian was right, but how could we do that to the people who already suffered at Rome's hands?

"I feel like there is a hand around my throat, tightening slowly…so slowly," I said.

"Your Uncle Saenunos loved frog stew. My mother made it quite often. You know the old tale about frogs in a pot? They say if you place a frog in a pot of hot water and slowly heat it, it won't notice the heat and will boil to death. But that's not true. They do know the pot is getting warmer. And when the feel they heat, they struggle and fight to survive. They use one another as ladders to climb out. They jump with all their strength. They fight not to become victims to someone else's appetite."

I turned back to my counting. "We are all frogs. And very soon, we will need to start jumping."

"Oh, Boudica. I fear we may already be too late."

After Vian and I had delivered the Roman his payment, and the man finished his meal, Prasutagus rallied our guard. We went with the Romans back into the city. The soldiers had our people in chains or placed in prison carts waiting to be transported.

The people of Venta wept and called out to us as we approached the horrible scene.

"Be calm, my people," Prasutagus called. "Be calm. Boudica and I have paid the debts of those we could. There must be no more violence here, children of Epona. No violence. Those who have no blood on their hands will be freed."

At that, the Romans began unchaining people.

But it was not just our menfolk, traders, or heads of house they had taken. I also saw old women, mothers, aged men, and young boys and girls. The Romans had taken anyone who had not paid—entire families.

"Now, what of your druids?" Procurator Vitus asked. "I understand there is some shrine hereabouts."

"Our druids have no source of income. Our temples are not like yours. The druids do not collect payment from everyone who visits," I snapped back.

"No?" the procurator asked in mock surprise. "Legate Vespasian has found the druids quite flush with coin in the west."

"That is the west, sir. Their ways are not ours. Our holy people have no money. They are foragers and farmers. And I have accounted for their share of taxes in my calculations," Prasutagus said firmly.

"Are they troublemakers?" the procurator prodded my husband. "In the west—"

"This is not the west," my husband said again, his anger getting the better of him. "The druids of the Greater Iceni are sacred. They speak for our gods. May I remind you again, Procurator, that the Greater Iceni are *allies* of Rome. I hope Rome has not forgotten."

"Oh, we have not forgotten," the procurator replied slickly. "Otherwise, King Prasutagus, these people's blood would flood the streets, and we would not be making bargains over wine." He gestured to his men to prepare to depart. "I hope my men find similar hospitality in Oak Throne, Queen Boudica. Already, the governor's patience with your northern folk is thin."

"Your men will have no issues in Oak Throne," I

replied stiffly.

"Well, I will be close by in Camulodunum if I hear differently," he said, then went to the door of his carpentum. He paused and turned to Prasutagus. "I hope to see you there sometime, King Prasutagus. You would enjoy the entertainments in Camulodunum. You should come to visit King Diras and Lady Julia. Make yourself more seen, *client king*. Perhaps things will improve next year if you visit Camulodunum more frequently." With that, he got into the litter and closed the door.

The legionnaire called to the other soldiers. They formed in rows, turning in sync, and began to march from Venta in time.

Everyone stood watching as they left. The sound of their footsteps, the rattle of their armor, rolled away from us like a bad storm departing.

Behind us, I heard people crying. Weeping women and children ran alongside the cart holding the prisoners we could not free. Rome said the men would work a year, but we all knew the truth.

They would never be back.

Prasutagus reached out and took my hand.

His fingers were ice-cold.

His body told me what his lips could not.

Perhaps not with swords or fire, but the Romans were coming for us.

One coin at a time.

CHAPTER 22

Cai arrived in Venta a week later with word from Bran. The Roman visit had gone much the same in Oak Throne as in Venta. The Romans had taken everything we had saved on behalf of *all* the Northern Iceni as Oak Throne's payment alone. While Holk Fort and Frog's Hollow had ruefully paid to keep the peace, a retainer in the south, a small farmstead named Willow Glade, had protested.

"Lynet said they could see the fire from Frog's Hollow," Cai told me. "By the time they arrived, everything was gone, including the families working the farm. There are reports from other farms that the young men and some of the young ladies were taken."

I'd been friends with Cai all my life and knew him to be earnest and steady—except when Pix dug into him. He'd been shaken by these events.

"What happens next year?" Cai asked, horror shadowing his eyes. "And the year after, and after that…"

I reached out and took his hand, squeezing it.

We both knew the answer.

IT WAS MIDSUMMER when storm clouds rolled in once more. This time, in the form of Lors, a Trinovantes chieftain with whom Prasutagus was friendly.

Prasutagus and I had been at the King's Wood when Pix and Artur appeared, riding hard, Chieftain Lors and a small band of Trinovantes warriors along with him.

Melusine, who had been laughing and joking with us, made a hasty retreat into her small house.

Tavish's gaze followed her, a worried expression on his face. The look betrayed the druid's heart.

Prasutagus and I stepped toward the chieftain.

"Prasutagus," Chieftain Lors said, slipping off his horse and rushing forward to meet us. When he saw Tavish, he bowed. "Holy one."

"Lors," Prasutagus said. "What's happened?"

The man shook his head. Then, I saw his clothing was soiled with soot and his hands and clothes caked in blood.

"It's over, Prasutagus. The Trinovantes are done, killed by our own king. It began with Maiden Stones... The Romans took the shrine. Chieftains Coel, Rotri, Brode, and I pushed back. Coel and Rotri are dead, and their villages are burned. Brode escaped by ship, but his people were not so lucky. As for my own people," he said, then shook his head sadly. "My wife, my children...all gone. It was the excuse they had been waiting for to eliminate us. They've been building their colonia, houses for retired soldiers, giving them tracts of Trinovantes farmlands. We were in the way. First, they cut the holy grove, taking the ancient oaks. Then, they came for the stones. When the maidens protested, everything fell apart. The Trinovantes people are running, hiding, or dying. The king—more like his Roman handlers—closed Camulodunum. I am shocked to hear these words coming from my lips, my father and brothers dead at his hands, but we must get word to Caratacus. Prasutagus, we must rise."

"Please," Tavish said. "Please, won't you come inside? You are wounded and weary," the druid said, gesturing to the roundhouse where the druids gathered.

A sick feeling rocked my stomach. The priestesses... my thoughts went to the sweet, innocent girls who had helped me bring Sorcha into this world. Maiden Stones was one of the holiest places in all our lands.

A wind blew through the forest, making the leaves

quake. The trees whispered. I could hear their voices on the breeze.

"Boudica, protect the oaks.

"Boudica, protect the stones.

"Boudica... Rise, rise, rise!

"Bring the fire!"

SEATED IN THE DRUIDS' small house, Chieftain Lors unpacked a harrowing tale, tears streaming down his face as he spoke.

"I told Arilla to take the children and run, but a Roman spotted her. He cut her down, his horse trampling over my small children. They were so little, five and four years of age. They died in the mud," he said, then wept.

After a few moments, he shook his head. "We waited too long to join Caratacus. We trusted Diras too much. I must try to get west to Caratacus."

"We must learn where Caratacus is first," Prasutagus said.

"Should we go to King Diras?" I asked Prasutagus. "Perhaps he doesn't know..."

"Boudica," Prasutagus cautioned. "This is not like before."

"I know," I said, "but there is no one else. If we do not speak on behalf of the Trinovantes, who will?"

Chieftain Lors looked at me. "Queen Boudica, with all due respect, I don't think there is anything left to say. We are conquered by our own king."

LEAVING the chieftain in the care of the druids, we returned to Venta. When we entered the city, Prasutagus stopped. "I need to…" he said, then paused, gesturing down a side street. "Madogh is staying with his sister."

I nodded. "I know it is hopeless, but we should go to Camulodunum. We have not seen the place with our own eyes for too long. We have no sense of what has happened to the Trinovantes. And I… I must try to see if there is some sign of the priestesses of Maiden Stones."

Prasutagus nodded. "I caution you not to hold out hope for them. But otherwise, I agree. We are doomed to failure, but you are right that there is no one else to speak."

I swallowed hard. "All we can do is try."

"Speak to Ewan," Prasutagus told me. "Tell him to be prepared to ride within the hour. Heavy guard."

I nodded, then the two of us went our separate ways. When I arrived at the roundhouse, I spoke to Ewan, asking him to muster the guard, then made ready to depart.

Prasutagus arrived a short time later. He hurried into our bedchamber and redressed.

"For the first time, I'm worrying that we don't have enough guards in the city or on the roundhouse," Prasutagus said as he dressed. It had not escaped my notice that he had daggers in his boots and vest, two swords on his hips, and pulled a bow from the wall. "When we return, I will call for more warriors to be stationed in the city. I'll train and armor them. I feel like I've been sleeping. Seeing Lors like that, imagining it was you and Artur, Sorcha, and Olwen," he said, shaking his head. "I will bring more guards into the city and king's house."

I said nothing, merely nodded. I, too, shared Prasutagus's fears.

I slid my daggers into my boots but wore no weapons on the outside. After all, I was Northern Iceni, and my people had been disarmed. I needed to play the part.

Prasutagus and I joined the others in the main chamber.

Pix waited, armored from head to toe.

Prasutagus paused. "Pix," he said. "I would like you to stay here with the children."

"Is that so, Strawberry King?"

"If something were to happen in our absence... I trust my family with you. I know you will keep them safe."

Pix looked surprised, and a softness came upon her features. "All right. I'll see to them."

"Why do you have to go?" Sorcha demanded angrily. "All of a sudden, everyone is going to Camulodunum. Why? We are not Trinovantes."

"No, but the Trinovantes people are dying," I told her.

"Their king should help them."

"Yes, he should. Perhaps he doesn't know what is happening to them. Someone must talk to him, tell him."

Sorcha crossed her arms. "Why does it have to be you?"

I smiled gently at her. "Because there is no one else left."

Olwen came to me.

When I moved to hug her, she gestured for me to wait. She pulled one of my hairpins from her pocket. It was a long, slender piece with the image of a horsehead at the top. She slipped it into my hair, careful not to poke me.

I smiled at her and touched my hair. "Look better now?"

She nodded and then hugged me.

With the household settled, we prepared to ride out.

"Ye be careful," Pix told me. "The whole countryside will be on fire. The Romans may not want ye poking yer nose into their business. It could be as Lors said. They have been waiting to take the land from the people. Ye may not find an ear to listen to ye."

"I know," I said sadly. "But we must try."

"Aye, Boudica," Pix said. "Yer eyes always search for peace, even when none is to be had. May Andraste ride with ye all the same."

With that, I mounted Druda, and we rode out.

We left Venta and rode throughout the day into the night, stopping only briefly to rest in a secluded glade away from the road, deep in the forest. When the sun rose in the morning, we set off again, working our way from the forest and back to the road.

Our banners fluttering in the breeze, we made our way down the road toward Camulodunum. The small farms that dotted the landscape in the distance were burning. Black smoke rose in billowing clouds in the countryside all around. The roads were empty.

This time, no one was fleeing. No one was running. Everyone was dying.

After an hour on the ride, we finally saw another

party, but they were not Trinovantes. Three riders hurried our way.

There was no missing the scarlet-colored banner they carried.

"Halt!" the lead man yelled. "Identify yourself."

"I am King Prasutagus, and this is my wife, Queen Boudica, of the Greater Iceni. We are riding to Camulo-dunum to see King Diras."

"Were you sent for?" another of the other soldiers asked.

"That is no business of yours, soldier," I replied angrily. "Your tongue wags before your mind engages."

The lead soldier frowned at the man. "We will escort you into the city. There is rebellious activity taking place throughout the region. It's not safe," he said, then motioned for us to follow.

As we rode onward, we began to see signs of construction. The Romans had expanded their roads and built vast farms on Trinovantes' lands. Slaves struggled under the hot summer sun and whip of the taskmaster's lash to lay bricks on a new road that veered from the main pass to the city.

"Where does this road go?" I asked one of the Romans.

"To the villas of the colonia."

"We shall see this colonia," Prasutagus said. Not waiting for the Romans to protest, Prasutagus guided his horse onto the route, the rest of us following. We rode for a time, and finally, the colonia came into sight.

Somehow, I imagined a small collection of houses near the city center. What I found before me, however, was much different. If I put four Londiniums side by side, it would not make up the size of the land taken by the colonia. Neat rows of villas sat along paved streets, red tile roofs glimmering the sunlight, with large plots of land around each villa.

"What is the purpose of this place?" Prasutagus asked one of the soldiers.

"Retired soldiers have been given their shares of land here, King Prasutagus. It is the custom."

"To take someone else's land? That is the custom?" I asked.

"A reward of land comes at the end of service to Rome," the soldier explained, confused by my reaction.

Prasutagus turned to me. "I have heard as much. Some Roman soldiers are given the reward of land after a period of service. It is used as an enticement to get men to join their legions."

"How can Rome give land that is not theirs?" I asked.

"Rome can gift land wherever the Empire rules," one of the soldiers answered.

"Has anyone asked the Trinovantes what they think about that?" I replied.

"They have," Artur answered. "That explains the smoke we saw on our way here."

"I've seen enough. Take us to the city," Prasutagus said.

The soldier nodded and then led us onward.

The Camulodunum we had seen when we came last was no more. Like Londinium, the city had grown tenfold. And every inch of that growth was Roman. As we rode into the town, we found Romans everywhere. In fact, there were hardly any of our people except those in chains. We rode down the street where the shine of Camulos once sat. In its place...

"By the gods," Artur whispered, looking up at a massive edifice.

"The temple of Claudius," one of the soldiers said, smiling at the building. He gestured to a tall statue of the emperor standing before a multi-columned building. It was taller than any house or fort I had ever seen.

"A temple to your emperor?" Artur asked.

"*Our* emperor," the man replied in annoyance.

"Then, he is worshipped in the same manner as your gods?" Artur asked.

"Of course. He is emperor."

"There was a spring on this site, sacred to Camulos," I said, my brow knitting in frustration.

"I know nothing of Camulos, but when Claudius came to this heathen place, he stabbed the banner of

Rome into the ground. A spring erupted from that sacred spot, so a temple was built here. Now, the spring of Claudius flows from the ground, filling an offering pool within the temple."

"Offering pool?" I asked.

"Yes, a sacred pool where people may leave coins or other valuables in honor of the emperor. The shrine is magnificent, but many other wonderful sites exist in Camulodunum. In fact, there will be gladiator fighting in the arena today. You should come to watch."

"And what are gladiators?" I asked.

"Gladiators are warriors who battle to the death," one of the soldiers told us. "It is a great show," he added with a grin.

My eyes went down the row. At the end of one lane, I saw the robed priestesses of Minerva before a smaller, but regally adorned temple. Like the temple of Claudius, pillars adorned the temple of the goddess. Standing on the steps before the temple was a beautiful statue of the goddess herself. Her gowns had been painted blue. Gold trim made her hair glimmer in the summer sunlight.

We arrived at the forum where we had met with the other kings and the emperor long ago. The place was teeming with Romans who gave us suspicious glances as we passed.

Prasutagus met my gaze for a brief moment, then we dismounted.

"Weapons," the legionnaire said, his hands extended.

Prasutagus removed all visible weapons and then motioned for his men to do the same.

"Two of your people only," he said. "We will see to the rest."

Prasutagus motioned for Artur and Ewan to follow us inside.

We entered the building only to be met with suspicious gazes and unfamiliar faces. All those smiling Romans who had lauded Prasutagus's ingenuity and flattered my beauty were gone. Instead, I felt like I had walked into a room full of vultures, all of whom studied Prasutagus and me.

King Diras sat on his throne surrounded by several hawkish-looking old men who spoke to one another while the king gazed absently at a spot on the wall. I scanned the room for Lady Julia, but she was not found.

"King Prasutagus and Queen Boudica of the Iceni," the page called.

When Prasutagus moved to correct the boy, I touched his arm.

"The error is telling. Let us see what else they tell us," I whispered.

Prasutagus nodded.

"King Prasutagus, Queen Boudica," King Diras

called, finally turning to us. "Welcome again to Camulo-dunum, my friends."

"King Diras," Prasutagus said, bowing.

"King Diras," I echoed.

"Why are you here?" the king asked.

"King Diras, we have come on behalf of our holy people," Prasutagus said.

"What holy people?"

"Of the Trinovantes."

"I thought you meant the Roman priests."

"No, my friend. Those honored by *your* people, the Trinovantes."

"What's wrong?" King Diras asked, looking truly confused.

I quickly glanced at the men around Diras. The king may not have known the matter, but one of the serpents at his side surely did.

"There is nothing for you to be worried about," one small man wearing a toga said, stepping forward and setting his hand on Diras's shoulder. "Just peasants complaining."

"That is not so," Prasutagus said firmly, then turned back to Diras again. "I have learned that a sacred temple of the Trinovantes people called Maiden Stones has been razed. It is an ancient holy place of your people. I am sure this cannot be true, but we wanted to inquire with you, King Diras."

King Diras looked confused, then turned the Roman. The sharp-eyed man leaned in and whispered in the king's ear.

When he stepped back, King Diras nodded and then told us, "The priests were hiding rebels there, so they paid the price."

I bit my lip, holding back my astonishment.

"Many of the Trinovantes are in full rebellion against King Diras," the Roman told us. "We are working hard to squash these rebels wherever they are found."

"Who are you?" I asked.

"I am Senator Marcellus Nipius Sorio."

"Where is Lady Julia?"

"I sent my mother back to Rome," King Diras told me. "She was always telling me what to do. But I have my own men, and I am king. I rule the Trinovantes, not her."

"Indeed," Prasutagus said.

"My people are rebelling against their king," Diras went on. "My friends—the Romans—are helping me end the rebellion."

"So we have heard," Prasutagus said. "We saw the fires from many villages and farmsteads as we passed."

"If they rebel, then they will pay the price," King Diras said.

"What ignited the rebellion, my friend?" Prasutagus asked.

The Roman senator moved to cut Diras off, but the king began speaking before the secretary had a chance.

King Diras smiled at Prasutagus. "First, they were mad because we needed some of their lands for the Roman soldiers to build their villas. Then, the chieftains were angry about paying back their loans. But everyone knows you have to pay back loans. After that, they began to cause trouble. Some of them even snuck into the city to cause problems. So, now, I will have all the chieftains beheaded, and my Roman friends will take care of my people and my cities. The traitors can be slaves and build my roads. You must be careful your chieftains don't act like mine did. But if they do, our Roman friends will help you."

Prasutagus nodded thoughtfully. "Thank you for your counsel, King Diras. I will heed your words carefully."

King Diras smiled, satisfied with the exchange.

Beside him, however, the senator wore a sour expression.

"You will stay and dine with me," King Diras said. "They will bring the meal soon."

"We would be delighted," Prasutagus replied.

Not long thereafter, the massive banquet table began to be set. Two men, who appeared to know something of our trade in London, approached Prasutagus. I held my cup of wine and listened. While the conversation started off amicably enough, soon they began questioning Prasutagus on what he knew of the resources in Trinovantes territory, namely where there were mines of silver and other priceless resources.

A young Roman woman, about sixteen years of age, approached King Diras. She wore a light blue gown, her dark hair pinned up, ringlets of curls gracing her shoulders. She eyed me carefully, then whispered in the king's ear.

A moment later, King Diras called to me. "Queen Boudica. Will you come here?"

I joined the pair. "King Diras?"

"Queen Boudica, this is Lucia. Lucia and I will get married this summer."

"Lucia," I said, inclining my head to her. "I bid you welcome to our lands."

Lucia looked me over from head to foot. The laughter in her eyes revealed her thoughts. Like many other Romans, she found our people...rough. "Thank you, Queen Boudica."

"Lucia has her women with her. You can meet them and be friends," King Diras said with a smile.

"Queen Boudica is very busy with her own affairs," Lucia told the king. "And it is nearly time to eat," she said, extending her hand to her soon-to-be husband.

"Oh, all right," King Diras said.

The king then descended his dais and went to the head of the table.

A servant rang a bell, calling the other guests to join. The servants settled Ewan and Artur at the foot of the table along with the other, lesser guests.

I met Artur's gaze, worrying how he might take the slight, but he gestured to me that he was fine.

Prasutagus and I settled in across from one another. Around us, conversation was soon underway about all manner of people whose names I had never heard, about trade in the territory, and about goings-on in the west.

Prasutagus and I suffered in silence, the Romans barely acknowledging us.

Lucia and three other well-dressed young women sat near the king, all of them laughing and giggling while Lucia refilled her husband's wine cup again and again.

At some point, I met my husband's gaze.

Prasutagus shook his head.

I nodded.

When the meal ended, a quartet of musicians appeared, and the Romans drifted off to drink or lie on chaises.

Prasutagus gently took my arm. "Boudica, there is nothing to be done here. Let's not waste more time. I will excuse us."

"Agreed," I said, then nodded.

Turning, I went to find a quiet place away from the crowd, only to accidentally knock a goblet of wine off the table. It spilled everywhere, including on the hem of the dress of one of Lucia's friends.

"Oaf," the girl cursed at me. "Clumsy fool. And this stola is new," she hissed at me, then looked for a servant. "You there. Water!" she shouted at one of the serving women.

"Careful, Flavia. She's a queen," Lucia said with a mocking laugh. "Wouldn't want to offend her."

"Queen of what? Dung heaps? My horse wears better clothes than her."

"Smells the same, though," another of the girls said, making them all laugh.

A Trinovantes servant rushed back with water and linen to clean the Roman girl's gown. "My lady," she said, her head bowed as she handed her the water.

"Never mind, I'll go change," the girl said, scowling at me. The girls departed, leaving the servant and me behind, both gaping.

I had never been one to compare looks or dresses with other women. The whole encounter left me confused, slightly embarrassed, and angry.

The servant turned and looked at me. "Queen Boudica. Your sleeve," she said, gesturing to my dress.

I almost told her not to worry about it, but I thought better of it.

"Yes. Please. Thank you," I said, motioning for her to step aside with me.

"Pay them no mind, Queen Boudica," the woman whispered to me. "They have no manners at all. They see all of us as swine."

"They are nothing to me. You are Trinovantes?"

She nodded. "The Romans took my family's farm. I don't know where the rest of my family has gone, but I ended up here. When I heard I would serve the king of the Trinovantes, I hoped… But as you already see, there is no hope here."

I sighed heavily. "Have you heard anything about the priestesses from Maiden Stones? What has happened to them? Is there any rumor?"

She nodded. "The Romans talked about it after the shrine was defiled. The priestesses went to the slave auction. A dozen men came with some druids to try to free them, but they were captured and executed. The druids' bodies hung in the square until yesterday."

"Are the priestesses still at the auctioneer's?"

"I don't know."

Setting aside the water and cloth, I took the girl's hands. "May the Great Mother watch over you."

"And you," she told me, then went on her way.

My gaze went to Prasutagus, who was speaking to King Diras. I then looked about for Artur and Ewan but didn't find them. Given no one was paying any attention to me, I slipped from the building and out into the street.

Romans were creeping about everywhere. I hurried from the building and headed back into the market-place. There, some Romans were drinking at a tavern. Others were playing games of dice. I passed them, going to the livestock yards, where human cargo waited to be sold.

Sad-looking men and women sat in cages. They looked at me with empty gazes. I scanned them, looking for the priestesses.

"My friend," I called to one of the women, "the priestesses of Maiden Stones… Have you seen them? Are they here?"

The woman looked away.

I began to fret. Any moment now, I was bound to run into a Roman.

"Anyone, please. I'm looking for the priestesses. Are they here? Has anyone seen them?"

"Nay, lady. They're all sold off," one gruff man said, not bothering to look up. "Gone. Just like everything else. Gone."

"Oi! You. What are you doing there?" a Roman called to me.

I stiffened my stance, squaring my shoulders, then turned to the Roman. "I'm looking to buy a maid," I replied with an annoyed but elevated tone.

"At this time of night? Creeping about like this, I'd say you're looking to steal."

"Hardly. My party is departing Camulodunum, and I was looking for a woman suitable for a maid."

"Oh, were you now?" the man asked, eyeing me over.

"Yes. I need a girl no more than twenty. Have any like that?"

"Got silver?"

"Of course."

The man waved to me to follow him.

We made our way from the cages and down a narrow alleyway. "In this building 'ere," the man said, pointing.

The hairs on the back of my neck rose.

"Just this way," he said, motioning for me to follow.

"Perhaps, I—"

The man grabbed me roughly and slammed me against the wall, his hand around my neck as he searched for my coin purse. "I'll take this pouch, fancy lady," he said, yanking the pouch from my belt. "And then I think I'll help myself to this one," he said, sticking his hands between my legs. "Scream, and I'll slice your throat."

I froze.

Northern Iceni.

I am Northern Iceni.

We were disarmed.

What weapons I did carry on me were out of reach.

"Oh, I bet you've got a strawberry-red cunny of fluff there," he said, laughing gleefully.

I tried to jerk away, but he squeezed my neck tighter, banging my head against the side of the building. For a moment, I saw stars. But I also felt a weird pinch at the back of my head.

The hairpin.

Reaching up, I pulled the horsehead hairpin from my hair. With one swift move, I stabbed the man in the eye.

"Ah," he wailed, letting me go. "You whore! You whore!"

I pulled the pin out of his eye and stabbed him in the neck, aiming for the fat vein. I then drew my knife from my boot, stabbed the man in the chest, then pushed him to the ground. Working quickly, I grabbed the hair pin, coin purse, and dagger, stuffing the blade back in my boot, then ran back to the forum.

As I went, I heard commotion amongst the Romans.

All at once, the city lit up in excitement.

Bells chimed.

Torches were lit.

People poured from their houses.

I turned a corner and nearly ran into Artur.

"Boudica," he said, looking me over. "We were looking for you and..." He paused, looking me over.

"There is blood on your hands," he said, lifting my hand in which I was clutching the hairpin.

Artur took the pin from my hand, stuffed it into his vest, they yanked out his waterskin. "Quickly, wash your hands," he told me.

"The governor! The governor has come! Governor Scapula is here!" a young man called as he raced through the streets.

Quickly washing the blood away, Artur and I then hurried back.

People poured out onto the steps.

Prasutagus, Ewan, and the other Iceni guard joined Artur and me.

"Boudica," Prasutagus said, eyeing me over. "What's wrong?"

It was then I realized my hair and clothing were rumpled, and there were tears in my eyes. "I'm fine. I'll be all right. Just call for the horses."

Prasutagus nodded, then motioned to Ewan.

"The governor," Prasutagus said, gesturing to the commotion. "He was not expected. When they heard he had come, they acted like a hive full of shaken bees."

"Something must have happened," I replied, willing my heart to be calm.

Prasutagus nodded.

I was still shaking.

Artur put his arm around my shoulders and pulled me close.

The clop of hooves and the clatter of Roman armor rang across the city as the Roman soldiers made their way toward the forum. Scapula rode at the front, a self-satisfied smirk on his face.

"Governor Scapula," Senator Marcellus Nipius Sorio called, stepping in front of King Diras to greet the governor.

"Cousin," Scapula greeted the man. "Bring out your best wine."

"What is it? What has happened?"

Scapula smiled broadly then gestured behind him. The soldiers moved aside so a single rider could come forward. Behind the rider came a man in chains.

His feet and face bloodied, his body broken, I barely recognized him at first. But then, I saw what had the Romans rejoicing.

It was Caratacus.

WE STARED in disbelief as the Catuvellauni king stood swaying on his feet.

"Tie him to the post," the governor said. "Let the

world see. The great terror of Rome has been captured thanks to our loyal friends, the Brigantes. We'll let you take in the night air, Caratacus. Tomorrow, you will be at sea," Scapula said with a laugh, then went inside, the Romans following him.

I watched as they dragged the Catuvellauni king toward the post.

Caratacus looked our way as he went, opening his eyes just a crack. He spotted Prasutagus and me.

"Prasutagus… Boudica… You must rise. Rise now! You must rise, or all is lost. They will tear down our gods. Kill our children. Burn the greenwood. You are our only hope. Rise up! Rise!"

"Shut up, you," one of the Roman soldiers said, hitting Caratacus with the butt of his sword and knocking him unconscious.

"Father, let's go," Artur said. "Let's go. The horses are ready."

Shaken, Prasutagus hesitated a moment, then nodded.

"The governor," I said, looking back to the forum. Would the man be offended if he learned we'd left?

"The rest of them hardly noticed we were here. Why would he be any different?" Prasutagus replied, then looked down at my clothes. "Is that blood on your sleeve, Boudica?"

I nodded. "It is. Let's go."

NOT UNTIL WE were clear of Camulodunum and away from the Roman road, back on the soil of our land, did I feel like I could breathe again. The others were silent as we rode into the night.

I reined in beside my husband.

"Caratacus…" I whispered.

"The Brigantes," Prasutagus replied. "What did the governor mean?"

I shook my head. "I don't know."

"Boudica, what happened to you?"

"I went to look for the priestesses. There was a slaver who… He's dead now."

"Are you all right?"

Was I? I hadn't had a moment to consider. But given all I had seen, everything others had gone through, the assault felt like nothing. "I'm fine."

"You didn't find them."

"No."

"Whatever was left of the Trinovantes people lies dead, drowned in the sacred spring of Camulos now defiled by the Romans."

"And now they have Caratacus."

"With him goes the west."

"Mona?"

"I don't know, Boudica. I only know that our little patch of this land is the only thing in the east that is not theirs. When they have finished the west, when it *all* belongs to them, we would be fools to think they won't come for us."

"Ah, Prasutagus, what do we do?"

My husband reached out for my hand. "To the north, they still play the game. Cartimandua has just delivered Rome a valuable prize. We must play harder if we are to survive."

"*Or* we must rise."

Prasutagus looked at me. "Without Caratacus to lead the west…"

"Are we too late?"

Prasutagus didn't answer. He merely shook his head.

My thoughts went to Mona and to Brenna.

Sister…

Sister…

Beware. The guardian of the west has fallen. They are coming.

CHAPTER 23

In the following weeks, word spread like wildfire of the capture of Caratacus and the role of the queen of the Brigantes in the matter. No one knew the details or could say for sure why, but Cartimandua had handed Caratacus to Rome.

In response, Cartimandua's husband whipped up a revolt against her and tried to take the Brigantes' queen's crown.

"Rome has come to her defense," Broc, Prasutagus's spy, told us. "The rebellion will soon be squashed."

"Why did she do it? And her husband...to lead a revolt against her. Is there no love between them?" I asked.

Broc frowned. "I don't know. But what I know for certain is that Rome had Caratacus on the run. He went to the Brigantes for help and ended up in chains."

With Caratacus delivered to the emperor, the resistance in the west quieted, and the call for the east to rise grew silent. The defeat of Caratacus was a major blow to those who would resist. And while our hearts broke for the Trinovantes, now, with Caratacus captured, the west had no leader except for the directives from Mona. To the north, Cartimandua's husband's rebellion was squashed with Roman help. Cartimandua was now firmly indebted to the Romans. With all hope of an alliance of the tribes undone, we turned once more to just managing and hoping the Romans would simply leave us alone.

And that was how it went for a while. But in the year 52, Roman hands grew greedy once more. It began with rumors from the southernmost Greater Iceni families that Romans had built an outpost just south of our lands.

And then, people began disappearing.

Families.

Farms.

Then, two children made it to Venta to tell a horrible story. Raven's Dell had fallen.

"It was the Romans," the tearful girl said. "They took the Chieftain Divin, his daughter, Brangaine, and anyone strong enough to work. The old people, the children…all dead," she said, then broke into tears. "And then, they set everything on fire. We only survived because we were out foraging. When we got back to the village, it was nearly done. We ran. We ran as fast as we could. We followed the streams and rivers to Venta. Elen of the Ways protected us."

I saw a flush of red rise up Prasutagus's neck. He wrapped his hands around the ends of his chair and did not speak.

"I am so sorry for what you have seen, what you have suffered," I said, going to them and embracing them. "You have traveled far to bring us such sorrowful news. Vian and Brita will see to you. Rest. Eat. You are safe here in the king's house."

"Thank you, Queen Boudica, King Prasutagus," the girl said, bowing to us.

I gestured to Vian.

"Please, come with me," Vian told them, reaching for their hands.

The pair departed with her.

I turned to Prasutagus.

He stared in front of him, his face a wall of rage.

"Prasutagus?"

"The governor is in Londinium in his new villa. After I see what is left of Raven's Dell, I will go there," he said, fury in his voice.

"I will come with you to meet the governor," I said, then asked, "For what possible reason would he take our people or attack our land unless he's trying to provoke a war?"

Prasutagus looked at me. "You may have to stop me from squeezing the answer to that question from Scapula's throat."

PRASUTAGUS RETURNED FROM RAVEN'S DELL, looking pale and shaken. What he saw moved him to action.

"It's all gone, Boudica. Every house. Every building. Burned to nothing. The Romans built a new outpost just south of the Greater Iceni border. And they are building a new road. If they continue on their path, the road will lead through the western corner of Greater Iceni territory toward Stonea."

"Is that the cause? To build their road? Rather than ask our permission, they just killed our people?"

"We will soon find out."

While I hoped never to return to Londinium, I found myself on a ship the next day.

The weather was not cooperative as we traveled from Yarmouth to Londinium. The winds blew, the rain came in, and the sea rocked our ship. It was a rough journey, leaving us cold and ill at ease. The trip up the Thames was no better. The river was swollen from the unrelenting rains. Thunder and lightning rocked the sky. When we finally made port, I was drenched. Vian, Pix, and Artur accompanied us on the trip. Pix, we soon discovered, did not have the stomach for rough seas. She'd spent much of the voyage hanging over the side of the ship.

"Let's get you to the villa," I told my friend, who looked pale, her stomach empty.

"By the Morrigu, if it be raining when ye return, I'll take the old path. Rather be lost in the sunny fields of the Otherworld for a spell than tossed about like a drowning kitten on the seas."

"Aw, it's sweet you think of yourself like a kitten," I told her.

Pix chuckled lightly. "Ye best not chide me. I could vomit any moment, and ye be wearing new boots."

I huffed a laugh.

"I will settle with the dock master and join you. I won't be long," Prasutagus told us.

Pix, Vian, Artur, Beow, and I walked through the sloppy city streets to our house. The rain had driven most of the precious Romans indoors, but the foreign traders and slaves still packed the streets, hauling carts or pushing through in the rain. We felt the warmth and heat from within as we passed the taverns.

"I say, ye can leave me here," Pix said, pausing by one door.

"Not on your life," I replied, pulling her onward.

"Boudica," Vian said, looking around wide-eyed. "It's so changed."

"And not for the better. Like a boil, growing and growing until it bursts."

"It's so...Roman. There is hardly sign we are amongst our own people anymore."

"*Are we* our own people anymore?" Artur asked.

None of us answered.

We arrived at the villa, and Eudaf ushered us in quickly.

"Queen Boudica," he said. "We were not expecting you. You must forgive us for a cold house and scarcely a jug of wine to be found."

Ede arrived a moment later. "You are soaked to the bone, my queen. All of you. Let me see to the fires at once."

"I can help," Artur told her, disappearing with the woman to the back.

"Please, don't worry yourself, Eudaf. We have urgent affairs with the governor. I am sorry to ask you to go out in the rain, but please, go to his villa and request an audience."

"Of course," Eudaf replied, then went to gather his cloak and hat.

"Pix, please, go to your chamber and take your rest," I told my ailing friend.

"Let me come with you. I'll see to your fire," Beow told Pix.

"I would ask ye to stay and keep me warm, pretty one, but I'm too ailing."

"I suspect my wife would not appreciate that, but I'm happy to help with your fire."

At that, Pix merely laughed, then the pair departed, leaving Vian and me.

"Come on, Boudica," Vian said. "We can fend for ourselves well enough. And we must get out of these gowns before we both catch our deaths. Surely there's a blanket to wrap up in. If not, these Roman drapes will do."

Within the hour, the whole house had transformed. Ede went to the market, returning with a cart full of food. Soon, the place was warm, the smells of meat and bread wafting from the kitchens, and friendly voices filled the house. All those who sailed with us had come to stay in whatever nook or cranny could be found. Given the weather, Prasutagus had not permitted the men to remain on the ship.

Finding the clothes we had packed were sopping wet, the maid Briganna went to a shop to purchase gowns for Vian and me.

"I did my best, but there was not much to choose from," the girl told me as she unpacked her purchases.

"There used to be an older woman in the market who sold fine embroidery. Perhaps we could ask her to come to the villa."

"Oh, Queen Boudica, I know the woman you mean. She died last winter. A coughing sickness went through the city."

"Her hands were blessed by the gods. I am sorry for it."

"As am I. For a fresh gown, you will only find the Roman style."

I frowned.

"Take a Roman gown," Vian told me. "The governor sees us as wild things dressed as we are. Dress as they do. Remind the governor without saying anything that you are a Roman citizen."

"All right. But you must do the same since you will accompany us."

Vian smirked at me. "Very well."

Eudaf returned with the news that the governor would see us in the morning.

"I did not see him but spoke to his man. He asked me the reason for your unexpected visit. I told him I was not privy to it."

Prasutagus merely nodded. "Thank you, Eudaf."

Since returning from Raven's Dell, Prasutagus had

grown quiet. He and Chieftain Divin had been friends for many years. The attack on the village and the loss of the people had shaken us all, but I could see that it had touched Prasutagus much deeper. He had barely arrived at the villa when he made ready to leave again.

"I will go to the slavers," Prasutagus told me. "Before we left, I sent Ewan to Camulodunum to search for our people. I can't wait here in comfort thinking my people may be in chains somewhere in this city."

"Let me come with you."

He shook his head. "No. I will take my men. I want to be seen with my warriors. I want word to travel back to the governor. Stay here. Rest. See to Pix."

With that, Prasutagus and his men departed, leaving the warmth of the villa and going back into the rain.

I went upstairs, finding Pix dead asleep under the blankets. I shook her wet clothes and then set them to dry by the brazier. Making sure her room was warm and that she was tucked in, I returned to my own chamber and opened the door to the balcony.

Rain pattered down, flooding the streets.

The sky rumbled angrily, lightning illuminating the dark clouds, turning them purple.

Taranis, I hear the wheels of your chariot turning.

Help us find a way.

Help us find a way to give back to Rome the poison she has given our people.

CHAPTER 24

P rasutagus returned late in the night looking despondent.

"Nothing. No sign of them. The slave markets are full of the Catuvellauni and Cornovii. Sad, sick, and broken. The slaver told me Rome keeps the strongest men, sending them west to build. The women are sent to Rome. The young, pretty ones are often plucked from the bunch to serve at the colonia." Prasutagus shook his head. "I am heartsick, Boudica. These are my people. I am responsible for them. And they are gone. Just gone. Like they have disappeared."

I held my husband. "We will pray to the gods. Don't give up hope yet."

"Our gods are silent," Prasutagus whispered. "I cannot hear them anymore."

"Listen to the thunder. Taranis is awake. He rolls

across the sky, seeing what has become of his children. He is angry."

Prasutagus turned and looked at me, a sorrowful expression on his face. "Is it him, Boudica, or Jupiter, the god of Rome, showing his strength? Like Camulos's sacred well, like Maiden Stones, our gods are falling to Rome—just like us."

I pulled Prasutagus closer but said nothing more.

My husband was a druid, a man of the gods. To hear him speak thus... It broke my heart to see hope fading.

THE FOLLOWING DAY, we woke before sunrise and prepared to visit the governor's villa.

I found Pix in the kitchens. She was sitting at the servants' table, a full platter before her.

"Feeling better I see?" I asked.

"Aye. After a full night's sleep on that big, soft bed and a full belly, I be a new woman. Why are ye wearing *that*?" she asked, frowning at the soft, pale green Roman stola.

"Strategy."

"Ye will catch cold."

"The rain is gone. The sun is out. Finish up. We're

leaving in a moment," I told her then returned to the main room where a sleepless Prasutagus, Artur, and the guard waited. Vian joined us, wearing a similar Roman gown in blue. But with her, she had a satchel strung bandolier style across her body.

"Ready?" Prasutagus asked me.

I nodded.

We made our way from the villa into the street. The Roman-style roads had been designed in such a manner that all the water had drained off overnight, leaving the road to dry under the sun. Once more, the Romans returned to the streets. They eyed us with great interest as we passed.

We made our way to the governor's villa. There, we were greeted by soldiers and servants who disarmed us then led Prasutagus, Vian, Pix, Artur, and myself deeper into the elaborate house, the rest of the guard remaining behind.

There was a great courtyard beyond the entrance of the place, the center of which was open to the sky. Fragrant flowers and fruit trees grew there. In the center of the space was a statue of a winged goddess wearing a helmet. A fountain of fresh water collected about her feet.

We were escorted across the courtyard, passing through a set of doors, and were led down a long hall which led to another set of doors. The servant gestured for us to wait a moment while he slipped inside.

I eyed the tiled floor below my feet and the elaborate wall hangings. A horse pelt hung on the wall. It was a strange, striped pattern, alternating black and white.

"Come," the servant said, gesturing for us to follow.

Within the meeting chamber, we found the governor seated at a long wooden table. His secretary sat at his own desk nearby. Soldiers stood just inside, guarding the doors.

The room was dim. Even though it was morning, the space was warm. Sun streamed in from the open edifices along the top of the wall. Beams of slanting sunlight made patterns on the floor.

"King Prasutagus. Queen Boudica. To what do I owe the pleasure of your visit?" Governor Scapula asked, barely looking up from whatever he'd been reading.

"Governor," Prasutagus said, stepping forward. "I have come to speak with you about an incident that has occurred at one of my southernmost villages."

"What kind of incident?" he asked in a disinterested tone.

"The village was sacked and burned. My people are dead. My chieftain and his daughter, along with the other men and women who were not murdered, are missing."

"Rebels, I presume? You need our help finding the culprits."

"The culprit is Rome," Prasutagus said angrily.

At that, Scapula paused and looked up at my husband. "Impossible," the governor said then looked to his secretary, the sniveling Ampelius. "Have we had any reports of problems with the Greater Iceni?"

"No, Governor."

"As I said, not us, Prasutagus. I suggest you look elsewhere for the culprits."

"I have witnesses," Prasutagus said, stepping closer to Scapula. "It was Rome. Are you calling me a liar? My people are dead!"

At that, the governor rose and the guards came to attention.

"Governor," I said, stepping forward. I took Prasutagus's arm, reminding him to be calm. "Your people recently built an outpost just to the south of this village. And there is a road being constructed that will pass through Greater Iceni territory. Perhaps your men there would know something about what has happened."

The governor eyed me from head to foot. "You are looking very well today, Queen Boudica."

My skin crawled. "Thank you, Governor. The city agrees with me."

"Yes, I've grown quite fond of Londinium. Now that Caratacus is enjoying Rome, I can enjoy my villa properly," he said then laughed. "Now, what is the outpost you speak of? I'm confused."

"We have a map," Vian said, gesturing to her satchel. "May I?"

The governor scanned the room, his gaze falling on a large but cluttered table. "You there. Slave girl. Clear that table then bring wine," the governor called to one of the servants. "You may place it there," he told Vian.

Vian and I moved to the table. When we did, I met the gaze of the slave clearing the space. I realized then I was standing face to face with Arian, a priestess of Maiden Stones. We held one another's eyes for a long moment.

"Stop gawking and work, worthless whore," the governor yelled at her.

Moving nonchalantly, I turned my back to the governor and stepped close to Arian.

"Say nothing," Arian whispered to me. "Say nothing."

Arian worked quickly, moving the clutter aside, then disappeared.

My gaze went from Pix to Prasutagus, both of whom had seen and recognized the priestess.

I shook my head ever so slightly.

"Now, show me," the governor said, gesturing impatiently to Vian.

Vian rolled out the map.

"Here is the location of the Greater Iceni border with the Trinovantes," Prasutagus told the governor. "And this is the location of Raven's Dell, my village. Your new outpost is here, a stone's throw from my lands. And this is the direction in which your new road is headed," he said, showing the path through Greater Iceni territory.

The governor frowned hard then looked at his secretary. "Ampelius?"

"I know nothing of this attack. It was not ordered by our people."

"Lawless Trinovantes," the governor said then. "Knock over a couple of stones and the whole countryside gets set on fire. Those are your culprits, Prasutagus. Not Rome."

"Governor," Prasutagus said. "There *are* witnesses."

"All the world will blame Rome. Why would we slaughter the innocent people of your village, Prasutagus?"

"Governor," Ampelius said carefully. "Is Raven's Dell a *Greater Iceni* village?"

"Yes, it is," Prasutagus answered hotly.

"Our men recorded it as a *Trinovantes* village."

"Are you telling me your men attacked my village by mistake?" Prasutagus's eyes bulged, and I began to worry that he might do something rash.

"Ampelius?" the governor snapped.

"So it would seem, Governor."

"The people of the village who were taken prisoner, where would they be?" Prasutagus asked through gritted teeth.

The governor looked to his secretary.

"Trinovantes captives are sent west. The men, at least. What women who are not sold to serve at the colonia are sent to Rome."

"A mistake, Prasutagus, that is all," the governor said nonchalantly.

"A mistake!" Prasutagus shouted. "My people are dead, Rome. The chieftain and his daughter are missing. How can you brush it away as a mistake?"

"You dare raise your voice at me?" the governor shouted at Prasutagus.

"I...I...I..." I began then swooned toward Artur. "I feel faint."

"Boudica," Artur said, holding me.

"I need a moment. Is there somewhere I can step away? I..." I said, looking about the room, spotting Arian. "Perhaps your servant can take me to the... I need to..."

The governor huffed in annoyance then waved to Arian to escort me away.

"Governor, I am responsible for the people of Raven's Dell," Prasutagus said stonily. "How do you expect me to tell the Greater Iceni that Rome is an ally when my villages are burned and my people enslaved.

This is not a mistake to wave away, and you know that." In my husband's words, I heard the edge of a threat.

I hoped the governor heard it as well, because Prasutagus was not wrong. Such an affront would lead to rebellion.

"I will have the men responsible for this error punished," the governor told my husband. "And I will send someone today to have your people recalled from the west."

"And the women. They must be found at once. These are my subjects, Governor. They rely on me for protection."

"I will send a rider to Camulodunum. See to it, Ampelius."

"Yes, Governor. At once."

"This business of your road," Prasutagus said harshly. "I have not agreed to its construction in my lands."

"This way, lady," Arian said quietly, leading me away from the room and down a hallway to a small privy located just off the main hall. Shutting the door behind us, Arian ensured we were alone then turned to me.

"Queen Boudica," she said, wrapping her arms around me.

"Oh, Arian," I replied, cupping her face. "I have searched for you and your sisters."

"I don't know where the others are. The governor spotted me at one the households in Londinium. He took a liking to my form and brought me here to use at his leisure."

"Oh, Arian. You must flee this place. Tonight, escape to our villa and—"

"No, Boudica. No. Not like that. I need your help. You know some herbcraft, do you not?"

"Some, yes."

"I need nightcap mushroom. Do you know it?"

"I..." I said then paused. I remembered Ula pointing out the mushroom once, warning me from it due to its deadly nature. "Yes."

"It doesn't grow in the city. I've looked in vain. But it *can* be found amongst the willows that grow along the Thames. It grows the morning following a full moon. Today, Boudica. By the gods, this very morning. Find the mushrooms and meet me in the afternoon at the market. I am always sent in the afternoon to purchase a cheese the governor prefers," she said, laughing ruefully. "Find the mushrooms and bring them to me."

"Arian? Do you mean to..."

"I will avenge my sisters and bring an end to Scapula," she said, holding my gaze.

I nodded. "I will see to it."

"And Boudica... Rome lies. They sent the soldiers to clear that village. They *knew* it was Greater Iceni. I heard them speak of it. They cared nothing about betraying the Greater Iceni. Believe *nothing* they tell you."

I pulled her into a tight embrace. "In Andraste's name, I will find the nightcap and deliver it to you. May the Maiden protect you."

"May she protect us both."

BY THE TIME I RETURNED, the tense conversation had ended. Prasutagus had agreed to let the Romans build their road through our territory to Stonea in exchange for a decrease in taxes.

"The procurator dips too deeply, Governor. We do not have the resources to keep pace."

"The Brigantes have no such issues," Scapula said dismissively. "But I hear you, Prasutagus. Ampelius will send a messenger when your people are recovered. In recompense for the village and loss of life, however..." he said then waved to Ampelius.

The man dipped into a chest on the table and from within pulled out a bag of coins.

"For the misunderstanding," the governor added.

The secretary went to give the bag to Prasutagus, but my husband didn't move.

Vian stepped forward, taking the sack.

"Ah, Queen Boudica," the governor said, briefly turning his attention to me. "Better?"

"Yes, Governor. Just…the heat."

He nodded absently then waved to one of the men. "Show the Greater Iceni out."

"Governor," I said, bowing.

The others followed suit, Pix elbowing Prasutagus hard.

My husband bowed, then we all turned and departed.

"The room smells like a fart," Scapula was saying as we left.

"It's the Thames, Governor. The river is stirred up today," Ampelius replied.

"Muddy, stinking country—" he was saying as the door swung closed behind him.

"Boudica," Pix whispered. "Where be Arian? We can't just leave the priestess—"

"Not now," I told her then looked at my husband. "Let's go to the docks."

Prasutagus did not reply.

"Prasutagus?"

"Hmm?"

"Let's go to the docks."

He nodded but said nothing else.

I studied my husband's face. Something had

awoken behind his eyes, something that had never been there before. In the depths of his vision, I saw rage.

I APPRISED the others of the priestess's request. Taking a small crew, we left Londinium and made our way downriver until we found a cove. We navigated the ship into a natural harbor. There, we found a small grove of willows growing on the riverbank. Their long tendrils gently brushed the surface of the water. Swans had taken shelter in the quiet cove, escaping the rough waves of the river. Pix, Prasutagus, and I set out, scouring the roots of every willow that grew for the mushroom. Finally, after a long hunt, Pix called to me.

"Boudica! Prasutagus! Here."

We joined her.

There, at the base of the tree, we found the small, red-capped mushrooms. With a gloved hand, Pix plucked one and turned it over. The gills of the mushroom underneath were dripping with a white liquid.

"Widow's tears," Prasutagus said. "This is the one."

Pix broke the cap. At once, the mushroom turned blue.

I opened a satchel and Pix began loading the mushrooms inside.

"Enough here to poison half the city," Pix said.

"Don't tempt me," Prasutagus said gruffly.

When we were done, Pix carefully pulled off her gloves and tossed them into the river.

"Let's go. We have Romans to kill," I said.

"Now, ye are finally talking sense," Pix said.

We returned to the city near midday.

"I will go to the docks then to our market stall. We must look as though nothing is amiss," Prasutagus said.

"I will take Vian and Pix and go to the market and buy a ridiculous number of frivolous items."

Prasutagus nodded then said, "Boudica, do not be seen making the exchange. They must have no reason to suspect us."

"Ye forget yourself, druid," Pix told him. "The death looks natural thanks to the mushroom. That is, no doubt, why she chose it."

Prasutagus frowned. "All the same."

"We cannot leave her here, Prasutagus. What about Arian?"

"If she flees immediately after his death, it could raise suspicion. I will have Madogh spirit her away before the new governor arrives."

I nodded. "I will tell her."

My husband turned to me, setting his hand on my

cheek, and kissed me gently. "No peacocks," he whispered in my ear.

"No peacocks."

Prasutagus turned to Artur. "Come, Son. We must spend the day looking busy and not angry. Let's go have an ale," he said, putting his arm around Artur's shoulder. The pair then departed.

Pix, Vian, and I returned to the marketplace, spending the morning picking through the goods for sale there: cups, pots, platters, jewelry, livestock. We saw it all. In the afternoon, we made our way to the food market. There, I spotted Arian. She was alone, dressed in a hooded cloak, a basket on her arm. Coming together at the cheese vendor's stand, Pix sampled the wares while Arian made her purchase.

"Ah, here for the governor's daily order?" the vendor asked with a smile.

"Yes. And, if you have them, a bundle of bay leaves. The governor has been feeling run-down of late. The cook thought they might help."

"Let me see what I have," the man said, turning to his hampers of goods.

I stepped near the priestess, discreetly placing the satchel in her basket.

"Leave the city," Arian whispered. "I will wait so no suspicion is cast on you. It will come slowly upon him. No one will suspect." Arian picked up a bundle of flowers and set them in her basket, covering the satchel.

"Our man will find you when it is done," I whispered to her. "We will get you out. Until then, may the Dark Lady Andraste hide you in the shadows." I turned to Vian and Pix. "It grows too hot. Let's get out of the sun," I complained loudly so the vendor could hear.

"I will be here tomorrow, ladies," the merchant called over his shoulder to us as we retreated.

As we walked away, I clenched my teeth and sent an earnest prayer to the gods.

Andraste, be with Arian.

Be with us all.

Avenge.

Avenge.

CHAPTER 25

W e departed Londinium the following day. I left the trinkets I'd purchased behind in the villa. They had no place in my home. I changed into my riding clothes, leaving the Roman dress behind. I hoped I never had to see it again. With that, our party set sail.

"Do you have any hope that they will find Chieftain Divin?" Vian asked Prasutagus gently.

Prasutagus shook his head. "No. Nor will they even look. I hope he is dead."

"May the Mother comfort him and you…" Vian said gently, setting her hand on Prasutagus's arm.

He gave me a grateful smile and then looked back out at the sea.

A MONTH LATER, the news came that the governor had succumbed to a lingering ailment. It was a messenger from Rome who brought the news.

"The governor had grown increasingly ill this last month. His heart gave out in his sleep," the Roman messenger relayed.

"We are very sorry to hear it," I lied. "Thank you for informing us. Who will take the command of the Roman forces now?"

"General Vespasian will rule until a new governor is named."

"What is the word from Rome? Any rumor regarding who will be sent next?" I asked, refilling the messenger's wine.

"Well," he began hesitantly.

"Come, friend," Prasutagus said. "We all know how Rome works. Everyone will already know who will be chosen. The emperor must have his favorites."

"He does, which is why it is hard to say. There will be many conversations underway. But we will know soon enough."

"Well then," I said, lifting my cup. "To our new

governor. May he have the strength and compassion of all your gods."

Word soon came that the new governor, Aulus Didius Gallus, who had once been a senator, had been chosen to rule over Britannia. With him came some shuffling of the staff at the governor's villa in Londinium. This provided Madogh with the perfect moment to effect Arian's escape. But when the pair met, the priestess had other ideas.

"She will stay in the governor's house," Madogh told us. "There, she can listen, learn, and report on what is happening. We have planned how she can pass the information on to me."

"She's not safe there," I said in frustration. "From one moment to the next, she may be turned out, sold, sent away, or the gods only know what."

"She knows," Madogh said. "She said…" He paused, a sad expression crossing his features. "She said that her life is over. Now, she will serve the gods and our people. She believes the gods placed her there deliberately. Now, she will do their will."

"But the risk to her."

"She wanted me to assure you that she is not worried for her person under the new governor."

"Why not?" I asked.

"Because Governor Gallus travels with his companion, a young gentleman named Brutus."

"Ah," I replied.

"She will stay as long as she can. She is brave to do it, but we have devised a way for her to escape if needed. But for now…"

"Do we know anything else about this Gallus?"

"He and the emperor are quite close, but Claudius has the man on a leash. Gallus's actions will be a mirror of Claudius's will. Soon, we will discover Claudius's plans for our island. There are rumors that the emperor's interest has turned elsewhere. Apparently, he complains bitterly about the expense being poured into campaigns here."

"Do you think they may withdraw? Could it be?" I asked hopefully.

"Time will tell, Queen Boudica."

And time did tell. Governor Gallus arrived in Londinium and stayed there. He never called a meeting of the client kings who remained—such as we were. He never rode into the countryside. He never visited Verulamium. He *rarely* saw Camulodunum. When he did, it was to take in the entertainment at the coliseum. He launched no campaigns. Made no wars. General Vespasian, who had terrorized the southwest, went home. Rome simply held what they had already won. Gallus raised taxes and built roads. Lots of roads. For the most part, in the west. The appetite for war faded.

Now, under Gallus, the Romans grabbed money and resources, including people.

At least, that was how it began.

With Gallus's arrival, we started to see a glimmer of hope. Claudius's interest in Britannia *was* waning. Madogh heard rumors that Claudius planned to withdraw troops from our lands to fight in other areas.

Hope was renewed.

And then, in 54, Emperor Claudius died.

The Romans went into mourning, and soon, word came that Claudius's stepson, Nero, had taken his stepfather's place as emperor of Rome.

"What kind of man is he?" Prasutagus asked Madogh.

News of a new emperor had rocked the Romans, but it also had an equally profound effect on us. All our hopes of a Roman withdrawal were put on hold.

"A self-important, lecherous drunk," Madogh replied.

"Ah, so like half the Romans we know," Prasutagus said.

Madogh nodded. "And…an ambitious one. Like his mother. They say Claudius's wife poisoned the old emperor."

"Why would she do that?" I asked.

"Nero has always been the preferred heir. But of late, Claudius had shown interest in promoting his blood over his wife's child. Apparently, his wife was not receptive to the idea. Our new emperor has the support of the people. They love their emperor, particularly when he gets drunk, races his chariot through the city, and plays the lyre for them. But more, he holds the Petronian guard in his command. They are Rome's most fierce fighters. If I were a natural-born son of Claudius, I would find somewhere to hide. Quickly."

I frowned. "He sounds like a reckless child."

"Yes," Madogh agreed. "That is the consensus."

"Children grow weary of things quickly. Let's hope he finds Britannia as expensive as Claudius was beginning to think it was," Prasutagus said, then asked, "Aulus Plautius... We hear nothing of him. What has become of him?"

I kept my expression blank, trying not to show any emotion. Prasutagus asked the question that had lived, unspoken, on the tip of my tongue for years.

"Retired from military life with honors. I heard he retreated to some family property away from Rome...a farm of some sort. Rumors swirl around his wife, but of him, I hear nothing."

"I am glad he can sleep well at night," Prasutagus said gruffly.

Madogh huffed a laugh.

Desperate to hide my feelings, I turned the conversation, asking, "Will this Nero replace do-nothing

Governor Gallus? Should we expect a new governor in Britannia?"

Madogh shrugged. "I don't know, my queen. There is no rumor, and Arian said the governor's house has made no changes. They do not act as if they expect to be recalled, although Arian said Gallus wishes it. Apparently, he hates it here and pines for home."

"Is it wrong for me to be glad he hates it here?" I asked with a laugh, which the others joined.

"May Taranis steer this Nero's attention in another direction. And may all the gods bring about the change we pray for...that the eagle flies from these lands, never to return," Prasutagus said, lifting his cup in a toast, which we joined.

But it was not to be.

Nero was not his stepfather. And it soon turned out the young emperor was ambitious. He didn't care about completing a quest Caesar failed, but Nero was smart enough to know that land meant resources, and resources meant wealth.

Rome was not going anywhere.

In the summer of 57, I rode north to spend time with my people. That summer, rumors abounded of people disappearing. Those Coritani who'd remained in peace under Rome's yoke were gone overnight. While I was in Oak Throne, Bran caught wind of rumors as to why so many had been recently taken.

"They are mining," Bran told me. "All along the south. The traders reported huge numbers of slaves being taken to work the mines."

To increase the trade and the prosperity of the Northern Iceni, Bran and I had concocted a plan to build a trading outpost along the Wash, just as Prasutagus and I had done in Yarmouth. Over the years, a prosperous trading community had begun to flourish at Sea Throne, as we named it. Any trader traveling our island's eastern coast stopped in Sea Throne. And because of that, money began to flow more readily into Northern Iceni hands.

And from our hands to Rome.

Roman tax was eating into everything we earned.

"They are sending captives to mine the rich silver, lead, copper, and tin all along the coast. And there is more."

"What more?" I asked, pouring us both another mug of ale.

"In the Fens, on the westernmost edge on the border with the Catuvellauni, they are mining iron."

"No wonder Scapula was so keen on keeping that land. There had always been rumor of iron but—"

"What our father and grandfather failed to use, Rome is stripping from the ground," Bran said, then frowned. "Maybe this is what they wanted all along."

"So many hands have flavored the soup now, it is

hard to discern what they wanted. Verica had his will. Aedd Mawr thought of his heirs. Claudius wanted to achieve where Caesar failed," I said, then shrugged.

"We fell right into it," Bran said sadly.

"Yes, but we are still alive. Our children are still alive. Others have not been so lucky."

"Speaking of children," Bran said, hearing a ruckus coming from the front of the roundhouse. A moment later, a gaggle of teenagers rushed into the room. Sorcha, Bellicus, and Caturin appeared, looking as though they had just been in a brawl.

"Sorcha, your lip is bleeding," I told her with a frown.

She gingerly touched the corner of her lip. "Yes, but Bellicus can throw me much farther than he could this morning."

"Where is Olwen?"

"With Ula."

I frowned harder then rose. "I better go before Ula plies Olwen with mushroom tonics to get her to speak for the gods," I told Bran.

"But Olwen doesn't speak at all," Bellicus said.

"Leave it to Ula to try," I said. I patted my brother on the shoulder, then turned to go. "Sorcha, ask Cidna for a damp cloth for that lip."

"All right."

With that, I departed.

Sorcha had begged to ride north with me. And where Sorcha went, Olwen followed. Caturin's request to join us came as a surprise, but it shouldn't have. The years passed. Caturin was fast on his way to becoming a young man searching for adventure.

Mara, however, had taken a different approach to her life. While I thought she'd eventually make her way to the King's Wood, love found her. Bruin, one of the young warriors in Artur's warband, had taken a liking to Mara, and she to him. They had been wed at Beltane and now had their own home in Venta. I was happy to see my niece settled into a contented life.

I made my way down the narrow streets, passing a Roman soldier.

The man gave me a formal nod and continued on his path.

When my gaze drifted down the lane toward the market, I saw more Romans there. How commonplace it had become. They were everywhere, like a fungus growing on a rotten log. I hurried my step, making my way to Ula's cottage. I was about to knock when I heard an odd sound coming from inside.

Ula was laughing.

And not in a *"you are all doomed"* sort of way, but a cheerful belly laugh.

Confused, I opened the door, finding Ula and Olwen sitting on the floor, the pair quickly exchanging Ogham staves. Olwen rubbed her finger along the lengths of the wooden stave, feeling the Ogham symbol engraved there, then handed it to Ula. Ula would sort through her staves and hand one back to Olwen, the pair grinning at one another as they worked.

"What are you—"

"Quiet, you," Ula scolded me, then continued.

Olwen looked up at me, her bright blue eyes shining as she smiled happily.

The pair persisted. I watched as they worked. Soon, I realized that they were conversing. While we had employed a tutor for the girls, Olwen could not follow the lessons nor learn to write. It wasn't that she was unintelligent, but she just couldn't get the ideas out. But my daughter could *see*. Born with a caul, neither Prasutagus nor I were surprised to discover she had been blessed by the gods with the sight. We tried other things to help her find a way to communicate. I had given her a lyre, hoping some of Brenna's gifts might have come to her, but that had come to nothing.

For the first time, she'd found a way.

But as I watched Olwen and Ula, I also saw something else.

Ula looked so...old. She was so tiny under her bulky robes. Her wrinkles seemed to have wrinkles. It would not be long now before we lost her. I ached at the thought.

Graymalkin, the kitten I had given Ula, was also reaching his elder years. He sat beside Ula, watching the pair exchange staves. Age had come for all of us. My daughters were teenagers, and my hair had strands of silver.

How had time run out on us all like this?

When they were done, Ula sat back, clapped her hands, and smiled.

"She is too bright for this world," Ula told me, tweaking Olwen's chin. "She can speak the language of the gods but not that of mankind. You will leave her here with me."

"What for?"

"So I can train her properly," Ula replied with annoyance. "One does not need to speak to do great magic. You just need the eyes to see, which she has. I see your druid husband hasn't taught her anything."

At that, Olwen and I both frowned at Ula.

Ula laughed. "Like a pair of croaking frogs, grousing in unison."

"Olwen, you could stay for a time if you would like. You can sleep in the roundhouse. I'm sure Bellicus would be glad of the company."

Ula grinned at Olwen. "Stay in Oak Throne. I will teach you how to poison the Romans."

Olwen considered it for a moment, then nodded.

"Only until Lughnasadh," I told them.

Ula frowned at me. "Samhain."

"Why?"

"Because I said so. Samhain."

"You will be careful with my daughter, Ula. More careful than you were with me. No climbing oaks covered in ice."

"Not the season for it," she said with a chuckle, but her laugh grew raspy, and she began to cough hard.

Grabbing a pitcher from the table, I poured her a mug of water.

She sipped and coughed and sputtered until it passed.

"I don't like the sound of that, and it isn't the first time I'm hearing that cough since I've gotten here," I told Ula.

"Was ill over the winter. Can't shake the cough. I have enough herbs, but an old body is slow to heal." She glared at me. "Stop looking at me like the Crone is looming. I know I am old."

"It's not that. It's just... Perhaps Bec can help. Have you spoken to her—"

"What do I need her for?"

"Or Dôn?"

"Dôn is as old as I am," Ula chided me with a wave. "You should pay her a visit before you go, Boudica."

"Why?"

"I already told you why," she said, giving me a knowing look.

"Then I shall make a tour of old women before I depart."

At that, Ula laughed. "Don't get too smart, Boudica. I see the white in your hair."

"Good. That means you haven't completely lost your eyesight *yet*."

Olwen snickered.

Ula puffed air at me.

I bent, giving Graymalkin a pat. "It is early enough that I can make it to the grove today. Want to come, or do you want to stay with Ula?" I asked Olwen.

She gestured to Ula.

"You see?" Ula said.

"Charmed her, did you?" I leaned down and kissed Olwen on the head. "Be careful. I'll be back after a time."

Olwen nodded, then scooped up the staves once more.

"Again?" Ula asked.

Olwen nodded.

And once more, they began their conversation.

I returned to the roundhouse where the others sat talking and drinking ale.

"I will ride to the grove today. Sorcha, you will accompany me. Anyone else care to join?"

"I will come," Bec said.

Bellicus and Caturin shook their heads.

"Good," Bran said. "I need strong labor anyway. We have work to do, boys."

"Now, I just have to figure out where Pix has wandered off to," I said.

Bec chuckled. "Really, Boudica? Do you have to guess?"

With Cai. Always with Cai.

I turned to Sorcha. "Get cleaned up and ready to go. I'll meet you at the stables."

Sorcha nodded, then began quickly scarfing down some food.

I headed out, going to Cai's small house. Part of me felt guilty bothering them, but I suspected it was a trip Pix would not want to miss.

"Pix," I called, rapping on the door. "I'm going to the grove. Want to come?"

There was some commotion within, and a moment later, Pix appeared at the door. Even though she had let her blonde hair grow long over the years, her long tresses did little to hide the fact that she was naked.

Through the open crack in the edifice, I saw Cai struggling to cover himself. He gave me a bashful wave.

"Going to the grove?" Pix asked.

"Pix," I said, frowning at her public display.

"What? 'Tis hot, Strawberry Queen."

Just then, a pair of Roman soldiers walked by. They

briefly looked my way to give a respectful nod, then spotted Pix. Both of them stared.

"Hey, Rome, want to mine for gold? I've got a pretty patch," she said, wiggling her hips at them.

The men chuckled and then hurried on their way.

"Don't tempt them. Get dressed and meet me at the stables," I said, then called, "Sorry, Cai."

"I was tired anyway," Cai replied, making me laugh. "I'll dress and ride with you."

"Good. Ye can rest in the saddle, then be ready for more riding tonight," Pix told him, then turned and closed the door.

With a shake of the head, I went to the stables. There, I found Druda sleeping. More often than not, I found my boy more eager to nap than to ride. Like all of us, age had found him. On the way north, his pace was considerably slower than usual, even if he was alert and ready. I suspect this would be his last trip to Oak Throne. Before I departed, I would visit the auction barns and see if any Northern Iceni foals were available.

"Dozing, old friend?" I stroked his nose. "How about a galivant through the greenwood?"

I brushed the horse down and was saddling him when Sorcha and Bec arrived.

"Lady Bec," one of the grooms said, then went about preparing a horse for her.

Sorcha bopped along behind Bec, an apple in her

mouth. She went to Ember, the blood bay steed Prasutagus had bought for her from the horse market at midsummer. The horse was as headstrong and wild as my daughter. The pair were a perfect match.

"Still eating?" I asked Sorcha.

She shook her head. "This is for Ember," she said, taking a bite of the apple before giving it to the horse.

I laughed.

It amused me to realize I was raising a miniature version of myself.

We departed within the hour. Cai enlisted four other men to ride with us to the grove. Still, the Northern Iceni were without arms. But Rome had begun to soften its gaze on our people. Hunters now wore their bows and hunting knives, unharried by Roman soldiers who no longer had Scapula breathing down their necks to punish our people. But swords...

Arixus had done well in the years since the disarming. If our people ever needed a blade again, they would not have far to look.

Only once had we been discovered. Bran paid the Roman such a hefty bribe that no word was ever spoken. But that same spring, the man had died of fever —or Arixus's abundance of caution. We were never sure which. But either way, the secret went undiscovered.

We arrived at the Grove of Andraste at the golden hour of the day. Warm sunlight shone down through the canopy overhead, making the leaves glimmer gold and green.

I closed my eyes and felt the gentle sway of Druda's step, heard the song of birds, and smelled the loamy smell of earth effervescing like a perfume from the forest floor. I had been away from the greenwood for too long. That younger version of me I saw echoed in my daughter had been like a wild thing in the forest.

I hardly recognized myself anymore.

We rode into the square. When we arrived, I was surprised to find the place so busy. Everywhere I looked, priestesses hurried about. More small houses had been built to accommodate what had become a large community.

Ula was right to send me here.

Dindraine was the first to spot me. In the passing years, the Catuvellauni priestess's hair had turned silver. She smiled when she saw me.

"Queen Boudica," she said, joining us. "As Dôn said, here you are."

"As Dôn said?"

Dindraine nodded. "She told us you would come today."

I scanned the grove, spotting Tatha, who was herding some pigs back into a pen.

She waved to me.

"This place... There are so many here."

"Many shrines to our holy goddesses have fallen, small and large. Arixus has sent the women here so we may begin again. From here, we plan the future. What you see before you are others like me, refugees… Catuvellauni, Coritani, Trinovantes, even some Cantiaci. The Mother has led them here."

"May she be praised."

Dindraine smiled, then turned her gaze to Bec. "My lady," she said, then her eyes moved to Sorcha.

"Dindraine, this is my elder daughter, Princess Sorcha," I introduced.

"Yes, I see you and Prasutagus in her features. Come, Dôn asked to see you. She is waiting."

Sorcha, Bec, Pix, and I followed Dindraine up the old path to the crown of ancient trees. With each step, I felt the tingle of magic in the air.

I looked back at my daughter.

She was looking into the canopy overhead. Blobs of sunlight danced on her features. But the red strands in her dark hair caught my attention the most. They glimmered like fire.

"Boudica," Dindraine said gently, gesturing before her.

There, Dôn sat at the center of the circle. Like so many times before, she waited. But, like Ula, time had caught her. She was a bent thing, leaning against her tall staff. She looked pale, unwell.

"Dindraine," I whispered.

"She's dying," Dindraine replied in a low tone. "She will be gone before summer's end."

"What will you do?"

"Andraste has given Dôn a vision. A counsel of nine of us will take Dôn's place. And from there, we will do what we can to save our way of life. But for now... She would see you alone. The rest of us will wait."

Leaving the others, I joined the priestess.

"Your footfalls are heavy now, Boudica. Too much walking on paved roads. You have forgotten to avoid stepping on every crossed branch and dry leaf," Dôn said, then looked up at me. I was startled to see the color of her eyes had faded to milky white with hues of blue.

"You are right about that, wise one."

"Now, you may call me ancient one, Boudica. Finally, I have earned the title."

I sat on the bench beside her, taking her free hand into mine. "I have left you on your own too long."

"Nonsense. I am overrun with people," she said with a laugh.

"Are you complaining? I would hate to have to compare you to Ula."

"Now, that is beneath you, Boudica," Dôn said with a chuckle.

I huffed a light laugh.

"I will be gone soon," Dôn said tiredly, "but I think I

have seen enough of this world. I will go to the other side and rest until the eagle has flown from this land."

"Will it leave? Have you seen, Dôn? Will we ever be free of them?"

Don stared into the fire. "Yes," she said. "I see a great bear in the sky and the sword of Avallach rising. When that time comes, Rome will become the story of grandfathers, and new legends will rise. I think I will come back then," she said, then laughed lightly.

"How long, Dôn? How long?"

"Too long. And the road between here and there is paved with ash and iron."

I looked into the fire. "And for now?"

"For now, the dark lady Andraste whispers your name."

"As she has for many years. I have tried to do my best and protect our people."

"Yes. By Epona, I know that to be true. We grew very close to finding a way to rid ourselves of them. On Mona, they work tirelessly to bring about a change, make Claudius grow bored, and send his gaze south of Rome. It nearly worked. But a mother's will—Agrippina, wife of Claudius, mother of Nero—was stronger than us all. One woman's desire to protect her son's fortune has changed the course of all our fates. One should never underestimate a mother trying to protect her child. That fire can burn the world."

"What should I do? What does the dark lady want of me? I had heard her call, but she riddles."

"Soon, her message will be clear. And when it is, when you finally hear it, act. Act."

"You riddle like her."

Dôn laughed. "I have spent a lifetime listening to her voice. Perhaps you are right."

I set my arm around Dôn's frail shoulders. "My heart is heavy knowing you will leave us soon. You were always there for me."

Dôn rested her head against mine. "I am ready, Boudica. I do not want to see what happens next."

We sat there for a long time, then Dôn straightened once more. "I will say farewell to you, Boudica, first queen of the Iceni. Now, send me your daughter, for the dark lady would whisper to Sorcha. Already, I hear Andraste in the flames," she said, gesturing to the fire before her.

For a moment, fear struck me. Andraste's messages were often ominous. My child… I looked back at Sorcha. As much as she reminded me of myself, Sorcha was not a thing of the greenwood. She was a firebrand.

"Farewell, wise one," I said, kissing Dôn on the head, then left her, rejoining the others. "Dôn will speak with you, Sorcha."

"Me?"

"We will see you below when you are done," I told her.

"I will speak to Dôn," Bec said, "and meet you after."

With that, Dindraine, Pix, and I headed back to the village.

"I be sorry to see the Crone about her," Pix said. "But I suppose death finds us all."

"Unless you slip through a mound and disappear for a hundred years," I replied.

"All the same, even foxes grow old, eventually."

"I will not ask what she told you, but, Boudica, is there any hope?" Dindraine asked.

"Ah, my friend..." I said, exhaling heavily.

"Then may our children and children's children live in easier times," Dindraine replied.

"And Andraste protect us all."

CHAPTER 26

Pix and I visited with the other priestesses and helped the women working to prepare some apples for baking. Bec and Sorcha returned later, but Dôn remained at the shrine. With sadness, I realized this was the last time I would see her in this world.

Sorcha, too, had been moved by her encounter. I could tell by the expression on her face that Sorcha had seen something that had unnerved her. Leaving the others, she went to Ember and stood patting the horse.

I joined her.

At first, I said nothing, simply fed bites of apple to the horse. After a time, however, I asked, "Are you all right?"

"Decidedly not," my daughter replied, meeting my gaze.

"What did you see? Andraste?"

Sorcha shook her head. She was silent momentarily, then whispered, "The Morrigu."

A chill washed over me, and my skin rose in gooseflesh. Why had such a potent goddess come to Sorcha?

"Sorcha," I whispered. "Why?"

"She said dark times are coming. She bid me be strong, bold, and bloody."

I went to my daughter and took her hand. "Whatever is coming, we will face it together."

Sorcha nodded, but I could tell she was rattled.

I smiled gently at her. "Remember, your father is a druid. Your grandmother was a priestess here, in this very place. You might be a princess, but the magic of this land runs in your veins. Listen to the gods. Many times, I have been stubborn and regretted not heeding their call. Listen to them, my little firebrand. Listen to their call."

Sorcha nodded. After a moment, she said, "I saw someone. I think… I think it was your sister, Brenna. She looked much like you—and me. She was on the shore of an island. There was blood in the water, and embers and ash floated through the air. I was afraid for her."

"Is she in danger? Did you sense that it's happening now?"

Sorcha shook her head. "No. I don't think so. It felt like…a glimpse into the future."

My mind drifted back, remembering the echo of a dream I'd had of Brenna.

"May the gods protect my sister and all the druids of Mona."

"I also saw a misty place. There was a fortress on a hill with many bridges. It was so green. There were mountains with tall, rocky spires. It was an island, I think. I have never seen such a place before. It was just a glimpse, but I saw myself and Artur there."

"The gods riddle. In my experience, over time, the riddles unravel. Wherever that place is, I am glad that Artur was with you."

At that, Sorcha gave a weak smile.

"Come on," I told her, putting my arm over her shoulder. "The priestesses have batches of cider ready. Unless Pix has finished it all, a cup will make you feel better."

"All right," she said with a soft chuckle.

As we crossed the square to join the others, I couldn't contain the question pricking at my heart. "Sorcha, in your vision with Artur on the island, did you see Olwen?"

Sorcha was silent for a moment, then said, "No."

While her answer may have meant nothing, tears still pricked at the corners of my eyes.

We spent the afternoon at the grove, then returned to Oak Throne at dusk. My heart felt heavy, knowing I would not see Dôn again. Leaving the others at the roundhouse, I journeyed to Ula's little cottage to search for Olwen, but neither she nor Ula was there.

Hedging a bet, I left the fort and went to the river, hoping to find them hunting herbs and flowers, but they were not there. My gaze drifted across the river to the Mossy Wood. Certainty settled in the pit of my stomach. That was, most definitely, where they had gone.

I made my way to the forest's edge. For all their grandstanding, the Romans still did not dare come close to the Mossy Wood. For that, I was glad.

I slipped into the forest, immediately feeling the change in the air. It was cooler here, and the air smelled of fern and moss. I tried to sense Ula and Olwen. Glancing about, I felt my daughter. Remembering the path, I made my way toward the cavern that led underground, back to the well at Ula's cottage, which was also the entrance to the Hollow Hills.

Making my way over mushroom-covered logs and around moss-covered boulders, I wound through the forest. I could feel the eyes of the woods upon me. They knew I was here. They were watching.

A soft wind blew thought the trees, making the timbers creak and the leaves rustle.

Soon, I smelled campfire smoke. And along with it, the scent of pungent herbs.

Of course, Ula was at it again.

I made my way through the woods, coming to the site. Ula sat on a rock, watching as Olwen stared drowsy-eyed into the fire. Ula looked up at me, motioning for me to be quiet. I sat down beside her on the stone. My daughter looked dazed. No matter what Olwen saw, she would not be able to communicate it clearly. But, perhaps, the message was not for us. Maybe it was for Olwen alone.

I plucked some long grass blades and sat, waiting and weaving, making a small doll, like those we prepared at Lughnasadh. When I finished, I handed it to Ula, who huffed a light laugh in thanks and stuck it into the robes of her cloak. Then, Olwen gasped loudly and looked up at Ula and me.

Tears rolled down her cheeks.

"Olwen," I said, going to her.

Olwen flung her arms around my neck and buried her head on my shoulder. She wept for a long time, then pulled back, sniffling.

"A vision?" I asked her.

She nodded.

Ula joined us. In a satchel, she carried the Ogham staves.

Olwen took them quickly, searched them, then pulled out the one she wanted. With a shaking hand, she gave it to me.

"Duir," I whispered. "The oak."

Olwen shook her head and pointed at the stave again.

Ula was less patient. She swatted me on the back of the head and then asked, "Have you forgotten everything, you stupid girl?"

I looked at the stave in my hand, then from Ula to Olwen. "The king. The father?" I asked her.

Her eyes welling with tears, Olwen nodded then took the stave from me and clutched it to her chest. She looked then toward the open gap of the cave. She rose. Bobbing her head and gesturing as she sometimes did, she went to the cave entrance and set down the stave. She then removed the silver bracelet she wore and laid it there. Her hands rotating around one another, fingers moving, head bobbing, she appeared to communicate something to the little people of the Hollow Hills. When she was done, Olwen rejoined us.

Ula set her hand above Olwen's heart. "You can ask, but sometimes there is nothing to be done. It is as the gods will."

"Ula…" I whispered.

"We don't need to know more. The message was for Olwen."

I looked back at the stave lying at the entrance to the cave.

Prasutagus…

MY DAUGHTER and I returned to the roundhouse without further discussing what had happened in the Mossy Wood. I didn't want to upset Olwen more. There, we met with Bran and Bec. They had gathered with the others at the table for the evening meal. I tried to convince Ula to join us, but you might as well have asked her to dine in Londinium. Muttering at me, she went back to her cottage.

"Olwen will stay in Oak Throne until Samhain," I told Bran and Bec, "if that is all right with you."

While Bran and Bec nodded in agreement, Sorcha looked annoyed. "Why?' Sorcha asked.

"She will train with Ula," I said. "Ula is working to help Olwen communicate. So far, she has had some luck."

"How, Boudica?" Bec asked.

"Using Ogham staves."

Bec smiled. "I can help you as well," she told Olwen. "Just show me how. I was once a priestess, even though it feels like ages ago. But I remember my Ogham."

Olwen smiled at her.

Sorcha, on the other hand, frowned. "But she will return to Venta just after Samhain, right?"

I nodded.

Sorcha looked at her sister.

Olwen gestured to Sorcha. I had seen Olwen make the same movement before, the sisters communicating in their own language.

"All right. All right," Sorcha told Olwen, then turned back to her meal. The images the Morrigu had shown Sorcha had unnerved her. Olwen, however, had already put her sadness behind her. The visions she had seen had rocked her at the moment but didn't weigh her down now.

But her message *had* touched me. Olwen had seen something concerning her father. The thought that something bad could happen to Prasutagus filled me with unspeakable dread.

"While Olwen will stay, the rest of us will leave in the morning," I told Bran. "Is there anything else I can attend to before I go?"

Bran shook his head. "No. I am off in the morning to Sea Throne anyway. The world keeps us busy, Sister."

"Yes," I said, looking at those gathered at the table. "But it is good to pause for a moment. Even if it is just a moment."

My family.

As always, Riona, Cidna, and Balfor fluttered around in the background. I was eternally grateful for their enduring presence.

My mother, father, Belenus, and Caturix were all dead.

Brenna was gone.

The next generation now sat at the table.

Aesunos and Saenunos had left us at war.

What kind of world would we leave Sorcha, Olwen, Bellicus, and Caturin?

EARLY THE FOLLOWING DAY, I paid a visit to the horse market. As I had hoped, there were several horses available.

"There are many fine steeds for you to choose from," Moritasgus, our stable hand, said. Moritasgus was old now, but he still had a sharp eye for horses. I had asked him to come along with me. "Indeed, many fine horses, but I think I know the one for you, Boudica."

He led me to a stall where we found a beautiful yearling. The horse's coat was a mix of pale gold and white, with a butter-colored mane and tail and a white blaze and boots. The curious creature, who had been chewing grass, paused when we came to see him. A tuft of grass sticking out of one side of his mouth, he looked at us with curiosity in his eyes.

"He is ready to ride. And he shares a bloodline with Druda. His father is Druda's brother."

"Truly?"

Moritasgus nodded. "He came over from Frog's Hollow with two others just last week. That filly there is Mountain's daughter," he said, pointing to another young horse with a dark brown coat and a blonde main and tail. "Probably the last he will ever sire, Lynet said. Mountain doesn't get around much anymore. His filly is a sweet thing. Very good temperament. She's a bit too calm for you," Moritasgus said with a laugh.

"I..." I began, feeling a pinch in my heart. "Let me have them both. Olwen can have Mountain's filly, but Druda's blood," I said, looking at the goofy creature studying me, "can come home with me."

With that, I paid the vendor for the horses, and Moritasgus and I led both animals away.

"I'll get a proper lead on him and prepare this handsome fellow for the ride to Venta," Moritasgus told me. "And I'll find a place for the filly in the stables," Moritasgus told me.

"Thank you, Moritasgus."

"Of course, Princess—I mean, Queen. Always my princess in my eyes, though," he told me with a wink, then we went our separate ways.

I returned to the roundhouse to say my goodbyes.

After packing up my things, I exited the roundhouse and prepared to depart.

Olwen stood alongside Bec.

I kissed her on both cheeks and then on her forehead. "Ula is the meanest creature I have ever known. Don't let her abuse you," I told my daughter.

Olwen looked puzzled. She shook her head as if to say my comment confused her.

"What? She's kind to you?" I asked.

Olwen nodded.

Bec laughed and then told Olwen, "Then you are the only creature in existence she has ever willingly been kind too."

Olwen shrugged, then smiled.

"Stop by the stables later. See Moritasgus. I have let you a gift," I told my daughter.

Olwen's eyes grew shiny with excitement, and she smiled at Bec.

"I'll take you," Bec reassured her.

Olwen smiled.

"Be well," I told them both, then added, "And send word if you need anything."

Bec nodded.

"Thank you, Priestess," I told her, taking her hand.

"You're welcome, Princess."

With that, I turned and mounted Druda, who huffed when I adjusted myself in my saddle.

"I'll try not to take offense to that huff, old man. I hope you aren't implying I'm too heavy."

Druda snorted.

Bran joined me then. "Safe travels, Boudica."

"And you, Brother."

Moritasgus joined us then, leading the yearling.

"Who is this?" Pix asked.

"That is my new horse," I said. "Druda's nephew, in fact. See, you won't have to complain about carrying me anymore, Druda," I said, patting the horse on his neck. "I've found another to take the burden from you."

"Handsome boy," Pix said. "Ye see him, Nightshade?"

Pix's irritable horse ignored both her rider and the yearling completely.

I took the yearling's lead from Moritasgus. "Thank you, my friend."

He nodded to me.

With that, I motioned that I was ready to go.

I gave the others one last wave, then we headed off.

While Druda had seemed irritable before, the newcomer's presence got his attention.

"You see, there was no need to complain. One last ride carrying your heavy passenger, then it will just be strolls around the city from now on."

Druda whinnied to the yearling, the younger horse answering him the same.

"Aye, gods, now there be two of them," Pix laughed.

I chuckled, then leaned over and pressed my cheek against Druda's mane while I hugged his neck. "No. There is only one Druda. My heart horse."

"Epona incarnate," Pix said.

Ignoring her, I continued to hug Druda, who knickered softly at me.

"I love you too, Druda. I love you too."

CHAPTER 27

When we arrived at the roundhouse in Venta, I saw that riders had come. Someone had sent messengers. I sighed, feeling less than interested to hear news. For once, I wanted things to stay quiet. I didn't want to learn what new tragedy had befallen. So, I stayed with Sorcha, and we took the horses to the stables. I wanted to make sure my newcomer had no issues with the others.

Isolde, the stable hand, greeted us with a smile. "Who is this handsome gentleman?" she asked, patting Druda's nephew.

"My new horse," I told her. "I'll be out tomorrow for a ride."

"Let me put him in a pen so the others don't pick at him too much the first night. Come along, handsome,"

Isolde told the newcomer with a laugh, leading the yearling away.

The rest of the herd strained their necks to look.

"What will you call him?" Sorcha asked me.

"No ideas yet. You have any?"

Sorcha shook her head and then said, "He's probably still green. I can ride him for you, get him settled in. I know you're busy."

Of course, she desperately *wanted* to ride him—green or not. And, given she was my daughter, likely *because* he was green. "Thank you. I would appreciate that."

"Ah, here are my girls," a voice called from behind us.

We turned to find Prasutagus.

"We are one short, though," he added.

"Olwen was taken by a hedgewitch."

"A hedgewitch?" Prasutagus asked.

I nodded, meeting my husband's gaze. But when I did so, I remembered Olwen's warning. Swallowing my feelings, I looked back toward the yearling so Prasutagus wouldn't see the expression on my face. "Ula asked me to leave Olwen in Oak Throne until Samhain. She has found a way to help Olwen communicate better. From what I have seen, it's working. Olwen will stay with Bran and Bec. They have promised to look out for her. And, though cantankerous and risk-taking as she is, Ula will not let anything horrible happen to her."

"I'm very curious to see what Ula has learned," Prasutagus said.

I nodded. "We are down one daughter, but our party increased by one horse," I said, gesturing to the yearling.

"So I see. I think that is Druda's bloodline," Prasutagus said, watching as the yearling tried to eat a leaf that had fallen into the water trough, only to get it stuck on his nose. He was now working furiously to get it off with his tongue.

We all laughed.

"How did you guess?" I asked my husband with a chuckle. I then looked back toward the roundhouse. "Messengers?"

He nodded. "News from Londinium," he said, then glanced at Sorcha. Usually, my husband would try to keep the children away from talk of politics, but today, he carried on. "Gallus has left."

"For where?"

Prasutagus shook his head. "He's gone."

"Permanently?"

"A new man, Quintus Veranius, has arrived from Rome to become governor. Gallus hopped on a ship the day the new governor arrived, taking all his people with him. They said he left with the merriment of a groom on his way to his wedding."

"What is the reason for the change?"

Prasutagus shook his head. "We have not yet heard. I'm guessing Veranius's motivations will be plain soon enough. Another piece of gossip finally made its way home."

"What is it?"

"Caratacus."

"Caratacus? But I thought…"

"He's alive and well, Boudica. Apparently, he gave an impassioned plea before the emperor. Caratacus begged for understanding and leniency. The emperor was so moved that he granted clemency and permitted Caratacus to live in Rome in exile. Apparently, Caratacus and his wife and children now own a small farm, grow hazelnuts, and raise sheep."

I stared at my husband.

Beside us, Sorcha burst out laughing.

We both turned and looked at her.

"It's so absurd, isn't it? I mean, it was all a lie. First, they came to help Verica and Aedd Mawr. Then, the Romans stayed because of the *terrible scourge* that was Caratacus. And now they're still here because…" She gestured to indicate what was plain— there was no good reason for them to still be here. "While our people sweat, bleed, and die, Caratacus sips wine and eats nuts. It's just…" She began to laugh again. "It's too rich, isn't it? It's just too rich. By the gods, I hope all these Roman cities burn to the ground one day," she said, then walked away, still laughing.

"Sorcha's right," I told my husband. "I feel sick. How quaint. He's reunited with his family and is living a contented life while he leaves his people to die."

"Perhaps he preferred the weather."

I frowned at Prasutagus.

"Well, Wife. It means nothing to us. Come, let's have our own wine and nuts and enjoy them without blood on our hands."

"I hope Caratacus chokes."

"May the gods hear your words."

WITH THE ARRIVAL of Governor Veranius, we began to see a shift in attitude from Emperor Nero. Aside from collecting coins, the Romans had seemed almost disinterested in Britannia. Governor Gallus's lackadaisical attitude led us to believe Rome's interest in our country was finally waning.

But Dôn had foreseen the truth.

Rome was not done with us yet.

Governor Veranius suddenly began to pull legions from the east to fight in the west.

Their target?

The druids.

Gallus had paid little attention to the druids aside from taxation. But now, Veranius pushed west with renewed vigor. When the Cornovii, Ordovices, and Silures pushed back, the Romans took their vengeance out on the holy people.

The effect on the country was chilling.

Given the Romans' affronts, I shouldn't have been surprised when a messenger arrived from the druids.

But the shape of the message was wholly unexpected.

It was just before Samhain when Pix, Sorcha, and I were working with the horses at the stables. I was riding the yearling—whom we had named Dice, because every time I rode him, it was a gamble on what would happen next—when they announced riders at the gate.

Prasutagus had gone to the King's Wood, and I had finally gotten Dice settled enough that he was trotting gently in circles around the corral.

"Figures," Sorcha grumbled. "Want me to go see who it is?"

"Artur will see to them. If it's the Romans, hop on, and we'll ride away."

At that, Sorcha laughed.

Wanting to get one or two more passes in before I had to give up training for politics, I clicked to Dice, and we took off in a trot. He was gaining speed when Artur led a small party into the king's compound.

There, I saw three white-robed druids.

And so did Dice.

Apparently, their fluttery robes were the scariest thing Dice had ever seen because he shied sideways, bucking in the process.

I was also distracted by the unexpected guests that I failed to hold on as I should have. Soon, I found myself lying in the dirt, the wind knocked out of me.

I lay there a moment, trying to catch my breath. As I did, I saw those same fluttery robes approach. Then, someone leaned over me.

"Some things never change."

Catching my breath, I whispered, "Brenna?"

My sister chuckled. "And here they told me you were a queen. Yet, I find the same wild princess I've always known."

"Hurts more than it used to."

Brenna laughed. "That, I understand," she said, then held out her hand, helping me up.

I rose, dusted myself off, then embraced my sister. "Aye, thank Epona," I whispered, pulling her close. I closed my eyes, taking in her scent and the comfort of her embrace. "It's been far too long."

"Yes," my sister agreed.

When we finally let one another go, I looked behind

Brenna to see she had traveled with an older gentleman
I recognized as Caoilfhionn, the arch druid, and a
woman just a bit older than Brenna and me.

"Arch Druid Caoilfhionn," I said, bowing deeply.

"Queen Boudica," he replied, inclining his head
to me.

"Boudica, this is Luadine, leader of the Order of
Bards," Brenna said.

"Holy One," I said, bowing to her.

"Merry met, Queen Boudica."

"We must speak, Boudica," Brenna told me in a
serious tone.

I nodded, signaled a groom to take Dice, then joined
the druids.

"Holy Ones, you are welcome to Venta. You've had a
very long journey. Please, let's go inside," I said,
gesturing to the roundhouse.

As we went, Sorcha joined Brenna and me.

"My eldest daughter," I said, introducing Sorcha.
"Sorcha, this is my sister, Brenna."

Brenna smiled at Sorcha. "When I saw her, my heart
stopped a moment. How like our mother you look,
Sorcha."

"My aunt Brenna? Can it be?" Sorcha said excitedly.

"I am so glad to finally meet you," Brenna told
Sorcha, reaching out for her hand, which Sorcha eagerly
took.

"My other daughter, Olwen, is in Oak Throne," I told Brenna. "We can ride to see her afterward."

"I…" Brenna began, then paused. "I hope I will be able," she said, the nervous tremor in her voice betraying her.

I paused a moment and turned to Artur. "Artur, will you ride to the King's Wood? Ask Tavish and Prasutagus to come. Tell him we have visitors from Mona."

Artur stared at the druids for a moment, then nodded. "I'll go at once," he said, then rushed back toward the stables.

Pix stepped beside me. "I know ye are happy to see yer sister, but this is not likely to bode well," she whispered.

I gave her a knowing look.

We made our way to the roundhouse, Balfor meeting us at the door.

"Holy ones," he said, bowing deeply. He turned to me. "Your meeting room is ready. We will have lodging prepared."

"Thank you, Balfor," I told the man.

I led the druids to the chamber. There, Ronat and Betha were working quickly to set out food. When we entered, they both paused to bow.

"Wise Ones," Betha said.

"Wise Ones," Ronat echoed.

Brenna smiled at them and then inclined her head.

Ronat stared at Brenna for a long moment. Eventually, Betha elbowed her daughter to get back to work.

"What?" Ronat whispered to her mother. "It's just… She looks just like Boudica and Sorcha."

"That's the queen's sister," Betha whispered. "Don't you remember? Now, bring the mead."

I chuckled lightly and gestured for the druids to sit near the fire. Betha appeared a moment later with goblets of mead.

The druids took the drinks and sipped slowly.

"King Prasutagus is at the King's Wood," I told them. "He will join us shortly with the druid Tavish. This is our elder daughter, Sorcha. And this is Pix, our guardian. I hope the journey from Mona was not difficult."

"I don't care much for traveling by sea," the arch druid told me with a light laugh. "But the gods were kind. We had calm waters and no Romans. What more can we ask for?"

"Much. We can ask for much," Luadine replied with a laugh that had a bitter edge.

Brenna shifted uncomfortably. "I remember the last time I was in this room," she said, looking around. "I nearly became the wife of Prasutagus quite by accident," she said, then laughed. "I will forever be grateful to the druid's interference, my sister's honesty, and a bit of good timing for the changes in my fortune. But I am delighted to see you well, Boudica," she told me, then looked to Sorcha. "And to meet my niece."

"I am sorry that I did not make it back to the land of the Greater Iceni before the passing of Ansgar. He was much-respected in our order," Caoilfhionn said.

"We were very sorry to lose him. He was like family to us," I replied.

"Now, this Tavish of Arminghall... He has not come to live in the king's household? That is irregular," Caoilfhionn said.

"Tavish prefers to stay with the others to help ensure their safety. We are inclined to agree with him."

"Yes," Caoilfhionn said. "Yes, I suppose there is some sense in that."

"Queen Boudica," Betha said tepidly. "We are ready."

"Please," I said, gesturing to the druids. "Come. You have traveled far. You must be hungry."

With that, we all adjourned to the dining table where Ronat and Betha had laid out the finest meal our house could serve, including many Roman-style dishes. As they ate, Luadine took note of the Roman serving vessels—which we had discovered held the heat of the dishes very well—as well as the Roman ingredients in the dishes.

"Your table serves very *modern* fare," Luadine said.

While her tone was not overly rude, the look Brenna gave her—then tried to smother—

told me what I suspected. The bard was not happy to see such things on our table.

"Venta is a great trading hub," I said. "We are fortunate to have access to goods from lands far and wide. Not everything has been to our taste, of course. But we've adapted."

"You even met Emperor Claudius," Brenna said brightly.

"Yes, when he greeted the eleven kings."

"The submission of the eleven kings. That is how it is remembered amongst the Romans," Caoilfhionn said.

"Like all things with Rome, what was offered and what was given are often different things. Yet, here we sit, our lands intact, our people free."

"An echo of Cartimandua," Luadine said to Caoilfhionn, who nodded.

At that, Pix caught my gaze. She raised and lowered her eyebrows.

As we ate, I noted that the druids avoided the rich Roman sauces and other unusual spices. I felt sorry for Betha, who had done her best to provide the kind of meal she would serve the governor, only to have the druids turn up their noses at it.

Brenna, however, seemed more conscious of the moment and tried everything.

"This is very good," she told Betha, spooning on one of the sauces. "What is it?"

"Garum, Princess Brenna."

"I like it," she told the cook with a smile.

May all the gods bless my sister.

We kept the conversation light, Brenna asking about the yearling I was riding. Finally, Prasutagus, Tavish, and Artur returned.

"Wise Ones," Prasutagus said when he entered. I could tell he'd been rushing to get here. Only now was he slowing down. He raised his hands to his forehead in a gesture of respect.

"Prasutagus," Arch Druid Caoilfhionn said. "It is good to see you again."

"Arch Druid Caoilfhionn. I am honored to have you here," Prasutagus said, then turned to Luadine. "And Bard Luadine. It is an honor."

"Prasutagus," she said, nodding to him.

When Prasutagus saw Brenna, he smiled. "Brenna."

"Prasutagus. Well met."

Prasutagus turned to Tavish.

"Wise Ones," Tavish said, bowing deeply.

Caoilfhionn studied him. "Tavish, is it? I'm sorry, but I don't remember you from Mona."

"I was one of many young men, Arch Druid. It's no surprise. But, yes, I trained amongst you until Rome came, then I returned to the Greater Iceni."

Prasutagus turned to Artur. "My son, Artur."

"Son?" the arch druid asked. "I was told the Greater Iceni line was comprised of two daughters, your eldest here," he said, gesturing to Sorcha.

"Artur is the child of my first wife, Esu," Prasutagus explained.

"Ah, then he is no blood relation to you," the arch druid clarified.

"No, but he is my son nonetheless," Prasutagus said stiffly.

"I see. No offense meant to the boy. He appears to be a fine warrior," the druid said dismissively.

Suddenly, I started to understand why Ula had left the holy people.

Prasutagus motioned for Tavish and Artur to join us at the table.

Artur and Sorcha exchanged a glance as Artur sat. In her look, my daughter sent love and sympathy to her brother—blood relation or not.

Artur gave her an appreciative smile then rolled his eyes.

I sucked back my lips, trying not to grin.

"I have never been to Arminghall Henge," the bard Luadine said. "Tell me about it," she said to Tavish.

Ronat and Betha served the others, and the conversation turned lighter for a time, the druid Tavish talking of the henge and of the King's Wood.

Arch Druid Caoilfhionn waved to Betha to take his still-full plate. I didn't miss the expression on her face when she realized he had not eaten.

"Holy one, a round of bread and cheese, perhaps?" she whispered to him.

At that, the druid nodded.

Looking defeated, Betha returned with a plate with simple fare that she set before the druid who finally ate. I understood his disdain for the Roman food, but it was an offense to the gods to refuse what a host offered. Arch Druid Caoilfhionn was undoubtedly aware of that. Did he think himself above the gods?

Once the meal was done, Sorcha and Artur retreated, both giving the druids their respect before making a hasty departure.

"They remind me of us with our brothers," Brenna told me, smiling in their wake.

I nodded.

"We are honored to have you here, Arch Druid," Prasutagus told the man. "But also surprised. Why have you made such a long journey to see us?"

At that, Caoilfhionn nodded slowly and stroked his beard. When he looked up at Prasutagus once more, he said, "Because our gods are dying…"

Prasutagus and I listened as the arch druid told us a tale of horror sweeping across the west. As had happened to Dindraine's order and at Maiden Stones, the Romans were toppling our shrines. But they were also actively butchering our people.

"They are cutting a path to Mona and sending us a message as they go," Caoilfhionn said. "With Caratacus dead, they believed the fight for freedom had ended. They have learned differently."

"The druids have now taken leadership in the wake of the void created by Caratacus's capture and death," Bard Luadine said. "We are organizing the west."

"I..." I said, then looked at Prasutagus, who also looked surprised. "Caratacus is not dead," I told the druids.

They both stared at me as if I had turned yellow.

"What do you mean?" Arch Druid Caoilfhionn asked.

"He pleaded his case before the emperor and was pardoned. He and his family have been living in Rome all this time."

At that, the druids sat in stunned silence.

"With all due respect," Brenna said, "we should not be surprised. Caratacus's greed brought Rome here, and it was his continued desire to retain his crown that fueled the rebellion. Ultimately, Caratacus's moves have always been about one thing—himself."

At that, the arch druid shifted, uncomfortable with the truth. "Be that as it may," he finally said, "we need help. The Greater Iceni have laid down in bed with the Romans. I barely recognize this house anymore. You have become something other than what you were. But now, you must shake off the mantle of Rome and help us. You *must* protect us."

"What would you have us do?" Prasutagus asked.

"Fight," Caoilfhionn replied. "Rally the east, Prasutagus."

Prasutagus looked astonished at such a direct order.

"The Romans have learned there are vast mines of silver and gold in Ordovices territory. They cannot get to it because the western tribes are united and pushing back. But now that the Romans have brought more soldiers west, the tribes struggle to stand against the Roman forces," Brenna explained.

"We will lose the western front without your help," Luadine told us.

For a long moment afterward, there was silence in the room.

Finally, I said, "When Caturix and the Coritani kings rose, it made no difference in the fight. In the end, my brother died, the Northern Iceni were punished, and the Coritani are no more."

"Are you so much in love with Rome, Queen Boudica?" Caoilfhionn asked me, a stern tone in his voice.

Unable to chain my temper, I retorted, saying, "How dare you ask me such a question? My brother is dead. My people are dishonored. Every day, Prasutagus and I shelter refugees from other tribes. How many priestesses have I endeavored to save from Rome's clutches? We have suffered grave insults from the Romans. And yes, there was a time when we thought to rise, but now... Our people are our chief concern, Arch Druid, before anything else. You may have been *so much in love* with Caratacus," I said waspishly, "but the Catuvellauni king always put himself first—no matter the risk to others. Prasutagus and I have always done the opposite. Our people come first, no matter the risk to honor, pride, or the sauces on our table."

Brenna shifted uncomfortably.

Behind her, Pix covered her mouth with her hand to suffocate a laugh.

At the other end of the room, where Ronat and Betha were clearing the plates, Ronat elbowed her mother, then the pair grinned at one another.

The arch druid shifted in his seat.

"Arch Druid," Prasutagus said. "We have heard rumors that Nero has little taste left for the campaign in our lands. In his last governor, we saw signs that interest was further waning. I am sick at heart to hear how our holy people have been treated. Aulus Plautius agreed our holy people would go unharmed, but his predecessors have not been inclined to keep that promise. If the Romans know you are actively leading the rebellion, you have placed a target on yourselves, on Mona, and on every druid and priestess on this island. Including those sheltered by the Greater and Northern Iceni."

"Which is why you must act," Bard Luadine said forcefully.

"Prasutagus, Boudica," Brenna said more gently. "We all understand your desire to protect your people. The Greater and Northern Iceni are lucky to have you. Other tribes have not been so fortunate and have suffered the whims of Rome. If what you say is correct, if Rome has grown tired of our island, perhaps that creates an opportunity. If the Romans suddenly find themselves at war with all the tribes at once, maybe that will be the final thing to convince Nero to leave."

"Or, they will send forces from Gaul, and that will be the end of us all," I replied.

"What we are asking is not easy. But soon, snow will fall, and the Romans will withdraw from the west, back to Verulamium. Come spring, we must have your answer," Caoilfhionn told us. "Rally the east. Get those Trinovantes and Catuvellauni chieftains who have survived behind you. Fight with us."

"You have given us much to think about," Prasutagus said.

"The time to act is closing," Bard Luadine said. "Do think it over. We need you. Now, I think Caoilfhionn and I should retire. It has been a very long journey to meet with such unexpected resistance."

"Indeed," Caoilfhionn said gruffly.

Prasutagus signaled to Balfor.

"Please, follow me," the housecarl told the druids.

Caoilfhionn and Luadine rose and left the chamber. Brenna lingered a moment, then whispered, "I should go with them, but I will meet with you later tonight." She then followed behind the others.

After they had gone, Tavish, Prasutagus, Pix, and I looked at each other.

"They are unchanged," Tavish said with a frown. "No offense to your sister, Queen Boudica."

"None taken. What do we do?" I asked Prasutagus.

My husband exhaled deeply. In it, I heard the weariness of his spirit.

"'Tis not what they said," Pix said, "but how they said it. They know nothing about the fight ye have waged here to keep yer people safe. Walking and talking like his cock is as big as an oak, the arch druid thinks highly of himself."

"He is the same as he ever was," Tavish said.

Prasutagus nodded.

"And how long were ye on that island?" Pix asked Tavish.

"Nine years, like all druids."

"And still, he didn't look down his nose long enough to see ye. If the arch druid cannot recognize members of his own order, how does he know enough to steer us all?"

"The druids speak for the gods," Prasutagus said.

"Anyone ever ask the gods if that's what they want?" Pix replied.

"Do you mean to tell me, after all this time, you don't think we should fight?" I asked Pix.

"Nay. Now, let's not be foolish. I did not say it were a bad idea, but I don't like that druid poking about in affairs he knows nothing about."

"I must get a man to Gaul before winter, see how well garrisoned the Romans are there. If more troops are coming from Rome to pursue the Ordovices' gold, there may be no hope. But if Nero is merely moving men from east to west, that will leave the east open and quiet."

I nodded. "Winter is upon us. By spring, we will know more."

"Agreed," Tavish said, Prasutagus and Pix also nodding.

"I honor our order," Prasutagus said, looking to Tavish, "but I have not sacrificed all these years to throw everything away just because the arch druid demands it. If we move, it will be because *we* deem the time right, not because we've been commanded."

Tavish nodded. "Agreed, my king. May the gods—and only the gods—guide us."

IT WAS VERY LATE that night when Brenna finally appeared. I was sitting in the main family room, resting by the fire, when my sister found me.

"Boudica," she said, embracing me. "I'm sorry. I fell asleep. The sea voyage was very long."

"Please, make no apologies. I am glad to set my eyes upon you again." I hugged her.

"Oh, Boudica. This is not the return I wanted to

make. As it is, we will leave in the morning. I will not be able to visit with Bran and Bec or meet Olwen or Bellicus," she said sadly. "You and Bran have suffered so much alone, and now I am passing like a cloud over the moon."

"Bran and I were sorry we could not share our griefs with you. When Caturix died, everything was in such upheaval. We couldn't get word to you ourselves. I know you learned of it through rumor, and for that, I am sorry."

"There is nothing you could do," Brenna said. "My heart aches to know my brother and Melusine are gone. It was such a tragedy."

"Well…" I said as I considered. I leaned toward my sister. "Melusine lives."

Brenna gasped and grabbed my arms. "Where? How?"

"There is no other way to explain it but by saying the gods intervened. She escaped the fall of Stonea and has been living here with us, in secret, in the King's Wood."

"May the gods be praised."

"There is more," I said. In a whisper, I added, "Caturix lives on…in his children." I then told Brenna of Kennocha and all that had happened.

"Caturin lives here training to be a part of the king's guard. Mara wed one of our warriors and lives in Venta."

"Oh, Boudica. My heart is so glad to know his children survived. But how sorrowful a tale... Father was always too eager to protect the line no matter what, and now... You are the queen of all the Iceni? Over Bran?"

"It was the only bargain we could manage to save the Northern Iceni from a terrible fate. As it was, our people were shamed, disarmed... But not entirely," I said, giving her a knowing look. "There is a cache at Seahenge. If it is ever needed, the druids are ready."

"Boudica, there is so much fear amongst the druids. They have read omens and seen signs. The gods grow quiet. All they see is fire before us. They truly believe that if you do not act, we will fall. In fact..." she said, then paused. "Sister, I have seen a vision of you on a battlefield before a great army. You stood between Rome and us, a shield in your hand. You held back the tide. I *have* seen you rise, Boudica."

I stared at Brenna. Could it be? "I...I don't know, Sister. We have sacrificed and suffered so much to keep the peace for our people."

"If it is as you say, if Rome wants to leave, perhaps a push is needed."

"Or it will be the end of us all."

"Wild as you are, Boudica, I know your heart will guide you. You will do what is right for the people. You have always loved them like they were part of our family."

I smiled gently at her. "I have missed you."

"And I, you."

"Will you play for me, Sister? Just once before you go? You can see what has become of me. I would love to hear what has become of your magic."

Brenna smiled and then pulled her lyre from her bag. "Won't I wake the house?"

I shrugged. "Who cares. Let them wake."

At that, Brenna giggled and then set her hands to her lyre. Then, she began to play. The song started with light, sweet notes. I closed my eyes, listening to her music. As she played, memories of days in the forest and on the beach with Gaheris came to mind. I remembered the sweet tastes of summer ales and the salty tang of Gaheris's skin. I remembered his laugh and the smell of his hair. I could feel the warmth of his embrace, remembering what it felt like to lie with him under the sun, skin upon skin. The melody continued, each sweet note taking me back to those lovely days and the sound of Gaheris's laughter, Mavis's call as she flew in circles above us, and Druda and Mountain racing down the beach. It was like I was there, living it again.

When I opened my eyes again, I was surprised to find tears trickling down my cheeks.

And I discovered I was no longer alone.

Everyone in the house had come—guards, the kitchen staff, Prasutagus, Pix, Sorcha, Artur. Everyone.

I looked up at Prasutagus, who also had tears in his eyes.

"Brenna," I whispered.

"'Tis sweet magic, the hand of a bard," Pix said, quickly dashing tears from her cheeks.

"I'm so sorry," Brenna said. "I didn't mean to wake you all."

Surprising us, Betha crossed the room and pulled Brenna into an embrace.

"Sweet lady, thank you. I haven't let myself think of my dear, dead man in twenty years. All those sweet memories flooded back at once. Thank you, Princess Brenna."

Around me, everyone spoke at once, thanking my sister.

"Let me get everyone a drink," Betha said. "We'll all need it."

Prasutagus sat down beside me, motioning for Sorcha to join us. He smiled at Brenna and said, "Here is something you will never hear a man say to a beautiful woman. I am very glad I *didn't* marry you, Brenna."

At that, Brenna laughed, then inclined her head to him.

I took Brenna's hand and squeezed it gently. "May Ogmios be thanked."

Brenna smiled at me and then returned the gesture. "And Epona be praised."

We shared a drink together, everyone speaking of what beautiful visions Brenna's song had evoked.

"What did you remember?" I asked Pix, who was decidedly quiet.

"I was a child again," she said with a smile. "I'd forgotten my mother's face until…" Pix said, then smiled sadly, her eyes growing watery once more. "'Twas good to remember. And ye, Strawberry Queen?"

"Gaheris," I whispered so the others did not hear.

"She woke some of our oldest memories of love. That is what everyone speaks of but doesn't know how to name."

I smiled wistfully, trying to hold on to the last of the memories.

It had felt so real.

I closed my eyes.

Ah, Gaheris, how I miss you.

Once everyone finished their drinks and thanked Brenna once more, they departed for bed again.

Before she left, Sorcha came to Pix and me, hugging us both very tightly.

"Good night," she told us, kissing us each on the cheeks before she departed.

Pix gave me a knowing look.

Apparently, the song had evoked something in Sorcha as well.

Before long, everyone had left.

While Brenna smiled wistfully, she looked tired.

"Does your magic work on you as well?" I asked her. She nodded.

"What did you see?"

"Caturix, Bran, you, and me with our mother."

I set my head on her shoulder. "That's a lovely thing to remember."

Brenna tilted her head, leaning against me. "Yes."

"You're tired."

"I am."

"You should go to bed."

"I should. But I think I'll sit here with you just a little bit longer," she said, taking my hand.

I closed my eyes. "I love you, Sister."

"I love you too."

WHEN I WOKE the next morning, I found Prasutagus missing. I rose and dressed for the day. Not discovering Prasutagus in the roundhouse, I went outside only to find he and Caoilfhionn returning from somewhere. The pair spoke as they rode, stopping before they reached the roundhouse.

I could tell from the look on Prasutagus's face that he

didn't like what he was hearing, but in the end, he lifted his hands in a gesture of respect.

Brenna and Luadine exited the guest house a few moments later, both ready to travel.

I joined them. "We will ride with you to Yarmouth," I told Brenna, spotting Pix and Sorcha coming from the stables. Sorcha was leading Dice and Ember behind her.

"Thank you, Sister."

The others appeared a short time later with supplies for the druids and to wish them farewell.

I joined Prasutagus as the others were saying goodbye.

"Off on an adventure this morning?" I asked.

"Caoilfhionn wanted to go to the King's Wood," Prasutagus said, then frowned. "We'll talk later, but I've promised nothing."

I nodded.

Kennocha and Caturin appeared from the barns. They looked at the party with curiosity.

"I will speak with them," I told Prasutagus, then went to Kennocha.

"Dawn's blessings," I called cheerfully, but Kennocha looked worried.

"Boudica... Druids?"

I nodded. "From Mona."

"Boudica, is that... Is that your sister?"

"Yes, and I think she would like to speak to you," I said, gesturing for Kennocha to follow me.

"I… All right," Kennocha said, then she and Caturin followed me.

Stepping aside from the other druids, Brenna joined us. "Lady Kennocha," Brenna called brightly. "Do you remember me?"

"Of course, Princess Brenna," Kennocha said, curtseying to her. She then turned to Caturin. "Caturin, this is Princess Brenna. She is the eldest daughter of old King Aesunos. Princess, this is my son, Caturin."

I could see Caturin putting together the pieces of what was left unsaid.

Brenna was his blood.

"Oh… I…" he stammered, then bowed.

"Hello, Caturin," Brenna said with a smile. "I am very pleased to meet you. That is a fine sword you have."

Caturin smiled at her. "It was a gift from Queen Boudica. I will join the king's guard when I am older. But for now, I train or help my mother with the animals."

Brenna smiled at Kennocha. "I remember your goats. How wild-eyed and playful they were."

"Kennocha sees to our livestock here. We are all grateful for her care," I said.

Kennocha gave me a soft smile.

"Well," Brenna said, touching Caturin's shoulder. "I wish you great fortune, Caturin. May the gods watch over you and keep you safe. Always."

"Thank you, Princess Brenna."

"Is your daughter here?" Brenna asked Kennocha.

"No, Princess. I'm sorry. She is in the city with her husband."

"Well, perhaps another time. May the gods keep you both," Brenna told them.

"Brenna?" Caoilfhionn called.

Brenna gave Caturin one last smile, then we left them, rejoining the party.

"My heart is much moved," Brenna whispered. "Thank you for looking after them."

"We feared Rome would come for them if they knew. It seemed safer to have them here."

"And Melusine… Caturix would be grateful."

"I hope so."

Brenna laughed. "He would not show it, but he would be."

Our party then mounted and set off for Yarmouth. As we went, I felt a cool breeze in the air. Autumn had come, and soon, winter. The druid's plea to us had been clear. While part of me resisted for the sake of peace, I sensed they truly feared for their order. And I felt that same fear deep in my bones.

Yet, I remembered Dôn's words. There was no

getting rid of Rome for many years to come. But dissuading them, lessening their numbers… Was it possible?

When we arrived in Yarmouth, we found the ship to take the druids back to Mona ready and waiting. It was a clear day. While cool, the dark blue waters of the sea were calm. Overhead, seabirds called and then circled.

We dismounted and went with the druids to their ship.

There were many traders in port.

But, thankfully, no Romans. There was something to fear if word got back to the governor that we'd received a delegation from Mona.

We walked with the druids to the ship.

"I wish you fair journeys," I told Caoilfhionn. "May Llyr give you calm seas, and Bel cast his sunlight in Rome's eyes, blinding them to your passage."

The druid inclined his head to me. "Thank you, Queen Boudica."

"Bard Luadine, I am very glad to have met you," I told her.

"And you, Queen Boudica."

"Prasutagus," Caoilfhionn said, taking my husband aside.

Luadine boarded the boat while Caoilfhionn and Prasutagus spoke in whispered tones.

"Sister, please send my love to Bran. I had desperately hoped to see him, but it was not in my hands," she said, glancing at the others. Then, she whispered, "I was only invited because they believed I could influence you to do as they say. Boudica, do what you think is right for the Iceni. Queen Cartimandua will not budge on her decision to protect the Brigantes like Brigantia herself. You would not be alone in your decision *not* to act against Rome. But if you see any path forward to rid us of Rome… Mona *is* in danger."

"If it comes to that, what can you do? Can you flee? To Éire or north?"

"Perhaps… But the druids will not abandon Mona. And in truth, I am one of them now."

I nodded, then took her hand. "Then may Epona guide us both."

Brenna embraced me. "Be safe, Sister. I love you."

"I love you too."

Brenna stepped back and looked at Sorcha. "How like my mother you look. But I see your own strong spirit in you, Sorcha," Brenna said, setting her hand on Sorcha's cheek. "Draw on that fire inside you when you need it. Do not forget."

Sorcha smiled at Brenna and then nodded.

Brenna hugged her tight and then let her go.

Before boarding the ship, she turned to Pix. "Watch them well."

"Aye, Princess."

And with that, my sister boarded the vessel, Caoil-fhionn following behind her.

We waited all together, watching as the druids cast off. When the wind seemed lacking, Caoilfhionn motioned to Brenna, who pulled out her small instrument. She strummed a few notes, causing the air to shiver, and an incandescent glow lifted from the strings of Brenna's instrument and filled the sails of the boat, pushing the vessel out to sea.

"Did you see that?" Sorcha whispered in disbelief.

I smiled.

"Yes, very glad I didn't marry your sister," Prasu-tagus said, setting his arm around my shoulders. "What I would have stolen from the world, Brenna's gifts and auburn-haired firebrands," he said, kissing Sorcha on her head. He chuckled. "Your hair is hot."

"It's the sun."

"If you say so, Firebrand. If you say so."

I went to the end of the pier, watching as the ship departed. My eyes on Brenna, I followed her until she was out of sight, a certainty in my heart whispering that I would never see my sister again.

CHAPTER 29

After the druids departed, Prasutagus and Artur stopped by the docking station to check on the men. At the same time, Sorcha got distracted by some kittens roaming about the docks, Pix joining her in the mischief. I was about to rejoin the men and ensure the horses were watered when I spotted a boat with a familiar pennant.

Menapii.

Reaching into my pocket, I pulled out the worn leather pouch and retrieved the Menapii coin. Brenna's music had evoked such visceral memories of Gaheris that I felt like he was alive again for a moment.

I clutched the coin in my hand and made my way to the ship.

As I approached, I distinguished the captain of their crew and approached him.

"Sir," I called.

The captain looked confused until another of his crew leaned toward him and whispered something. At that, the man's eyebrows shot up. He bowed to me and then said, "Queen Boudica. What can I do for you, great queen?"

"Help me with a riddle, I hope. Is this the coinage of your tribe?" I asked, reluctantly handing the coin to him. The moment it left my fingers, I felt desperate to get it back, as if I were clinging to the last piece of Gaheris.

"It is," the captain said, turning the coin over. "It is somewhat old, though," he said, handing it back to me.

"Can you tell me when this coin was made?"

"Cativorix, the king on your coin, only ruled from forty to forty-three, before the Romans disposed of him when he got in the way of their invasion."

"I see."

"Our tribe's situation is no better than yours. Caesar took the first cut. Aulus Plautius finished the job, disposing of our king."

A sick feeling rocked my stomach.

"Cativorix was our last king," the captain continued. "Now, we are Roman, like you," he said, handing back the coin.

"I see. Well, thank you for your time. Please, don't let me keep you," I told him, then turned and made my way from the docks toward the horses. As I went, I slipped the coin back into the pouch and stuffed it into my vest pocket, where it lay against my heart.

Aulus Plautius finished the job.

When they were building up forces in Menapii territory for the invasion *under Aulus.*

Aye, gods. Could it be?

No. Aulus would have told me.

Wouldn't he?

My stomach felt like someone was twisting it. I pushed the thought aside. All I knew was the coin was Menapii. It could have come from anyone, in the pocket of one of our people or a Menapii raider. There was no way to know.

There would never be a way to know for sure.

Gaheris was gone. Dead almost as many years as he'd been alive.

As I tried to push the thoughts from my mind, I went to the horses and began leading them to the water trough. But no matter what I did, the ache didn't go away.

I set my head against Dice's neck and closed my eyes.

"Ah, Gaheris," I whispered. "I hope you are in the Otherworld waiting for me. My heart will not be whole until I am with you again."

My heart felt heavy as we rode back to Venta. Pix and Sorcha chatted loudly, two orange kittens sticking their heads out of Sorcha's satchel, watching the world with bright eyes. They were cute, fluffy little things. I wasn't surprised when Sorcha said she wanted to bring them home. Naturally, Prasutagus agreed. There was little Sorcha wanted that he ever said no to.

We had almost arrived back at the city when Prasutagus reined in beside me.

"Boudica, I will go to the King's Wood and speak to Tavish. Want to come?"

I shook my head. "I've had enough of druids for the moment."

Prasutagus raised an eyebrow at me.

"Present company excluded."

"I was glad to see Brenna again. She looks well."

"Yes."

"I saw you with the Menapii. Anything?"

I shook my head.

Prasutagus reached out and took my hand, giving it a squeeze. "I love you."

I smiled at him. "And I, you."

At that, Prasutagus gestured to Artur, and the pair

trotted off toward the King's Wood, leaving us to return to the roundhouse. As we rode through Venta, Pix and Sorcha left me to visit Aden, the saddle maker's son, with whom Sorcha was always laughing and joking. Their friendship piqued my motherly curiosity, but Pix assured me they were only friends.

I rode on to the roundhouse with the guard.

When we arrived, I left Dice to Isolde and went inside. Not stopping to talk to the others, I went to my bedchamber, where I lay down and promptly cried myself to sleep.

IT WAS a week before Samhain when visitors arrived again, this time in the form of Bran, Bec, Bellicus, and Olwen.

Having planned to take the trip north to retrieve Olwen, I was surprised to see them.

"It has been too long since Bec and I came to Venta, and Bellicus has never been here. We thought we would come and see your city and bring Olwen home."

I smiled at them. "You are all most welcome." I went to Olwen, who was mounted on Mountain's filly. "My sweet girl, welcome home."

Olwen smiled at me and then dismounted.

"Did Mountain's girl give you an easy ride?" I asked her.

Olwen nodded.

"She is so lovely," Bec told me. "We have named her Uilleann."

"The Ogham for honeysuckle?"

Bec nodded. "It was Olwen's idea."

I looked at my daughter, who nodded and then curled her finger, making the Ogham sign for honeysuckle.

"Oh, Ula," I whispered to the absent woman, then hugged my daughter tightly, making her laugh. "Come, everyone. Let's go inside. There is a chill in the air."

We headed into the roundhouse. It was early morning still, and Sorcha, who had spent the day before sparring with Pix and Artur, was still abed.

Olwen looked about and seemed to be listening for her.

"Sleeping," I told my daughter.

Olwen nodded, then turned to Bellicus, motioning for the boy to come with her, then they both set off with mischief in their eyes. Sorcha was in for a startling awakening.

"Prince Bran, Lady Bec," Vian greeted them, appearing from the formal meeting chamber, her fingertips covered in coal from writing. "I am so glad to see you both."

"Merry met, Vian," Bran told her with a smile. "I just saw your family a fortnight ago. All are well."

At that, Vian smiled. "I'm glad to hear it."

Prasutagus joined us a moment later, covered from head to toe with mud.

"King Prasutagus," Bec said with a laugh. "You are positively…grubby."

At that, Prasutagus laughed. "You must forgive me, Priestess," he said, then smiled at Bran. "It is good to see you, Bran. I had an…incident with Kennocha's goats this morning. I'll return in a moment," he said, then motioned to Balfor. The pair departed, leaving us chuckling.

Ronat brought everyone a warm, honeyed herb drink and then went to prepare the morning meal.

"Boudica, your last messenger relayed that you had news," Bran said, a worried expression on his face.

Then, I told Bran of Brenna's visit and the news from Mona. As I recanted the tale, a refreshed Prasutagus joined us. Bran and Bec listened carefully as I relayed the druid's plea.

"What will you do?" Bran asked me and Prasutagus.

"We will wait until spring," I told him. "Then, we will see what the Romans are planning. Only afterward can we decide."

"Brenna said Queen Cartimandua is not budging. We would be alone in rallying forces," Bran said.

Prasutagus nodded. "The Trinovantes chieftains— what's left of them—will not be hard to convince. Already Chieftain Lors is eager to fight. The Trinovantes have suffered much. The destruction of Maiden Stones, taking of their lands, burning the villages… that was the end of their patience. They may have a king, but he is Rome. The Catuvellauni survivors feel much the same. A week back, I spoke to Chieftain Adirix. He is ready to rally alongside anyone who will fight. After the *mistake* at Raven's Dell, my patience is in tatters."

"Then, you are considering it?" Bran asked.

Prasutagus looked at me.

I nodded.

"Yes," Prasutagus said. "But only considering."

Bran exhaled deeply and then looked toward the fire burning in the brazier. He shook his head. "Dôn has passed," he said quietly. "We are without guidance in the lands of the Northern Iceni."

"There is Arixus," I told him.

"And all his swords," Bran said.

We heard Olwen, Sorcha, and Bellicus laughing in the back of the house.

"And then, there is that," Bec said, looking toward the children.

I nodded. "And that is all that matters."

Bec, Bran, Bellicus, and the warriors from the Northern Iceni stayed with us a few days, all of us venturing into the city to visit the market. Bran and Bellicus left with new boots in the Gaulish style, lined with lambskin and designed to withstand the brutal winters. Bec and I both came away with new cloaks, hooded, lined, and beautifully embroidered. The craftsmanship was so well done that I purchased similar cloaks for my daughters, the kitchen staff, Kennocha, Mara, Vian, Pix, and even Ula.

"It is a pity you were not here last year," I said. "I spent last season shivering."

"I am relieved to be in Venta, Queen Boudica," the dark-haired woman told me, then lowered her voice. "I am Cantiaci," she said. "We fled to Trinovantes territory when I was younger, but the troubles found us there as well. I spent the last season trying to sell at the colonia at Camulodunum, but Roman women do not like our styles," she said. "So, my daughter and I came here. We are only two months in your city, but thus far, we are very happy."

"You are most welcome here," I told her. "We are very grateful for your skills."

"The Romans are rubbish. I know they will come for half my profits, but as long as the Queen of the Iceni likes my cloaks, I suspect I will make enough of a living to survive," she told me, giving me a knowing smile.

"Hmm," I mused. "Have you been to King's Wood? The grove of the druids?"

"No, we have not yet had a chance to pay homage."

"Would you go there upon my request? I would see the druids warmly dressed for the winter. Druid Tavish may decline, but tell him I insist. Please see they have what they need, and I will provide the silver."

"Queen Boudica," she said, then bowed deeply. "I am truly grateful."

"May the gods bless you."

"And you."

With our packages in tow, we left the market.

"It really is a well-made piece," Bec said, smoothing her cloak. "Even Ula won't be able to find a reason to complain."

I laughed. "When have you ever known Ula not to complain?"

Bec chuckled, then turned serious. "She has grown so old, Boudica. We will see to her. But she is so stubborn and difficult. I hope she survives the winter."

"The world will not be the same without Ula in it. And now that Dôn has gone…"

"Let's hope Ula is too stubborn to let the Crone take her."

At that, we chuckled, but there was still sadness in both our voices.

When we finally returned to the roundhouse, it was

late afternoon. We found Bran there, picking food from the table.

"I'm glad my stomach reminded me to stop spending," Bran told me, his mouth full. "I am light on silver, Wife. You'll have to lend me your coin pouch," he told Bec.

"Mine is empty," she replied.

"Then we will spend Boudica's wealth."

I chuckled.

They stayed one more night, all of us gathering for the evening meal. Kennocha, Caturin, Mara, and her husband, Bruin, also joined us. The others gathered around the table, laughing and talking. Olwen smiled happily at the scene. I was filled with a strange mix of emotions.

On the one hand, I felt so happy seeing them all gathered there. On the other hand, a genuine sense of dread lingered in my stomach. There was a charge in the air, like the feeling just before a storm rolled in.

Something was coming.

"Boudica?" Prasutagus whispered, taking my hand. "Are you all right?"

"I…" I began, realizing my eyes were wet with unshed tears. "Yes. Just happy to see all of us together."

"I know you better than that," he whispered.

I gave him a soft smile. "I know you do," I told him, then kissed his hand and said nothing more. Instead, my gaze went to Sorcha, Caturin, and Bellicus, who were competing in a silly game Pix had taught them, trying to set a biscuit on their forehead and then drop it into their mouths.

Great Mother, thank you for this moment.

"Enjoy it, Boudica. Because the storm is gathering," a gravelly voice replied.

Andraste.

Bran's party left early the following morning. I waited with them as they prepared to ride out.

"To think," Bec said, "it all started in Venta, didn't it?" she said, looking toward the city. "Who knew what would come of that Beltane celebration? All our lives were transformed."

"They were," I agreed, then hugged her. "Be well, Priestess."

"You too, Princess," she told me and then mounted. "Bellicus," she called to the boy, who was still busy making jokes with Sorcha and Caturin.

Bellicus said goodbye to the others and then mounted.

I went to Bran.

"Send word if there is any news."

I nodded to him. "May the gods watch over you, Brother."

"And you."

With that, Bran gestured for them to ride out.

Out of the corner of my eye, I saw Cai give Pix one last kiss before he mounted his horse and joined the others.

Pix joined me. "Now the winter comes."

I nodded.

"At least I got one last ride before the snow fell," she said with a laugh, then slapped me on the shoulder.

"Ouch," I complained.

"Yer bones are getting brittle, old lady," Pix told me, then turned to Sorcha. "Come on, ye. You too, Caturin. Get yer spears," Pix told them, then headed to the stables.

Olwen joined me, pressing her cheek into my shoulder.

"I'm sad too," I said with a sigh. "Come on. Let's see if Ronat has any honey cakes left. We can eat our way to happiness again," I told my daughter, then we headed back inside.

THE WINTER WAS LONG, cold, dark, and miserable. All news ceased to flow, and the winds blew in and snow along with it. The elders said it had not snowed so much or been so cold since they were children. All activity ground to a halt for months on end.

For us, the cold was miserable.

For the Romans, it was worse.

I gladly smirked when they passed through, shivering in their too-thin garbs.

When spring finally arrived, the warm air melted all that deep snow, leading to flooding. The rivers Tas and Yare both flooded their banks. Prasutagus, Artur, and all the rest of the king's guard worked tirelessly to prevent damage to the docks and houses along the river.

Prasutagus had left early one spring morning to try to save a dock on the Yare when riders were announced.

I was surprised when Madogh and Arian appeared. Their horses were covered in mud. Both were soaked to the bone and looked road-weary.

Madogh helped the priestess from her horse, then the pair rushed to join me.

"Queen Boudica," Madogh said hurriedly.

I gestured for them to follow me inside, passing Balfor on the way.

"Balfor, the king…" I said.

He nodded, then hurriedly left the roundhouse.

I led the pair into the meeting chamber. Olwen and I

had lingered there that morning, Olwen sewing while I worked. My daughter looked up when I entered, her gaze going from Madogh and Arian to me.

"Olwen, sweet one, do you mind…"

She nodded and collected her things. As she moved to go, she paused and looked at Arian. Olwen raised her hands to her forehead in a gesture of respect, then left the chamber.

"How did she…" Arian began.

"She is a special child," I said. "Now, are you hurt, either of you? Do you need medical attention or—"

"No, Queen Boudica," Madogh said. "We are well. It's only…Governor Veranius is dead. He died at Verulamium."

"How?" I asked, looking from Madogh to Arian.

"Not me," she said, "this time." She smirked. "But they do suspect the druids. As soon as the thaw began, the governor started pushing west. He ordered the legions to attack one of the druid strongholds. The morning after the attack, they woke to find the governor's face had turned blue. His tongue, fingers, and toes were all black, and he was as stiff as a board. Poison or curse, they cannot say, but the druids are blamed. Nevertheless, it was enough to make them pull back to wait for further instruction from Rome. I think my time in Londinium is done."

I nodded to her. "You are welcome in the King's Wood or north, if you wish, in the Grove of Andraste."

"Thank you. I will… Let me think on it," she said, then glanced at Madogh.

Unsure of the meaning of their exchange, I asked, "Is there news from Rome?"

Madogh shook his head. "I will sail from here to Gaul and see what I can learn. I just wanted to get Arian to safety and the news to you and Prasutagus before I departed," he said, looking back at the priestess.

This time, I saw it.

There was affection between them.

"You have our eternal thanks. I have sent for the king. Come, warm yourselves by the fire, and I'll find you something to eat and drink," I said, then moved to leave the chamber.

When I was at the door, I heard Madogh whisper, "I will ask her about staying with my sister when she returns. I'm sure she'll agree."

I smiled lightly but said nothing. I merely went on my way. Madogh had lived in service to Prasutagus and me, skulking about wherever we sent him. Arian had done the same for her own reasons. The pair, it seemed, were well-suited to one another.

After requesting food, I returned to the meeting room.

"Everything in Londinium is in upheaval," Arian told me. "The Romans are abuzz about what the emperor will do. Many believe they will begin to recall their forces."

"What do you think?" I asked Madogh.

He shook his head. "I am not certain, my queen. Broc has been in Rome, trying to learn what he can, watching where troops are being dispatched. That news of the gold mines in Ordovices lands has whet Nero's appetite. But this death... It will be a deciding factor. Now, they will either push hard or retreat. We will not know until the new governor comes."

Prasutagus joined us later that morning after Madogh and Arian had something warm to eat and a chance to dry up. Madogh shared with my husband his plan to go to Gaul.

"Broc will ride from Rome to Gaul with news as soon as there is any," Madogh reassured the king. "And my contacts may know something. I will report back as soon as I hear."

"As always, go safely," Prasutagus said, then turned to Arian. "We must see to your comfort as well. How can we help you, Priestess?

"I..." Arian said, then turned to Madogh.

"With your blessings, King Prasutagus and Queen Boudica, Arian and I will wed before I leave for Gaul. Arian will stay with my sister until my return. Then, we will see to our own home."

"Oh, that is wonderful news," Prasutagus said, then smiled.

"May the Mother bless you both. Of course, you have our blessings."

"I am not done working on your behalf yet," Arian told us. "I, too, have contacts in Londinium. Madogh and I will continue our work."

Prasutagus and I grinned at the pair. "Let's have some blueberry wine to toast the couple," he said. "For, all the gods know, we should snatch every happy moment we get during these uncertain times."

As it turned out, my husband was right.

Uncertain was the theme of the moment. But it didn't take long for the storm clouds to roll in. The first warning of the coming storm came from an unexpected source.

A trading ship arrived in Yarmouth carrying an unexpected messenger.

"Queen Boudica," Balfor called to me, finding me in the stables. "There is a messenger at the gate for you."

"Who is it?"

"I cannot rightly say. He rode in with some people from Yarmouth. He said only that he has come from Rome and will only speak to you."

I frowned. "I don't like this," I said, feeling suspicious.

"Nor I, but he says to tell you he is a trader."

"A trader of what?"

"Well, that's the thing," Balfor said, looking confused. "He said he's a trader of roses."

I stilled.

Aulus.

Had Aulus come?

Certainly, Balfor would have recognized him.

Setting down my bucket, I wiped my hands on my apron, pulled it off, then quickly made my way across the courtyard.

Balfor whistled to the gate, and the men opened the edifice, letting a robed and hooded man within.

My hands shook.

Would Aulus dare such a trip?

I quickened my step.

When the young man dropped his hood to reveal his shaggy-cut, golden-blond hair, I was disappointed. Did I really think Aulus would come here just for me? How very stupid of me. That said, while the trader was Roman in appearance, I didn't know him. I slowed my step.

"Search him," I called to the guards, who quickly frisked the man for weapons, removing his daggers and a sword.

"I don't know you, sir," I told him.

"Queen Boudica. I carry a message for the rose of Britannia from one invested in your welfare."

Pix, who had appeared out of nowhere, stepped to my side.

I gestured for the man to join me. Leaving the guards, we walked away from the gate toward the vegetable garden where Ronat and Betha were working, tidying up the beds of vegetables and pulling weeds.

"Who be ye?" Pix asked the young man.

"My name is Atticus. I serve Aulus Plautius," he said, looking around to ensure no others could hear us. "Queen Boudica, I must be brief and gone from this place before I am recognized. Aulus Plautius sends you warm greetings but also a warning. There has been a shift in Rome. Emperor Nero is determined to complete —as swiftly and brutally as needed—the work General Plautius started. In Rome, Gaius Suetonius Paulinus is named Governor of Britannia. General Plautius sent me to warn you. Governor Paulinus makes Scapula look like a tame kitten. General Plautius said to look after your sister. As well he said to tell you that his offer remains. Although he was unclear on the offer, I assume you understand his meaning."

I nodded. "Thank you, Atticus. Won't you come inside for a moment's rest?"

The man shook his head. "A ship departs for Gaul this afternoon. I must be on it. I have traveled half the world to relay the governor's warning to you. I hope it will be of use to you."

"It is. Please, express my deep gratitude to Aulus for his warning. I know the risk he has taken to send you here. I am beyond grateful. While I must decline his offer, please tell him I think of it often."

Atticus nodded.

"Here, ye," Pix said, handing her full water skin to the man. "Have that and this," she added, giving him a sack hanging from her belt. "I was about to go out. It be full of rations."

"Thank you," Atticus told Pix. "Queen Boudica," he said, bowing to me, then returned to the gate. There, he met with the guard. After he reclaimed his weapons, he pulled up his hood once more and then departed.

"What did all that mean to ye?" Pix asked.

"Paulinus is coming for the druids. Mona is in danger, as are the rest of us. Rome will cut our throats if we dare get in the way. This time, they will get what they want or die trying."

"What will ye do?"

I frowned, not having an answer.

"And the governor's offer?"

"That was personal." I paused. "Aulus asked me to go away with him. He offered to take me from here before he left."

"But ye stayed."

"Of course I stayed. I would not have you taking my spot in Prasutagus's bed," I told her with a wink.

Pix chuckled, then asked, "Did ye consider it?"

"For a heartbeat. A world without war on a picturesque villa surrounded by grapevines and endless sunshine? Yes. For just a heartbeat. But no more than that."

"I bet twas a pretty heartbeat."

"It was."

"I was about to ride to the King's Wood. Prasutagus will not be back until nightfall. Want to come with me? I promise not to pepper ye with questions."

I nodded. "Yes," I said, seeing that beautiful vision dance before my eyes again. I saw fields with waving shafts of grain and row upon row of grapevines, I heard myself and Aulus laughing together and tasted wine in my mouth. I felt the summer sunshine on my bare arms, dressed in a Roman-style gown. I felt his hand on my skin and the ease in my heart—not being responsible for anything or anyone. I closed my eyes, holding on to the image, knowing, *knowing,* that Aulus still loved me. I let my mind relish the idea for just a moment, then let go, absorbing the true content of Aulus's message.

It had been a warning.

The next wave of the Roman invasion was about to begin.

CHAPTER 31

Aulus's warning was echoed in the coming months. For most of the spring, we saw no change in Roman behavior. They simply held the line. But what Aulus warned us of, Madogh confirmed. Forces began to amass in Gaul. Governor Paulinus and a man by the name of Agricola were coming, and with them, additional forces.

The Romans arrived in Londinium in autumn and began at once gearing up for a massive assault on the west.

But unlike his predecessor, who seemed to forget that the Iceni existed, aside from taxing our people into poverty, one of Governor Paulinus's first acts was to summon Prasutagus and myself to Londinium.

"And what is the nature of the summons?" Prasutagus asked the Roman messenger.

The man stood before us in the formal meeting hall, his helmet tucked under his arm.

"To assess the Norther and Greater Iceni," the man replied.

"Assess us for what?" Prasutagus asked, irritation peppering his voice.

"Loyalty, King Prasutagus."

At that, Prasutagus tightened his grip on the arms of his chair.

"I am sure the new governor will find all in order in Northern and Greater Iceni territory," I said congenially.

"Hardly, Queen Boudica. Already, we've had to replace the lax Roman soldiers garrisoned in Oak Throne. Your northern province lacks oversight."

"As Governor Scapula knew well, the Northern Iceni did not rebel as a whole. Only a small segment of our people acted out of order and met with Rome's swift retribution. The Northern Iceni have been loyal since they've been under my rule. We are client rulers, not conquered peoples."

The Roman sniffed loudly and then rolled his eyes. "That is for Governor Paulinus to determine."

"That is what was sworn to Emperor Claudius himself," Prasutagus said stiffly.

"Well, Claudius is no longer with us, is he?" the man said, then handed Prasutagus a scroll. "Can you read Latin, or should I—"

"I can read Latin," Prasutagus retorted hotly.

"Good, then you will read there what is expected of you. Good day," the man said, then brusquely left the meeting chamber, breezing past Balfor, who rushed to catch up with him.

"A prig, that one," Pix said in irritation. "Want me to track him and let a faerie arrow find his back on his way to Londinium."

"In my mind, I can imagine nothing better," Prasutagus said. "Each iteration of Rome that arrives at my doorstep gets progressively worse. Who knew Aulus Plautius would be the best of them?" Prasutagus said without looking up from his scroll.

Pix and I exchanged a quick glance then I asked, "What does it say?"

"We have a week to get to Londinium. And... And they want the outstanding interest on the loan given to us by Rome."

"Loan? What loan?"

"The twenty-million sesterces loaned to the Greater Iceni under Governor Plautius," Prasutagus said, confusion in his voice.

"That was no loan. That was given to us as compensation for staying our hands in the opening conflicts."

Prasutagus shifted the scroll so I could see. "What he says we owe."

When I saw the number, I gasped. "He cannot be serious."

"I guess we'll find out next week."

"Prasutagus, if he demands that payment…"

"Then we will be destitute. I will refuse to pay it and send a messenger to Nero myself."

"That will only anger Governor Paulinus."

"Do I have a choice?"

I scanned over the document. There was no mention of the money given to Caturix, only that *loaned* to the Greater Iceni. Thank the gods for that. But the conditions of the funds were very much misconstrued, as was his manner of suggesting we had failed to repay the loan, plus interest, when it was never presented as anything but a gift.

"What if they ask about the money given to Caturix?" I asked Prasutagus, unable to hide the fear in my voice. The gods only knew where that coin had gone because it certainly wasn't in Oak Throne.

"If that happens, Boudica, then we might as well do as the druids ask because Rome will come for all that is ours either way."

WE MADE our way to Londinium on the appointed date, unsure what to expect from Governor Paulinus. In the days before our departure, Sorcha made an impassioned plea to join us.

"Londinium is a hard place, Sorcha. I would not have my daughter there," Prasutagus told her.

"Father, I can fight well. I even disarmed Pix this week."

"'Twas an accident," Pix quipped.

"Liar," Sorcha told her with a wink.

"I am not. She can manage herself, and I will not leave her side," Pix reassured Prasutagus.

"Nor I," Artur said.

"Please, let me come. I want to see. May the gods forbid it, but if anything should happen to you or Mother, I will be the queen of the Greater Iceni. I must know what I am facing. Secluded in Venta, I only see a sliver of the world. Let me play my part. I am no meek princess waiting for some *fruitful* marriage contract," she said, rolling her eyes. "Those days are done. One day, I will be a leader. I must listen and learn."

In the back of the room, Vian cleared her throat and said, "I was little older than Sorcha when you took me to Camulodunum."

Sorcha gave Vian a grateful smile.

Knowing we'd been defeated, I turned to Prasutagus.

Prasutagus sighed. "Very well, but you will do as we say. And no sneaking about."

Sorcha's face lit up in a smile.

"Sorcha," I said in all seriousness. "Londinium… It is not like here. You will see things that will disturb and upset you. You must prepare yourself."

She nodded. "That is why I want to come," she told me. "I don't want to be ignorant of what you're facing anymore."

I was proud of her. Sorcha was sensitive to Artur's position in the house but knew she would be the next queen. It was good that she wanted to learn, even if we, her parents, didn't want to expose her to the world's harshness.

So, with Sorcha along with us, we made our way to Londinium under heavy guard. After considerable discussion, we decided that it was best that Artur stayed in Venta. The Roman summons was odd. If it were somehow a deception… With the city on high alert and the king's house well-guarded, Artur taking charge, we left Venta feeling anxiety over what lay ahead of us and for those we left behind.

The only bright spot in an otherwise unfortunate trip was seeing Sorcha's delight in being at sea.

"I can imagine adventuring beyond the horizon," she said. "Do women captain ships? Maybe I can have my own merchant vessel."

"What will ye trade?" Pix asked.

Sorcha paused. "I don't know. Maybe my sword... I could be a mercenary or an assassin." She laughed.

"And to think, the fey sent me to look after ye, when the firebrand has so many better adventures in mind," Pix told me.

"Why don't you go together? Sail to Éire and meet the kings of Tara."

"Or to the Isle of Mists," Sorcha said. "I could find Scáthach's secret training school."

"Scáthach is long dead, I'm afraid," Prasutagus told her.

"Perhaps, but surely others keep her traditions."

"They do," I said. "I have met one from the Isle of Mists—Cien, sister of Chieftain Lynet of Frog's Hollow."

Sorcha grinned excitedly at Pix. "When do you want to leave?"

Pix merely laughed.

We sailed throughout the day and night, traveling up the Thames the following morning to Londinium.

As we neared the city, Sorcha grew quiet as she watched the landscape change. Suddenly, everything had become far more...Roman.

When we drew near the city, we got a closer look at the bridge across the river, which was nearly complete.

"They built *that*?" Sorcha asked.

Prasutagus nodded.

"And the gods allowed it?"

We didn't answer.

Sorcha's eyes took in Londinium, disgust in her expression.

"It is not what you expected," I said.

"No."

"Worse?"

She nodded.

"We warned you."

"I know. It's just seeing and imagining..." she said, watching as Roman soldiers unloaded a boat full of raggedly dressed and bound captives, pushing and kicking them to make them move faster down the dock. "Who are they?"

I shook my head. "Dobunni, maybe. Cornovii."

Sorcha stared but said nothing more.

We made port, the others tying up the ship, then made our way to the villa where Eudaf greeted us.

"King Prasutagus, Queen Boudica. Welcome. A messenger from the governor's villa was here an hour ago asking for you. We told them you were expected today. They ask that you come to the villa upon your arrival."

"Well, I hope the governor will be patient enough for me to have something to drink and to wash my face," I replied in annoyance.

"From his reputation, I quite doubt it," Eudaf said,

then led us inside.

"Eudaf, this is our daughter, Princess Sorcha."

"Princess," Eudaf said, bowing deeply.

The house smelled of baking breads and roasting meat. Ede brought us all some wine, and we took our rest, Sorcha exploring the place.

Not long after our arrival—barely half a goblet's worth—there was noise at the gate.

"I shall go see," Eudaf said, then departed.

He returned a few moments later, looking annoyed.

"A messenger from the villa. I've asked him to stay in the courtyard. He is here to escort you to the governor's villa."

I looked at Prasutagus.

"Then he will enjoy us perfumed by sea air and sweat," Prasutagus said, setting down his goblet with an annoyed huff. "Sorcha? Pix?" Prasutagus called.

"We're going?" I asked Prasutagus, feeling annoyed. "As we are?"

"As we are," my husband replied.

Along with Sorcha, Vian, Pix, and our guard, we made our way to the governor's villa. Four Roman soldiers had come with the messenger to escort us.

We were immediately led inside the governor's villa and escorted to a small meeting chamber overlooking the Thames.

"Well, if all goes awry, ye can jump out the window," Pix quipped.

"Or toss him out of it," Prasutagus grumbled.

A few moments later, a stout man brusquely walked into the room. He went to his desk, then turned and looked at us. He was a short, muscular man with a heavy black brow and black and silver hair receding from his hairline. He had a long nose and sharp grey eyes.

His gaze danced from Prasutagus to me, flicking briefly behind us at Sorcha, Vian, and Pix.

He huffed a laugh and then turned to Prasutagus. "Chieftain Prasutagus, I presume."

"King Prasutagus," my husband corrected him.

"And your wife, Boudica, is it?" the man asked, looking at me.

"I am Queen Boudica of the Iceni."

He huffed in amusement. "I am Governor Paulinus. I have been reviewing the notes of the previous governors —if you could call them that—in charge of this part of the empire and have found some serious financial discrepancies concerning the Greater Iceni's payment of taxes and repayment of loans. Rome does not abide thieves," he said sharply, then looked at Prasutagus. "What do you have to say for yourself?"

I could see from the look on my husband's face that Prasutagus wanted to strangle the man.

"Governor Paulinus, the Greater Iceni have paid our assessed taxes, even when they were raised without warning, with no default. I received your missives regarding the taxation on the gift given to our people by Emperor Claudius through Aulus Plautius. There is a misunderstanding in your records, Governor. That was a gift, not a loan. No interest was owed and no payment was expected."

Paulinus laughed. "That is a good story, Prasutagus. Did you come up with that tale on the way from Venta?"

"It is no lie, Governor. Write to Aulus Plautius yourself. He will confirm what we are saying here."

"You would instruct *me* to write to Aulus Plautius?" the man asked Prasutagus, venom in his voice.

"If you will not, I will send a messenger myself. I would think the empire would be more organized in its record-keeping. The sums you mention were clearly a gift from Claudius in appreciation of our leniency toward Rome during the initial invasion," Prasutagus replied stiffly.

"Are you insinuating our emperor bribed you?"

"I insinuate nothing. It was a gift, as Aulus Plautius can confirm."

"I am not interested in the opinion of former governors of this realm. Emperor Nero has called in your debt, Chieftain."

"*King*. And that is impossible," Prasutagus said bitterly.

"Is it? You question our emperor?" Paulinus asked hotly. "Men have found themselves clapped in irons for less."

"We know that very well," I retorted, "and have seen it with our own eyes. You are asking for a return of funds—and a great sum—that no one ever, not once, insinuated was to be repaid. Let alone with interest."

"'Tis robbery," Pix muttered angrily.

"Tell your servant to mind her tongue," Paulinus snapped, glaring at Pix. "I say, Prasutagus, you are quite the cuckold. Are there no men in the Greater Iceni lands?" he asked, then laughed.

Prasutagus turned red, and I saw murder in his gaze.

"You have been granted a grace of one year to make the full payment. But the interest is due when the procurator visits," Governor Paulinus said. "That is all I can offer."

"Governor, you cannot possibly expect us to repay a gift—" I began, but Paulinus cut me off.

"Pay your debts, woman, or we will take what you owe in land or people. Now, you are excused," he said, then waved to a servant to escort us away.

"Chieftain," the man said, gesturing toward the door.

But Prasutagus didn't budge. "You know it was not a

loan. As does your emperor," he told Paulinus coldly. "You would dip your hand into Greater Iceni coffers and lands after the loyalty we have shown Rome?" he said, a dark edge on his voice. In it, I heard a warning.

And so did Paulinus.

"Would you threaten me, Chieftain?" Paulinus said, meeting Prasutagus's gaze. "You have a daughter, I see. I suppose you imagine she will lead your people once you're dead. Pay your debts, Briton, or there will be no Greater Iceni left for the girl to rule. Now, go. I have far more important matters to consider."

I looked from Paulinus to Prasutagus then set my hand on my husband's arm.

"Come, Prasutagus," I whispered.

"Yes, yes, listen to your women," Paulinus said with a laugh, then turned to his secretary, who had been sitting at a table nearby, scribbling notes. "I dare say it is a good thing Roman women know to hold their tongues and are beaten when they don't."

The secretary chuckled.

"Prasutagus," I whispered harshly, pulling on his arm.

Enraged, my husband turned, then we all left the room.

Sorcha, who had never seen her father disrespected in all her life, looked back at Paulinus with fire in her eyes.

I kept moving forward, my hand on Prasutagus's arm, my heart beating hard in my chest.

Rome had finally found a way.

They would choke us with a tax we could not afford. When we couldn't pay it, they would take our lands and people.

Or force us to rebel against them.

Either way, Rome could win it all.

CHAPTER 32

Prasutagus was silent as we returned to the villa.

While I'd expected Pix to chatter on endlessly in annoyance, she, too, said nothing.

All of us realized the magnitude of what was happening.

Rome was playing the endgame.

When we arrived at the villa, Prasutagus excused himself and went upstairs to our private bedchamber.

Pix, Vian, Sorcha, and I sat in the house's main room, all of us stunned to silence.

Finally, Sorcha broke the barrier, looking at me with the embers of flames still in her eyes. "Mother," she said softly.

I met my daughter's gaze. "He thinks he can

maneuver us, that we will fall into his hands. He is wrong."

"He is a spider," Vian said. "He began weaving before he set foot on this island."

"Yes," I said, looking into the flame of the brazier burning there. "But he is not the only one who is plotting." I looked back at Sorcha. "You do not need to fear."

"Oh, I don't," she said with a hard laugh. "I only hope that one day, I can wrap my hand around that man's throat and watch the light fade from his eyes."

"If I don't get there first," Pix said with a laugh that Sorcha joined.

But my gaze went to Vian, who held a warning glance in her eyes.

Now, we would have to dance to Rome's tune, or, like so many others, the Iceni would fall.

Leaving the others behind, I went upstairs, where I found Prasutagus sitting at the end of the bed, staring out the open balcony doors. His mind was very far away. Moving quietly, I sat beside him.

We remained that way for a long time, then Prasutagus said, "I will arrange for the sale of the villa. That will help us raise funds to pay the interest. Once it is done, Eudaf, Eda, and Briganna can come to Venta."

I studied my husband's face. Rather than frustration or sadness, I saw he was smothering rage.

"And after?"

Prasutagus looked at me. "We will never be able to repay that gift in one year. Boudica, they are coming for us. By the time we are done paying, nothing will be left of the Greater Iceni for Sorcha, Olwen, or Bellicus. Make no mistake, he is coming for the Northern Iceni as well."

"We must speak to Bran."

Prasutagus nodded.

"And we will whisper to the oaks, the stones, and the brotherhood that tends them," I said.

"And to Camulos's children who have already fallen to the eagle, even though their king sits on the throne," Prasutagus said, referring to the Trinovantes.

My heart pounded in my chest.

Is this really happening?

"Prasutagus?" I whispered.

My husband set his hand on my cheek. "We gambled. For many years, we stayed a step ahead. Now... Now, we must draw a new hand and begin again, or else end up neighbors to Caratacus in Rome."

"May all the gods forbid it."

"You may need to call all of them, Boudica. Because, if the druids are right and our gods are dying, it may take all of us working together if we are going to survive."

PRASUTAGUS DID NOT SLEEP MOST of the night. It was the grey hour before dawn when he rose. He sat for a long time at the side of the bed.

"Prasutagus?" I whispered.

"Boudica, will you write to Aulus Plautius?" he asked. "We will send a messenger to Rome before we depart. Tell him what has happened and ask him to help us."

"I…" I began, then said, "Yes. I will see to it. But he may not be able to do anything."

"I know," Prasutagus said darkly. "But we must try everything we can think of," he said, then turned and looked at me. "Perhaps Aulus can convince Nero it is better to keep the Iceni quiet. We have no way of knowing what influence, if any, Aulus still has. But if he has even a little, it is better to try than do nothing."

"Yes."

"I will take Eudaf and go to the forum, speak to the men there about the sale of the villa. Then, I will go to the market. We must increase our prices at every port to weather this storm."

"What else can I do?"

Prasutagus shook his head. "Prepare the missive," he

said, then looked at me. "Use whatever influence you think will work best."

"Prasutagus…"

"Boudica, I am not blind to the affection Aulus holds for you. He sent us a warning, and he did not lie. I am sorry to ask you to use it to our advantage, but we must try for our daughters' and our people's sake."

"I will attend to it."

"Thank you," he said, leaning back to kiss my cheek. "We will return to Venta tomorrow. I want to stay in Londinium, go to the taverns, listen, and see. If Paulinus is squeezing us, what else is he up to? Broc is here. I have not yet seen him, but he has made himself known. I will meet with him as well."

"Be careful, Prasutagus. Paulinus may have eyes on you."

"He already does," Prasutagus said, gesturing for me to accompany him. We went to the balcony. A man was peddling furs from a small table in the street below. The pelts were nothing special, and the man made little effort to entice early-morning buyers. And he *especially* made every effort not to look up at Prasutagus and me. "He's been there all night," my husband whispered. "Another man comes and goes, gathering a report. Watch yourself if you go anywhere today. You will likely be followed."

I nodded.

With that, Prasutagus dressed and made his way downstairs.

When he was gone, I went to the desk in our bedchamber and pulled out some parchment. I stared at the blank page before me.

Aulus…

I closed my eyes, remembering that last moment when he'd come to see me in Venta.

And then, I made my plea.

There was little use, but Prasutagus was right.

We had to try.

AFTER I PREPARED THE MISSIVE, I set it aside and dressed to go out. Downstairs, I found the others lingering, but Vian was running calculations, her mind working hard. She barely noticed me.

Sorcha and Pix both looked up when I entered.

"I'm going out," I told them. "Want to come?"

Pix and Sorcha both nodded.

"Vian?"

She waved some fingers at me.

"If Prasutagus returns, there is a letter waiting upstairs."

Vian merely nodded, then the three of us departed.

"And where are we going?" Pix asked as we made our way from the villa.

"For answers."

We left the villa, making our way down the streets of Londinium.

"Look happy and distracted," I whispered to the others. "Oh, your father won't mind if we spend a little," I told Sorcha with a laugh. "A new dress or two never hurt anyone."

"Perhaps a new horse?" Sorcha said, playing along.

"And a pair of blades?" Pix suggested.

"If you mean earrings, perhaps," I said, laughing loudly—and stupidly—as we passed the fur vendor who picked up our trail and followed behind us.

"I love the color vermillion," I said, turning the corner. "I do hope I can find a gown in that shade," I said loudly as we turned from sight. I gestured to Pix. "Grab him."

When Paulinus's spy turned the corner, Pix grabbed him by the collar.

When the man went for his dagger, Sorcha acted quickly, bashing the weapon from his hand.

I picked up the blade and set it on the man's neck.

"What did Paulinus instruct you to do?" I asked the man, who wriggled to get free but didn't answer.

Pix held the man by the throat and then punched

him in the nose. Blood leaked down his face. "She asked ye a question."

"Again, why were you sent?" I demanded.

"To watch," the man choked out.

"You have been watching, but it wasn't Prasutagus you followed. Why did you follow us?"

"I was… I was instructed to… to grab the princess."

"Why, you dirty sod," Sorcha said, kneeing the man in the groin.

"Paulinus sent you to grab my daughter?"

"Y-yes," the man choked out.

"And do what with her?" I said, pressing a knife into his throat.

The man didn't answer.

"And do what with her?" I demanded again.

Again, he didn't answer. And this time, I realized why. He would not say what was too horrific to tell. And suddenly, he'd come to understand what might happen to him if he spoke the truth. Paulinus had sent the man to snatch Sorcha and kill her.

"Let's go for a walk," I said, gesturing to Pix. "All of us."

Pix grabbed the man roughly, quickly binding his hands behind his back, then the three of us turned and headed toward the governor's villa, pulling the man along with us. The only amusing part of the affair was that such rough behavior had become so commonplace in Londinium, no one barely batted an eye at us. To our luck, we arrived at the governor's villa just as the man was preparing to ride out. He was at the gate with three other well-dressed Romans.

As we drew nearer, Paulinus's guards stiffened.

"Hold there," one of the men called to us.

"Hold yerself, Rome," Pix replied, and we pushed forward.

When the guards moved to intervene, I called out, "Governor Paulinus! Governor!"

The governor only briefly flicked his attention my way, thinking me little more than rabble.

"Get back, you," one of the soldiers said, stepping toward me.

"Would you place your hands on the Queen of the Iceni?" I spat at the man, then called once more. "Governor!"

At that, the governor paused and waved for the men he'd been speaking to be silent. He motioned for us to come forward.

"Ah, Chieftain Boudica?" he said. "How can Rome assist you this morning, Chieftain?"

"I have a gift for you," I told him, then gestured to Pix who shoved the cutthroat forward.

The man stumbled on the Roman-paved road, falling at the governor's feet.

Paulinus looked from the man to me.

"A gift from the emperor's loyal client queen to Rome. And to show my loyalty, I return him to you intact…a much better gift, I think, than what you planned for me and mine. Next time, Rome, I would prefer earrings or perhaps a nice vase to show Rome's continuing friendship, lest there be some sort of *misunderstanding* between us."

As he pulled on his gloves, the governor's lips curled into a smile. "I see no misunderstanding here, Chieftain."

"Why, I should—" Pix began, but I motioned for her to be silent.

"Be careful on your ride, Governor. Our forests are full of old, dangerous things. The fiercest, of course, are mother bears. There is nothing they will not do to protect what is theirs."

Paulinus gave me a sly smile. "Or they will die trying. Good day to you, Chieftain," he said, motioning for his men to take the assassin away. Paying me no more attention, he mounted his horse, the others doing the same, then rode off.

One of the Roman soldiers came forward to usher us off, but Pix gave him a stern look, and he backed away.

I motioned to Pix and Sorcha to depart.

"We should not have brought you," I told Sorcha as we made our way back into the city.

Sorcha shook her head. "No. I'm glad you did. I've

been a child. I never knew what you faced. Now, I see what you are up against. I cannot be a child any longer."

"You see the game they play."

Sorcha nodded. "Yes. They will take what is ours either by taxation or inciting rebellion."

"Yes."

"What will we do?" Sorcha asked, looking from Pix to me.

"We will play the game," I replied, "until we reach the end of the road."

"And then?"

"And then, we will bring fire."

CHAPTER 33

We departed Londinium the following day, with a heavy sense of dread. The sky, it seemed, felt our mood. Dark clouds had rolled in, turning everything grey and blocking the sun. In the distance, thunder rumbled.

When I had told Prasutagus what had transpired with the assassin, the air about him grew cold, and my husband's gaze grew dark.

"We must start to prepare. You must speak to Arixus, tell him to increase his output, and we will do the same in our lands," Prasutagus said.

"The Romans may suspect."

"Not if we are careful," Prasutagus said. "Now, every step we take must be weighed and measured, and our treasures shielded," he said, looking to Sorcha.

"Protected from harm, yes. But not protected from the truth. Sorcha is the future of our tribe. She should see every step we take, understand our choices, and know our allies and enemies. If we fall—"

"If we fall, Boudica, nothing will be left for Sorcha."

"Not necessarily. Look at King Diras. Look at Verica's heirs. They thrive because they have learned to play the game—although, Diras's achievements are actually his mother's. We must let Sorcha see. She is not a child anymore."

Prasutagus eyed our daughter, who was playing some sort of hand game with one of our warriors, the pair counting numbers on their fingers and then racing to slap one another's hands. They laughed loudly as they competed.

"It is hard to realize. I still see my little girl."

"Yes."

"When I think of what Paulinus tried to do... It never occurred to me that they would target her."

"He is trying to provoke a war."

"He has. He just doesn't know it yet."

"Then, are we giving him what he wants?" I asked Prasutagus.

"He wants the Greater Iceni to rebel. That is not what we're planning."

I held my husband's gaze.

No. That wasn't what we were planning. It was not the Greater Iceni alone we hoped to persuade to rise with us. It was the east. *All* of the east.

"We will bide our time," Prasutagus told me. "Make our plans."

"And how many insults will we suffer between now and then?"

"More than we can name."

WHEN WE RETURNED TO VENTA, Prasutagus and Vian quickly got to work ensuring that the Greater Iceni would have ample finances to pay the coming tariffs. And we planned for more.

"I will ride to Chieftain Lors," Prasutagus said, speaking of the Trinovantes chieftain. "We will speak of the new governor. I sent Madogh to find Chieftain Adirix of the Catuvellauni. He has been in hiding."

I nodded. "When you return, I will ride north to Bran and Arixus."

"It will take time, but we must prepare. I will have Artur come with me. But before I go, however, I must speak to Tavish. I do not trust the Romans to leave the

King's Wood in peace. I'm going to advise Tavish to move the druids."

"To where?" I asked in surprise.

"The druids walk the lines of power. To the north-west, there is a small but ancient grove dedicated to Elen of the Ways. It is a sacred, secret temple of the druids, known only to those who walk our path—or to the hunters Elen leads there. They will be safer hidden in the woods, away from the city."

"But the people... Won't they be frightened if the druids flee."

"By now, the people will have heard the rumors coming from the west. They will understand."

I was not so sure. The druids were a symbol of our power, of stability. In the north, the priestesses of the Grove of Andraste gave comfort to the Northern Iceni. If they were to flee...

I didn't argue with Prasutagus but merely nodded. While I understood Prasutagus's reasons, I was not sure Tavish would be so quick to agree. It was for the druid to decide.

With the plan settled, Prasutagus prepared to depart.

"Watch yourself while I am gone. Arian spotted men in the city who were watching the king's house—they lie under the dirt now, but more will come. I will lose any who follow me, but you must be wary. Don't let the girls go anywhere without a guard."

I nodded. "I will pray to the gods for your safe return. My druid husband," I said, touching his cheek.

"My Strawberry Queen."

With that, Prasutagus kissed me, and then he and Artur rode off with a small band of warriors.

I went to the wall and watched them ride away, my eyes on Prasutagus. Nearby, a murder of crows lifted off, cawing loudly as they went. The birds flew in the same direction as my husband, following Prasutagus from Venta and into an unknown future.

WAITING for Prasutagus to return proved painful.

Instead of wondering how talks were going and fearing we'd be found out, I dragged Pix and Sorcha to the courtyard where I took out a training spear and squared off against my daughter and my bodyguard.

"I am far too rusty," I said. "Gaheris would laugh if he saw me now."

Sorcha's brow furrowed. "Who is Gaheris?"

"I..." I said, then paused, realizing my daughter would have no reason to ever know nor hear Gaheris's name. "He was the son of Chieftain Lynet and a good friend. He taught me how to fight. And if he had not died, you probably would have looked like him."

At that, Olwen, who had come to watch us work, laughed and then signed the symbol of Beith, or birch, the first of the Ogham.

I nodded to her. "Yes, he was my first love."

Sorcha laughed. "That's impossible. I can't imagine you with anyone but Father."

"That's because they have soul magic," Pix explained. "Yer parents are bound in the old ways and have been lovers for many lifetimes."

Sorcha paused. "Is there really such a thing?"

Pix nodded. "Ye should ask the druids. But 'tis true. When you meet your soul match, ye will know."

Sorcha's brow scrunched up as she considered. While I'd never seen Sorcha show any sign of affection for anyone, she was certainly old enough, and plenty of the young men in Artur's warband had taken notice of her.

"Bah," she finally said. "No one has time for that now," she said, then pulled her sword. "All right, *Chieftain*," she told me with a knowing look, "you'd best firm up your grip. If you hold it like that, I'll have your spear —and you—on the ground before you know it."

At that, I laughed. "All right, Firebrand," I told her. "Do your worst."

Sorcha's worst left me feeling achy. That night, I had

Brita fix me a bath. Afterward, Pix gave me a drink laced with medicinal herbs.

"Ye will be glad of this later. Drink it all," she told me.

"I don't remember things hurting this much," I replied, rotating my shoulder.

Pix laughed. "Just wait until ye are my age," she told me with a wink, tapping her mug against mine.

But, as sore as I was, I returned to the square the following day, and the next, and the next, and continued to practice until my arms began to feel stronger, and my hands remembered how to twirl, thrust, and jab with my spear.

Two weeks later, just after Sorcha and I had finished a bout, Pix appeared from the stables driving a war chariot, Dice harnessed to the front.

"Been working him off and on," she told me, driving in a circle around Sorcha and me. "He was skittish at first, but now, he hauls it with the ease of a mule hauling sacks of grain. Young as he be, he picks up speed quickly. Get on. Both of ye."

"Pix," I said with a frown.

"I know, Boudica. Northern Iceni be horse people, not chariot riders. But ye can be quicker and more deadly in battle in a chariot."

"Who said anything about a battle?" I asked her.

"Paulinus. Or did ye miss that message?"

I frowned at her.

"Hop up, ye. Don't be stubborn. And ye too, Sorcha."

Sorcha grinned. "Finally! I've been begging for months."

Sorcha and I mounted the chariot with Pix, who clicked to Dice. The horse started trotting—quickly. I held on tightly.

"Now, the chariot is light, so the horse can pull ye fast. With both hands free, you can battle easily. Ye just need to learn to keep your balance."

My father and uncle preferred chariots, and even the Romans used them occasionally. Still, I was never one for it, choosing the saddle. All the same, I could see the point Pix was making.

With Olwen safely behind the manned walls of the roundhouse, we rode from the king's house down the streets of Venta.

As we went, I spotted unfamiliar eyes on me.

One man, who looked Gaulish, sat at the tavern, smoking a pipe and observing us as we went by. The moment we passed, he hurried from his table.

"Ye see him?" Pix asked me.

"I did."

"Come on, Dice. Show us what ye have," Pix said, then snapped the reins, coaxing the horse to go faster. We raced away from Venta, moving faster than any spy could follow. We rode down one of the roads that led to Yarmouth but made a turn at the sunflower fields, disappearing down a lane into the crops. We reappeared on the other side in a field of grass. Pix rode across the field, stopping to plant five spears in the ground, then made her way to the end of the row.

"Now, ye will drive," she told me.

"What about me?" Sorcha asked.

"Ye will have your own job," Pix told her, then turned back to me. "Swerve between them like this," Pix said, waving her hand, showing me that she wanted me to lace around the spears.

"The turns are very narrow," I said with a frown.

"That they be, so ye best learn how to make the turns without flipping over yer pretty apple cart."

I switched places with Pix.

"And ye," she told Sorcha. "Ye will hop off at the third spear and remount when your mother drives by once more."

"While the chariot is still moving?" Sorcha asked in surprise.

Pix nodded.

I frowned at her. "She's going to break her leg."

"Nay, she will not. But she will learn to hop on and off the chariot long enough to break *someone else's* leg. Now, walk on," Pix said, gesturing for me to get Dice going.

We began our practice. Training from morning until night, we worked in the chariot. Sorcha grew increasingly good at mounting and dismounting while I worked on driving.

When we returned to the roundhouse, we were all exhausted, including Dice.

As we drove through Venta, I didn't see the spy again.

Later, I discovered why.

I was sitting alone in my private meeting chamber that night, nursing a drink and trying not to whine about my sore arms, when Broc appeared.

I had only met Prasutagus's man a handful of times and hadn't even known he was in Venta. And there he was, standing at the door of my chamber, unannounced.

"Broc," I said, moving to rise.

"Rest, my queen. You worked hard today."

"I..."

"Paulinus's man spent half the day looking for you. He noticed the chariot wheel tracks and discovered your training by chance. He'll be waiting for you tomorrow to help the princess with her target practice."

With that, the man bowed and then disappeared.

Pix and I looked at one another. Pix then laughed and leaned forward, and clinked her cup against mine.

Saying nothing more, she finished her drink and then poured me another.

Today had been a good day.

TRUE TO HIS WORD, Broc left the spy exactly where he had told us. Bound, gagged, blindfolded, and tied to poles, the cutthroat and two other strangers were waiting. I recognized one of the men. He had come with Erbert when the man had delivered new cattle. Erbert had acted oddly that day. Even Betha and Ronat had mentioned it.

"Well," Pix said with a grin. "Seems yer man has given ye something to aim at."

For the first time, however, Sorcha balked. "But they are…they're…"

"Alive. Yes. And sent to kill us," I told her. I set my spear aside and took Sorcha by the shoulders. "May the Morrigu watch over us, my firebrand. All these men have come to Venta to watch us and take advantage of us if they may. Even this man found his way into the king's compound," I said, gesturing. "What if he returned while we were away? He could have killed Olwen, Vian, Caturin, Kennocha, or others. What you must learn to do next is not easy, but let the dark lady

Andraste and the Morrigu guide your hands. You must learn now or perish later."

"Ye know what to do," Pix told her. "Where to strike to end it quickly. I have taught ye that."

And with that, we began. First, we started working the chariot, racing back and forth across the field. I learned how to safely gain speed and make turns without risk.

On our next pass, Pix handed Sorcha a spear. "The first man," she told her.

Saying nothing, Sorcha merely balanced herself and waited until we were in range. And then, she launched the spear. Her aim was true, the spear piercing the man in the heart.

We wove through the spears. When we turned, Pix handed Sorcha a bow and quiver.

"Aim for the throat," she told her, then nodded to me.

We set off once more. Dice raced hard across the field, pulling the chariot quickly.

As we approached the second man, Sorcha shot and missed. Then shot again and again until finally, she hit her mark.

When we again turned the chariot, Pix instructed Sorcha to take the reins. "Ye will take the last man, Boudica. And be ready to remount the chariot once more when we come back. Ye be slow, Strawberry

Queen. And they will kill ye if you stay that way. Get faster."

We set off once more.

When we neared the third man—the man who'd come with Erbert—I hopped off the chariot, raced to the man, then shoved the point of my spear between his ribs to his heart. Yanking it back, I turned and prepared to get back on as the chariot drove by.

Pix was right.

I was slow.

I tried to catch up and hop on as Sorcha approached, but failed.

"Stay there. We will turn back, and ye will try again," Pix called.

Sorcha had made it look so easy. But she had youth on her side.

All I had was rage.

For Caturix's death.

For the treatment of the Northern Iceni.

For the insults Bec, Dindraine, Arian, and so many other women I loved had suffered.

For the tragedy of Maiden Stones and the assaults made on the druids.

For the death of Chieftain Divin and his daughter and for all the others who had fallen to Rome for no reason other than Rome's ambition.

When the chariot rushed toward me again, I braced

myself, gripping my spear tightly as Gaheris had taught me, then hopped back on.

It took me a moment to steady myself, but I managed.

Pix clapped me on the back. "There ye are, Strawberry Queen. Now, we just need to add scythes to your chariot wheels, and we will be ready to harvest Rome."

WE TRAINED DAY AFTER DAY. Sometimes Broc would leave us bodies for target practice. Other times, we only had straw dummies. But with each passing day, our team of three grew better, stronger, and more ready for what would come.

When Prasutagus finally returned almost a month later, he also had news.

"Paulinus is moving west, setting up his new outpost in the western-most regions of Catuvellauni territory. He has left his procurator behind to begin squeezing the rest of us. They say the new procurator is a vile creature. They even gripe about the heavy taxation in the colonia."

"May the gods forbid the usurpers pay taxes for the stolen land they live on," I replied waspishly.

"And the chieftains… What did they say?"

"They listened closely, particularly to what I shared about our visit from Mona. The Trinovantes and the Catuvellauni agree. They will be with us when we choose to act."

"*When*? Not *if*?" I asked Prasutagus, who met my gaze.

"If we have enough support, so we don't meet the same end as Caratacus or Caturix, then yes."

"And if not? If the support is not there?"

"We all see what Paulinus is doing. This year's payment on our *loan*, and Aulus Plautius's silver tongue, if he is inclined to help, may buy us a little time, but not much. Hopefully, it will be enough."

"I must ride north before the winter turns."

"In the spring, I will seek out what is left of the Coritani."

"Oh, Prasutagus, we must move so carefully. If Paulinus catches word… Already, Broc has delivered spies to me like a cat dragging back its kills," I said then told him how we'd been keeping ourselves entertained and handling Roman spies in his absence.

But Prasutagus merely laughed. "General Boudica," he said, touching my chin.

"Better than *chieftain*."

Prasutagus huffed a laugh, then pulled me close.

"Now, General. I have been in the field for far too long. What is your command?"

"Well, Soldier. First, I command you to remove your trousers. Then, I demand that you attend to me promptly, as Lord Cernunnos decrees."

"That, my Strawberry Queen, is a command I will happily attend to as many times as you ask."

CHAPTER 34

I rode out the following week to meet with Bran in Oak Throne while Prasutagus continued his work fostering support.

I arrived at Oak Throne just before the Roman procurator was due to visit the Iceni people. Upon my arrival, I met with Bran and Bec. Bellicus and Sorcha sat with us as I shared what had happened in Londinium.

"What of the money given to Caturix?" Bran asked, looking pale. "Boudica, I have no idea where that money is. It's at the bottom of the Fens for all I know."

"Maybe the Romans have it. They can hardly ask for money they stole back," I replied.

"I don't put it past them, Boudica," Bec warned.

"All the same, this Paulinus is a brutal man. He has come to finish us, one way or the other."

"What will we do?" Bran asked.

"For now, we bide our time. Tomorrow, however, we will ride to Holk Fort, where I will ask Arixus to increase production."

"Boudica," Bec gasped. "Will it come to that? Will they not roll over us as they did to all the others?"

"Not if we work with the druids and coordinate. A rising tide in the west matched by one in the east...the Romans crushed in the middle."

"Won't they just bring more warriors from Gaul?" Bellicus asked.

"If they think it's worth it," Bran told his son. "Will they, Boudica? If we can manage it, could such a rebellion get them to withdraw?"

"There were indications that Nero was wavering in his dedication to staying here. Gold in Ordovices lands prompted him to continue. But if the cost is too high..."

"This is a huge gamble," Bec said.

"I saw that man," Sorcha told Bec. "That Paulinus. My mother is right. He has come to end us, one way or the other."

"They sent someone to kidnap Sorcha while we were in Londinium. Paulinus is trying to provoke a war, one he thinks we cannot win. We have danced to Rome's tune for more than a decade, long enough for our children to grow into adults. Soon, the song will end. We must be ready."

"Then we will ride out in the morning," Bran said. "And we will be ready."

THE FOLLOWING MORNING, we departed from Oak Throne under heavy guard. The new Romans who Paulinus had stationed in Oak Throne had gotten word of our travel and arrived with the cheerful news that they had come to protect us.

"We will ride with you to Holk Fort, Queen Boudica. The roads are not safe. We will serve as guard."

"The roads are not safe…in disarmed Northern Iceni territory…where I am queen?"

At that, the Roman soldier shifted.

I laughed. "What is your name, soldier?"

"Quintus Severan, Queen Boudica."

"Quintus Severan, I hope your sword is sharper than your tongue because you are a terrible liar. Come with us, all the same. They have excellent ale and pretty women in Holk Fort. You are welcome to join our party."

As Bran and I rode, Sorcha fell back to ride beside Quintus Severan.

At first, I found my daughter's actions confusing.

But then, I watched her work.

I hadn't known Sorcha to be capable of flirting, but there she was, all the same, laughing lightly and smiling at him. She was purposely softening the Roman.

"Perhaps Sorcha can find the chink in their armor that I could not," Bran said, looking over his shoulder.

"I suspect ye lack the tools," Pix told him.

At that, Bran and Bellicus laughed.

We arrived at Holk Fort around midday. From the walls, they announced Bran and me...and the Romans. When the gates of the fort swung open, the place was quiet. Naturally, the people here wanted nothing to do with Rome. And until we left, Holk would likely stay silent.

I flicked a gaze at Bran, who gave me a knowing look.

As we rode through the town, it wasn't fear I felt. These people, who had suffered so much under Saenunos, were no longer afraid. They were angry.

And they had every right to be.

Rome had taken their weapons.

And now, the eagle's talon slipped deep into their pockets, leaving hard-working people scratching for coin when they should have been prospering. The wealth Claudius had promised us had come to fruition, just as he'd said. The late emperor had failed to mention that once the coin started to flow, Rome would be there to collect.

I found Arixus and two other black-robed druids waiting when we reached the roundhouse.

"Queen Boudica," Arixus told me politely then turned to the others. "You are all welcome in Holk Fort."

"Thank you, Arixus. Would your brothers please see to our escort? Our Roman friends rode with us to ensure our safety. Let's reward their trouble with an ale, shall we?"

At that, one of the druids came forward and gestured to the Romans. "If you will," he said stiffly.

"I will find you later," Sorcha told Quintus Severan. "You have to show me that card game."

At that, the Roman smiled at her and nodded.

My stomach turned, knowing what the Roman was likely thinking, but I knew my daughter better. She was up to some game—but it wasn't cards.

Arixus led us into the roundhouse, leaving the Romans behind. The place was tidy. So tidy I realized the roundhouse had been going unused. The druids did not stay here, merely meeting at the roundhouse when needed. All the same, it was there that I found Fan, Finola, and Aterie the younger.

"Queen Boudica," Fan said with a smile, emerging from the back. "Welcome back to Holk Fort."

Finola followed her holding Aterie's hand. It was

hard to believe ten years had passed since I'd seen his father killed before my eyes.

"Aterie," I said with a smile. "You are nearly as tall as your mother."

At that, the boy smiled abashedly. "Queen Boudica."

"Vian sends her love," I told them all. "We are preparing for the procurator's visit to Venta, so she could not get away."

"Ah, Queen Boudica, I'll never be able to repay you for what you've done for my girl. But for now, let me get you some ale and something to eat. Poor Bran," she said, looking at my brother. "The gods know, Cidna's dough gets worse as she ages. You all are probably fighting the collywobbles day and night. Let me get you a proper meal."

At that, Bran laughed, then said, "My thanks."

Fan was right. Cidna's eyesight was deteriorating terribly, and she was much slower in the kitchen than she had been. Still, Bec and Bran could not convince her to set her spoon aside. So, she underbaked and burned her dishes for them night and day and would likely do so until the day she died.

Bran, Sorcha, Bellicus, Pix, and I settled in alongside the druid.

"What news?" Arixus asked.

I told him all we had heard and seen regarding the new governor. "How long do we have?"

"We are watching two fronts. In the east, we are dancing to Rome's tune and drowning in debt. Prasutagus rallies the displaced chieftains of the Trinovantes, Catuvellauni, and anyone else he can find. In the west, Paulinus is marching toward Mona."

Arixus nodded. "We have heard much the same… Our order has always remained out of the way, but we, too, had a messenger from Mona."

"How?" I asked, surprised.

"Your fey woman is not the only one who can walk the old paths," Arixus said, then grinned at Pix.

"I'm not fey, ye know. I just be lost in time. There be a difference."

"As you say," Arixus told her with a grin. "The druids are anxious to protect themselves and the holiest places in our lands."

"Avallach?"

Arixus nodded. "The priestesses are using the old magic to keep Avallach hidden. But Mona is too vast, and the druids have had signs that the island will fall. I do not know if we can prevent it, but we must try, or all the wisdom of our people will be lost. We will continue our work at Seahenge, increasing our output. We will find you more men for your army, my queen. When it's time, you need only call upon us."

"Arixus… I know I don't need to impress on you the

importance of secrecy. No word must get to the Romans about what we are doing. If it does…"

"Then it will be over before it begins. As it is, Queen Boudica, the path ahead of us is not easy."

I swallowed hard, then nodded.

"Doom and gloom, doom and gloom," Fan said, returning once more with a tray of drinks. "For once, I wish someone would say it will be a fine harvest, a mild winter, and a warm spring. But those days are behind us, I suppose."

At that, we all chuckled.

"I could take ye through the mound to the fair ones," Pix offered. "Nothing but blue skies, summer wine, and fornication to be found with the fey."

At that, Fan laughed. "That's a tempting offer. I won't answer now when my heart is full of dread. For sure, I could use a little summer wine…and Finola's father has been dead a good many years. Andraste's toe, I've worked up a sweat just thinking about it. Let me go get the bread," Fan said with a laugh, which we all joined.

"I like a good bit of dread," Sorcha said, picking up a tankard. "It's motivating."

"Motivating you to do what?"

She shrugged. "To be ready to kill every Roman bastard that crosses my path," she said, then lifted her cup. "To Condatis, may he drown the Romans in their own tears."

"To Condatis," we all called, lifting our mugs in a toast.

As I drank, my gaze went to Arixus. He was observing Sorcha. A pinch of sadness marred his expression, which filled my heart with the sort of dread that did not motivate me, but devastated.

Arixus, Bran, and I spent the night whispering while Bellicus, Sorcha, and Pix went to get the Romans drunk and talking.

"Four Coritani chieftains have visited Holk," Arixus told me, "their druids along with them. They had hoped to find refuge in the north, but Cartimandua has her own troubles, and the Brigantes are unsettled. The chieftains are living in their own territory in hiding."

"What about to the north of Brigantes territory? The Caledonian Confederacy?"

"From what I have heard, the painted people of the north frighten the Romans as all the people of our isle once did. There are some there who would form an alliance with you, Boudica, but they cannot cross Brigantes lands to do so. The politics of the northern tribes are complicated."

"What of the Parisii on the coast?"

"There are no more Parisii. They are Brigantes."

"What happened?"

"Cartimandua," Arixus said with a light laugh.

"If we free ourselves of Rome, I hope we don't need to worry about the Brigantes queen."

"Not unless you cross her," Arixus said.

"Or run to her for help, as Caratacus did," Bran said.

"I suspect there is more to that tale," Arixus said dryly.

A map before us, the three of us talked until late in the night about where we might find allies. The moon was high when Bellicus, Pix, and Sorcha finally returned. Bellicus ambled to bed, but Pix and Sorcha joined us, smelling of ale.

"You smell like a tavern," I told Pix.

"Nay, nay," she said drunkenly. "Two taverns piled on top of one another."

I frowned at her and then turned to my daughter, who seemed in far better shape.

"What?" Sorcha said innocently. "It's not hard to dump your cup under the table and then call for another round," she said, then looked at Pix. "Given how old you are, I thought you'd have learned that by now."

In reply, Pix hiccupped.

We all chuckled.

"Next time, tell Bellicus," Bran said.

"Oh, he knew. He just liked the ale," Sorcha said with a laugh.

"Well?" I asked her. "Anything from the Romans?"

"They had word that the procurator will be coming with more forces this time and to expect the villagers to be disruptive. Already, they have been told to shackle anyone who falls out of line. All troublemakers will be sent to Verulamium and onward to the west. And then there are other rumors…"

"What rumors?"

"That they will go home soon. All of them were talking about it, making their plans. They all believe that they will start withdrawing once Nero gets the resources he's after in the west. They have all heard it costs the empire too much to stay here. They expect the troops will soon be drawn down and called back to Gaul. They do not expect the Romans to leave entirely, but they don't expect there will be more of a push north or elsewhere. The tribes, as they see it, are subdued. Now, we can just go back to being a trading outpost."

"Nero wants to leave," Bran said hopefully.

"But not until the west is crushed and drained of resources," Sorcha said.

I looked at Arixus. "A push might be what they need," I said.

"Or it might be what is needed to make them stay. It is a gamble," he replied.

"Before she passed, Dôn shared with me a vision she had. They will depart eventually and fully, but not for some time. But that doesn't mean we can't get them to draw down. There is no way they will leave Londinium or Camulodunum now."

"Unless there is no Londinium and Camulodunum," Arixus said, his eyes on the flickering fire of the brazier. After a moment, he turned his gaze back to me. He held my glance.

Understanding his meaning, I nodded.

"We will be ready, Boudica," Arixus said. "You may depend on us."

Seated in the chair beside Sorcha, Pix let out a loud snore, startling herself awake. "What?" she called, then went back to sleep.

I chuckled, then turned back to Arixus. "I thank the gods for you, Arixus, since the fey sent *her* to *protect* me."

Seemingly in reply, Pix snorted loudly, making us all laugh.

WE DEPARTED EARLY the following morning, Pix, Bellicus, and the Romans all looking groggy.

"Will you have enough to pay the procurator?" I asked Arixus. "They tell me Paulinus has brought some new man who stays in Camulodunum. His reputation proceeds him. By all reports, he is a difficult man."

Arixus nodded. "We sold iron to the Cornovii in secret. We have more than enough to pay whatever Rome thinks the poor village of Holk Fort owes. We will not do anything to whet their interest," Arixus reassured me.

"And the work at Seahenge?"

"Remains secret."

"May Condatis keep you, all your brothers, and all those wanderers who have found their way to you."

"And you, Queen Boudica. May the dark lady Andraste guide you and the Morrigu ride at your side in the coming days."

"Thank you, Arixus," I said, lifting my hands in a gesture of respect.

With that, the druid bowed to me, and we rode out again.

"You know," Bran said, patting the duffle bag full of oat cakes, bread rounds, cheese, and more Fan had given him, "I never think Cidna's food is off until I eat elsewhere. But I have to say…"

I laughed. "The same, Brother, the same."

WHEN WE RETURNED to Oak Throne, I had my party prepare to depart for Venta. We would ride through the night, returning by morning.

"You are welcome to stay longer," Bec told me. "You know that, of course."

"There is too much happening. I don't want to leave Prasutagus on his own. There is no telling what could happen next, everything being so on edge."

"Perhaps that is how they want you to feel," Bec considered. "In which case, you are more likely to say or do something you should not—and get caught in the action. You must be careful, Boudica. We all trust you, but whatever befalls you befalls us all."

I pulled my friend into a hug. "Then may the gods protect and guide me," I said, hugging her tight before letting go again. "Now, I have one last stop to make before we depart," I said, then turned to Sorcha. "I'll return shortly. Make sure the horses are ready?"

Sorcha nodded.

Leaving the others, I made my way quickly to Ula's cottage. To my surprise, the door was open. I could hear her inside sweeping.

"Ula, are you moving?" I asked, poking my head inside.

"Bah," she told me. "Just sweeping away the stink of Rome that swept in when you showed up."

"Will it make you happy to know I'm planning a rebellion and hope to murder as many Romans as possible? In fact, Arixus suggested I burn down Camulodunum and Londinium while I'm at it. Would that suit you?"

At that, Ula paused. "That's what the druid said?"

I nodded.

"Then what are you doing standing around here?"

I huffed a laugh. "I wanted to see if you wanted to come with me. Pix has taught me to drive a chariot. You can ride beside me."

"Bah," she huffed again but set her broom aside. Her hands on her hips, she looked me over from head to foot. "You're too soft, Boudica. Get your spear arm trained."

"I *have* been training."

"Yes, but not with that," she said, then pointed toward the wall.

There, propped in the corner, I saw… "The spear Gaheris made for me," I said with a gasp. "How?"

"Never mind how."

"No, Ula. How? It was buried with all the rest."

"So it was."

"Ula…"

"The little people of the hollow hills traded. That is all you need to know."

I went to the wall and took the spear. It had been cleaned and mended. Holding it in my hands, I felt Gaheris's spirit near me once more.

"Ula," I whispered, looking from her to the spear. "Thank you."

She nodded curtly. "All things that are yours will find their way back to you," Ula told me. "That was the message of the little people. And when that happens, you will know what to do. The land itself is with you, Boudica. But the times before you are dark. Let them embolden you, not crush you."

"Ula…"

"I am old, Boudica. I am old and tired and ready to die. But I will stay until it is done. Now, go on with you. Taranis's chariot wheels are turning, the Morrigu's crows are cawing, and I hear axes on the grinding wheel. I have done all I can do. The rest is up to you."

Setting the spear aside, I embraced her.

"Ah, get off me, girl," she said, but she didn't push me away.

How little she felt in my arms. "I love you, Ula."

"Now, don't get ridiculous," she said gruffly.

After a long moment, I let her go. I took the spear once more and exited the hut. I had just started my way down the road to rejoin the others when I heard Ula behind me.

"Boudica."

I turned and looked back at her.

She inclined her head to me, gave me half a smile, then went back inside.

A moment later, I heard her sweeping again and cursing at her cat.

"I love you too, Ula. I love you too."

CHAPTER 35

We returned to Venta in time to prepare for the annual tribute about which Prasutagus was growing increasingly, uncharacteristically irate. My husband had always endeavored to remain calm and balanced despite our difficulties. Still, of late, I noticed he was unnerved.

Late one night, as the end of the harvest approached, I lay in bed beside my husband, listening as he sighed and rolled, sleepless.

"Prasutagus," I said gently. "It will be all right. You and Vian have prepared as well as you could."

"It is not for myself that I worry," Prasutagus said. He pulled me close. "It is for my people. Some have had a lean year. Some will be defiant. They do not have the sheen of title to protect them."

"We have very little left ourselves, *Chieftain*."

"Because of *that*, the shield we have held before them is damaged, broken. My father taught me that my duty was to my people and my family before all else. Now, everyone and everything I love is at risk. With each disgruntled Catuvellauni or Trinovantes chieftain I speak to, each druid who whispers to me, I place my people in more danger."

"Prasutagus, if you're having doubts—"

"Yes. I do. I doubt myself. I doubt my gods. I doubt my advisers. I doubt when I decide to act. I doubt when I decide not to act. But all I want is to keep you safe. It is all I can think of. What if something were to happen to me? Would Rome sweep in and take everything from you?"

"Please, don't say such things," I whispered.

"I cannot sleep. The thought plagues me. I see you and my daughters alone against all the empire. It is an image that haunts me. I can't escape it. It fills me with dread."

I entwined my hand in Prasutagus's. "We are soulbound, my love. We will be together always. No matter what happens. One day, death will take us. That is inevitable. But I will find you again."

"I have seen you in my visions with such black hair —raven dark—your eyes the color of thistles," he said, kissing me on the back of my head. "How will I know you without all these wild, orange curls?" he asked with a light laugh.

I chuckled. "You are one to talk."

Prasutagus pressed his cheek against my head then sighed heavily.

"I love you," I whispered. "Whatever happens, we will weather the storm together, and when it is all done, we will find one another once more."

"Yes, I love you too."

"Good. Now, go to sleep, or I will start slipping a sleeping draft into your ale."

"You can try, Wife, but not much gets past a druid."

"You forget that I was taught by Ula. I know all the herbs you can't taste or smell."

He chuckled. "Then I consider myself forewarned. Now, if only there was a way to help me relax so I could sleep," he said, his hand gently cupping my breast as his lips danced across my neck.

"Are you trying to seduce me, King Prasutagus?"

"Is it working?"

"Yes, but keep at it," I said, rolling over and kissing him. Soon, we lost ourselves to passion, after which my husband finally slept soundly.

PROCURATOR DECIANUS CATUS arrived in Venta just before Samhain in a carpentum surrounded by Roman soldiers.

More.

Invariably, there were more.

Prasutagus and I went to the wagon door to greet the man, only to discover him sleeping.

Slumped to one side, his toga hiked up to his knees, drooling heavily, an empty wine goblet jiggling in his hand, the procurator napped.

Obviously embarrassed by the situation, the Roman soldier signaled to us to wait a moment while he leaned to shake the procurator awake.

"Procurator," the man whispered, shaking the man's shoulder. "Procurator Catus," he said a little more firmly, jostling him again. "We are in Venta. The local color is here to greet you."

"I say," the procurator said, pulling himself together. "Should have known. Smells of horse shite," he said, then pulled his toga down.

"It's his own breath blowing back on him," Sorcha quipped from behind us.

I smothered a laugh.

With a heavy groan, the procurator hefted his bulging frame out of the wagon, righted himself, then joined us.

"Procurator Catus," Prasutagus said politely, bowing.

The rest of us followed his lead.

"Prasutagus, is it not?" he asked with a sniff. "And Boudica," he said, looking me over. "Tawny," he added under his breath.

"Would you come inside, Procurator? You will be weary from your long ride from Camulodunum," I said.

Morfran landed on the roof of the procurator's wagon and cawed loudly at the man.

The sight of him caught the attention of everyone gathered.

The Romans looked unnerved.

"Shoo, you," the procurator said, then signaled to one of his men who lifted his spear.

"No," I called, stepping toward the soldier.

Artur whistled to the bird, which flew back to him.

"What in the—" the procurator began.

"It is my son's bird, Procurator," Prasutagus said, smothering his annoyance with the man.

Morfran had settled on Artur's arm once more. The raven gave the procurator another loud squawk and then took off, flying away from the king's compound.

Artur watched him go, frowning.

As did Prasutagus and Pix.

My husband knew the signs as well as I did. Morfran spoke for himself, but a raven was the creature of the Morrigu, and the goddess had made her voice heard.

She'd given us a warning.

"Better to have a dog, boy," the procurator told Artur. "Dogs are good for something rather than a brainless squawking bird. Come along then, Prasutagus," the procurator said, then headed toward the roundhouse.

Artur's face twisted with annoyance. Morfran had been Artur's companion these many years. As well, Artur had an affinity for birds, having trained a flock of ravens to carry messages and do his bidding. But he bit his tongue.

My husband and I turned, falling into step with the Roman.

"Like he owns the place," Sorcha grumbled, then left us, joining Artur.

I entered the roundhouse, following Prasutagus, who guided the procurator to the formal meeting room. There, wine and food had already been laid out, and Vian waited to review any accounting. Balfor stood at the door, waiting to attend to us.

"I have spoken to Paulinus," Procurator Catus said, sitting at the table. He motioned to Balfor to pour him a drink.

Balfor was surprised but did not complain and simply served the man.

"He tells me you sold your villa in Londinium," the procurator added.

"Yes," Prasutagus said crisply. "There seems to be some confusion over the gift of funds given to the Greater Iceni by Emperor Claudius. We were given a gift of twenty million sesterces in appreciation of our cooperation, as Aulus Plautius can confirm. Governor Paulinus is under the impression it was a loan, which it was not—"

"There is no false impression here, Prasutagus. Emperor Nero asked that the loan and outstanding interest be paid. And no amount of Aulus Plautius's whispering in the senate will change that..." he said, giving Prasutagus a knowing look. "However, the emperor did agree to postpone the full payment by three years. That, the whispering did accomplish," he said, then drained his cup, gesturing for Balfor to refill it again.

I took the pitcher myself and poured for the man. "The emperor is generous to give us a reprieve, but I hope he understands that we were not expecting the gift to be recalled."

"A misunderstanding on your part, I'm sure. But Aulus Plautius assures us that the Greater Iceni people are masters of ingenuity and will perform if given a chance. So, his whispering has bought you that," the procurator said, then laughed. "But that does not excuse you nor your people of their annual sums due. As well, we expect the interest on the loan to be paid this year. I trust I will find your payment ready, as well as the payment in Oak House, when I arrive there," he added, giving me a hard look.

"Oak Throne. And, yes, my brother Bran will have everything ready."

"Oak *Throne*," he said, then laughed lightly. "You people do like your trees. Now, the funds?"

Prasutagus gestured to Vian, who gave the man a parchment on which she had tabulated Venta's due.

"It is all here for you, Procurator, including the interest," Vian told him.

Procurator Catus stared at Vian. "Your daughter?" he asked Prasutagus.

"No, sir. Vian is my secretary."

"A woman?" the procurator replied, then laughed. "I thought you had druids for such things."

I scowled. "Our people find that women's minds are as sharp as men's. But, back to the point, you will find all in order," I replied, gesturing to the parchment.

The procurator blew air through his lips. "*I* find that Briton women talk too much. In Rome, Prasutagus, we teach our women to be docile and silent. You will find that life is more peaceful when women are taught their place, subservient to their men," he said, then rose, stuffing the scroll into his gown. "You should send your son to Rome to be educated, Prasutagus. We will refine the barbarian out of him so your people have a proper king in the future, like King Diras. Now, have your people bring your chests," he said, gesturing to our payment. "My men will collect from the city now. I trust there will be no violence."

"As long as there are no surprises, there will be no violence. My people are prepared to pay what has been asked, but more than that... I hope Rome remembers that the Greater Iceni are friends to Rome."

Procurator Catus merely laughed and then rose. He slugged the last of his wine and then turned to Prasutagus. "As for your taxes, I can only say that my men will do their jobs. Let us hope your people will comply."

At that, Prasutagus frowned.

"I might as well tell you now that I am also charged with taking your druids into custody."

"What did you say?" Prasutagus asked coldly.

"Your druids at the King's Wood," he said, then paused. "I say, I was right before about the trees. Paulinus has ordered that all druids be taken into custody for questioning until your holy people on Mona cease stirring up rebellion."

"You have no right to take any of my people, Procurator. Not you, nor the governor. My people have done nothing wrong. The druids here answer to me, not to Mona."

"Good, good, well, they can inform the governor of that when the druids are delivered to Londinium," Procurator Catus said, then moved to depart, but Prasutagus grabbed his arm, stopping him.

"Prasutagus," I said, stepping toward the pair.

"My people will not be touched. If the governor wants them, he will have to take me along with them, or by all the gods, there will be a reckoning."

"You would set a hand on me?" the procurator hissed.

"You would set a hand on all that is mine to protect?"

At that, the procurator laughed, then unexpectedly grabbed me by my hair, yanking me toward him. "Hand, boot, or blade," the procurator snarled back at my husband. "Do not tempt Rome."

"Unhand my wife or prepare to meet your gods," Prasutagus said, his dagger drawn.

The procurator merely smiled.

"Prasutagus," I whispered. "No."

"You're right, Queen Boudica," Procurator Catus said. "Your women *are* smart. Because you know that with a snap of my fingers, I will call every Roman waiting outside into this house and murder all of you— your children, your household, everyone, right down to that bloody bird. If I kill you, the Greater Iceni lands are mine. If you kill me, the Greater Iceni lands are mine.

Either way, Rome wins. Your wife understands that. Aulus Plautius always spoke well of you, Queen Boudica. Now I see why. So, go ahead. Try it, Prasutagus. We will see who wins. Otherwise, put your dagger away. Your queen will ride with me to the King's Wood to collect your druids. And you will be a good boy and stay here and make sure your pig farmers, and witches, and whores pay their taxes, or I will murder every single one of you."

With that, the procurator let me go.

"Boudica," Prasutagus said.

"I'm fine," I said stiffly. "Just do as he asks. I will go to the King's Wood with him."

"If your druids give me any trouble, you will find their corpses waiting for you," the procurator said, then motioned for me to walk on. "I certainly hope your brother is more amenable than your husband, Queen Boudica."

I said nothing and merely followed behind him.

When we stepped into the hallway, I found Sorcha and Olwen waiting.

Sorcha stood, blade drawn, murder in her eyes.

"Your girls?" the procurator asked me.

"Yes."

"Very fine-looking young women. Very fine. Send them to Rome. Get them good husbands. If you put them in the right beds, you could make something out of them and yourself, Queen Boudica," he said, then turned and made his way from the roundhouse.

Turning, I caught Olwen's gaze and signaled to her to find Pix—who had gone out that morning—and send her to Arixus with a warning. If the Romans took the brothers of Condatis prisoner, as they planned to do to Tavish and the others, we were all finished. Willing my mind to remember what Ula had taught me of Ogham and my fingers to obey, I signed to Olwen repeatedly until Olwen nodded, then rushed toward the back of the house. Sorcha quickly followed behind her.

Outside, I found the Romans waiting.

The procurator merely signaled his men, and they began to disperse back into the city.

"Into the carpentum," Catus told me roughly, then turned to the driver. "As I told you earlier."

At that, the driver merely nodded, and a guard formed up to join us.

Feeling the rage boiling, I slipped into the wagon and took my seat.

The Roman wedged himself in across from me, closed the door, then knocked on the wall of the wagon.

A moment later, the wagon turned to go.

"You are lucky to have such good friends in Rome, Queen Boudica. Paulinus was ready to make the Greater Iceni bleed and be done with it, but Aulus Plautius—who hates everyone," he said with a laugh, "extolled us of your virtues. I wondered why until I set eyes on you. Tawny, indeed. The tawny rose of Britannia," he said then laughed, and laughed, and laughed.

WHEN WE ARRIVED at the King's Wood, I heard some confusion amongst the soldiers. I moved the curtain aside and looked out but couldn't see what the matter was.

When the wagon stopped, I slipped out before the procurator could protest.

There, I found Tavish standing alone before the central fire ring.

Otherwise, the place was empty.

My gaze immediately went to Melusine's cottage, but there was no sign of her.

"Tavish," I said, fear in my voice.

Overhead, I heard a caw.

I looked up to find Morfran there.

I turned back to Tavish.

The druid met my gaze and held it.

Once the Roman squeezed himself out of the wagon, he surveyed the little community and signaled to his men. "Search the houses."

"I really must protest," I told the procurator. "You have no business here. To harass this place is the same as harassing your own temples. You would not let outsiders harry your priests of Mithras, Minerva, or any other of your gods."

"Our priests do not conspire against their supposed friends and allies," the procurator said dismissively then turned to Tavish. "Who are you?"

"I am Tavish, high druid of the Greater Iceni."

"Where are your people?"

"I am alone here."

The procurator's lip curled into a frustrated sneer, then he turned to his men. "Anyone?"

"The houses are empty, Procurator," one of the men called.

Overhead, Morfran cawed loudly once more.

"The whole country is accursed with these bloody birds," he said, then turned back to Tavish. "The others… Where are they?"

"My order disbanded some months ago," Tavish said. "For fear of Rome, they have fled. I, alone, remain."

At that, Procurator Catus laughed. "You expect me to believe you, druid?"

"I do not care what you believe, Rome. I speak the words of the gods."

"Bind him," the procurator said, gesturing to one of the soldiers.

"You will not," I said, my anger getting the better of me. "This is an offense to the gods and to the Greater Iceni. You have no evidence of misconduct against this man. What you're doing is an act of war."

"Snuffing out rebellion where it breeds is an act to prevent war," the procurator retorted angrily. "Now, bind him, and find the others," Catus called to his soldiers.

Fear gripping me, I moved to protect Tavish, but he shook his head. "Of the ways," he whispered, then gestured to Morfran.

The raven cawed loudly and then dived toward the Roman soldiers advancing on Tavish. With the men distracted, Tavish turned and fled toward the forest.

"What the— After him!" the procurator called.

The soldiers raced into the woods behind Tavish.

"What is the meaning of this?" the procurator demanded of me.

"You tell me! Do you think I had any inkling that the procurator of Rome, a man charged with little more than carting himself around the countryside to collect coin, would have the audacity to take my holy people into custody? It is as the man told you. The druids have fled in fear. Only Tavish, who we depended upon for religious council, remained. And now..."

"Waspish woman. Do you expect me to believe you?"

"Why wouldn't you? I am a client queen of Rome. I am an ally to the emperor. I have spurred the other tribes of this island on Rome's behalf. I stood in Camulodunum and swore my fealty to the empire. I may not have been born in Rome or dress or behave as Roman women do, but I am every bit a Roman Briton—as you call us. Prasutagus and I have been a model of how to behave in the presence of your leaders and soldiers. Emperor Claudius relied upon us to keep the peace. We have done everything that Rome asked only to be treated thus. The druids have fled. And that is because the empire has failed to keep its promise to the Iceni—because of you, not because of me. I will not stand here and be insulted by you. I am a queen. You're here to collect the taxes. So, collect them and leave the ruling to your betters," I said, then turned and walked away. I went to one of the Roman soldier's horses, mounted, then rode away from the King's Wood.

As I went, I prayed to every god that would hear me.

Cernunnos, protect Tavish. Hide him in the forest.

Elen of the Ways, protect Melusine and the others.

Bel, protect Bran and the people of Oak Throne.

Condatis, protect Arixus and the people of the Greater Iceni.

Andraste, keep the grove secret, safe.

And Epona… protect all the Iceni from foolishness and greed.

I found Prasutagus in the market when I returned to Venta.

He hurried to me.

"Boudica," he said, holding the horse's reins as I slipped from the saddle. "What happened?"

"He went to take the druids into custody, but they were gone. Tavish, alone, remained. He stayed long enough to tell me they were at the shrine of Elen of the Ways before he, too, slipped Rome's grasp. You sent Morfran to warn them?"

Prasutagus looked confused. "No. Morfran has been with us," he said, pointing to the trees nearby. "Watching over Artur."

"But there was a raven in the King's Wood. It attacked the soldiers so Tavish could flee."

"It was not Morfran."

"The gods themselves," I whispered.

Prasutagus nodded.

Great Morrigu, Lady of Ravens, may you be praised.

My hands still shaking, I turned to my husband. "Aye, Prasutagus… There was tension, and my tongue got the better of me."

"My knife nearly got the better of me," Prasutagus said, then looked toward the Romans making their way through the market. "We must keep things calm. If we give in to our anger now, unready as we are, we will surely die."

"Where is Pix? Did Olwen relay the message?"

Prasutagus shook his head. "I don't know. The girls went to find her."

"If the Romans take Arixus…" I said, trying to keep the panic from my voice.

"Be calm, Boudica. Be calm," he said, pulling me close. "Pix will reach him in time."

"And if she does not?"

"Then I will finally get to bloody my dagger. Because if that man ever lays a hand on you again, I will burn it all to the ground."

Procurator Catus returned an hour later in a sour mood. He checked in with his men, who had nearly finished collecting the taxes.

Prasutagus and I waited in the market where the people could see us.

The procurator, acting as if nothing was amiss, joined us. "My men will ride to Oak House now."

"Oak *Throne*. My brother is prepared to meet you. I am very certain the Roman soldiers stationed there can vouch for the conduct of the Northern Iceni people."

"Your druid slipped us, Queen Boudica. All the men saw in the forest was a stag."

"Rome is in the wrong to make such an affront on

my holy people," Prasutagus said. "I will make a complaint to Paulinus on the matter."

Procurator Catus laughed. "Complain all you want, Prasutagus. But until these meddlesome druids are quieted, no one will be interested in what you say. And if we find that druid of yours, we will clap him in irons and let him perform his heathen magic at our new coliseum in Camulodunum. Let us see how he does against lions," he said, then turned and crawled back into his wagon.

Prasutagus and I remained until the coin had been collected and the Romans were on their way. The soldier whose horse I had borrowed came to collect his steed.

"Queen Boudica," he said, inclining his head to me.

When I studied the man's features, I realized he was a Gaul.

"You are on the wrong side of the channel," I told him.

"I am on the wrong side of everything, Queen Boudica," he replied, then mounted his horse and rode off without adding another word.

Prasutagus and I watched him go.

"Conscripted man," Prasutagus said. "Many Cantiaci, Regnenses, and Atrebates have joined the Romans. Fight for Rome, make a wage, and in the end, hope to retire to some colonia where you can drink wine and forget all the horror you have brought to others."

"Everyone is just trying to find a way to survive."

"Yes," Prasutagus agreed. "But I can tell you one thing. I look forward to sticking my dagger into that bloated man's throat."

"If I don't get to him first."

At that, Prasutagus laughed and then pulled me close, kissing the top of my head. "May the Morrigu hear your words."

CHAPTER 36

Whatever Aulus Plautius said on our behalf bought Prasutagus and I the time we needed to prepare for what was beginning to feel like the inevitable conclusion to this madness. The governor's army pushed west, but his minions continued to press on the east with unwavering cruelty. With each season, stories of families found butchered, villages razed, or worse reached our ears.

It was early spring in the year sixty that I began to be plagued with terrible dreams.

Each morning, I would wake screaming.

"Boudica," Prasutagus said gently, holding my shoulder as I tried to calm down. "It's all right. It was just a dream." My husband rose and went to get me a goblet of water. When he returned to the bed, he handed it to me. "The same again?" he whispered.

I nodded.

Every night for the last month, I had seen the same dream.

Blood in the water.

Waves lapping upon the shores, carrying bodies.

At first, I thought I was reliving memories of the past, of Gaheris and those from Frog's Hollow.

But then, the dreams grew clearer.

It was not the Wash I was seeing.

I walked barefoot on a rocky shoreline. The water had felt cold, the rocky pebbles poking my feet. The bloody water had swirled around my ankles, staining the length of my white dress. Overhead, ravens had cried and what looked like embers danced across the sky.

But they were not embers.

Flaming arrows fell all around me, striking those close by who died with deafening screams.

I lifted my lyre and strummed a hard note.

The water before me twirled and rose into a spout which sped across the waves toward the ships that approached, crashing into them. But there were too many of them. They came like waves crashing onto the shore.

"Brenna," I whispered to my husband.

"Is it happening now, or is it a vision of what will come?"

I shook my head. "I don't know."

"I must try to get a messenger to Mona."

"Oh, Prasutagus," I whispered. "How? The Romans are everywhere."

"Madogh has people amongst the Brigantes who will take him across."

"The risk is too great. For Brenna, I would do anything, but we already lost Broc," I said. A year had passed since Broc had gone to Gaul and never returned. "Madogh is a father now. We cannot ask it of him."

"The gods have shown you a warning, Boudica."

"Why show me and not the druids?" I asked. "They must know already."

At that, Prasutagus paused. "Boudica, when did you see this happening? Was there snow or blossoms? What did you see about you?"

"I..." I began, trying to remember. "I don't know. The water was cold, and there was a crescent-shaped moon in the sky."

Prasutagus looked away for a long moment. "I, too, dreamed," he finally whispered. "There was so much darkness."

"We must make ready," I said, a waver in my voice. "I do not want it, but we must make ready. When the snow thaws, they will begin to push west once more."

Prasutagus pulled me toward him. We lay back down in our bed, entwined in one another's arms.

"In my dream, my shield was bent and broken. My sword was cracked and shattered. And yet, I stood before all of the Greater Iceni, faces I see in Venta and beyond each day, and waited as arrows arched across the sky, all of them trained on me," Prasutagus whispered.

"What happened next?"

Prasutagus kissed my shoulder. "Darkness, and then, so much…green. I was in an ancient forest with you, but your hair was the color of raven's feathers."

"Prasutagus, if we fail…"

"Then we will die. And our children will die. And the Greater Iceni will fall to Rome."

"We must not fail."

"We must not fail," my husband echoed. "But if we do, I will find you in the next life. You will be mine again, Boudica. Even if I have to fight Gaheris for you," he added with a laugh.

"And I, Esu."

"Life after life," Prasutagus said, lifting my hand and kissing my fingers.

"Life after life," I repeated. "May our souls be bound."

We fell silent once more, both of us feeling the heavy weight of destiny on our hearts.

IT BEGAN with the news that Governor Paulinus had broken the line against the Silures and Ordovices and was pushing across the mountains west—toward gold and Mona.

Then, pleas from the west came. A network of whispers started, all the voices asking for the same thing.

Rise.

Rise.

Along with the voices to the west came one from the east.

Prasutagus frowned as he read a message delivered by Roman soldiers.

"What is it?" I asked.

"Catus has summoned me to Camulodunum."

"For what purpose?"

"He wants to speak to me about building a road from Camulodunum to Yarmouth. I am to come at once." He crumpled up the note and tossed the parchment onto the ground.

"At least he asked," I replied.

"I suspect he realized that I might notice if they build a road across the heart of my territory. Raven's Dell was just a small corner, so…"

I frowned.

"What will you do?"

"I will go. But I will make him pay for what he wants. If he can choke me in fees, I can do the same to him."

"As long as you don't literally try to choke him."

"No doubt, I will be tempted."

"I can come."

Prasutagus shook his head. "I will take Artur. Stay here. Keep things quiet. I will return as soon as possible."

Summoning Artur, the pair made ready to depart.

I went to Artur. Morfran was sitting on his shoulder. "He looks ready for an adventure."

"He is jealous of the attention I've been showing the other birds," Artur told me, stroking the bird's feathers.

"I'm sure Procurator Catus will be happy to see him again."

At that, Artur laughed.

Ready to ride, Prasutagus joined us, Sorcha and Olwen escorting him, both girls with their arms wrapped around his waist, trying to prevent him from leaving.

"But there is work to do. And riding. And digging holes. And… and mucking out the stables. And… and…" Sorcha went on.

"And?" Prasutagus asked. "You've listed everything there is to list."

"And... archery training! You know I need work, and you did promise me you would help."

"Ah," Prasutagus told her. "That is true. We will practice when I return."

"Promise?"

He nodded.

"Don't be long."

"I won't."

"And be careful," Sorcha said, finally showing her true reason for wanting to delay her father.

In reply, Prasutagus merely kissed her on the top of her head. "Your hair is hot."

"You always say that."

They both laughed, then Prasutagus turned to Olwen. Meeting her gaze, he stroked her cheek. "Pretty one. Be safe while I am gone."

Olwen nodded then signed to him, making the symbol of Luis, for the Rowan tree, which was a symbol that reminded one to listen to their intuition and of protection. Many times amulets of Rowan were worn to protect the wearer.

Prasutagus nodded slowly. "I will be careful."

Olwen nodded.

Prasutagus gently held her cheeks then kissed her forehead and then her nose, making Olwen laugh.

Leaving the girls, he turned to me. "Be safe," he told me.

"And you."

"Don't start any wars while I'm gone."

"That's a very big ask."

Prasutagus laughed and then pulled me close. "I love you, my Strawberry Queen."

"And you, my May King."

At that, he gave me a kiss and then mounted his horse.

He then waved to the guard to ride out.

Olwen joined me while Sorcha ran to the walls of the roundhouse and climbed the stairs to the palisade, watching them depart.

She waved to Artur who returned her gesture, then remained in place, watching them ride away.

"Honey cakes?" I asked Olwen.

She nodded.

With that, the pair of us turned to go back inside the roundhouse but then Olwen paused, turning to watch as they closed the gates of the roundhouse. She looked from them to me and then signed the symbol for Duir.

"He'll be all right," I reassured her with a soft smile.

Olwen nodded, forcing a smile on her worried features, and then followed me inside.

Goddess. Mother. Let him be all right. Watch over my husband, and bring him home safely to me.

EARLY ONE MORNING a few days later, Pix, Sorcha, and I had risen before the sun and left the roundhouse. Making sure we were not followed, we rode into the woods to visit the secret shrine of Elen of the Ways. Tavish and the others had taken leave there, sheltered from Roman eyes, kept hidden by the goddess of the forest.

"I am surprised ye did not become a priestess of the forest goddess," Pix told me as we meandered down what amounted to little more than a deer path in the woods.

"The Northern Iceni care only for Andraste and Epona. And my father cared only to make sure I married someone who assured his alliances held firm," I replied.

"Was that why he permitted you to marry a chieftain's son?" Sorcha asked, curiosity in her voice.

"Yes…albeit begrudgingly."

"Did ye never think to serve the gods?" Pix asked me.

"After Gaheris died, yes. But then I met Prasutagus."

"What about ye?" Pix asked Sorcha.

Sorcha laughed. "Me?"

"Would ye follow the path of your grandmother,

aunt, and father and serve the gods? Or will you wed some handsome prince?"

"The Romans have killed all the princes and destroyed all the groves. I will count myself lucky if I live to see my next birthday. Other than that, I make no plans besides learning how to throw my daggers and strengthening my sword arm."

"Ye cannot go wrong with that," Pix replied with a laugh.

While Pix joked, I felt deep sorrow at Sorcha's words. The world I had grown up in was gone. Arguments about who would marry which Catuvellauni king, Prasutagus, a chieftain's son, or a princess felt like it belonged to another world. At Sorcha's age, I had already given my heart to Gaheris and dreamed of being the lady of Frog's Hollow. My daughter just wanted to live one more year.

The peace Prasutagus and I had bought for the Greater Iceni had allowed our children to grow up. But more than that? The dreams that came with true peace did not exist.

Instead, there was only death and darkness.

Exhaling a deep, sorrowful sigh, I continued, looking for the small markings that led us to the forest shrine deep in the woods.

It was midmorning when I finally caught sight of the jumble of rocks that was the home to the followers of the forest goddess and lady of paths, Elen of the Ways.

Moss, ferns, and even small trees grew on the boulders. The place looked like nothing, a nondescript spot in the wilderness, except the air around the site shifted. The sunshine looked far more golden, glistening on the green leaves of the trees. The beams of light slanted sideways here, giving everything a gentle, golden glow.

Overhead, the birds grew quiet, and there was no sound save that of the rustling leaves.

"Greetings to the forest and the horned goddess of the ways," I called, gesturing for the others to stop.

A barely recognizable path led down a slope from the forest into the stones. At the top of the hill was a single monolith. On it were carved swirling designs and the rough face of a woman with antlers on her head, her eyes as round as an owl's.

I dismounted and then went to the stone, setting my hand thereon.

"Elen of the Ways, thank you for keeping those I love and honor safe. May you guide all my people on your ancient paths to safety."

A moment later, a pair appeared on the path between the stones.

Tavish and Melusine made their way from the rocks to join us.

"Boudica," Melusine called happily, hurrying to us.

She pulled me into an embrace. "By the gods, I'm glad to see you," she said, holding me tightly. When she finally let me go, she embraced Pix then turned and looked at Sorcha. "How you have grown. I see Brenna in her face," Melusine said, turning to me.

"Yes," I said simply, then turned to Tavish. "My friend," I said, embracing him.

"I am glad to see you, Queen Boudica," he said, then looked over our party. "The king?"

"Called to Camulodunum," I replied, trying not to show my disgust.

"Ah," Tavish said. "I pity him."

"As do I."

"Come," Melusine said. "There is much to discuss."

"You must forgive our rustic ways," Tavish told us. "We druids have returned to nature once more."

Melusine and Tavish led us deep into the jumble of rocks that twisted and turned, eventually leading us into an elaborate cave system in the side of a cliff. It looked like a rock wall with a few crevices from the outside. But inside, many chambers led deep into the land. I saw several other druids from the King's Wood and some strangers.

I paused, not expecting to see anyone outside of our own people.

"Elen's paths have led many of our holy people to

safety," Tavish reassured me. "We welcome those who find us here."

The outsiders stared at me.

I could see fear and uncertainty in their eyes.

"They are welcome in Greater Iceni lands," I said.

Tavish gave me a soft smile, then he and Melusine led us away from the others. We wound around a narrow tunnel and then upward to the rocks at the top of the cliff. A thin crack in the stones let in sunlight in a private chamber. We found a small cot on the floor and some benches around a rough table there.

"Please," Melusine said, gesturing to the table as she poured Sorcha, Pix, and me drinks. "Strawberry wine," she said as she poured. "There is a field near here where strawberries grow in plenty in the summer. We collected what we could last summer. We have a distillery and storage below ground."

"Are ye not worried about disturbing the little people of the hollow hills?" Pix asked.

"You are right to ask," Tavish said. "These caves have long been a sanctuary for the followers of the old ways. If we do not venture too deep into the caverns, the little people leave us be. They are not ignorant of what plagues these lands. I think... I think they wish to help us."

I nodded slowly.

"Boudica," Tavish said in all seriousness. "Two days ago, druids of the Cornovii passed this way. The tale they spun... The Romans are advancing on the west at an alarming rate. The druids of Mona are pushing on the people to fight back, but the force that is coming for them... They came to plead their case to you and Prasutagus. They have already gone to Venta to seek an audience with you."

"I will look for them when I return. I expect Prasutagus to return within the week."

"The druids bid the east to rise. Forgive me for being so blunt, but what are you waiting for?" Tavish asked me.

Tavish's question hit my heart hard. I had posed that question to myself many times. "The longer I stay my hand, the less the Iceni bleed. If we can continue to dance to Rome's tune, we can prevent the people from dying. That is all I want, to keep our people safe," I said, then paused. "Somehow, I want to believe we can find a way to prevent war, but I feel the change coming. It is an itch on my skin I cannot shake. I sense it in every shadow and hear it in the whispers of the wind. One insult too many... But we are too far past that now, aren't we? Look at you, my friends. Sweet Melusine, your father, your people, the druids. I just..." I said, then looked at Sorcha. "It is a risk. We have to make sure we have the allies we need in place. If our combined forces are not enough, we lose it all. So until we are ready, we dance."

"And lose ourselves, piece by piece," Melusine said, reaching for my hands. "We all honor you here, Boudica. May the gods guide you to know what is right."

I squeezed her hands.

Tavish nodded. "You will find the allies you need. I am sure of it."

"All this talk of war, and no one said a thing about this brew. 'Tis excellent wine," Pix said, swirling the liquid in her cup. "Ye have done well holed up here like one of the Picts."

At that, Tavish laughed. "What do you know of the painted people of the north, Pix?"

"Only that ye dare not cross them, for the fey have given them faerie darts for their arrows."

"Is that so?" Tavish asked with a laugh.

As the pair continued to jest, I rose and went to the crevice and looked out.

Sunlight shimmered through the trees, casting blobs of golden light.

I closed my eyes and listened to the sounds of the forest.

Melusine was right.

We were dying bit by bit.

"Boudica…

"Protect the oaks.

"Protect the stones," the soft voice of the greenwood whispered, but then, in a rough and loud voice, it added, *"Protect the people! Duir! Duir has fallen."*

I swayed as a vision flashed through my mind. I saw Artur and Prasutagus riding, my husband slipping from his horse. The image flickered once more, and I saw Prasutagus lying before a fire.

I recognized the place.

It was the ruins of Raven's Dell.

I swooned, stumbling toward the wall and banging my head on a stone jutting out there.

"Boudica," Pix said, jumping up.

"Mother," Sorcha added, rushing toward me.

Tavish and Melusine joined them.

"Queen Boudica, what is it?" Tavish asked, frowning at my head. "You're bleeding."

My head ached, and for a moment, I felt confused. Dark spots appeared before my eyes, and I struggled to stay upright.

Melusine hurried across the room, taking a cloth from a basket and wetting it. She hurried back and pressed it against the cut.

"Boudica, what did you see?" Tavish asked.

"I..." I began, trying to remember. I gasped, then turned to Sorcha. "Your father," I said, feeling a chill wash over me. "Prasutagus is ill. He's in the ruins of Raven's Dell. I most go there now."

"Boudica, ye be certain?" Pix asked.

"I saw him. He fell from his horse. I recognized the ruins of Chieftain Divin's roundhouse. I must go. Now."

"I will come with you," Tavish said.

"Aye, gods. We must go quickly. He looked fevered," I said, then turned to hurry from the cave, but my legs felt weak and black spots danced before my eyes.

"Ye be half faint. Really, Boudica, ye know better," Pix scolded me, then took my arm and led me from the cavern."

"It doesn't matter. If we ride hard, we can reach Raven's Dell tomorrow morning."

"Boudica—"

"Pix!" I said, turning to her. "We must not delay," I told her, holding her gaze. Prasutagus's dream haunted me. I would not tempt the gods.

Pix nodded. "All right. Come on. Ye too, Sorcha."

"Mel," Tavish said, holding a moment to speak to the princess. "Keep everyone quiet. We do not know what this means, but don't let anyone travel from this place until we know what is happening. And be safe," he whispered.

"And you," she told him.

Tavish grabbed his things while we went to ready the horses.

"Mother," Sorcha said, worry in her voice. "Olwen

will worry if we don't come home as planned, and Vian will send someone out looking for us."

"Banshees be cursed," I swore. She was right. I looked to Pix. "Pix…"

"Sorcha be right. I will ride back to Venta and tell them. Ride with the druid. Follow Elen's trail. I will find ye," she said, then hopped on her horse and clicked loudly, speeding off.

As I watched her go, worry washed over me. Being on the road without a guard was a bad idea. I turned and looked at Sorcha.

"We'll be all right," she reassured me. "We both know our weapons, and we will have Tavish. Besides, Elen will not let anything happen to us."

"Yes, I'm sure you're right," I told her, reaching for her hand.

"Mother, what *did* you see?"

"Your father is ill. That is all I know."

A few moments later, Tavish returned, Melusine with him.

She handed me a parcel. "Food, in case it takes longer than you expect."

"Melusine…"

She smiled at me, took my hand, and squeezed it. "Be safe, Boudica," she told me then stepped back.

Tavish quickly mounted the horse a druid had

brought for him. "Follow me," he said, then we turned and rode away from the druid's grove.

Elen, watch over Prasutagus.

"Boudica...

"Daughter of oak...

"Daughter of stones...

"For yourself, you should save your prayers," an ancient, gravelly voice replied.

Andraste?

"By the pricking of my toes, something wicked your way goes..."

CHAPTER 37

We made our way through the forest at a quick clip. Like the air around the shrine, our path felt...different. Everything seemed brighter and more colorful, the sunbeams more golden. As we rode, the passage of time felt off. It did not dim as it should. We paused to rest and water the horses when we reached a creek.

Sorcha took Dice so I could refill our waterskins.

At the side of the stream, I found a large boulder. On it had been carved the face of Elen, a rudimentary image of a woman with owl eyes and deer horns. Spirals and other symbols I didn't understand marked the stones.

I reached out and touched the face of the goddess.

"Can you read the symbols?" Tavish asked me.

I shook my head. "I have learned the Ogham, but no more."

"Elen is one of the most ancient goddesses in our lands. She guides those who would travel on the lines of power across. These are maps for those who can read them," he said, touching the stone. On it, I saw raised dots that formed a diamond shape.

"I have seen these before," I said, touching the symbol but not understanding what I saw.

"Give me your coin pouch, my queen," he said. "For a moment only," he added with a soft smile.

I handed my pouch to him. He dug through the coins, pulling out one of the Iceni coins that bore the image of Prasutagus on one side. It was coin created before we had wed. On one side of the coin was my husband's face. On the other side was a horse in honor of Epona, along with other embellishments.

"Here," Tavish said, gesturing. "Look familiar?"

On the coin was the same diamond-shaped symbol as on the stone.

"The very same. What does it mean?" I asked.

"The markings on the coin are a map of the stars. The diamond. The figure of the horse. Look to the sky tonight. You will see Epona and the diamond there. These symbols help our people keep to Elen's ways so we may more easily traverse the country under her watchful eye. Your husband just made it a little easier to find the map for those who know how to read it," he said, then laughed lightly.

"Tavish," I said, looking about. The world around me seemed so bright, the green more amplified, the surface of the water sparking with iridescent light. The shimmering sunlight on the forest floor was golden. "I cannot describe what I am seeing, only that I feel it."

"Time and space work *differently* on these roads."

"The sun has barely moved. It's like no time has passed at all."

Tavish nodded. "That's correct."

"But how will Pix—"

"Your guardian knows the paths as well as any druid. She will find us," he said, then looked to Sorcha, who was speaking gently to the horses who had finished drinking. "I think we are ready now," he said, then turned to me. "Boudica, I hope I did not offend you before with my bluntness. These are dark times. I have seen many terrible omens these past days," he said then paused. "We should get to Prasutagus."

"Tavish? What did you see?"

Tavish frowned but said nothing more. "Let's ride out. Princess? Ready?"

"Yes, Wise One."

With that, Tavish nodded, and we mounted once more.

Once we were in the saddle, I closed my eyes and sent my thoughts to Prasutagus.

Hold on, my love. We're coming.

LATER THAT DAY, we neared a crossroads. As we approached it, we heard another horse riding hard toward us.

Tavish gestured for us to stop.

I gripped my spear while Sorcha pulled her bow.

A moment later, however, I spotted Pix on a fresh horse.

"Finally," she said. "Near travelled to faerie and back lookin' for ye."

"Venta? Everything all right?" I asked hurriedly.

"Word has not yet reached them about the king. Vian has closed the roundhouse and set the guard on watch."

"Let's waste no time," Tavish said, then clicked to his horse, the rest of us following hard behind him.

Making our way down the narrow path through the forest, I noted a shift in the land around me as we went farther south, closer to Trinovantes territory.

Tavish eyed the sky then gestured for us to pause when we drew near an ancient tree.

"We must leave the ways now," he said. "But we will be easier to see. Go quiet, and follow me."

We turned away from the forest and toward a nearby steam. Tavish led us across the shallow creek to the other side. As we passed the water, I felt momentarily dizzy. The sky overhead moved strangely, the clouds shifting quickly across the sky. For a moment, everything spun around me, and then, I found myself by the stream not far from Raven's Dell. We followed the water back to the village. I recognized the place. This was where the Morrigu appeared to me.

Back then, I'd rejected her message.

In search of a peaceful solution, I had disregarded the battle goddess's demands.

Had I been wrong?

Had I been wrong all this time?

Regret and despair filled my stomach.

But my sense of fear and worry for Prasutagus outweighed everything else. I glanced back at Sorcha. She was biting her bottom lip, her eyebrows scrunched together.

We followed behind Tavish, finally reaching what remained of Raven's Dell.

It was a shock to see the place.

The little village was destroyed, most of the buildings burned to shells. The roundhouse had been reduced to ashes. Despite all our searching, we had never found Chieftain Divin, his daughter Brangaine, or any of the others.

Prasutagus's guard stepped forward at once.

"Hold there!" Ewan called.

From the roof of the house, Morfran cawed noisily at us.

It took Ewan a moment to recognize Tavish, but then he spotted the rest of our party, "Queen Boudica," he said, rushing forward. "Princess Sorcha. The king... How—" he said then looked from Pix to Tavish. "He's inside. Please, come at once, Wise One."

Tavish nodded, then hurried within.

Leaving the horses to Pix, Sorcha and I rushed behind Tavish. There, on a makeshift cot, I found Prasutagus, Artur at his side.

"Mother," Artur said, a pained expression on his face when he saw me.

"My king," Tavish said, kneeling beside Prasutagus to examine him. "When did he grow ill?"

"On the way back from Camulodunum," Artur said. "He complained of feeling cold, which was very unlike him. The next thing we knew, he slipped from the saddle. We found him burning and sweating. Then, he began wheezing violently, as if he could not catch his breath. We hurried him here. We've been trying to cool him down."

"Is he lucid?" Tavish asked.

"Barely," Artur replied.

"My king?" Tavish said, calling to Prasutagus. "My king?"

Prasutagus merely groaned.

Tavish opened Prasutagus's mouth and looked within. He then opened Prasutagus's eyelids, which had rolled back.

"Prasutagus," I said, kneeling beside him, taking his hand. "My love, do you hear me? Prasutagus?"

"Boudica," he whispered softly then wheezed hard.

His skin was burning hot.

"Father," Sorcha said, joining me, setting her hand on Prasutagus's arm. "Father, we're here."

"He's scorching with fever," I said, touching his forehead. "His lips... Do they look swollen to you too, Tavish?"

The druid nodded.

I turned to Artur. "Was he unwell on the ride from Venta or during his meetings?"

"He was irritable," Artur said, "which seemed unlike him. But given the circumstances, I didn't blame him. When we arrived, the talks began amenable enough, but then he and Procurator Catus had a terrible argument. Afterward, Prasutagus left in a rage."

I looked around at the others. While I wanted to know the reason for the argument, I would not ask in front of the men.

Tavish removed Prasutagus's boots, looking closely at his feet. Once he had done that, he gestured for me and Sorcha to step aside. He pressed his ear to Prasutagus's chest and listened.

My stomach quaked as I saw my husband lying there, pale as snow, sweating, groaning, wheezing, and struggling to stay conscious.

"His heart is beating rapidly," Tavish finally said.

"He sounds like he is in pain," I whispered.

Tavish gave me a knowing glance then lifted Prasutagus's tunic, inspecting his skin. The druid then studied my husband's fingers.

"Why are you looking at his hands and feet?" Sorcha asked.

I had not questioned the druid, but the moment Sorcha asked, I knew the answer. I turned to Artur. "Did you dine with the Romans?"

Artur shook his head. "No."

"What about drink? Did he drink anything?"

"I had nothing, but Catus and Father drank wine," Artur said.

"Did you actually see the Roman drink?" Tavish asked Artur.

"By the gods," Ewan whispered, the others realizing the implications of what was being asked.

Artur paused as he thought back. "I...I don't remember. My eyes were on my father as the conversation grew tense."

"Is there any sign, Tavish? Can you see any sign of poison?"

Tavish frowned hard. "I'm not sure, Boudica. Are

there any ailments in Venta? Has Prasutagus been exposed to anyone who has been ill?"

"No, but he was at Yarmouth two days back. He mentioned a ship of traders was unwell."

Tavish looked up, his glance going behind me to Pix. "Will you look?"

She nodded then knelt beside the king. "Aye, Strawberry King, ye are sweating like a virgin on her wedding day," Pix said, cutting the tension. "Be easy, now. Let me have a look," Pix said. Like Tavish, she inspected his hands, feet, and mouth. She then instructed the druid to help her remove my husband's tunic. He groaned when they moved him.

"Prasutagus," I said gently. "It's all right. We are just trying to find the cause of your ailment. It's all right. They will be done in a moment," I said, feeling my tears threaten. "You're all right. We're all here with you."

When they rolled Prasutagus on his side, I saw that his back was a wall of red. A large, bumpy rash had taken over the surface of his skin.

Sorcha gasped.

Pix gently lifted his arm, seeing the same rash in Prasutagus's armpit.

"Quickly, now," Tavish said. "We need to mix a draught of angelica, mung root, and spring berries. Pix, go to the stream and bring back mud and clay. Someone else go with her. Sorcha, into the forest. Find new fern fronds. Quickly now. You men, scour the forest floor for spring berries. Go at once. Bring as many as you can."

With that, everyone quickly departed leaving Artur, Tavish, and me on our own.

"Artur, what did they argue about?" I asked.

"Boudica," Artur replied, fear in his eyes. "They spoke of the money gifted to King Caturix. The procurator accused Prasutagus and you of hiding your debts from Rome. There was a terrible argument between them, Prasutagus telling the procurator that neither he nor you ever saw that sum, and for all Prasutagus knew, the Romans had it. The procurator told father," he said then paused, "that he would act upon Rome's rights and take from the Northern Iceni land equal to the value of the money loaned to King Caturix. Then, there was some argument about how *all* of the Greater Iceni's land is owned in half between Prasutagus and the emperor. The procurator said it was part of the submission agreement you agreed to before Emperor Claudius. Catus warned he would collect what was Rome's, whether father wanted to give it or not. And... he called you and Prasutagus traitors."

"Traitors," I said with a gasp.

At last, Rome had turned the knife on us.

I turned to Tavish. "*Was* he poisoned?"

"He has had a reaction to something. I cannot determine the source. It is as if his body is fighting against something foreign, as some do when they are stung by a bee or eat food that their body rejects."

"He ate nothing in Camulodunum," I confirmed with Artur. "Are you certain?"

He nodded. "He only ate what we packed with us, but he drank the wine."

"Does the king normally have a reaction to certain foods or herbs?" Tavish asked me.

I shook my head. "None that I know of."

"Bring the king's ration bag," Tavish told Artur then turned to my husband once more.

"Tavish," I whispered.

But at that same moment, Prasutagus began to wheeze heavily. His breathing became rattling and rapid, as if he were suffocating.

"My king," Tavish said, trying to hold him. "My king. Boudica, find the blue flask in my bag. Quickly."

Prasutagus's body began to shake, and his face grew red.

"Prasutagus," Tavish called, panic in his voice.

I handed Tavish the tonic. He quickly wet a cloth with the liquid and placed it over Prasutagus's nose and mouth. I had seen Ula use the same trick before. The fluid within helped clear the airways. But still, Prasutagus strained, his face growing redder, tinging with purple.

"He can't breathe. It's like he's choking. Prasutagus?

Prasutagus?" I called, reaching for him, tears running down my face.

My husband began to convulse. Tavish and I held him so he didn't hurt himself.

But a moment later, Prasutagus grew still and silent.

His gaze drifted to me for a single moment. When his eyes met mine, a light smile danced on his lips. His glance then shifted behind me. He smiled. Then, his gaze grew glossy, and his hand slumped to his chest.

"Prasutagus?" I whispered.

"My king?" Tavish said in alarm.

"Prasutagus?"

Tavish touched my husband's throat and wrist, then set his head on Prasutagus's chest.

I took Prasutagus's hand, but it had gone limp.

"Tavish?" I whispered.

The druid sat back, a look of disbelief on his face.

Tavish and I stared at Prasutagus, who now looked at some far-off place that neither of us could see.

"May Esu be waiting for you," I whispered. "May she guide you to your ancestors. May you find your father and mother and be at peace, my love," I said, tears streaming down my cheeks as I leaned forward and closed my husband's eyes.

I heard a noise behind me.

Looking back, I saw Artur standing there, Prasutagus's ration bag in his hand.

Setting the bag aside, he knelt beside me, wrapping his arm around my shoulders and pulling me close, both of us weeping.

"I have the ferns. The others are coming with—" Sorcha began as she entered the hovel, a bouquet of fern fronds in her hand. When she saw us, however, she stopped.

"Sorcha," I whispered.

My daughter stood frozen. I watched as she took it all in, then she began to shake her head. "No," she whispered. "No. No, no, no," she said. Dropping the bright green ferns on the ground, she turned and fled from the hut.

I rose and went to the door. "Sorcha!"

Pix and Ewan had come with buckets of mud. Pix looked from Sorcha to me.

When she saw my face, she knew.

Pix's features screwed up, her lips pursing, brow flexing, as tears came to her eyes. "Aye, by the Great Mother. No," she whispered then looked in the direction Sorcha went. "I'll go after her," she said, setting the bucket aside, then headed in the direction toward which Sorcha had fled.

I looked back into the room.

His eyes closed, Prasutagus's face was turned in the direction of the open casement—toward the forest, toward the trees. He had died with his eyes on his family and the land that he loved.

Artur was weeping, his head on his father's chest.

Beside him, Tavish had begun to pray in a low tone.

Outside, Morfran squawked, and squawked, and squawked.

The men returned.

Behind me, they whispered amongst themselves.

I looked over my shoulder at them, shook my head, then went back inside.

The king was dead.

And with his passage, the cracked shield that had protected us crumbled into dust.

CHAPTER 38

Death unmoors you. Suddenly, the person is just gone. Their plans, their dreams, all of it vanishes overnight. Everything is undone.

As I stood there in what remained of Raven's Dell, I thought of my world before Rome had come. I remembered my first meeting with Prasutagus. Gaheris had recently died. My dreams of a life with him had just been shattered. But back then, I still recognized the world around me. Now, I was a stranger to this world. I stared absently at the charred ruins of Raven's Dell. The only color left amongst the blackened buildings was the bright green fern fronds Sorcha had dropped when she'd fled.

My husband was dead.

Either by accident or poison, that was not yet clear.

Prasutagus was the king.

While I was a client queen of Rome, I knew the Romans well enough to know that they did not honor women's rights like men's. And Rome had already told Prasutagus they wanted the money Caturix owed.

They were coming for us.

Now, there was nothing to stop them.

The men prepared a litter with which we would take Prasutagus back to Venta.

Finally, sweaty and looking miserable, Ewan came to me. "Boudica, we're ready. We'll attach the litter to his horse."

I nodded.

On the other side of the square, Artur sat beside Sorcha, who had stopped speaking. My daughter sat on a charred bench, staring at an empty firepit.

I went and sat down on the bench beside Sorcha and pulled her toward me.

Still, she said nothing.

Artur held his sister's hand. We sat in silence.

After a time, Prasutagus's men went into the house to collect the king.

"I will help," Artur said. He kissed Sorcha's hand, then let her go, joining the others.

Sorcha and I merely sat and waited.

After what felt like an eternity, Pix appeared, guiding

the way. Soon, the others came carrying Prasutagus's body.

A small sob escaped my lips. I covered them with my hand.

Sorcha turned, burying her face into my arm.

I pulled her close, holding her as I watched the man I loved being carried to his litter.

After a long moment, I patted Sorcha's hair and said, "Come, we will find some young oak, fern, and flowers. We will adorn him as the king he is—a son of Cernunnos, a druid king, father of the Greater Iceni, and of the greenwood. We will not let him be dragged to Arminghall like some damned dead animal."

With that, Sorcha and I went into the forest, collecting what oaks, ferns, and flowers we could find. My mind was shattered, lost to grief. Distracted, I wandered a little farther than I had intended. I found myself alone in the forest, standing in the middle of a circle of mushrooms.

The scent of flowers, the warmth of summertime, and the gentleness of the air all told me I had inadvertently stepped into an in-between place. I was about to turn back when I heard a soft voice call.

"How now, Queen Boudica of the Greater Iceni?"

"I am Queen Boudica of all the Iceni," I replied tiredly, then turned.

Behind me was a stand of hawthorn trees. There,

amongst them, I saw a familiar shape. The faerie prince. He looked the same, dressed in his green tunic, his raven-dark tresses shimmering in the sunlight, light glinting off the silver crown on his head.

And I told him my name.

Again.

Never eat and drink with the fey.

Never accept faerie gifts.

And never tell them your full name.

Banshees be cursed!

He looked at me from between the branches. His eyes flashed silver.

"A widow now," he whispered. "Why don't you leave this world, Queen Boudica of the Iceni? The eagle has you wrapped in its claws. Soon, it will pick your bones clean. Leave this violent place and come with me to the summer and sunshine."

"I cannot," I whispered, desperately wishing I could say yes, that I could escape the pain of what would come next.

He stepped toward me, a playful smirk on his lips. "Just for a while... Come with us, eat, drink, and rest. We can open the gates to you, take you far from here. Or, maybe you would like to visit somewhere where the sun shines on fields of grapes and be with one you have known for many lifetimes."

The thought of Aulus in that moment made me feel ill.

"No," I whispered.

"Come away all the same. Come away from the pain."

"Mother?" Sorcha called from somewhere afar. "Where are you?"

The sound of her voice, and the sad tone therein, pulled me back from the strange brink on which I was standing.

"No," I said, then moved to leave the faerie ring and break the spell. But I paused a moment and looked toward the fey creature. "Do you know?" I asked. "Do you know the truth? Did the Romans poison Prasutagus?"

"Queen of oak... Queen of stone..." the man said, his voice fading as he drifted away, blending into the trees. "Queen of ash and iron... What do *you* think?"

And then, he was gone.

I knew what I thought.

And the very whisper of it filled me with murderous rage.

"Mother?" Sorcha called again, appearing not far from me. She looked around as if she could not see me. "Mother?" This time, there was panic in her voice.

"I'm here," I yelled back. "I'm here," I said, stepping from the circle. "Sorcha—"

Sorcha jumped. "Mother," she said, looking around in confusion. "Where did you—" Then she saw the ring of mushrooms. "You dared a faerie ring?"

"Accident."

"But you... You were not here, and now—"

"Ula is right. Don't tempt fey things."

"Banshees be cursed," Sorcha whispered in a low tone, her voice full of amazement. Then, she looked at the bundles in her hands. "I have all I can find."

I nodded. "The same. Come."

Sorcha and I returned to our party. The men waited patiently as Sorcha and I arranged Prasutagus's litter. When it was finally done, I nodded and then stepped back.

"Let us take the king to Arminghall," I said. "We will see him to the gods before the sun rises."

"My queen, no one will blame you if you delay—" Ewan began.

"My friend, it is not for myself that I rush," I said, then looked around at all the others. I paused a moment, then said, "When the Romans first came, Prasutagus and I passed through Raven's Dell on our way to Camulodunum. There, by the stream, I had a vision of the Morrigu. She warned me then that the eagle would come for us. Prasutagus and I danced to Rome's tune to keep everyone safe, sacrificing more than we wanted. But now, the Morrigu is right. The king is dead. Rome will come. I cannot delay even to send my husband to the gods as I see fit. Word will spread at once that he is dead. It cannot be helped. And then, they will come. Like rain in spring or snow in winter. We must make ready."

"What will we do?" Artur asked.

"We will rise."

CHAPTER 39

After some discussion, we decided that Artur and Pix would ride ahead to the king's house to collect Olwen and the rest of the household. We would not have common gossip reach them before the news came from someone they loved.

"Olwen..." Sorcha said, tears threatening.

"Artur and Pix will see to her," I said gently. "We will be together soon."

But even as I said it, I remembered when Olwen had given me the Ogham stave. My younger daughter had already seen something. Perhaps she didn't know when or how, but she knew.

Not that it would lessen the pain of loss.

My own relationship with my father had been strained. But Olwen, Sorcha, and Artur loved their father. As I loved my husband. As the Greater Iceni loved their king.

"Ewan," I said, joining the guard. "Please, pick two of your men and send them north immediately. I am sorry to ask them to miss the funeral rites, but I must get word to Bran. Bran must be told that Prasutagus is dead. And that he must make ready in case Rome comes."

"They will, won't they?" Ewan whispered.

I paused.

"My queen?"

"The next few days will shape the future of our world. Bran needs to be ready."

Ewan nodded and then spoke to his men. Two of our most trusted warriors prepared to ride out. They stopped first, paying their final respects to Prasutagus, then departed quickly.

"Boudica," Tavish said, "I will travel the ways back to the shrine and collect the druids. We will meet you in Arminghall."

"Tavish. No. The Romans are hunting you."

"We will risk it for Prasutagus's sake. We will see the king to the pyre."

I nodded to him. "Very well."

Tavish left us then, mounting his horse and departing once more.

Once the others had set out, I went to Sorcha, took

her hand, and met her gaze. "Let's get your father to Arminghall."

She stared at me. "It doesn't feel real. Why don't I feel anything? It doesn't feel real. Do you feel like that?"

I nodded. "The pain will come later. And it will be more than either of us can stand. For now, we must ensure your father goes to his ancestors with honor."

"And after?"

"After is another matter. I love you, my daughter. Now, let's go."

With that, we rode out.

The ride from Raven's Dell felt like it took forever. It was a long, dark, and somber ride. Time slipped away. I endeavored to replay all the happy moments I had shared with my husband, but whispers invaded my every thought.

Rome.

Rome.

Rome.

The Seelie prince had whispered to my heart.

The Romans had poisoned Prasutagus. Their silent act was one of war. My mind twisted and turned, spinning around what must happen next. It was too much. My heart ached. My husband was gone. My daughters, grown though they now were, were fatherless.

"Aye, Andraste, be with me," I whispered.

We arrived at Arminghall in the dead of night.

Much to my surprise all of Venta was there.

The henge was lit with torches. And everyone—everyone—had come. The thousands of people who lived in the city stood waiting for their king to arrive.

In the center of the henge, I could just make out the shapes of Tavish and the other druids.

Word had been spread.

And the people had gathered.

The King of the Greater Iceni was dead.

As we rode toward the henge, the people of the Greater Iceni grew silent and bowed as we passed.

We made our way to the druids.

A pyre had been erected.

Pix waited with Artur, Olwen, Vian, and the others from my household. Everyone's eyes were wet with tears.

I dismounted quickly, waiting for Sorcha, then we joined Olwen.

Over and over again, my daughter signaled the symbol for Duir, then she broke into a soundless sob.

"Oh, my sweet girl," I said, stroking her hair as I held her. "My sweet girl."

Sorcha hugged her sister. "We are here," she reassured Olwen. "We are here."

Artur and Balfor joined the warriors and unhitched the litter. They prepared to take Prasutagus to the fire.

Those in the crowd wept.

Melusine stepped forward. She rarely showed herself in public. But tonight, she stood at the gate of the henge, uncovered, a torch in her hand, and began to sing.

Light is behind, all our hopes are shed
  The great heart of the forest has fled
  Now, run wild
  Under the moon and oaks this night
  Now, run wild
  Our sacred paths have bled
  Hope is behind, raven's wings beat instead
  Epona's children, wake from your beds
  Now, run wild
  For the stars fall this night
  Now, run fearless
  There are clouds ahead
  Happiness is behind, the path of iron ahead
  It is time to raise up your heads
  Now, run wild
  Children of stone and light
  Now, run fearless, for there is naught but night
  There is naught but night.

Her voice rang loudly and clearly, the melancholy song ringing across the fields. I imagined it reverberating across the land, touching every heart in Greater

Iceni territory, awakening in them the same thing that was awakening in me.

A desire to fight back.

A desire to take everything back… my home, my gods, my people, my land, all of it.

All of it.

The men carried Prasutagus's body to the pyre.

Once he was laid thereon, Tavish began to call to the gods in a strong, firm voice.

But I didn't hear anything.

The druids raised their hands in unison and chanted sacred prayers.

But still, I heard nothing.

All I saw was the flames of the torches.

I stared into the fire. Watching, and watching, and watching.

When Tavish lifted a torch and moved toward Prasutagus's pyre, he paused and looked at me.

I inhaled slowly, deeply, taking in the last breath I would ever take in a world where my husband still existed.

Then, I nodded to the druid.

With that, Tavish lit the pyre.

The dry twigs and logs, imbued with pitch so the flames would burn faster, quickly caught.

Around me, I heard people singing the funeral lament of our people.

But I did not hear the words.

All I saw was the flame encompassing my husband's body. I stared into it until I could feel the fire looking back at me. In the flames, images began to take shape. I saw Camulodunum with the temple of Divine Claudius and the neat rows of the colonia built with the sacred rocks of Maiden Stones. In my vision, Camulodunum in flames. And beyond that, deeper into the fire, I saw more. I saw the governor's villa, the basilica, the stone walls, and the temple of Mithras in Londinium burst into flames.

Burning.

Burning.

I saw them burning.

And something inside me that I had built a wall around began to melt, fading in the wake of that heat of Prasutagus's pyre. It faded until there was nothing between Rome and me other than the raw, raging fire that I had imprisoned within me. It burst forth, touching every inch of my body. I felt it burning within me, a rage I hadn't known I was smoldering.

I felt the fury of my ancestors and heard the thousands of angry voices of those who had died face-down in the mud. A thundering cacophony of voices that all demanded one thing of me.

"*Rise.*

"*Rise.*

"Rise, Queen Boudica of the Iceni.

"Rise!"

And then, after them, a single soft voice whispered in my ear, the sound and feel of it as gentle as a lover's touch.

"Boudica," Prasutagus whispered, "rise."

Deafened by the sound, I flung my hands to my ears and let out a wail so loud, so powerful, that when it had left me, I dropped to my knees, panting.

"Boudica," Pix said, bending to take my arm. "Boudica?"

Breathing deeply, I sat there, rocking myself back and forth until I felt the pieces of myself come back together again. When I finally emerged from that darkness, I realized it was nearly dawn.

Heavy fog blanketed the nemeton.

My skin, clothes, hair, and everything else were wet from the morning dew.

The pyre smoldered.

Confused, I looked behind me.

The people had gone.

The druids had gone.

Everyone had gone but Pix.

"Pix?" I whispered.

"Ye would not be moved. Nor did ye hear any of us. The druid said to leave ye until the gods were done speaking. Are they done?"

I nodded slowly, my eyes on Prasutagus's pyre.

"Good. Now, there will be time enough to say what they spoke to ye. But for now, ye be grieved and exhausted. Let me get ye home and to bed. And after, we will do what must be done."

"Pix," I whispered.

"Nay, Strawberry Queen. Say nothing now. I don't need a vision to know what the gods want from ye. But ye must rest if ye hope to see it done. I be here for ye. From now to the very end."

"Promise?"

"Aye, Boudica. From this life to the next, and the next, and the next."

CHAPTER 40

I t was a somber ride back to the roundhouse. Given the hour and the mood in Venta, no one was about. The fog was dense. I was soaked and cold by the time we finally got home. Pix led me to my bedchamber, but I just couldn't... not without Prasutagus.

I shook my head then slipped into the girls' room. There, I found Sorcha and Olwen curled up in Olwen's bed.

Feeling exhausted, I lay down on Sorcha's pallet.

"Rest ye now," Pix told me. "If there is need, I will wake ye."

I closed my eyes.

Oh, Prasutagus...

I felt a sharp pain in my chest.

Aye, gods. Why? Why?

The misery that racked me was more than I could bear. My love. My children's father. Gone. Just, gone. I hadn't felt like this since Gaheris had been taken. Prasutagus was my partner, my love. How could I face what came next without him?

Tears slipped down my cheeks.

Why?

Why?

Rome.

That was why.

Rome had taken Prasutagus from me.

Sobbing softly, trying not to wake the girls, grief and rage overwhelmed me.

Eventually, I cried myself to sleep.

As they had for the past weeks, my dreams haunted me. Again, I was on Mona, seeing what Brenna saw. But something about this was different.

Before, I had felt like I was seeing the future.

Now...

It was just past dawn.

I was running from the beach, away from the water, toward a cluster of houses. A bell was ringing in the distance. Shortly thereafter, someone sounded a carnyx. The sound of the war horn echoed across the island. Everywhere I looked, I saw people running.

I raced toward a ring of stones that sat on a lonely hilltop above the small village. My lungs burned in my chest. I could feel the sense of panic rippling through me. When I got to the stones, I dropped on my knees and looked into the well that sat within the circle of stones. A moonwell…

Suddenly, Brenna's face appeared in the water.

"Boudica," she called to me. "Boudica, do you hear me? Boudica!"

"Brenna?"

"The Romans! The Romans! They are gathering. They will come for us. Boudica! Boudica, help us!"

With a gasp, I sat up, finding Pix standing at the end of the bed.

"Boudica," she said, and I realized it was not the first time she had called my name.

"Pix?"

"Procurator Catus is here with a guard. He is demanding to speak with you. Now."

I looked toward Olwen's bed, but the girls were gone. "Where are they?"

"They went into Venta with Artur and Vian."

"The procurator is here? Now?"

"Outside the gates. We did not let him in, despite his threats."

"The Romans have gathered their forces along the coast in the west. A launch on Mona is imminent."

"How do ye know?" Pix asked, aghast.

"Brenna. We need to get rid of the procurator. I will

buy us time. The moment the Romans are gone, we must start sending riders—to Bran, to the chieftains, to Arixus, to everyone."

"Boudica—"

"I will raise the east and try to draw the Romans away from Mona. We can still manage it. But we must act now."

Pix nodded. "I will gather the men and get everyone organized."

"The minute you see Artur and the girls, get them safely stowed away from Roman eyes and behind these walls."

At that, Pix nodded and then departed.

I rose, pausing just a moment to splash some water on my face. I could still smell the smoke of the funeral pyre in my hair and on my gown.

Grabbing my spear, I turned and made my way from the roundhouse. The wind blew across the square, blowing my skirts about me.

Overhead, Morfran called to me. I held out my arm.

The bird landed thereon.

"Queen Boudica," one of the guards called. "The Romans want to enter."

"Train your bows on them. Draw your swords. Open the gates," I replied, walking with purpose.

The gates swung open, revealing that my men—not just my men, but the people of Venta—were guarding the entrances to the king's compound. Men and women, young and old, boys and girls with swords, hammers, bows, spears, and more stood before the gates of the king's house.

Procurator Catus waited before a large party of Roman soldiers.

More.

More than ever.

The people moved, letting me through.

When I reached the Romans, Morfran squawked loudly at Catus, then rose off, flying to Artur, who had just appeared, Vian, Sorcha, and Olwen along with him, from the direction of Arminghall.

"What is the meaning of this?" Procurator Catus asked me angrily. "I will not be denied entrance."

"You *have* been denied, Procurator. What do you want?"

"Where is Prasutagus?"

"Breath in the air. You can still smell him on the wind."

At that, the procurator started at me. I read his expression, trying to find surprise there. There was none.

"Well," he said, shifting. "I mourn your loss, Queen Boudica. Your husband and I did not always see eye to eye, but Prasutagus was well-respected by Emperor Claudius. Now, we have important business we must discuss. A point of contention and confusion arose between your husband and myself at our last meeting. We must further discuss the matter."

I waved toward the tavern nearby. The place had cleared out with the arrival of the Romans. The benches at the tables outside the tavern were empty. "Have a seat," I said, willing my hands to be steady and still. Willing myself not to kill every last Roman standing there.

I had to delay.

I had to act stupid.

I had to get the procurator to think I knew nothing of the manner of Prasutagus's death nor of the Roman assault on Mona. I was just a widow in mourning. I had to play the game now. And yet, my anger rolled inside me, the edge of it so thin, my hands shook.

With an annoyed huff, the procurator sat down at one of the benches.

I lifted a mug from the table, sloshing what liquid there was therein to the ground, then poured the Roman a drink from the pitcher of ale sitting there. I set it down hard, the liquid spilling over the top.

He looked at it, a disgusted sneer on his face.

"What, sir? Not to your liking. Just a simple, unpolluted ale shared between friends," I said as I poured myself a cup then set it aside, not drinking. I stared at him with intensity. I wished he would crack in half.

Lifting the cup, he looked up at me from under his bushy black-and-white brows. His gaze flicked to my drink, which I had not touched, then to his own cup again. Then, he set his cup back down without drinking.

Gripping my spear hard, I asked, "What do you want?"

"What Rome is owed, Queen Boudica. I am sorry for your loss, but perhaps your husband did not have a chance to share our concerns regarding the coin loaned—"

"Gifted."

"*Loaned* to both yourself *and King Caturix*. I am well aware that you and Prasutagus have done your best to pay on your debt, but this matter of keeping your brother's loan a secret… I did not think you so low, Queen Boudica. And to discover that you have lied and deceived, after the Northern Iceni were given special exemption after their little rebellion. Horrible. Horrible. And you call yourselves allies to Rome?"

"What do I know of the coin given to Caturix? Rome took over Stonea, where my brother held his seat. That money was there, in the fort. Have you had your men check the cupboards? Maybe if Scapula hadn't stolen that fort from me, I would have found it. But he did. I don't have that coin."

"Lies."

"What? You think my brother gave me the coin

before he led his rebellion? Or maybe he had it on his person? I didn't see it when I cut my brother's corpse from a pole. Maybe the crows ate it along with the rest of his body. We don't have that coin, Procurator. For all I know, Rome has that money and is fleecing the Iceni like common vagabonds because you are failing at your war in the west," I said, slapping my hand on the table, making the man's cup quake, the ale spilling over.

The sight of it was enough to remind me of what I was supposed to be doing. I was supposed to be calm. I was supposed to be biding my time. I was supposed to be placating the man. My rage was causing me to fail miserably.

The procurator met my gaze. "You will pay that coin. Every cent of it. The money owed by *all* of the Iceni. If you do not, I will take your lands, your people, your horses, and anything else I want. Do you hear me, woman? Your husband is dead. You are queen no more. You fail us one time, and we will sweep over you as we did the Catuvellauni."

I squeezed my hand around my spear and said, "A fortnight. You must give me a fortnight to collect the coin. I must take from every hand. Give me that, and you will get your money."

Thinking he had won something, the procurator rose. Setting his fists on the table, he leaned toward me. "Fail, and I will have you in chains, tawny."

Avoiding his gaze, I looked away.

My eyes fell briefly on the man's belt on which he wore a dagger.

A chill washed over me. My hands shaking, unable to hide the emotion in my voice, I hissed, "Where did you get that?"

There, hanging from the procurator's belt, was a dagger like no other. Made of ancient metal, the flower of Scáthatch on the hilt, was Gaheris's blade.

"What?" the procurator asked in annoyance.

I stepped back, willing my heart to be still, but my breathing was so hard, my nostrils flared. "The dagger. Where did you get that?"

"Oh," he said, pulling the blade from his belt.

My emotions betrayed me. The man had seen something painful in my expression.

He smiled sickly. "That is my treasure. It is the reason I came to this bloody island. When was it? Forty-one or forty-two, perhaps. Aulus was sending spies all along the coast to find the best place to land for the invasion. We didn't want to make Caesar's mistakes, of course, so we were sending landing parties up and down your coastlines. One party came back with a tale. They had found a very nice spot to land in the Wash. That's Northern Iceni territory, isn't it?" he asked, a twinkle of macabre glee in his eyes. "Yes. I believe it is. They encountered a small band of villagers. Nothing too much for our men to handle. Slaughtered them, of course, but came home with a few prizes. Some coin, brooches, weapons. The men gave Aulus Plautius this dagger. He wore it for a time then lost it in a dice game to Titus Carassius. Titus lost it in a game of cards to me. Handsome design, and the blade never gets dull. I... Do you recognize the blade?" he asked, smiling vindictively.

I extended my hand. "Give to me," I said, barely able to breathe.

"What?"

"Give it to me."

Catus laughed. "You can't be serious."

"Give it to me, you steaming pile of dung," I screamed at him then moved quickly, pressing the tip of my spear against the procurator's neck.

The Romans moved toward me, but Catus motioned for them to hold.

"You are making a mistake," Catus whispered to me. "You are smarter than this. Press that spear in, and you will unmake your world."

"Give me the dagger," I hissed, pushing the spear until it cut the man's skin, making him bleed.

"Thank you," he whispered to me. "You men there," he said, quickly moving away from me. "Take them," he said, gesturing to Sorcha, Olwen, Artur, and Vian. "And bind the queen."

"Oh, no ye don't," Pix said, pulling her sword and rushing forward.

"Kill them," Catus said, gesturing to the crowd. "Kill them all. Kill anyone who resists then see to the king's roundhouse," Catus called.

Pushing the citizens aside, the soldiers stepped in between the procurator and me and grabbed me.

"Boudica," Pix called, fighting to get to me.

"Kill her!" Catus called. "Bind the queen and bring her there," he said, pointing to the hitching rail outside the tavern. "That boy and the secretary. Bind and gag them and throw them in the wagon. As for the girls..." Catus said then turned and looked at me. "Ah, tawny. You have no king to protect you now.

"Men, it was a long walk from Camulodunum. You look very thirsty. The queen assures me the drink here is unpolluted. Let's see if her daughters are the same. The Greater Iceni are horse people. Ride their princesses until they're broken," he called with a laugh.

The Roman soldiers grabbed Sorcha and Olwen and started pulling them toward the tavern.

"No! No," I screamed, but someone hit me hard on the back of the head.

Dark spots swam before my eyes. One of the Romans yanked my spear from my hand and threw it aside. When I looked back, trying to see my daughters, one of the Roman soldiers punched me in the face again and again.

Through the blood and pain, I saw Pix fighting to get to me.

"Boudica! Boudica!" she screamed as nearly a dozen Roman soldiers moved to stop her.

"Pix, get out of here! Get out of here!"

"Sorcha!" Artur screamed. "Sorcha! Olwen!"

A Roman hit Artur hard, knocking him to the ground. Another grabbed Vian roughly.

Around me, everything ignited at once.

The people began to fight back.

Pulling their swords or grabbing anything handy, they began to beat the Romans, trying to stop them.

My head spun. My face felt like it was on fire. Blood poured from my nose.

All around, people were fighting, and screaming, and dying.

I tried to find my daughters in the crowd.

"Mother! Mother!" Sorcha screamed as she fought against the Romans who held her. For a moment, I caught sight of Olwen. She sobbed soundlessly in terror as the Romans pulled her toward the tavern.

"Olwen... Sorcha..."

I pushed the soldiers aside and ran toward my daughters, but four men intercepted me.

Then, I lost Olwen and Sorcha in the crowd. I was unable to see them, but I could hear Sorcha screaming.

Yanking me hard, the Romans pulled me toward the hitching post.

"Bind her. Bind her by the wrists!" the procurator called.

I fought back, but there were too many of them.

A moment later, I was being tied to the wood, my wrists roughly bound with rope.

Catus pulled out Gaheris's blade, showing it to me once more.

He grinned at me then came behind me. Yanking my dress, he used the dagger to cut open the back of my gown.

"Here. Give me that," he said, speaking to someone I could not see.

All around me, I heard confusion and screaming as people fought and died.

Then, I heard the boom of fire.

"You would tempt Rome, Queen Boudica?" Catus called to me. "Now, feel what it means to be Rome's servant," he said with a laugh.

There was a sharp crack, and then I felt the lash on my back.

Again and again, Catus cracked the horsewhip on my back as he laughed, and laughed.

Inside the tavern, I heard Sorcha screaming and crying.

I couldn't see what was happening to my daughters, but I knew.

I knew.

May the maiden be with them, I knew.

Aye gods, I knew.

I felt it in the pit of my stomach.

In that moment, I wanted to die.

I hoped they would die.

I wanted them to die rather than face such an assault.

"They are innocent. Innocent," I whispered.

But Catus merely laughed and cracked his whip. "Not anymore," he howled.

The pain on my flesh was nothing compared to the pain in my heart.

Over and over again, the procurator lashed me.

I couldn't feel my skin anymore.

My mind grew numb from the pain. For a moment, I thought I would black out.

"That should be enough," Catus finally said then told one of his men. "I think they've learned their lesson. Make ready to go," he said then came before me once more.

His white robes marred with speckles of my blood, Catus shook the bloody whip before me then dropped it. Leaning down, he met my gaze and held it.

"You have a fortnight, Boudica. When you fail to pay —which you will—I will have all that is yours. You have forgotten who your master is. I hope this served as a reminder," he said then slipped the dagger back onto his belt. "Who knows, Queen Boudica. In nine months' time, perhaps your family will look far more Roman anyway," he added with a laugh. "By the by, I have Prasutagus's son and that *female* secretary of yours. Deliver the coin as agreed, and you can have them back. Fail, and they will die."

With that, the man departed.

I felt sick, my stomach threatening to heave at any moment. The pain was so horrible it made my head spin.

But worse, far worse, was the soft sound I heard in the distance: Sorcha weeping.

"Girls. My girls," I whispered.

I heard the Romans call to one another, and a moment later, they moved off.

Then, everything went black.

CHAPTER 41

"Queen Boudica," a soft voice called. "My queen? Boudica? She's coming around. Ready the draught."

I opened my eyes. Overhead, I saw many bundles of dried herbs hanging from the rafters. The familiar scents of herbs, flowers, and mushrooms perfumed the place.

"Ula?" I whispered.

"Queen Boudica," a soft voice said again. "It is Ariadne," she said, taking my hand gently. "It is Ariadne and Rue. You are with us at my midwifery in Venta."

I opened my eyes. Ariadne, who had delivered Olwen, sat on a stool beside the bed. Rue, the Catuvellauni priestess I had saved from the slavers in Londinium, was with her.

"Try not to move," Ariadne told me. "We have cleaned your wounds, put on healing unguents, and bandaged you, but you must move as little as possible. Rue has a tonic for you to stem the pain."

"My girls… Where are my girls?"

"They are here with us, my queen."

"I need to—" I began, then moved to rise, but the pain was nearly unbearable. "Ahh," I gasped.

"Mother?" Sorcha called from the other room.

"She's awake," Rue called to her.

Sorcha burst into the room, her face red from crying. "Mother!"

"Sorcha," I said, moving to get to her, but she waved her hands at me.

"Don't move. You must not move."

Ignoring her, I sat up. "Oh, Sorcha," I said, reaching for her and wrapping my arms around her. "Oh, my girl. I am so sorry. I am so, so sorry. I could not—Where is Olwen?"

"She was distraught, so we gave her something to help her sleep," Ariadne told me.

"Here," Rue said, handing me a tonic. "Drink this. It will help with the pain without numbing the mind."

I took the drink, then looked at my daughter as I set my hand on Sorcha's face. Her dirty cheeks were marred with streaks where tears had run. "Oh, Sorcha…"

"I will mend. Do not think of it. I will mend," she

said, choking on her words as she struggled to catch her breath. "Ariadne has looked after Olwen and me. We will mend." My daughter was trying to be strong. But who can be strong in the face of what she endured? My girls had been innocent. Now... The Romans had taken that from them in the cruelest way possible.

"Sorcha," I said, tears trailing down my cheeks. "My daughter."

"Ariadne and I have cared for them, my queen. There is no long-lasting physical damage," Rue told me. "And we have given them both tonics of moonberry, so no fruit can be born of such vileness. It is only the heart that takes time to mend. I shared my experience with your daughters. They will recover in time. But it does take time."

"When I have killed every Roman, I will be fine. Then, I will be better," Sorcha said, seething. "I memorized every face. Every soldier. I know them all, and I will find them."

"Sorcha," I said, my hands shaking as I smoothed her hair. "Pix and the others? Where is Pix?"

"She managed to escape before they killed her, but she is wounded. She's resting with Olwen," Ariadne told me.

"Ah, gods," I said, covering my mouth with my hands. "They have Artur and Vian. I must—" I said, then moved to rise.

"Boudica, you *cannot*. You must rest," Ariadne protested.

"The people… How many people have been killed? The city? The servants at the king's house? Please, I…" I said, then looked down at my torn gown. "I need a cape. I must go check on the others. There is work that must be done now. I cannot delay a moment," I said, then looked at the women. "Prasutagus's death was no accident. Rome will move on the Iceni if I do not act quickly. Pain or not, I must act now."

"Mother," Sorcha whispered. "*Did* the Romans poison father?"

"Yes."

Sorcha sat back, a stunned expression on her face.

"If you are determined to move about, you must let me wrap your chest to hold the bandages more tightly in place," Ariadne told me. "Sorcha, help me get your mother's dress off."

Rue returned a moment later with a simple green gown and an odd cloak made in a patchwork design. "It is unusual, I know," she told me when she saw me eyeing the mantle. "It was a gift from an old woman here in Venta. She was dying. She made the cloak to thank me for treating her as best I could. It has squares of all the gowns she wore over the years and patches from her husband's, son's, and daughter's clothes—all of whom had gone before her. She told me she put protective spells in every stitch. You must take it, Boudica."

"I cannot," I replied.

"I am alive because of you. If you had not intervened that day, I would have been sold to slavery. I know what you must face now. This woman's spellwork will protect you. Take it, Boudica, with all its blessings upon you."

Swallowing hard, I nodded.

After Ariadne had rewrapped my wounds and the women helped me change, I donned the cloak. Rue hurried to the corner where she retrieved my spear.

"One of the men brought it."

"Thank you," I told Rue, then turned to Sorcha. "Stay with Pix and Olwen. Watch over them. I must go to the roundhouse and see what the Romans have done. I won't have you there."

"Mother…" Sorcha began to protest.

"No, Sorcha."

"There is a guard outside waiting for you. Many of the king's guard were killed in the fighting, but warriors are already gathering, my queen," Ariadne told me.

"Good. Soon, I will call them all."

Leaning against my staff, I went to the second chamber, where I found Olwen and Pix were sleeping. Pix's eye and the side of her face were bruised and bloody.

"She was knocked unconscious in the battle," Rue told me. "It's probably the only reason she's still alive."

Olwen slept on a small cot by the fire. How tiny she looked lying there. In her sleepy face, I saw her baby features. But she was grown now. A child no more. Rome had taken the last of her innocence.

"I will be back for them," I said, turning to Sorcha. "Watch over them."

Sorcha nodded.

With that, I exited the midwifery, Rue following behind me.

"I will come in case there are wounded," she told me. "I sent a boy to fetch the druids. Until they arrive, I will do what I can."

Outside the midwifery, I found a dozen Greater Iceni soldiers, all of whom were wounded in some manner or other. Amongst them, I spotted Ewan.

"Queen Boudica," he said, hurrying to me. "My queen," he said, dropping to his knee.

Behind him, the others did the same.

"Queen Boudica, please forgive us. We could not get to you and the princesses. We tried. Many men died. My queen… My queen…"

"Rise, Ewan. Please. Rise, all of you. I cannot bend to lift you. Please, rise."

As the midwife said, many people had gathered— not just the guard, but men from Venta, the blacksmith and his sons, horse vendors, silver makers, so many, men and women alike—all with swords. Everyone was looking at me.

I cleared my throat and said, "The Morrigu has taken flight. The raven will now chase the eagle. These many years, we have endured insults to protect our lives. No more. Now, we will follow that fiery goddess all the way to the end," I said, then turned to Ewan. "Close the city. Man the walls. Kill any Roman found in Venta."

Ewan nodded, then began calling to the others, shouting orders.

Turning, I made my way to the roundhouse. In the distance, I could see that one of the buildings was on fire.

My hands shook.

Every step I took was painful.

But it didn't matter. Prasutagus was dead. My girls had been defiled. My son and friend had been taken.

Now, there was only vengeance.

I ARRIVED AT THE ROUNDHOUSE, finding exactly what I had expected. The granary was on fire, as were the stables. The guard was all dead. The horses had fled to the corral, where they bucked and kicked wildly in panic.

The men from the horse market hurried to the animals. Raven, old as he was, had herded all of the other horses to the far end of the fence, away from the fire. He paced back and forth, keeping them away from the flames.

I spotted Dice and Ember dancing anxiously behind Raven.

I scanned the herd but didn't see Druda anywhere. "Druda! Druda?"

There was no reply.

"Gods, no," I whispered. "Druda!"

Finally, I heard a whiney coming from the stables.

"No," I cried. "They are trapped in their stalls."

A moment later, Isolde, who, from her appearance, had suffered a fate not much different from my daughters and myself, appeared from the burning stables.

"Queen Boudica! Help! Help! The horses!"

We hurried across the square. The stable was ablaze. The back of the barn was entirely on fire.

"The horses in the back… I can't get to them. There is still time for those in the front, but I need help," Isolde said tearfully.

Grabbing saddle blankets or whatever else they could find, the men dipped them into the water trough, soaking them, then headed into the blaze.

When I moved to go, Beow held me back. "No,

Queen Boudica," he said, giving me a firm look. He then raced forward with the others.

A few moments later, Uilleann, Olwen's horse, came racing past.

After her came several of the other horses.

"Druda! Druda!" I called.

Again, he whinnied. I could hear panic in the sound.

I rushed into the burning building, covering my mouth with a corner of the cape.

The whole stable was on fire.

The men worked quickly, freeing as many horses as possible, but those in the back of the stables...

Finally, I spotted Druda. He was in a stall in the back.

"Druda!"

The roof overhead shifted, and beams began to fall.

"Get out," Beow called to the men. "Get out!"

The others hurried away.

"Druda!" I called one last time, catching sight of my horse for a moment. I met his gaze. He called out to me in a sweet, loving knicker, then Isolde pulled me away.

A moment later, the roof of the stable collapsed.

We hurried away from the falling timbers, trying to get clear as the fire engulfed the place.

"Druda!" I screamed, watching the fire take the stable. "Oh, no," I whispered, tears streaming down my cheeks. "Not like that. Not like that... Druda..."

"My queen," Rue called to me from the roundhouse door.

"Go on," Isolde told me. "I'll collect Uilleann and the rest."

I hurried across the square to the roundhouse, meeting Rue, who stood barring the door.

"Rue? What is it?" I asked, looking behind her.

"Boudica," she said gently, meeting and holding my gaze.

She didn't have to say more.

"No," I whispered.

Rue stepped aside, and the two of us entered the house.

I found my home in a complete state of chaos...and carnage. As we made our way through, I stepped over several members of the king's guard, including the young men who had joined Artur in his warband. I paused when I came upon Newt, the boy who had gone from scrubbing pots in my kitchen to protecting my life.

I bent and put my fingers to his neck, feeling for signs of life.

He was gone.

Turning down the hallway, I went to the formal meeting room. It had been looted. All of our gold, coins, silver pieces...everything had been taken.

Working my way around the house, I found more bodies.

"Brita? Betha or Ronat?" I asked Rue.

She shook her head. "I have not found them."

We crept through the quiet building.

Finally, before the door to my bed chamber, I found Balfor. He had been stabbed in the chest. He lay in a pool of blood, his sword still in his hand.

Not far from him lay a dead Roman soldier.

Balfor had been trying to protect the room.

Instantly, I knew why.

"Rue," I called, gesturing to her to come with me as I pushed open the door.

My bedchamber had been looted, but the bed remained in place.

"Help me," I told Rue. "We must push the bed aside."

Working together, we pushed, but the strain of the work made my back burn with searing pain. Swallowing my screams, I pushed past it and shoved, revealing the secret chamber hidden under the bed.

"Queen Boudica," Rue said in puzzlement.

Bending, I opened the door to the hidden cavern below.

"Brita?" I called.

There was movement, and a moment later, Brita appeared. "Queen Boudica?"

"Thank the gods. Come. Come out," I told her.

"What is that place?" Rue asked.

"It holds the treasure of the Greater Iceni. The gold of Prasutagus's ancestors is stored in secret below. At least, what is left of it…which is not much."

Brita appeared first, climbing the narrow steps with a torch.

Rue bent to help her up.

Behind her came Betha and Ronat. Betha wept as she made her way.

"Come on," Rue told her. "Come out. They're gone," she reassured her.

The moment Betha saw Balfor's body, she began to weep loudly.

I looked into the vault once more. "Kennocha?" I called. "Caturin?"

"They're not here, Boudica," Brita told me. "It all happened so quickly. It was all Balfor could do to get us below. I haven't seen them."

"By Andraste," I cursed, then turned and hurried from the roundhouse. Outside, the men were working with the horses and the other livestock, trying to get them settled…including a small herd of goats running wild about the square.

Pulling up the hem of Rue's dress, I raced across the square to the small house in which Kennocha and Caturin lived.

"Kennocha! Caturin?" I called, flinging open the door.

I found Mara on the floor, her brother's head in her lap. Not far from her, Kennocha lay in a puddle of blood, a stab wound in her stomach.

Caturin coughed lightly.

"It's all right," Mara said gently. "It's all right. I'm here."

I hurried to them, lowing myself to join Mara.

"I came just after the men opened the gates," Mara said sadly. "I found them..." she said, tears streaming down her cheeks. "My mother is—" She sobbed. "She's gone. Caturin..."

Mara pressed her hand against a wound on Caturin's stomach. Blood squelched through her fingers. The boy had gone pale white.

"Caturin," I said, taking his hand. "Caturin?"

How like my brother he looked.

"Queen Boudica," he whispered softly.

"Don't try to speak," I told him. "Rest now. Rest. Go gently, dear one. Go gently."

Mara smiled softly. "Our mother waits for you," Mara said, tears streaming down her cheeks. "You will see her in a field full of flowers beside a sunny meadow. You'll know her. All the goats will be with her," Mara said with a brittle laugh. "It's all right, Caturin... You can go to her. Boudica and I are here. We will watch over you as you take your rest."

"Mara..." Caturin whispered.

She bent, kissing him on the forehead. "I'm here."

Caturin grew very still. He was silent for a long time, then whispered, "I see old Ansgar. He beckons me... And Mother... Mother is here with a man. They are waving to me. He looks like you, Mara..." With that, Caturin exhaled deeply, then grew still, his hand slipping from Mara's grasp.

At that, Mara clutched her brother, holding him against her chest and weeping loudly. I wrapped my arms around them both, holding them and sobbing.

Caturix, I have failed you.

We sat there for a long time. Finally, I heard someone at the door behind me.

I looked back to find Ewan there.

"Boudica," he whispered.

I kissed my niece on the side of her head, then went to Kennocha. I closed her eyes and set her hands on her chest, then walked from the small house.

"The people have collected outside the king's compound. They are waiting for you," Ewan told me.

"The ravens," I told Ewan, referring to Artur's trained birds. "Send them now, as Artur planned."

Ewan nodded, and then departed.

Blood on my hands and dress, I gripped my spear and made my way to the wall of the king's house, climbing up the rampart.

Tears stained my cheeks.

When I went to wipe them away, I realized I had accidentally marred my skin with the blood on my hands... Caturin's, Kennocha's, Newt's... I didn't know whose. Perhaps, all of them. All of them. The blood of all my people was on my hands.

Below me, the people of Venta had gathered. All of them.

From the looks of some of my warriors, they had done as I had asked and dealt with the Romans who had ventured into my city on this awful night.

Overhead, the sky was now full of stars.

Behind me, the stables still burned. Under the burning ashes lay my beloved friend, the last echo of a life I had almost lived at Gaheris's side.

Far in the distance, I saw the last remaining curl of fire from Prasutagus's pyre spiraling up into the night sky.

"People of the Greater Iceni," I called loudly, the wind blowing Rue's patchwork cloak around me. The torches on the wall flickered. "I stand before you this night to speak of something that we cannot see, we cannot touch, and barely recognize its presence until it has been taken from us. Freedom. To know freedom's worth, to truly feel it in our hearts, we must also know the yoke of slavery. And that is what we have become, Epona's children. Link by link, the Romans have enslaved us with their friendship, their favor, their goods, their jewels, their gems, and then their taxes. We have tried to walk beside the eagle, to live in a world where they and we coexist in peace. In the process, we have forgotten what we are. Northern Iceni, Greater Iceni... For many years, we were two people, but in the eyes of the gods, we are all Epona's children. We are the horse people. We are the people of this land. We are the children of our gods. For too long, we have tried to dance to Rome's tune. For too long, we have fought to support and uphold *others'* rights—those of Verica, those of Aedd Mawr—while ours were chipped from us bit by bit.

"Those who came here offering us friendship have robbed us. They have taken our lands, our wealth, our priests, our families, our blood... They have taken your king. And in the west, Rome launches on Mona. They would pull down our gods, and as they have done to Camulos, would set their own gods on top of them. They would take our world and make it theirs.

"For years, Prasutagus and I have struggled, suffered, and strained—you along with us—to keep a fragile peace. We ransomed our very souls to Rome on behalf of harmony. While the Catuvellauni bled and died, we kept our heads down and smiled and paid our taxes to keep the peace. As long as they did not come for us, we kept the peace. But it was an illusion. It was a lie.

The Romans were biding their time. We thought we had gambled and won.

"But there is no winning against Rome.

"Rome never wanted peace.

"They have played a long game with the Iceni, and because they did not come for us with swords and fires, we thought *we* had won.

"But nothing was further from the truth.

"Rome is a rot that has taken over this island. It grows like a fungus along the Thames, taking over our ancient forests, choking the greenwood, and silencing our gods.

"They have deceived us.

"Manipulated us.

"Lied to us.

"They did not want peace. They wanted peace *for now*. They wanted peace as long as it was convenient for them. They wanted the east quiet while they dealt with the others. First, Caratacus, then the western tribes, and now our druids.

"This accord they sold us was a lie. And we—no, *I*—believed it. I wanted it to be true because I wanted you to live. I wanted you to thrive. I wanted you to survive.

"But the peace we provided bought Rome the time it needed to take this island, to make it theirs. And to become strong.

"Rome's peace with the Iceni was never meant to last. It was only for a time.

"It was an illusion.

"They want our lands.

"Our children.

"Our wealth.

"Our world.

"And now, they have come for it.

"If I could change the flow of time and go back, I would stand at Togodumnus's and Caratacus's side, spear in hand, and tell you to fight. I would put aside the grudges between our tribes and bid you all to rise as one. Together. But I cannot change the past. I cannot. Rather than rising, we bargained for your peace, for your children. We sacrificed to make that dream a reality. And for a time, we thrived. But now, Rome has shown its true face. Now, we can no longer stand aside.

"Now, we must rise.

"We must rise, children of Epona.

"And with us, all the east will rise.

"We will take back our homes.

"We will take back our gods.

"We will set fire to all that is Rome. We will burn their gods, their soldiers, their men, their women. We will show Rome that not only are we the people of the horse, but we are the children of Andraste, Cernunnos,

Bel, Taranis, Elen, and of the Morrigu! We will show them what it means to be from this land, of this blood.

"We will rise.

"So, rise, Greater Iceni.

"Rise!

"And bring fire!"

At that exact moment, Ewan loosed the ravens.

With screaming caws, the birds flew out into the night sky. An unkindness of ravens, hundreds of black birds, flew around me, spreading across the land.

All of them had been trained to deliver one message.

When the ravens of Venta flew, there was but one message for the east.

War.

CHAPTER 42

They began to arrive the following morning and over the next few days. Greater Iceni, Northern Iceni, Trinovantes, Catuvellauni, Coritani, druids, and more...so many more. Warbands, families, farmers, the disenchanted.

They all came to make war.

Bran was the first... with blood on his hands and a story to tell.

"It was the caw of the raven that woke me. At first, I thought I was dreaming, but then Bec heard it too. We went outside and found..." Bran said, then paused as he shook his head in amazement.

"What?" I asked.

Bran handed me his sword.

Not *a* sword.

His sword.

"Our weapons. All of them. Laid upon the ground in neat rows. Shining, as if they had all been freshly polished, the leather mended, the blades sharp. The sound of the raven made the Romans come to see. When they realized..." Bran said then shrugged. "There are no Romans in Oak Throne anymore. We killed them all, save one, whom Ula and the other women took to the Mossy Woods to give to the little people of the Hollow Hills in thanks," he said, setting his hand on his sword. "The land itself speaks, Boudica."

"It will take all of us to see this done. And with a little luck, perhaps we can save Mona as well. I only hope we are not too late."

My brother and I stood on the walls of Venta, looking out at the field beyond the city where the armies gathered.

Standing in silence, Bran took my hand.

Soon, a party of Fen folk drew near.

"Queen Boudica," one of the men of the Fens called up to me. "Stonea is yours again, my queen. The Romans went to sleep in the bog and will not rise again. The ancient fort of Saenuvax is yours once more."

I bowed to him. "You are welcome in Venta. I thank you for this news."

The man returned the gesture, then he and his warband rode into the city.

"Boudica, if the Romans find out we are amassing before we attack…" Bran said.

"Paulinus has his men in the west. What forces they can summon, we will outnumber."

"Artur and Vian?"

"They are in Camulodunum. I will go for them tonight."

"How will you get them out? The Romans will lock up the city. They will execute them before our armies can get close."

I smiled at my brother, then put my hand on his shoulder. "I have a plan."

They arrived throughout the day. Their fires sprung up all across the fields surrounding Venta. The city lit up with the sounds of hammers, the puff of smoke from forges, the whirl of axes being ground and swords being sharpened. I had emptied the cache of weapons we'd stored and worked with the others to begin to make ready.

At midday, Arixus and his druids arrived with a dozen wagons covered in tarps. They drove through the city to the wonderment of the people of Venta, the sunlight glinting on the swords, axes, shields, and arrows, gifts from Condatis to the Northern Iceni.

As they rode, the people called to them.

"Prayers to you, Wise Ones!"

"Blessings upon the brothers of Seahenge!"

"Blessings upon the brothers of Condatis!"

Arixus's order had always kept themselves apart.

Now, they were receiving an outpouring of love.

"The druids of Holk Fort," Sorcha said, joining Bran and me.

I looked behind me, scanning the crowd gathered there. I spotted Pix, but I didn't see Olwen.

"Olwen?" I asked Sorcha.

She shook her head. "Still abed. She will not rise."

I frowned but said no more.

Sorcha's anger drove her, but I worried for Olwen. Olwen had always been one step apart of this world. What she had suffered forced her to the heart of the cruelty of *this* world. If we survived, she would have much to overcome.

"Come, let's greet Arixus," I told them, then we all descended.

Behind the druids came the warriors of Holk Fort, armored like the gods themselves and ready to battle.

I went to the wagon Arixus was driving.

"Arixus," I said, greeting him. "May the gods bless you."

"I received your summons, Queen Boudica. But I have arrived in Venta to hear the worst of news. Prasutagus murdered and you and..." he said, his gaze going briefly to Sorcha.

"The Romans poisoned Prasutagus. My husband has

gone to the ancestors. My daughters and I... Like our people, we will heal, or we will die. But now that choice is in our hands," I said, looking behind him at the massive army that was gathering.

Arixus bowed to me and then turned to Bran. "King Bran, I have brought you the treasure of your lands. Shall we see it into Northern Iceni hands?" he asked.

Bran paused a moment, surprised by the use of the title. He looked from Arixus to me.

"The Romans do not define us anymore," I told my brother. "Bran, son of Aesunos and Damara, *you* are the rightful king of the Northern Iceni. I bow to you, my brother and my king."

Bran coughed nervously, then nodded to Arixus. "Let me summon them."

"Ride on to the king's roundhouse. We will meet you there," I told Arixus.

He nodded then gestured for the others to follow him.

Bran jogged up the stairs along the wall and went to the parapet. He pulled his horn and sounded it, summoning the Northern Iceni.

Sorcha, Pix, Bran, and I met Arixus in the king's compound once more. There, Arixus and the other druids pulled the weapons into position. They prepared to distribute the arms to the Northern Iceni. Bran and Pix went to help them.

"Mother," Sorcha said. "Artur and Vian..."

"They will be recovered before sunrise."

"How?"

I studied my daughter's face. "I'm going to Camulo-dunum. Tonight."

"Tonight?"

"Want to come?"

Sorcha stared at me in disbelief. "Can I murder the procurator?"

"Right after I get that dagger back."

Sorcha's brow flexed. "What is that dagger?"

"That dagger..." I said, then paused, catching my emotions. "That dagger is the blade of Gaheris, son of Lynet and Roland, a family heirloom passed down by his female ancestors from the holy Isle of Mists. It was given to them by the warrior maiden Scáthach. That dagger started this war. And with that dagger, I will end it."

"Then it was the Romans who killed Gaheris?"

"Yes," I said through gritted teeth. Long ago, I had told Aulus about Gaheris and his death. He'd said nothing, but Aulus knew he was responsible. He had sent the spies who had killed Gaheris. He had known, and he hadn't told me.

Another lie.

Another Roman lie.

Perhaps Aulus loved me, but not enough to admit his fault.

But of course, he hadn't. Aulus *did* love me, which meant he knew me well enough to know that if I had learned the truth, I would have burned down the world.

Sorcha's gaze went to the Northern Iceni pouring into the king's compound.

"When do we leave?" Sorcha asked.

"I will summon the chieftains. After discussing the plan, we will depart."

"What about Olwen? Mother, she's—"

"I will go see Olwen. I know she is in pain, but Artur's and Vian's lives are in danger. I must get them back."

Sorcha nodded. Her gaze turned to Arixus and the druids. "I'll go help them," she said, gesturing.

I nodded.

Seeing the others had everything in hand, I made my way into the roundhouse. The bodies had been cleared, and Brita, Ronat, and Betha had done their best to scrub the blood away. But still, the air felt polluted. The place had been spoiled by what had happened here.

If I survived whatever came next, something would have to be done.

I slipped down the hallway to the girls' bedchamber.

I rapped gently on the door. "Olwen, it's me," I said, then entered.

Inside, Olwen sat on her bed, staring at the wall.

Sitting beside her, I struggled to find the words to comfort her. Always, my daughter had lived in another world. She saw and felt things none of the rest of us saw. And then there was the unspoken. Often, my daughter saw what would happen before it came to pass. For such a gentle soul, it was too much. I feared what she might do to herself, and the mere thought of it broke me.

"Do you remember when you gave me the hairpin to wear to Camulodunum?" I asked her.

For a long moment, she was still, but then she turned and looked at me. Her bright blue eyes were red from weeping. She nodded.

"A man attacked me in Camulodunum. The Romans had disarmed us, but because I had that pin, I fought him off and escaped. But you knew that would happen, didn't you? You knew I would need it."

She nodded.

"And your father?"

She shrugged slightly.

"You knew something was coming for him? Something bad?"

She nodded, tears slipping down her cheeks.

"Do you see something now? Something of the future?"

Once more, she nodded, and this time, she began weeping hard.

I pulled her toward me and kissed her on her head. "I love you, Olwen. What has happened to you and Sorcha…it is horrible beyond all measure, but it is not the end of you. Please, know that. You have a long life before you. But"—I pulled back, cupping her face in my hands—"right now, you may want to crumble into a thousand tiny pieces and blow away in the wind. I know what that feels like. I have been in that dark place. My daughter, the path before us is laid with ash and iron. But we must walk it, or we will all perish. This is our last chance. I am not asking you to be like Sorcha or forget what has happened, what you have lost. But I am asking you to be strong *just for now*. Just for a little while. Our pain, our grief, our terror…they are ours. But right now, Artur and Vian are in mortal danger, and Mona will fall if I do not act. I will put my pains aside, those of my body and my heart, and do what I must. Just for now.

"Soon, the army will leave Venta. I need you with me. I don't know what will happen, but I know that if we fall, the Romans will come to Venta, and they will… I cannot leave you behind, Olwen. And it is too much to ask you to go forward. I am sorry to ask it. I am sorrier than I can say. I am at a loss. I must leave with Tavish for Camulodunum tonight. The army will follow. I need you to ride with Bran. And yet, I cannot ask it of you. Oh, Olwen…"

My poor child had been defiled, her father murdered, and now I asked her to put her pain aside for a time. What kind of mother was I?

Olwen leaned forward, grabbed my hands, then whispered in a slow, halting voice, "Go... get... Vian... and... Artur."

"Oh, Olwen," I said, putting my arms around her and pulling her close. "I love you so very much."

I held my child for a long moment, then rose once more, feeling the pinch of pain in my back, but I ignored it. I wiped my eyes then held out my hand for my daughter. "I will address the chieftains now. Will you come with me? Let's show them that Rome cannot break us."

Olwen nodded, took my hand, then rose.

With that, we left the roundhouse.

I found Pix waiting outside.

She looked from Olwen to me.

"Ye well?" she asked me.

I eyed her face, which was now varying shades of black, purple, and yellow. "About as well as you."

At that, Pix laughed. "Well enough to kill some Romans then."

"Let's get to it."

Pix grinned. "I thought ye would never ask."

CHAPTER 43

Leaders of warbands, chieftains, and druids alike gathered at the king's house under a hastily erected tent.

"Tonight, we will begin our advance on Rome," I said. "We will take them unaware, in their sleep. And we will strike in a manner they will not expect. We will strike Camulodunum first. Our forces will be split. We will first attack the residents of the colonia, drawing the guard from the heart of the city. Once they are distracted, the rest of our forces will sweep in. We will take the city, moving inward from the gate, until the entire place is ash.

"Kill the Romans. All of them. Loot what you want. Burn the rest.

"King Bran will lead the assault on the city, the Greater and Northern Iceni following him," I said, gesturing to my brother. "Chieftain Lors of the Trino-vantes and Chieftain Adirix of the Catuvellauni will lead the attack on the residences of the colonia. The chieftains will strike first, the rest of us to follow.

"We should expect Rome to send reinforcements from Londinium.

"As you advance, keep in mind that many of our own people have been taken as slaves by the Romans. Free who you can when you can. As for the rest… Let us repay their taxes with the sword."

At that, the others around us nodded.

"Boudica? And you?" Lynet asked.

"I will leave directly with a small band of warriors. We must slip into Camulodunum before the attack. Artur, my son, along with my secretary, Vian, were taken as hostages. The Romans will kill them. We will retrieve them."

At that, Lynet nodded.

One of the druids of the Trinovantes stepped forward. "May Camulos protect us all and guard us as we free his city from the filth that has desecrated it. And may all our gods be with you. Tonight, we take back what has been stolen from us!"

Bran turned to Lors and Adirix. "We will depart in two hours."

"We will be ready," Chieftain Lors told him.

"And we," Chieftain Adirix agreed.

With that, the men departed to prepare their warbands.

Bran turned to me. "Trinovantes and Catuvellauni working together. You have done something impossible, Boudica."

"It was Prasutagus," I said, feeling the pinch in my heart. "It was his doing. I'm simply taking the mantle now."

Bran studied my face. "I still don't like this idea of you going into the city."

I gave my brother a soft smile. "Artur is a man now, but when he was a child, I made him a promise. I promised him I would always come for him. I will keep that promise. But, Bran, if anything happens to me, fight on. Continue on. I am just one person. In the grand scheme of things, I don't matter. You must fight on, no matter what."

"Don't say such things."

"We fight for our people, our lands, our children… and for *our sister*. What we do here may save Brenna's life. So, no matter what, fight on."

At that, Bran nodded.

Across from us, Bellicus and Sorcha worked busily tightening each other's armor.

Bec hurried across the square with a basket of rations in her hands, distributing them to the warriors.

"Oak Throne?"

"I left Ula in charge."

"Ula?"

Bran nodded, a serious expression on his face. "For all her cantankerous ways, she loves the people of Oak Throne. She promised she will do what she can to keep the fort safe. Tatha has come from the grove to help. Dindraine is overseeing things there." Bran's brow scrunched up. "It was strange. I…" he said then paused. "Dindraine warned me that the path to the Grove of Andraste would not be the same anymore. In fact, she told me I might not be able to find it at all, that the path would be closed to many. I'm not sure what she meant, but when I left the grove, the air felt strange. And when I looked back, I couldn't see the crown of trees on the hill anymore. It was like—"

"Magic."

"Magic," Bran said with a nod.

"I am glad to know the dark lady Andraste has protected her holy site. I only hope those on Mona have been able to do the same."

Bran nodded.

"I must prepare to go now."

"I will go speak with Arixus. And I will see you soon…in Camulodunum."

"In Camulodunum."

With that, I returned to the roundhouse to prepare. I slipped into my bedchamber, redressing in a simple tunic and trousers. When I opened the trunk to pull out my leather jerkin, however, I was overcome by Prasutagus's scent.

The perfume was so sweet and so palpable that I paused and knelt to the ground, ignoring the pain in my back. I lifted one of my husband's tunics and pressed it against my face, soaking in his smell. I had done everything I could to block the pain of Prasutagus's death. The loss of my husband was a wound that would never heal. Coupled with all that had come after, I did not have the luxury to grieve. I knew that I was blocking the pain away, because if I let it take me now, I couldn't do what came next. I needed to be strong now... for my girls, my people, and for Artur and Vian. In a heartbeat, all of this could go wrong. I didn't dare let the pain in.

But in this place, alone, I allowed myself a tiny moment.

"Prasutagus," I whispered, my voice choking out his name.

He felt so close.

It was like he was standing in the room.

I inhaled and exhaled once more, then set the tunic aside and picked up my leather jerkin. I slipped it on, feeling the pain on my back but pushing past it. I laced up the bodice then pulled my hair back into a long braid. When I was done, I descended the steps into the Iceni vault.

The chamber, which had once looked like a dragon's horde, was now nearly empty.

Crossing the space, I went to a box sitting on the ledge and opened it.

Within was the torc my husband had given me as a wedding gift. I had only worn it a few times, but now...

I pulled it out and placed the heavy item on my neck.

Closing the lid, I went back upstairs where I found Pix waiting.

"Ye stocking up on gold? Planning to flee to the Éire?"

"Not a bad idea. We could take the treasure and go wed the kings of Tara and begin again."

At that, Pix huffed a laugh then looked me over, nodding affirmatively when she saw I was ready. "Tavish sent me to find ye."

"Help me?" I asked, gesturing to the bed.

We slid the bed back in place, then I picked up the patchwork cloak Rue had given me, fastening it with a brooch, and grabbed my spear.

I nodded to Pix, then the two of us made our way from the roundhouse. I had turned the corner to exit when I crossed paths with Melusine, who was coming from the kitchens.

"Melusine," I said, pausing.

Melusine smiled. "I have been Bergusia for so long, I

barely remember Melusine now. But I cannot tell you how many Coritani have embraced me, glad to know that the rumors I was dead were not true. The chieftains want me to return to the Coritani when this is done. I am the only surviving royal left of the Coritani people."

"To be queen?" I asked.

She nodded. "Yes, but I am far more Bergusia than Melusine now. My place is with Tavish," she said, handing each of us one of the ration bags she had in her hands. "I will ride with Bran and see you again in Camulodunum," she said, moving her cloak aside to reveal her smithing hammers on her belt. "I am no warrior, but if I can pound steel, I can pound flesh."

I hugged her. "We shall see you again soon."

Melusine nodded, then we went outside.

There, I found Olwen and Sorcha watching the commotion.

Pix and I went to my daughters.

"Olwen, you will stay close to the others. Bellicus has been charged with watching over you until we are reunited." Like my daughters, Bellicus had grown seemingly overnight from a wild boy to a warrior. With a sword on one hip and an axe on the other, Bellicus was ready for battle. But until then, his father had given him an important task, one Bran said he readily agreed to. "Stay close to him. Understand?"

At that, Olwen nodded.

"I've given her my dagger," Sorcha told us, pointing to the dagger hanging from Olwen's belt. Otherwise, the girl had no adornments hanging from her pale pink gown. Her long, hay-colored hair hung loose. This night, I felt the otherworld close to my child.

I set my hand on her cheek then leaned forward, pressing my forehead against hers. "Stay safe," I whispered, kissed her forehead, then let her go.

Bec joined us, putting her arm around Olwen's shoulders. "Will you help Melusine and me distribute the rest of the rations?"

Olwen nodded.

Bec met my gaze. "Be careful, Princess."

"And you, Priestess."

And with that, Pix, Sorcha, and I left them. We went to the horses where Ewan, Tavish, and Madogh waited.

"We are ready, my queen," Tavish told me.

I was about to mount Dice when I spotted Mara across the square. She was working hard herding Kennocha's goats back into their pen.

"A moment," I said then went to her.

"Foul little beasts, come on, before I let the men roast you," she said, frustration in her voice.

I clicked to some of the wayward goats, shooing them into the pen. Once they were all inside, Mara latched the gate.

QUEEN OF ASH AND IRON

"Thank you, Boudica," she said then looked me over. "You're leaving now."

I nodded.

"Bruin is there," she said, pointing to her husband. "He will ride with Bran."

"And you?"

Mara inhaled and exhaled deeply. "I..." she said, setting her hand on her stomach. "I have no place with you right now. Bruin would have *us* here and safe."

"You're with child?"

She nodded.

I looked back toward Kennocha's house. "Did she know?"

"Yes," she said, her eyes welling with tears.

"Ah, Mara," I said, pulling her close. "She will watch over you and your unborn. Yes. Stay in Venta. Stay safe."

"Boudica," Mara said, a nervous tremor in her voice. "If something goes wrong..."

I smoothed her hair, pushing it behind her ears. In her face, I saw the shadow of my brother once more. "In the great house, under the bed in my chamber, there is a trap door. There is a vault under the roundhouse. That is where all the wealth of the Greater Iceni is hidden. If anything happens, if we fail, take it all and flee."

"Boudica," Mara said aghast.

"Do as I say. Go to Yarmouth and buy passage on a

567

ship. But have faith," I said then smiled. "The gods are with us. I will see your little one born and know my brother lives on in you both," I said, tears coming to my eyes.

Mara hugged me. "May the Mother watch over you."

"And you, my sweet niece."

With that, I let her go. I rejoined the others, then we made our way to the gates of the king's roundhouse.

Everyone stopped, bowing to us as we went.

I met my brother's eye.

Bran set his hand on his heart and then bowed to me.

I returned the gesture.

I spotted the druid Arixus on the walls as we rode out of the compound.

I lifted my hands to my forehead in a gesture of respect.

To my surprise, the druid did the same.

Then I turned and faced the path before me.

Hold on, Artur. I'm coming.

CHAPTER 44

Tavish led us on a path that took us from Arminghall Henge to what was left of Maiden Stones, not far from Camulodunum. By the time we arrived, it was dark. The little buildings had burned, and the stones were gone. Maiden Stones was utterly decimated.

"What happened to the pink stone that sat at the center of the shrine?" I asked.

Tavish shook his head. "No one knows."

I frowned.

We drew close to the city. Securing the horses, we left them behind then went into the city on foot.

We worked quickly and quietly, rushing across the landscape in the darkness. As we drew closer toward Camulodunum, Tavish lifted his arms and began to whisper. From the folds of his robe, fog began to roll out toward the city, hiding our approach.

Pix, Sorcha, Madogh, and I watched in amazement.

Once the mist had occluded our approach, Madogh gestured to us. "This way."

While part of the city closest to the Romanized center was roughly walled, mainly to keep the Trinovantes rabble from annoying the Romans, the area around the colonia and the rest of the compound was not. Moving quietly, we slipped into the city. After sneaking through a weak section of the wall, we wove down the narrow streets toward the king's house.

Pausing when Roman patrols passed, we hid in the shadows.

"They have Artur and Vian in the king's house," Madogh told us.

"How will we get in?"

"The servants' entrance. There are Trinovantes slaves who will let us into the building, and will flee with us thereafter."

"The king? Lady Julia?" I asked.

"The lady has not returned. The puppet king and his Roman wife have chambers upstairs. We will leave them there for the Trinovantes people to deal with."

Moving quickly, we rushed through the streets toward the king's house.

When we turned a corner, however, we found

ourselves face to face with a Roman soldier and a woman in a compromised position.

A quick glance at the girl told me she was Trinovantes.

The man jumped away from the woman and moved to raise the alarm, but Madogh sent a dagger flying, silencing any sound the Roman may have made.

Horrified, the woman stood, frozen, against the wall.

Madogh and Tavish hurried forward, grabbing the Roman and dumping him into an empty rain barrel nearby.

"Ye be Trinovantes?" Pix asked the girl.

Even in the darkness, I could see that her wrists and neck were raw from bindings.

She nodded mutely.

"Get ye from the city. Now. Go," Pix told her in a harsh whisper. "The Morrigu is coming."

At that, the girl ceased trembling and stared at Pix.

Pix nodded to her, gave the girl one of the knives from her belt, then gestured to her to get away.

At that, the girl rushed off.

"Madogh," I whispered to the man. "Are you sure they are in the king's house?"

He nodded. "Positive."

In the cover of darkness, we made our way through the town until we reached the building. When we got there, I heard a familiar caw.

I looked up on the top of the building to discover Morfran.

"Morfran?"

The bird called at me once more.

"That is why I am certain," Madogh told me with a sly smile. "This way." Madogh led us around the villa to the back where boxes, carts, barrels, and other supplies sat waiting. There was no sign of a guard.

We hid in the darkness.

Madogh whistled lightly, imitating the sound of a nightbird.

A moment later, a small, dark-haired boy—perhaps no more than six years of age—appeared.

He peered into the darkness.

Madogh stepped into the light.

Spotting him, the boy gestured for him to follow.

Madogh signaled to our party, and we headed into the building.

"'Tis too easy," Pix whispered to Madogh.

"No, maiden. Rome is sleeping. In their arrogance, their eyes are shut to the possibility of rebellion."

We slipped inside, the boy leading us down a narrow hallway lit with torches set in sconces on the walls. As we went, we passed a Trinovantes woman carrying a basket.

Madogh paused.

She removed the drape over the basket, revealing bread rounds heaped therein. She nodded to Madogh.

The spy lifted one of the rounds, revealing a set of iron keys underneath.

The woman leaned forward and whispered to him.

He nodded, took the iron keys, then motioned for us to press on.

When Tavish passed the woman, she inclined her head to him.

"Flee, sister. Flee the city," he whispered.

She nodded then met my gaze, inclining her head to me.

Behind me, Pix plucked up a round of bread, broke off a hunk, and took a bite.

At that, the woman merely laughed and shook her head.

We followed Madogh as he led us down a narrow stairwell under the building. At the bottom of the steps, two Roman guards lay unconscious. Madogh fiddled with the keys, finally finding the right one to unlock the door.

He opened the door to reveal a long, narrow dungeon. The place stank of human waste, and the sense of misery and despair was overwhelming.

"Aye, gods," Pix whispered.

Sorcha stepped forward. "Artur?" she called in panic. "Artur!"

"Sorcha," I whispered, reminding her to be silent, but she could not. Not in the face of such misery.

My daughter hurried from cell to cell, searching for her brother. "Artur? Vian!"

"Sorcha," a soft voice whispered from the back.

Sorcha ran to a cell at the back of the hall, looking in through the small window. "Here. He's here," she called to Madogh, gesturing for us to hurry.

"Vian," I told Pix, the pair of us searching, going from cell to cell, looking for the missing girl.

"Vian?" Pix called, but there was no answer.

"Banshees be cursed."

Finally, Madogh got Artur's door open, and Sorcha and the spy rushed within.

I hurried after them.

They had shackled Artur to the wall. He hung there, his face a bloody mess, his body bruised.

"Artur," Sorcha said, racing to him. "Hold on. We will unlock your bindings."

Artur looked up, his gaze going from Sorcha to me.

Tears pricked at my eyes. I smiled gently at him and set my hand on his cheek, meeting his gaze. "I will always find you," I whispered.

"Mother," he said in a small, soft voice.

"Pix, check the guards' bodies for keys to the cuffs," Madogh told her.

"I'll help," Sorcha said, then slipped from the cell.

"Artur, where is Vian?" I asked. "She's not here."

He shook his head. "Catus left. I heard him tell King Diras he was going to take her with him to Londinium."

"Ah, gods," I hissed in frustration. "What will we do?" The thought that Vian—and Gaheris's dagger—were out of my reach filled me with despair.

"We will find her," Tavish reassured me.

But I had my doubts. Catus would learn of the attack on Camulodunum and kill Vian in punishment. The thought made me sick.

Sorcha ran back a moment later, keys in her hands, and began unlatching Artur's binds.

"Help him," Madogh told Pix, the pair supporting Artur's weight.

From somewhere outside Artur's cell, I heard a soft voice call. "Boudica? Queen Boudica?"

Leaving the others, I went into the main chamber and listened once more.

"Boudica?" a male voice called softly again.

I hurried across the space to another cell and looked in.

There, in the dim light, I saw a man similarly chained to the wall. I could barely make him out, and his hair had grown very long. "Divin? Is that you?" I whispered in disbelief.

"Boudica," he moaned.

"Sorcha," I called.

The girl sprinted across the room, keys in her hand, and opened the door. We went to the chieftain.

"Divin," I said, aghast. "By the Mother, we have been searching for you."

"I have been here since they took Raven's Dell. Boudica…"

"Let's get you down," I whispered, Madogh appearing once more with the keys to the cuffs.

We unchained the man, but he fell at once to the ground. He was a fraction of his former size, having been starved and beaten. His condition left me in a state of shock.

"Divin," I said sadly. "We must carry him," I told the others.

"No," he whispered, his voice raspy. "No… I have dreamed of the greenwood. The ancestors call me from the other world. Leave me. Leave me. But my daughter, Brangaine… The queen has her as a slave. My daughter… Boudica, save my daughter."

I nodded. "I will. I will."

Divin smiled at me. "I see the Morrigu standing behind you, Boudica. May she watch over you," he whispered, then closed his eyes and did not open them again.

"Shite," Madogh swore. "The queen's chambers are upstairs where it will be swarming with guards."

"Take Artur and go," Tavish told Madogh, Sorcha,

and Pix. "Boudica and I will get Brangaine and be right behind you."

"But—" Pix began in protest.

"It will be easier if it is just the two of us. Go."

Pix frowned.

"Meet us at the end of the tavern row," Madogh told Tavish and me.

Tavish nodded then turned to me. "Come on."

I looked back at Pix.

"Fine. Go on with ye," she told me. "I'll look after these two."

With that, we all made our way from the dungeon. But Sorcha slipped away from us for a moment and began opening the cell doors.

"Sorcha," Pix said worriedly.

"Distraction," she said. "It will draw the guards away from upstairs."

At that, we hurried out. Madogh led the others outside while Tavish and I made our way deeper into the king's house. Tavish bent, snatching a helmet, sword, and cloak from one of the Roman soldiers. He put the helmet on and threw the cloak over his robes.

We made our way down the hallway. We turned into the kitchens, finding the slaves hard at work there.

They paused when they saw us.

I scanned the room to see Catuvellauni, Trinovantes, and even Gaulish faces looking back at me.

There was a long silent moment, then I stepped forward and asked, "The maid, Brangaine, daughter of Chieftain Divin. Where is she? How can I get to her?"

The servants looked from Tavish to me.

"There is a servant stairwell. There," one of the women said, stepping forward. She had long dark hair and dark eyes. Her looks were vaguely familiar. "There are guards in the hall outside the queen's chambers. I…" she said, then paused. "I will help you, my queen." She turned and looked back at two other girls. "We will."

I looked at all the other servants there. "A reckoning is upon Rome. On silent wings, flee the city," I told them.

With that, the other servants set their work aside and hurried from the room.

The girl who'd spoken met my gaze. "Follow me," she said.

She snatched a kitchen knife, the other girls doing the same, then the three women led Tavish and I upstairs.

"The slaves are kept in the first door on the left," the girl told me. "There will be three guards. We will go now. They will not expect anything from us."

The courage in the girl's eyes moved me.

"May the Morrigu go with you," I whispered.

Tavish turned to me. "I will help them," he said,

adjusting the cloak around his druid robes then slipped quickly up the steps behind them.

Moving quickly and quietly, I followed, peering around the wall to watch.

The Roman guards seemed confused at the women's sudden appearance, but the dark-haired girl spoke sweetly to the Romans, luring the men to her. The other girls joined her.

Keeping his head low, Tavish also approached.

When the Romans got close, the girls acted.

Pulling her blade from the skirts of her gown, the dark-haired girl stabbed one of the Roman soldiers in the chest. The others moved to do the same. When one of the soldiers evaded a girl's grasp, Tavish grabbed him, then slid his blade across the man's throat, silencing him.

My spear in my hand, I slipped across the hallway and opened the door to the dark, dank chamber.

Within, a dozen women were sleeping on narrow cots.

Looking sleepy-eyed, one of the young girls sat up. The poor child was barely ten years old.

When she saw me, she gasped and wiggled toward another woman.

"It's all right," I whispered. "I'm not here to harm you," I told the little girl.

Soon, they all woke.

"Brangaine?" I called into the room. "Brangaine, are you here? Brangaine?"

"Here. I'm here. I... Queen Boudica?"

"Come with me now. All of you," I said. "Come now. You must leave Camulodunum."

A moment later, the dark-haired girl appeared behind me.

"Annisha?" she called into the room. With a gasp, she ran to the young girl who'd first spotted me. Immediately, I realized the similarity in their looks. "Annisha. Come. We must go. Queen Boudica has come to free us."

Brangaine hurried across the room to me. "Queen Boudica," she said, a desperate look on her face. "My father!"

"Aye, sweet friend, he is with our gods and the ancestors. We were too late."

"Oh," she breathed sadly, her hands covering her mouth.

"His last words were to tell me of your whereabouts. Now, come. All of you. We must go. Now."

We hurried down the steps, but when we got to the kitchens, we saw a dozen soldiers racing toward the dungeons.

Tavish gestured to us to be still and silent.

Soon, we heard shouting coming from that direction.

"We must get to the tavern row," Tavish told the dark-haired girl.

"This way," she told us, gesturing for us to follow.

We turned and raced down another hallway, passing linen washing tubs. The smells of soap and lye filled the air, linens hung from lines stretched across the room.

Leading us through the maze, we hurried to a door that exited out into a small courtyard.

"Over the wall," the girl said, pointing.

"Let me go over first. I can help," Brangaine said.

"Me too," the dark-haired girl said, following her.

The two quickly scaled the wall.

"Annisha, right?" I asked, lifting the little girl. "Over to your sister. Ready?"

"How did you know she was my sister?" she asked me.

I smiled lightly. "I can just tell. I have a sister too," I said simply, feeling pain in my heart.

Brenna...

Brenna...

I am setting the world on fire to save you.

Brennna...

I lifted the girl, helping her over, then the others after her.

Once they were all across, Tavish helped me across, the druid following quickly behind me.

We hurried to the tavern row where Madogh and the others would be waiting. As we made our way, however, Tavish's steps slowed.

He stopped, staring down the row that led to the temples.

"Tavish?" I whispered, hurrying him on.

The druid didn't move.

Looking back, I gestured to Brangaine. "Last tavern in the row. Look for Pix."

The girl nodded, then led the others away.

"Tavish," I said, rejoining the druid.

"Boudica," he whispered, his eyes wide in wonder. "The gods whisper to me. I hear Camulos. He is so *angry...*" Tavish said then stepped forward. Tossing the Roman robe, helmet, and sword aside, the druid lifted his arms and began speaking in a language I didn't understand. His voice was soft at first and then grew louder, and louder, but with it, the wind began to blow.

Stronger and stronger, the wind began to whip around us, rattling the trappings of the buildings.

Then, I heard a groan in the air. From somewhere across the city, I heard a woman's laugher. It rolled on the wind.

Overhead, I heard the cries of ravens.

A flock of them flew across the city, cawing loudly as they went.

And then, the ground trembled.

Somewhere within the city, a voice cried out in fear.

Wind whipped around the statues before the great temples to the Roman gods.

Tavish spoke louder, his voice carrying on the wind.

At one of the temples, I heard a shriek. A winged goddess on her pedestal seemed to come to life. Her wings fluttered, and she fled from her place before her temple.

In the sky on the distant horizon, lightning clashed between the clouds and thunder began to roll.

The winged goddess cried out in pain and fell to the ground, becoming stone once more.

Laughter—wild, maniacal laughter—danced on the wind.

Tavish turned to me, a glimmer of bright white light lingering in his eyes. "They have come. We must go," he told me. He rushed toward me, grabbing my arm, then the pair of us hurried down the lane.

"Tavish," I whispered.

"The gods are awake, Boudica. They are with us. Here, all across this island, in Mona, they are with us. All across our lands, they rise up. They rise up. They wake all of us who have been sleeping. It is time. They whisper doom to Rome. In the senate, far away, Great Epona shrieks for her children, crying for those taken so far from their homes. Tamesis turns her waters red. Taranis rolls across the sky. Our gods are battling the Roman usurper gods who choke their sacred places."

I looked toward the skyline.

Once again, thunder struck. This time, I saw a flash

of red in the clouds. Amongst it, I could have sworn I saw a man on a chariot.

Tavish and I ran, finally meeting up once more with the others at the tavern. I nodded to Madogh, and our party slipped from the city back into the night, crossing the grassy fields toward the treeline.

But behind us, the wind blew and the ravens cawed, and within the gust I heard the sound of the Morrigu's laughter.

CHAPTER 45

On the outskirts of Camulodunum, we rejoined the others.

An army like I had never seen before waited for my call.

Rue, who had ridden with us, saw at once to Artur's wounds. She cleaned the wounds on his face then set about touching his tender ribcage.

"Broken or cracked," she told him. "I would tell you to rest, but... Lift your arms. I will bind you as best I can."

Artur nodded then turned to me. "Vian..."

"We will get her back."

"Boudica," he said gently, his gaze going to Olwen and Sorcha who stood beside their horses. "I'm so sorry. I tried to get to them, to you... I have failed the one duty left to me in the wake of my father's death," he said, sounding miserable. "Your cries will ring in my ears until the day I die."

"No," I told him. "No. You will not carry that blame with you. That blame is upon Rome. I will snuff the light from Catus's eyes and wipe Rome from this island. They are to blame. Not you nor anyone else."

Artur frowned.

"Listen to your mother," Rue told him. "From queen to farmer, there is no one the Romans have not defiled with their filth. Use your anger to fuel your sword. Do not let it lie in your heart."

"Yes, Priestess," he told her.

A flicker of a smile crossed Rue's face at the use of the title. In the wake of Rome's death, everyone was reclaiming what was theirs.

Rue clapped Artur on the shoulder. "Your face is a mess. Nothing to be done about that. All the better to frighten them," she said then turned to me. "Done."

I nodded to her, then went to Brangaine.

"Brangaine, the women with the supplies are at the back of the army. Join them there or fight if you wish. There are enough weapons. If you do not wish to partic- ipate, take the others back to Venta."

"Raven's Dell—"

"Is no more. Burned to the ground. I am sorry, my sweet girl."

Brangaine swallowed her tears and then nodded. "I

will talk with the others," she said, looking back at the girls. "Some will want to stay and fight. *I* want to stay and fight."

I smiled at her. "Then stay and fight."

At that, she and the other girls left me.

I went to Bran.

"Are you ready?" I asked him.

My brother nodded. "Are you?"

"Then, it's time."

Bran turned to Bellicus and gestured to the boy.

Bellicus said something to Olwen, then the pair went to the field before the army. Olwen held a torch aloft.

The flickering red of the fire reflected on her face.

Bellicus pulled three arrows from his quiver. He lit them then sent them flying into the air in rapid succession.

When it was done, they rejoined us.

"Olwen, you must go back with Bec, Melusine, Rue, and the others now," I said, gesturing to the wagons at the very back of the army. "We will find you when it is done."

Olwen nodded then took my face into her hands and kissed me on the forehead. She then did the same to Sorcha. When she was done, she signed the sign for Straif, the blackthorn tree. The Ogham symbol was one of the dark goddess Cailleach and represented triumph in darkness and times of death.

I nodded to my daughter.

She gave me one last smile, then she and Rue retreated.

Sorcha and I mounted our horses and waited. Pix, who was wearing every weapon she'd ever purchased, reined in beside me, Tavish along with her.

After a long moment, we heard a carnyx sound.

The somber horn echoed across the fields surrounding the quaint houses of the colonia.

The retired Roman soldiers had come here, taken our lands, made homes out of our sacred trees, sacred stones.

They had burned, looted, and stolen Trinovantes lands, villages, and farms, to make their Roman dreams a reality.

All the while, King Diras sat in Camulodunum listening to the whispers of Rome. In a way, it was not his fault. Some men were like wolves, and Diras was easy prey. They had twisted the boy into a bastardized version of a Trinovantes leader. Ancient Aedd Mawr, who I had seen but once as a girl, was a noble king. I remembered him coming to Oak Throne, his long white hair fluttering in the breeze. I'd thought him a druid until my father said otherwise.

A year later, Cunobelinus, the father of Caratacus and Togodumnus, had taken his lands.

Again, the carnyx sounded.

Then, in the distance, we saw them.

The army of Catuvellauni and Trinovantes began their advance.

An alarm rang up in the city. From our vantage point, we could see a flurry of activity as those soldiers stationed in the heart of Camulodunum—which, for all intents and purposes had become Rome's capital in our land—rushed to save the Roman retirees from what they likely guessed to be a noisy little uprising.

As I watched, I realized just how poorly manned Camulodunum actually was. Paulinus had pulled almost all of the Roman soldiers west. I kept waiting for the scarlet banners to flutter to life and the lines of armored soldiers to appear from nowhere.

But they didn't come.

Our horses pranced anxiously as we waited.

And waited.

And waited.

Soon, I smelled fire on the wind.

The city below us grew quiet save the ringing of a warning bell as the citizens shuttered their houses and barred their doors.

They thought they would be safe.

They were wrong.

I looked down the line and spotted Arixus and his brothers. The druids of Condatis all wore black robes and rode black steeds. They had painted their faces a mix of blue and white in a menacing appearance that made their faces look like skulls. They had also similarly painted the outline of bones on their horses' coats.

I set my hand on my heart and bowed to him.

He returned the gesture.

Then, I turned to Bran and nodded.

Bran edged his horse forward, then turned to face us.

"Children of Epona, are you with me?" he called.

At that, a fierce scream lit up the forest.

"Children of Cernunnos, are you with me?"

Again, the warriors screamed.

"May Bel sharpen his sword and Taranis ride in his chariot. Tonight, we take back our lands. We take back our freedom," he said with a scream, hoisting his sword.

One of the brothers of Condatis sounded a carnyx.

From the city below, I could have sworn I felt the people take a breath as they realized.

"Kill every Roman!" Bran screamed, then turned his horse and led the charge.

I snapped Dice's reins then set off, Pix and Sorcha with me.

We had nearly reached the city when they realized they were being attacked on two fronts.

What happened next came as a blur of blood, iron, and fire.

Per our plan, Bran and Arixus led the warriors

systematically through the city while my warband kept to the back of the army to guard the rear.

The reason why was soon plain.

The attack had just begun when the men from the outpost near what was left of Raven's Dell appeared. A party of no more than fifty men rode hard toward us.

But we were ready.

"Now, now," I screamed to the men and women of Venta who followed me. My spear firm in my hand, I led the advance.

Riding hard, we rode toward the Romans who had been taken off guard by the sight of a massive army besieging the city. Taking aim, I hurled my spear at one of the infantryman's faces. He raised his shield, but he was too slow. My spear knocked him from his feet. He fell to the ground. Galloping quickly, I bent and grabbed my spear then turned Dice and rode back again.

Sorcha and Pix had dismounted and were fighting side by side. Screaming angrily, her auburn-colored hair glowing in the light of the fires from the buildings of Camulodunum, Sorcha worked her sword like she'd been born with it in her hand.

I remembered that little girl always carrying her wooden dagger. I saw them in double-vision.

When I advanced again, I saw the Romans pulling into a defensive stance. Outnumbered, they formed a circle, using their shields to protect themselves, jabbing with their spears between the cracks.

But my people would have none of it.

Using our sheer numbers, we pressed into the Romans, breaking their formation. At once, we began quickly dispatching the soldiers.

Slipping from Dice, I joined the fray.

When one soldier turned to run, I went after him. I stabbed the Roman in the back of the neck, piercing his skin at the base of his skull.

Turning, I engaged another fighter. It was then that I discovered what Pix had warned me of all along. The Romans were heavily armored and well-trained. Even conscripted soldiers had been drilled by their generals and taught to fight. The man, thinking me an easy kill, came with his sword and shield ready...but he was wrong.

Working with great speed, I attacked. Using the length of my spear, I swept at the man's bare legs, knocking them out from under him. When he fell, I jabbed him in the neck then turned to fight the next man, who stared, aghast. Before he lifted his shield, I gripped my spear firmly and pierced his eye, shoving the point in deep.

Yanking the spear back, I shook the blood off, then looked to discover that the Roman reinforcements were already finished.

Whistling to Dice, I mounted the horse then hurried to the others to regroup.

In the city, the sounds of screams grew louder as fire began to engulf all of Camulodunum.

Some of the Romans tried to flee the city.

They had not expected us to be waiting.

Rushing forward, we cut down the stragglers trying to escape. As the Romans tried to hurry away, they became laden down with the wealth or slaves they were trying to drag along with them.

One of the slavers raced from the burning city, driving a wagon full of human cargo. The passengers screamed for help.

Pix, Sorcha, and I raced to catch the man before he escaped.

Driving his pair of horses hard, he hurried down the road. I launched my spear at him but missed.

"Pix!" I called.

Pulling a dagger, Pix tried to take out the driver, but he turned the wagon in time, and the weapon bounced off the side of the wagon.

Sorcha bent low in her saddle, kicked her heels into Ember's side, and raced forward. She slipped her feet out of the stirrups and pulled them up onto her saddle. Balancing herself, she edged Ember in then jumped into the front of the wagon.

My heart leaped to my chest. "Sorcha…"

Racing forward, my heart pounding in my chest, I was surprised when the wagon driver was suddenly sent flying from the cart, causing Dice to leap over him.

When I got to the wagon, I found Sorcha had taken the reins and was trying to slow the wild horses.

"Mother, get Dice in front. Help me calm them down or the wagon will tip on the curve," Sorcha called to me, pointing ahead to a bend in the road.

Leaning in, I edged Dice ahead of the wild horses then tried to slow his pace and theirs. The panicked animals, seeing Dice was slowing, assumed there was no need for fear anymore. If Dice was calm, they could be calm. They slowed their step.

Once the horses were settled, Sorcha pulled them to a stop then rushed to the back of the wagon. A heavy iron lock and chain held it closed.

"Get back," she told the people then yanked her sword from its sheath and dropped the blade on the chain.

It hit with a resounding clang.

The metal fell to the ground.

Pix and I dismounted and hurried to help Sorcha.

Inside were at least two dozen frightened women and children.

"Queen Boudica," one of the women cried then rushed forward, wrapping her arms around me. "My queen."

"My queen. My queen," voices called from within.

"Greater Iceni," I said with a gasp. "All of you? Greater Iceni?"

"We are," the old woman said tearfully. "From the coast. Our village was raided, our men killed or shipped off. Oh, my queen."

"Aye, gods," I whispered. "Come out. All of you. Come out. Quickly now. Our people wait amongst the trees. Go there," I said, gesturing as Pix, Sorcha, and I began helping them from the cart.

Fury gripped me.

"I will escort them back to the others," Sorcha told me.

"I will go with her so she doesn't get herself killed when she comes back to join ye," Pix told me.

"Come. This way," Sorcha told them, grabbing Ember's reins. The captives hurried alongside Sorcha toward the forest.

"Firebrand, indeed," I said then slipped onto Dice once more.

"Come on," I told the horse. "Let's see what awaits us next."

The battle continued throughout the night.

When the sun finally rose, I paused a moment to see most of the city was now engulfed in flames.

It was late in the morning when Bran and his warriors began to pull back.

My brother rode to join me.

"Those still alive have withdrawn behind the walls around the innermost part of the city. We will regroup then finish them after a moment's rest," he told me, looking me over. "Boudica," Bran said, his face covered in ash and splatters of blood. "You all right?"

I nodded. "You?"

Bran nodded then looked back toward Bellicus. Like us, the young warrior had fought throughout the night. Unlike Bran and me, who were both in need of rest, Bellicus looked eager to keep fighting.

Sorcha and Pix joined us, Sorcha going to her cousin.

The pair laughed with one another, showing each other their wounds.

"Perhaps we should—" Bran began, but then we heard the Trinovantes warhorn calling for reinforcements.

"Lors."

Bran turned his horse. "Quickly. Quickly. Regroup now," he called. "We must reinforce Chieftain Lors."

Gathering us all, we raced across the field, other warriors joining us as we went.

When we reached what was left of the villas, we discovered that Rome had sent reinforcements—such as they were. Barely two hundred men had taken the field against the Trinovantes and Catuvellauni.

"They've come from Londinium," I told Bran, recognizing the legion's banner.

"If this is all they sent, then Rome has no idea the size of the force we have rallied."

With that, we rode hard into the fray.

Whatever the Romans had expected to encounter, this was not it. Our army swept over the Romans like a wild river rushing over the rocks.

"The cavalry," Pix said, pointing.

Directing our horses, we led our warriors toward the mounted soldiers.

The Roman soldiers had the benefit of experience.

But we were people of the horse.

Bellicus raced headlong toward one of the Roman soldiers. The man readied to meet him but was caught off guard when Bellicus quickly climbed out of his saddle and launched toward the man, knocking him from his horse. Sorcha moved similarly, crawling up into her saddle and blasting off a barrage of arrows into the huddled mass of soldiers.

Moments later, the rest of our riders engaged the soldiers.

Setting my reins aside and directing Dice with the force of my knees alone, I engaged one of the soldiers. Spinning my spear over my head, I whacked the man hard on the side of the head, rendering him unconscious. When he slipped from his horse, I jabbed him through a weak spot in his armor and left him to die. I turned then, seeing another man fleeing the battle. Clicking to Dice, I rode him down. Hoisting my spear, I took aim and let the weapon fly. It struck the man in the back, piercing his armor. He fell to the ground.

I fetched the spear, then turned the horse to rejoin the others, but it was already done.

There were no Romans left to fight.

Clicking to my horse, I rejoined Bran.

"By Andraste's toe," Bran swore. "Is that all they think to muster?"

"Paulinus has everyone in the west. Perhaps that's all there is to send. And if that's the case, we must finish Camulodunum and move on to Londinium quickly before Paulinus realizes."

At that, Bran nodded.

With the reinforcements destroyed no sooner than we had arrived, the rest of us returned once more to camp.

There, Bran and I joined with Chieftain Lors, Chieftain Adirix, Tavish, Arixus, and the others. We stood over a patch of earth on which Chieftain Lors was drawing with his spear. Runners with food and drink were working through the camp where our people now took their rest. I saw Rue and Melusine, Olwen with them, working through the crowd, tending to the wounded. More warriors had arrived overnight. I saw warbands whose pennants or colors I did not recognize.

I turned back to the others as they worked through the plans for the assault on the center of the city.

"We have finished it here," Chieftain Lors said, indicating the villas where the retirees lived. "They were spread at quite a distance and it took the night, but there is no one left."

"The city is finished here," Arixus said, showing where he had led his own attack.

Bran nodded then stepped forward. "We have pinned those who survived the initial onslaught here. They have withdrawn behind the walls surrounding the king's villa and the temples. A final push will be needed to kill or capture King Diras and restore Camulos's city."

"The temple of Divine Claudius sits upon the sacred well of Camulos," Tavish said. "We must see it destroyed. It is Camulos's will."

The others nodded.

"Good. Good," Chieftain Adirix said. "An hour's rest, and we will have them. The Coritani have gone into the city to catch any stragglers."

With that, we went our separate ways.

Taking a round of bread from one of the passing women, I went to a tree nearby and sat. When my back touched the tree, a stinging sensation swept across my body, the ache and pain reminding me it was still there. I slipped my hand into my vest and pulled out a small vial Ariadne had given me to stem the pain. Sipping the tonic, I closed my eyes. Soon, I would not feel the pain anymore. Opening my eyes slowly, I stared off into the distance, watching the city burn.

I remembered the moment I first saw the Roman army. It had been so impressive. The sheer size of the force, the elephants, and Aulus Plautius. Now...

I closed my eyes.

Prasutagus...

The ache in my heart reminded me that I had no business calling my husband yet. When it was done, I would let myself feel the pain. But even as I thought the words, I remembered Dôn's prophecy that the eagle would reside on our island for many years to come. Could I change the tide of fate? And if not, could I at least squelch Rome's hold on my lands? As I watched Camulodunum burn, I felt my fury rise once more.

"Great Mother, Lord of the Forest, be with me."

I rose and joined Arixus, who was looking out at the fire.

"Queen Boudica," he said, inclining his head to me. "We should go soon. We must finish them and be on to Londinium. Rome will not sleep once they have heard what we have done here."

"My thoughts exactly. I was coming to rouse the others now."

"More have come," Arixus told me, gesturing to the army behind us. "More Catuvellauni. They stand shoulder to shoulder with the Trinovantes they once killed. Now, we all only have one enemy."

"Will we succeed?" I asked Arixus.

"What does it mean to succeed?" Arixus replied. "We cannot wipe Rome from the face of the earth."

"No, but we can crush Roman's hold on this island," I said. "We must break them enough that they limp away, their hunger to stay here any longer shattered."

Arixus nodded. "If that is your hope, we must rally now."

"Yes," I said, nodding.

"Boudica," Arixus added. "When this is done, those who survive will look to the Iceni—to you—for guidance. Show them what it means to be a leader. Remind them that there can be peace and cooperation between the tribes."

I set my hand on his shoulder. "Thank you, my friend."

The druid and I joined Bran.

"We must rally the men, finish the city," I said.

Bran nodded. "I will rouse the men. You will speak to Lors and Adirix?"

I nodded then went to the men, leaving Bran and Arixus to ready the Iceni.

"Chieftain Lors," I called to him. One of the women

had just finished wrapping the chieftain's forearm with a bandage. "Are you well?"

"Well enough, Queen Boudica."

"We must finish the city now then prepare to ride on to Londinium."

"Good. I am anxious to have King Diras's head hanging from my saddle. But, Boudica, why Londinium? Shouldn't we just ride west to meet Paulinus."

"I am very certain we will meet the governor before this is done. But first, we must cripple Rome. Here, we have taken the heart by destroying Camulodunum. Now, we must go to Londinium and take the head. Londinium is the source of Rome's wealth on our island. Finish it, and we finish the supply of gold and silver to the continent. We must push on Nero, make him see there is little reason to stay here. If we can wipe Rome's holdings from the map, perhaps it will be enough to make him rethink his occupation here."

The chieftain nodded slowly as he considered. "The Catuvellauni are anxious to retake Verulamium."

"We will in time, but you are right that we must track Paulinus's movements. We have taken them by surprise here. Can you send riders west—fast horses, loyal men—to discover Rome's movements?"

The chieftain nodded. "I will see to it. We have them

now, Boudica. But we must be wary. If they bring rein-forcements from Gaul, we may not be enough."

"If we can swing the tide of this war in our favor, maybe we can find allies in the north."

"Brigantes?"

I nodded.

"Unless they're too busy killing one another. After what she did to Caratacus, none will trust Cartimandua."

I paused as I considered. "Perhaps. Let's win the campaign first, and then we shall see what our neigh-bors to the north decide. I'll ride in with Bran."

"I'll speak to Adirix and prepare some riders to go west. We'll arrange for an advance force to watch the road to Londinium."

"Thank you," I said, then turned back just as Bran sounded his horn once more, gathering the warriors of the Northern Iceni.

Pix joined me. "Will be short work of it. Best to just set fire to the place and be done with it."

"I agree, but the Trinovantes want Diras."

"What do they want with him? That boy hardly knows what's going on around him."

"They blame his inaction."

"Then they blame a child."

"All the same…"

Pix frowned but said nothing more. We were of the

same mind on the matter. Diras hardly knew where he was or what his responsibilities were, but that didn't matter to the Trinovantes. They had suffered and died while their king sat and did nothing to save them. It was Rome's fault, but Diras had become the focus of their anger.

A spear in one hand, shield in the other, I joined Bran, Tavish, Arixus, and the others.

"King Bran. Queen Boudica. Wise Ones," the chieftain said, bowing to us.

"Chieftain," Arixus said then gestured to the city. "Claim your city and by so doing, reclaim your lands. We are with you."

At that, the chieftain smiled then turned back to his people. "Trinovantes," he called to them.

In reply, a scream rolled from the warriors.

"Camulos calls. Let us take what is ours!"

At that, one of the druids sounded the carnyx, and then the warriors of the Trinovantes rushed into the city.

"Hold!" Bran called to the Iceni.

Once the Trinovantes had swept into the streets, Bran nodded to me.

"Children of Epona! Advance!" I screamed, and with that, we rushed behind our Trinovantes brothers.

When we finally made our way into the city, it was madness. The Trinovantes were scaling the walls of the king's compound. What Roman soldiers remained inside were fighting back. Arrows and javelins were hoisted over the walls toward us. A band of Trinovantes had brought a sharpened log with them and were heaving it against the gate.

Pix pulled her bow, wrapped the tip with a cloth, and lit it.

"Ye see? Back there where ye rode that creature?" she asked me, gesturing with her chin to an area just inside the compound where the Romans had stored grain and hay.

"It was called an elephant."

Pix nodded. "Let's motivate the Romans to open the gate. Sieges don't last long when things be on fire."

With that, she launched her flaming arrow toward the hay. And then another, and another, and another, until the grain and the haystacks were blazing.

"Boudica," Bran said, calling for me to join him. We raced around the back of the army, meeting with Cai and some others who had brought a wagon filled with casks.

"Mead?" I asked him.

He nodded.

I looked at Pix.

"Clever, handsome boy. Now, let's crack this place open like a nut."

Pushing the wagon to one of the side gates, we worked together, making ready. With a hearty heave, we drove the wagon to the door of the side gate and retreated. Readying their flaming arrows, the others began to shoot at the barrels of mead. It took several shots, but the first barrel cracked open, and the liquid within ignited. A moment later, there was a giant whooshing sound, a flash of blue, and the barrels—all at once—burst into flame. The force of the blast was so intense that it knocked the gate from its hinges, the burning doors blasting into the city.

At that exact moment, the Trinovantes bashed off the gate.

There was a loud cheer, and the warriors rushed in.

"Let's go!" Bran called, and hurried into the compound.

The Trinovantes made their way to the king's house and forum. We made our way to the temples.

Roman soldiers stood on guard in front of their holy places, but as soon as they saw the size of our forces, they raced inside.

Our own warriors raced after them.

At the foot of the temple of Divine Claudius, the Romans fought back, defending the sacred temple.

We hurried to engage them.

My spear in one hand, a shield in the other, I blocked the blow of a Roman who rushed me then jabbed, trying to pierce the Roman's armor. My first attempt failed, my spear bouncing off his breastplate.

The man attacked again, trying to stab around my shield. I realized his short sword didn't have the length to reach me. When I attacked again, I waited for the man to extend his sword arm. Then, using my spear length to my advantage, I turned quickly to the side and thrust into the soldier's armpit, and deeper, into his chest.

He fell at once.

Around me, pairs battled as our people sought to free Camulos. At the other temples, I saw the priests running away, carrying their sacred relics with them. But our fury had no bounds. Sick to death of insult upon insult, our warriors paid no heed to whether it was soldier or priest they found. All were given the same grizzly end.

Some of the warriors broke through the Roman line, making it to the large bronze doors. Others joined in, trying to break down the doors.

Inside, I heard frightened cries.

But my eyes went to the statue of Claudius, standing there, smirking as he looked down on the city he had taken—not through force or bloodshed—through smiles and lies.

"Pix!" I called. "Rope!" I said, gesturing to the statue.

We left the fray, gathering up what rope we could find and lashed it about the statute. When the others saw what we were up to, they came to help.

Soon, we had lashed Claudius firmly.

All of us in place, Pix yelled, "Heave!"

We pulled.

"Heave!"

Again, we tugged.

After a dozen more tries, Claudius finally came loose from his pedestal. The statue tilted back and forth a moment.

"Fall. Fall, damn you," I yelled.

Then, the statue hit the ground, breaking into a thousand small pieces.

At that, a cheer lit up the sky.

Bran, looking sweaty, joined me. "Boudica, we cannot break in," he said, gesturing to the temple. "The door is too thick, and there are no windows."

"Burn it."

Pix grinned, then stepped forward. "Bring fire!" she called to the others.

At that, the others cheered, and at once, people set about setting the temple on fire. For a moment, I paused, thinking of those trapped within. But when I did, Sorcha's sobs again rang through my mind.

I turned and walked away.

I set my gaze toward the forum. "Come on," I told Pix and Bran. "Let's see what the Trinovantes have found."

We made our way to the forum. We discovered that the Trinovantes had sacked the building and were looting the place. But more than that, the Trinovantes warriors were covered in blood. Roman men in their togas and Roman women in their stolas lay dead on the ground. That included the waspish young Roman woman who had cursed me for spilling wine on her dress. She lay, her eyes staring blankly. Her lovely lavender-colored dress was stained with her blood.

Chieftain Lors and his men dragged King Diras and Queen Lucia to the balcony above the square.

As my eyes drifted upward, I remembered Aulus looking down at me from the same spot.

If I knew then what I knew now, I would have drawn an arrow and shot him.

"Trinovantes," Chieftain Lors called in a loud voice. "I bring you a gift!" he said with a laugh. "Won't you all bow to your king, the blood of mighty Aedd Mawr?"

At that, the crowd laughed.

"And what about his beautiful wife, Queen Lucia?"

At that, they hissed.

"King Diras, your people come before you with complaints. Do you finally hear us?" the chieftain asked, shaking the young man, forcing him to look upon Camulodunum as it went up in flames. "King Diras, the blood of your fathers has been bleeding, the priests of your forefathers' gods have all been murdered, the virgin daughters of your chieftains have been raped, and the wives of your subjects have been sold as slaves.

What say you, great king of the Trinovantes tribe, Celtic king of the ancient people of Camulos?" he asked him, the chieftain's voice growing rougher and angrier as he spoke. "What say you, king of our tribe, the last of the line of noble men? What do you say to your people now?"

Diras looked horrified. In his gaze, I could see that he understood, perhaps for the first time, that maybe he had done something wrong. For the first time, he realized what he was supposed to be, what he was supposed to have done, who he was supposed to stand for. But it was only for a moment, and then it was gone.

"I… I want to go back to Rome," the boy stammered.

"He wants to go back to Rome," the chieftain chided. "Well, let's send him back, shall we?"

The Trinovantes cheered.

My heart moved with pity, I stepped forward to speak, but Pix held my arm. "Nay, Strawberry Queen. 'Tis bigger than your compassion now."

The chieftain pushed Diras over the rail, lifted his sword, and relieved the king of his head.

Beside them, Queen Lucia screamed as red blood splattered all over her gown.

A female warrior who had been holding the queen looked to the chieftain.

He nodded to her.

The Trinovantes warrior maiden pulled her dagger,

stabbed Queen Lucia in the chest, then tossed her body over the balcony, bringing cheers from the crowd.

"Burn it all down," Chieftain Lors called to the army. "Burn it all."

"Let's get ready to ride to Londinium," I told Bran.

My brother nodded, then Bran, Pix, and I retreated from the scene. Bran sounded his horn, calling for the Iceni to fall back.

We made our way from the city.

Behind us, the whole place was soon engulfed in flame.

As we walked, I spotted something at the heart of one of the infernos.

There, the wooden effigy of Camulos stood untouched by the fire.

The god's face stared out at me from the flames.

I raised my hands to my forehead.

Soon, there would be nothing left of Roman Camulodunum.

Camulos would rule once more.

CHAPTER 46

We set off first thing in the morning for Londinium. As we gathered in a field not far from the city to regroup, I finally got a sense of the vast number of people who had come: Greater and Northern Iceni, Trinovantes, Catuvellauni, Coritani, Cantiaci... by the tens of thousands.

Pausing our horses on a hill above the field, I looked out at the army in wonderment.

"We have a real chance, don't we? A real chance," Sorcha said, looking out at the scene. "I have never seen such an army."

"Nor I," Pix said, then turned to me. "Ne'er in my long life."

"Let's hope it is enough," I said, then rode to the front, aware that this massive army was all looking at me.

Pulling my horn from my belt, I sounded it and then gestured for the army to move out.

Turning Dice, I set off toward Londinium.

And vengeance.

IT WAS midday when one of Lors's advance riders returned. His horse lathered with sweat, the man looked relieved to see us.

"Queen Boudica, King Bran, Chieftains," he said, bowing to all of us. "Thank the gods I have found you. The Romans sent reinforcements. A legion is marching from Flag Fen. They are not far behind me. Cavalry and infantry."

"Did they see you?" I asked.

"No, Queen Boudica."

I turned to Lors. "What is between here and the road to Flag Fen. Any place suitable for an ambush?"

The chieftain considered and then nodded. "Yes, the forest of Brookwood. The road cuts through the forest. Many sacred trees were taken when they carved their road," Lors growled, then turned to one of his men. "Get Brecan," he told the man, who rushed off and then turned back to us. "The forest lies in Chieftain Brecan's lands."

When Chieftain Brecan joined us, we apprised him of the situation.

"How far is the forest?" I asked.

"Three leagues to the north on the road."

"And the Romans?" I asked the rider.

"Double that."

"We can take the Trinovantes," Lors said, turning to Chieftain Brecan, who nodded. "We will ambush them in the forest and regroup with you before Londinium. There is no need to take the entire army."

I nodded. "Very well. The Romans also reveal themselves with this move. They don't know Camulodunum is finished, nor do they know the size of our army. We must do what we can to prevent Paulinus from learning the truth."

"What are you thinking, Boudica?" Tavish asked.

"We must send an advance party into Londinium and burn the ships. All of them. We can choke off their retreat by the river and delay word reaching Gaul. If Catus thinks this is just a little uprising, he won't call for reinforcements. But if he learns the truth, he may send to Gaul."

"I will go," Tavish said. "If you permit it, my queen."

I inclined my head to Tavish. "I would be grateful to you."

Tavish turned to Melusine. "Want to come?"

Melusine smirked. "I wouldn't miss this for anything."

"May the gods watch over you," I told them, trying to swallow the fear and worry I felt for Melusine. But I reminded myself that she was not the sheltered princess I had once known. Melusine had suffered and had come out the other side a stronger version of herself. She didn't need my worry.

With that, Melusine and Tavish departed.

Chieftain Lors turned to me. "We will meet you again soon."

"May Camulos ride with you," I told him, then the chieftain departed.

"Spread the word of what is happening," I told Cai and Artur. "Make sure the others know we are not being abandoned. Trust is still fragile. We will ride on."

At that, Cai and Artur departed.

"Mother," Sorcha said. "Vian?"

"We'll find her," I said then searched the crowd behind me for Madogh. I signaled to him. The spy rode to join me.

"Queen Boudica."

"Will you go to Londinium? Catus took Vian with him. We need to find out where she is—and anything else you can see."

Madogh nodded to me. "I will see it done," he said then rode off in great haste.

"You have done well," Arixus reassured me. "Give the others a moment, let the news spread as to why the Trinovantes are pulling off, then signal for the army to march on."

Taking the druid's advice, I waited for all parties to be reassured before sounding my horn again. Turning my horse, I began my path again toward Londinium.

"Don't look back," Arixus told me. "Show no lack of confidence. Remember, the gods are on your side."

And with that, we rode forward, the great Celtic army following me.

BY NIGHTFALL, we reached a vast field half a day's ride from Londinium. We settled there for the night. I sent scouts ahead to Londinium to see what waited for us on the road and in the city beyond, and then waited for news from the Trinovantes.

We had the advantage. I only hoped we were able to act upon it.

Some tents were erected, and after a long day's ride, I went to see Bec and check on Olwen. With each step we took closer to Londinium, my mind went to Vian. The news would surely reach Londinium of our approach. What if Catus fled? What if he murdered Vian out of spite? The thought filled me with dread.

At the back of the camp, I found some tents for people to receive medical treatment and get something to eat. There, I found Bec and Olwen handing out rations and filling horns of ale.

"Olwen," I said, approaching her.

She nodded to me, then handed an older warrior a round of bread.

"Bless you, Princess," he told her, patting her hand, then turned to me. "Queen Boudica," he said, bowing, then went on his way.

Olwen joined me.

She looked me over from head to toe, inspecting me.

"Dirty. Hungry. Thirsty. Tired. Otherwise, intact."

Olwen gestured for me to follow her. She poured me an ale, grabbed two bread rounds from a basket, then motioned for me to follow her.

Spotting Bec, I called to her.

"I'll join you in a moment," she told me.

We went to one of the tents, where I found Sorcha and Bellicus seated alongside Artur, all three eating.

Olwen and I settled in with them. I took a large bite of the bread and then immediately paused, inspecting it. I looked at Olwen. "Did these come from Oak Throne?"

Smiling, she nodded.

I laughed lightly. "Burned and raw at the same time. Leave it to Cidna to give us all collywobbles while we fight for our lives."

Bellicus laughed. "You should be used to it by now, Boudica."

In truth, I was. The idea that it was Cidna's food nourishing me after a long day's battle warmed my heart. "Properly baked food never tastes quite right."

At that, the others laughed.

I turned to Olwen, pushing a stray hair behind her ear. "Are you well? Is it not too much for you?"

She took my hand and kissed the back of it, then gave me a soft smile.

It was too much for her... Too many people, too much noise, too much light, but she would not say so. Not now.

I set my hand on her cheek. "Brave girl. My brave girl. Your father would be very proud of you," I told her, feeling that aching pinch in my heart once more.

Olwen felt it too. Her eyes grew watery, and she nodded, setting her head on my shoulder.

I stroked her lengthy hair, then exhaled deeply and drank my ale.

"Boudica," Artur said. "When we attack Londinium, how will we know where to find Vian?"

"The procurator will be in the governor's villa. I

hope he keeps Vian close." *And that he doesn't murder her. And that he doesn't flee.* But I did not voice my worries to Artur.

"And if he is not there?" Artur asked.

His question plagued my heart. "I'm not leaving Londinium without her."

"Her, that man's head, and that dagger," Pix said, sitting beside us.

"Is there word of Governor Paulinus?" Bellicus asked.

Bec and Bran joined us.

I shook my head. "Riders have gone forth to see. We may hear something by morning."

Bec handed her son another round of bread.

"Shall we toast?" Bellicus asked, lifting his cup. "To the end of Rome."

"And to family. May the Mother and the Horned One protect you from this day until your last," I added.

"To family," we called, then lifted our cups in toast and drank.

My mind went to Vian once more.

Pix, reading my expression, tapped her cup against mine. "Ne'er you worry, Strawberry Queen. We'll get her back. We'll get her back."

THAT NIGHT, my sleep was fitful. Despite my desperate need for rest, I barely slept. My back ached, I could not get comfortable, and my dreams were filled with screams.

I saw Mona as I had seen it through Brenna's eyes. Everything was on fire: roundhouses, temples, sacred trees. Druids lay dead on the shoreline, the walkways, and the grassy knolls. Everywhere I looked, people were screaming, fighting, and dying.

"Brenna? Brenna!" I searched the scene for my sister, unable to find her anywhere. "Brenna!"

"Boudica?" Pix called. "Boudica, wake ye. Boudica?" she asked again, shaking my shoulder.

"Pix?"

"Yer dreaming, and a rider has returned."

"I..." I said sleepily, then sat up. "Yes. All right. A rider from where?"

"Sent by the chieftain. He's speaking to Bran now. The Trinovantes met the legion and were victorious. They ride to meet us now. 'Tis near dawn."

I nodded, then looked across the tent at Olwen and Sorcha, who had slept side by side that night, the pair holding on to one another.

"Just like when they were girls," Pix said, giving them a smile.

"What girlhood they had left in them, Rome has taken from them," I said bitterly, then looked up at Pix. "The chances of getting Vian back... They may have already started evacuating Londinium, and Catus is a coward. Despite what I told Artur, we have no idea where to find her."

Pix crossed her arms on her chest as she considered. "Where would ye keep her?"

"With me, in case the enemy got close. I'd use her like a shield."

"Then ye know where to find her."

I frowned.

"Come on. Eat something and make ready. We will ride soon, and ye have the largest army in history behind ye, General Boudica," she said with a laugh. "Ye will get her back."

CHAPTER 47

Later that morning, Chieftain Lors arrived. Not long after, Madogh returned with news from Londinium. Calling all the leaders together, we listened to the spy's report.

"Reinforcements arrived in Londinium, but it was scantly an army compared to our numbers. They were in the city only an hour before they retreated. Some of the Romans went with them, but not many. Others tried to flee on the Thames, but all the boats were burnt. Smoke rolls from the river where burning vessels drift like ghost ships down the Thames."

"Who rode in? Did you see who had come?" I asked.

"It was the governor, Boudica."

"Then he has pulled back from Mona," I said, feeling relief wash over me. "But he left Londinium? Are you certain?"

QUEEN OF ASH AND IRON

Madogh nodded. "He entered the city, spoke to the procurator, then left. A call went out through Londinium for the people to flee with the army, but most ignored him. Instead, they are boarding up their shops and packing their market wares."

"The procurator? Where is he?"

"He tried to leave by boat, but there was none to be had. He and the governor had a very loud argument in the courtyard of the governor's villa. The governor told the procurator to stay in Londinium and face the consequences of the fire he started."

I huffed a laugh. "Paulinus has more sense than Catus."

"The procurator sent runners for a means of transport down the Thames, but all the boats were burned. Our handiwork, I presume?"

"Tavish. Any sign of the druid?"

Madogh shook his head.

"And Vian? Did you see her at the villa?"

Madogh nodded. "Catus paraded her in front of Governor Paulinus. The governor struck the procurator and told him that his stupidity had undermined the safety of the entire east. Afterward, she was taken away. I moved in to retrieve her but could not find a way."

"How many people are still in Londinium?" Catuvellauni Chieftain Adirix asked.

Madogh huffed a laugh. "Most of them, Chieftain.

The people are not frightened. They are angry about the ships but believe it's just a warband causing trouble. So, they are boarding up their homes and shops, drinking ale, and waiting for the soldiers to handle the problem."

"They will learn the truth soon enough," I said. "Thank you, Madogh. Let's prepare to ride out. We will take the city full force, riding in from the north where the walls are unfinished. Let's show the Romans our *little* warband."

At that, the others laughed, and we made ready to depart.

Soon, horns sounded as we rallied the army to prepare to move out.

Pix joined me as I made my way back to Dice.

"City fighting, close quarters. 'Tis not easy, Boudica. Ye need to be ready for it."

"I only have one target. And right now, I'm happy enough to kill him with my bare hands."

"That may be, but he will have his guards about him. And ye can be certain, they will be many of the same men who were there when they put a lash to ye. Get your sword ready, Boudica. Ye will need it."

I mounted Dice and then motioned for Pix to come with me. We rode down the line until I found Lynet.

"Boudica," she said, bowing to me.

"Lynet," I said. "When we enter the city, I want you to come with me."

"Of course. But…"

I inhaled deeply and then said, "Procurator Catus has something that belongs to you."

Lynet shook her head in confusion.

"Your dagger. *His* dagger."

"Boudica…" Lynet said with a gasp.

"And a story that went with it," I told her, repeating what the procurator had told me about the attack on the Wash. As I spoke, the others around Lynet listened. Finally, they learned the truth of what had happened that terrible day so many years ago when we had all lost something dear. When I was done speaking, Lynet's face was as hard as stone.

"I am with you. And as many of the warriors of Frog's Hollow as you need."

The others nodded.

I inclined my head to her and then looked over the party of warriors. I recognized many of the men with whom Gaheris and I had been friends. They were there with their grown sons and daughters. With them, I recognized another face. Age had changed him, and a blond beard now graced his chin, but I'd know his eyes anywhere.

"Tristan?" I asked, smiling at him.

He inclined his head to me.

"You are a child no more. Your family would be very proud of you."

He smiled at me and set his hand on his heart.

I looked at the others, scanning the faces of people I had known all my life. In a life unlived, I would have been one of them. Now...

"Frog's Hollow," I called, "will you ride with me toward vengeance?"

At that, they rose up in cheer in reply.

I turned to Lynet. "Come. Let's get your dagger."

With that, we began our ride toward Londinium. The day passed quickly, and the sun began to set as we approached the city.

Much to my relief, Melusine and Tavish rejoined us unscathed.

"It is done," Tavish told me. "Merchant ship and Roman barge alike, nothing is left floating in the Thames."

I eyed the druids over. He and Melusine had blood stains on their clothing, but neither was injured.

"All well?" I asked.

Tavish nodded. "Thamis be thanked. We're wet and tired, but it is done."

I paused as I considered his words. I had never approached Londinium by land, but by river, we had come many times. On every occasion, I had seen people fishing, trapping, and birding all along the Thames shoreline.

"The river...is the water high?"

Tavish shook his head. "No."

Considering, I nodded. "Thank you, Tavish."

The other leaders of the warbands joined me as we made our approach.

"The city walls are incomplete," Madogh told us. "The northern face is not yet done, and there are pockets to the east and west that are weak where they have not yet finished the gates. Also to the east, part of the wall fell in the last heavy rain. The city can be breached there."

"They will concentrate their forces to the north, try to prevent us from getting into the city," Chieftain Finan of the Coritani said.

I nodded in agreement. "We will send the brunt of our army there to meet them. The Trinovantes can attack from the east, breaking through the walls where Madogh indicated. Once they are through, they can maneuver from behind and pinch the Roman forces in between."

"There will be resistance in the city. Some of the citizens are retired soldiers. They will fight back," Madogh warned.

"No matter. We will see to them," Chieftain Adirix said confidently.

"Bran will lead the attack to the north. I will take a smaller warband into the city by other means. I have an appointment with the procurator. I'd hate for him to miss his payment."

At that, the others laughed.

"When the sun rises again on Londinium, may there be nothing but ash, and may the gods go with you all," I told them.

"And with you," the others replied.

I turned to Bran, taking his hand. "Go carefully, Brother. The Romans fight like a machine."

Bran nodded. "You are going for Vian?"

"Yes."

Bran huffed a laugh. "Tell me about your plan later. I don't want to worry about you now."

I smiled at him. "I will see you again soon," I told him, then gestured to Lynet, Madogh, Artur, Pix, and Sorcha.

"Along with a band of warriors from Frog's Hollow, we will go for the procurator. Let's just hope we don't need to swim."

Madogh cocked an eyebrow. "What do you have in mind, Queen Boudica?"

"Let's find our own way into the city."

LEAVING THE OTHERS BEHIND, we rode with two dozen warriors from Frog's Hollow to the Thames. When we reached the river's edge, we passed the horses off to some of the women and elders who'd ridden with us so they could take the animals back. People would soon begin fleeing the city. I wouldn't risk leaving the horses behind.

We went to the river's edge. As I remembered, the bank of the Thames was passable by foot, with many rocky shoals that extended out into the water.

"There is a ramp leading down from the governor's villa to the river," Madogh told us. "The servants use it to fetch water and toss rubbish. Deliveries from barges are also taken up the ramp. There is a gate. On the other side, it leads to a servants' entrance."

"Let's go," I said.

Working quickly and quietly, we made our way in the darkness toward the governor's villa. As we went, we passed a family rushing away from the city. They were Atrebates by their dress. Sorcha and several others trained their bows on them, all of us pausing a moment.

Then, I saw the fear in their eyes.

I gestured for my people to lower their weapons, then motioned for the people to pass.

"Our own people are not our enemies," I said.

Working along the river, we heard the sounds of warning bells and screams ringing in the city. Bran had begun the assault. Now, the Romans would see what had come for them.

We hurried along the river's edge, finally spotting the villa. From where we were, I could see the docks. They had all burned, as had the few boats that remained and the construction on the great bridge across the Thames. The druids had set fire to it all. The smell of smoke lingered in the air.

Moving silently, we made our way toward the governor's villa.

From within the city, I heard panic and mayhem. People were screaming in fear, calling to one another. Soldiers shouted for men to cover the east gate.

Madogh signaled for us to wait then slipped up the ramp to check for guards. The ramp was to one side of the house, leading to a gate at the back of the villa.

We waited in the darkness until he finally returned.

"They have pulled some of the guard from the house to defend the city against the Trinovantes' assault on the east wall. Still, go cautiously. Catus will not have let them all go," he said, then motioned for us to follow him.

We slipped up the ramp toward the house. When I finally got to ground level and could see the chaos in the city, a strange sense of joy lit up my heart. The Romans had finally seen what was coming for them. And it was too late to flee.

"Halt! Who goes there?" a guard called from the back gate of the villa.

Sorcha silenced the speaker with an arrow.

Madogh raced forward, quickly scaling the gate. A moment later, it opened from the inside. Madogh gestured for us to keep low and be quick. We hurried within, entering a courtyard where crates of food sat and laundry hung to dry. Hurrying across the square, we slipped into the house.

There, we encountered two more guards.

Artur and Pix charged forward, engaging the men and ending them quickly. In the next chamber, Roman servants worked quickly preparing crates of what looked like gold and silver. Half a dozen Roman soldiers guarded the room.

We rushed them, the warriors of Frog's Hollow making quick work of all but one of the guards who Madogh grabbed and pinned against the wall.

"Where is the procurator?" Madogh asked the soldier who spat at him.

I pulled my dagger and pressed it against the man's neck. "Talk or die. Where is the procurator?"

"Upstairs in his bedchamber, hiding under the bed," he said with a laugh.

"What is all this?" I asked, gesturing to the crates.

"The procurator has a ship coming for him from an outpost upriver. He's fleeing to Gaul."

"There was a girl with him, a girl he took from the Greater Iceni. Where is she?"

"How would I know?" the man replied tartly.

I pressed the blade in, cutting his skin.

"I don't know," he replied quickly. "But if she is anywhere, she is with him."

"I know you," Sorcha said from behind us.

I looked over my shoulder to see my daughter staring at the man. For a flicker of a moment, I swore I saw fire in her eyes.

"Sorcha?" I whispered.

"I know you..." Sorcha repeated.

And then, I knew what she meant.

I looked back at the soldier. "You were there? In Venta?" I hissed at him.

"I... I..."

"Hold him," I told Madogh.

The spy took one shoulder, me taking the other, and we pressed the Roman against the wall.

With a scream, Sorcha stabbed the man between the collar bones on the exposed part of his chest. Over and over she stabbed until the man began to slip from our grasp.

I let him go, his lifeless body crumpling to the ground.

Turning, I set my hand on my daughter's shoulder and met her gaze. "Sorcha?"

Steely eyed, she met my gaze, flecks of blood all over her face. "Let's find Vian," she said. She shook the blood from her dagger, then sheathed it once more.

We ran from the chamber and began working our way through the villa, cutting a path through the guards as we made our way up the steps. Flinging open door after door, we found many notable Romans hiding within. We made no distinction between tradesman, merchant, or soldier. They were Roman, so they were doomed.

"They are in the villa! The villa is under attack!" a panicked male voice screamed as Artur kicked in one of the doors to the bedchambers.

Five guards raced out.

Tristan and the other men of Frog's Hollow rushed forward to help Artur and end the guards.

"Boudica!" Artur called to me, gesturing to the room.

I pushed forward.

There, I found Procurator Catus. He held Vian before him, a dagger—Gaheris's dagger—at her throat.

When he saw me, his eyes grew wide and his nostrils flared. He stepped back, dragging Vian with him.

"Come closer, and I'll cut her throat," he told me.

"Let her go," I told him.

"I'm warning you, Boudica. I'll cut her throat. Get out of my way. Let me out of this room."

"After what you have done? How can you possibly believe I will let you slip away?"

"Because this girl's life depends on it," he said, pressing the dagger against Vian's neck. Droplets of blood slipped down her throat.

"Boudica," Vian whispered tearfully.

"Take another step closer and I will—" Catus warned.

A moment later, the man's words came to an abrupt halt as a dagger smashed into his eye.

I gasped and looked behind me to find Lynet, her arm still extended from the throw.

Turning back, I watched as Catus stood still for a moment, as if his body was still processing his death, then he dropped Gaheris's dagger. His grip on Vian loosened, then he fell to the ground.

Lynet, Artur, and I raced forward.

"Vian," Artur said, reaching for her.

Vian moaned sadly then wrapped her arms around him. "Artur... Thank the gods. I thought you were dead."

I bent down, picking up the blade that had once belonged to my love.

I turned to Lynet. "May the blade come home once more," I said, giving it to her.

Lynet took it from me. Staring down at the dagger, her eyes grew misty. She wrapped her hand around the handle and closed her eyes. "Thank you, Boudica," she whispered.

Pix bent, yanking the scabbard from the procurator's belt. She handed it to Lynet who sheathed her family heirloom.

I went to the window and looked out at the scene unfolding in the city below. There, I saw both Trinovantes warriors and Iceni.

"Bran broke through," I said.

"Let's help him finish the job," Lynet said.

"Stay with me," Artur told Vian, who nodded.

With that, we left the governor's palace, clearing it of whatever Romans we found. In the city streets, the merchants and others tried to fight back. One group of heavily armed men rushed our party, but they were quickly overcome. In the confusion of the fray, I watched as many of the Trinovantes warriors hunted down and killed Roman men and women alike... priests and priestesses, merchants, slaves...

Pix read the expression on my face.

"The red rage of the Morrigu has them. There is nothing to be done, Boudica. The goddess is shrieking for vengeance, and she does not care who stands in her way. Soldier, senator, merchant, or slave, if they have the blood of the eagle, she will devour them. Come. The city is on fire. Let's leave this place before we get trapped."

We hurried from the city, passing warriors as we

went. Pix was right, Londinium was turning into an inferno. The impressive basilica, the townhouses where we once stayed, the temples… All of it was going up in flames.

We exited the city from the north and retreated across the fields, rejoining the others. When we got there, Lynet and her warriors went to help with the wounded, while I took Vian to the tent that had been erected for me.

Olwen rushed to join us, wrapping her arms around Vian.

"Olwen," Vian whispered in a shaky breath.

"Are you hurt at all?" I asked Vian. "Do you need Rue or another of the healing women?"

"No. No," Vian said. "Oh, thank the gods," Vian said, kissing Olwen on her head and weeping. "Thank the gods," Vian said, reaching for Sorcha who also wrapped her arms around the girl. "Thank the gods," she said again, smiling up at me.

I returned the gesture.

Reassured she was unharmed, I walked to the edge of the camp and looked down over the burning city.

Pix joined me. Studying my expression she asked, "Why do ye not look happy?"

"Did Paulinus underestimate us or did he leave Londinium to burn?"

Pix paused as she considered. "He didn't reinforce

the city, but he also told the people to flee."

"Then he knew we were coming. He knew they would die."

Pix nodded slowly.

"The others would have us march on Verulamium next. Do you think Paulinus will be waiting there?"

Pix crossed her arms as she considered. "'Tis nothing there save an old hunk of rock. It means little to anyone except the Catuvellauni. If I were Rome, I'd pull back, wait for more reinforcements, then try to engage us on the open field."

"Why the open field?"

"Ye see how the Romans fight. Taken off guard, they can be defeated. But there be a reason Roman rules the world. Ye should keep yer advantage. If ye can pounce on Paulinus before he's reinforced, ye can defeat him."

"Delay the attack on Verulamium and chase Paulinus?"

Pix nodded.

"It will be hard to sell that to the Catuvellauni."

"What does it matter if it be hard? It be the truth. And right now, all that matters is crushing Rome. That hunk of rock will be there when it is done. Ye have cut the head and heart of Rome from this land. Now finish the body—the governor's army."

I nodded slowly. Pix was right. "Yes. And may the gods be with us."

CHAPTER 48

With Londinium burning, the army rested and recovered, the wounded receiving treatment. Exhausted, I went to my tent and lay down. When I finally woke the next day, my body ached and all I wanted to do was go back to sleep, but there was work to be done.

Leaving Olwen and Sorcha, I splashed water on my face, pulled on my cloak, and headed out into the early morning air. It was foggy that morning, a dense bank of mist rising off the Thames. The city below, however, still burned. The fire from it would have been evident for miles around. Flakes of ash covered the ground like snow.

Feeling groggy, I went to the meeting tent. There, a map of the country had been laid out.

I stood staring at it, considering Paulinus's moves.

Governor Paulinus was not alone. There were other generals, other legions, spread along the coast. If the governor worked quickly, he could summon all his forces to his aid. Pix was right. We had to stop him before he could get reinforcements. Chipping off Rome piece by piece, we could win this war. But if we let them regroup…

My gaze went to Mona.

If Paulinus had ridden from the west, did that mean he had abandoned his assault on the druids or had he left soldiers behind?

Or worse yet, had the island already been defeated? Had we risen too late?

A boy arrived, carrying along with him a bowl filled with meat, bread, and cheese. "This is for you, Queen Boudica."

"Thank you," I told him, ruffling his hair.

To my surprise, Vian appeared out of the mist, wrapped in Artur's cloak.

"Vian. Why aren't you resting?"

"I tried," she said, then looked at my map. "Catus took me from Venta to wound you. Doing so, he made one mistake."

"What's that?" I asked.

Vian picked up the wooden tokens lying in a basket beside the map and started placing them thereon. "He took the most observant woman in Britannia into his workspace. In so doing, he showed me every card he held," she said as she worked. "And let me hear every word between him and the governor."

"What did you hear?" I asked.

"The second legion controlled by Poenius Postumus, stationed on the Isca," she said, setting a token in Dummonii territory, "has refused the governor's call to send reinforcements. Postumus bluntly told the governor he had his own problems. No reinforcements are coming from him," she said, running her finger along the southwest coast. "Paulinus hurried his cavalry to Londinium. The bulk of his men are behind him, marching back from Mona," she said, setting down more tokens. "Right now, Boudica, they do not have the men. If you can strike before they regroup, you will easily overtake the governor. But even if they do manage to combine forces, you have them outnumbered at least five to one. Act quickly."

"Vian," I began, then paused. "Mona?"

At that, Vian shifted her gaze.

"Vian?"

"Finished. That was the word he used. The governor said he would have to go back and mop up what he missed thanks to the rebellion, but otherwise, Mona is done."

I stared at the map. "We were too late. We rose too late."

"Surely, there are some survivors. The governor withdrew in haste once he heard the news from Camulodunum. It is not a total loss. Some of them must have survived."

"And are now flung to the wind," I said, gripping the side of the table.

Brenna...

Ah, Sister...

Vian and I both looked back at the map. "Move quickly, Boudica, and you will have him. Then, whatever happened to Mona, we can rebuild and start anew."

I scanned the map then nodded. "Yes. Yes, you're right."

Now, if I can only get the others to agree.

"WE SAID we would march to Verulamium, so we will march to Verulamium," Chieftain Adirix said angrily, pounding his fist on the table, making the tokens shake. "I did not rally my people simply to avenge the Northern and Greater Iceni and liberate Trinovantes and Atrebates. We will march on Verulamium."

"I am not disagreeing, Chieftain," I said—again. "I

am only saying we have the advantage now. If what Vian is saying is true, we should not delay. We should cut off Paulinus before he is able to gather the full strength of his forces. We take out the general and his cavalry, and then we can meet the infantry on their own —and whatever else they want to throw at us. Victorious, we will return to Verulamium and finish the Romans there."

"I honor your love for your ancestral home, but Verulamium has lost its strategic importance since the time of Aulus Plautius. Retaking your capital is a matter of honor, one none of us disagree with, but Queen Boudica is right that we must strike the Roman army now while they are weak," Arixus told the chieftain.

"You have my word, we will free the fort, and the Catuvellauni will rule themselves once more," I told the chieftain, but he was unmoved.

"No. If you do not march for Verulamium, I will withdraw my men. You can take on the Romans on your own."

"Then you lose either way," Chieftain Lors pointed out.

"I will not be chided by the Trinovantes," Chieftain Adirix replied.

"Even when I have more sense that you?"

At that, Chieftain Adirix puffed out his chest and moved toward Lors.

"Are ye cocks so small?" Pix asked them, stepping between them. "Or did ye forget, we all have one enemy now? And it's not one another. Ye would be wise to listen to Boudica."

"Chieftain," Vian said respectfully to Chieftain Adirix. "It is simply a matter of numbers. Boudica should move on the governor now."

"Numbers or not, if she bypasses Verulamium, then she can take on the general without me."

"If Paulinus regroups with his infantry, and we don't have the Catuvellauni?" I asked Vian.

She frowned. "I greatly dislike those odds."

"Adirix, your personal quest may doom us all," I told the Catuvellauni chieftain with a frown.

"I'm not changing my mind."

"How fast can we get to Verulamium?" I asked.

"By this afternoon."

"Summon your men. We must end it quickly then move at once to intercept Paulinus. I need riders tracking the governor's movements. Now. Rally in haste," I told them.

With that, the leaders and chieftains departed.

"Boudica," Bran said, nervousness in his voice.

"I know. But we can either help the Catuvellauni or die trying to fight the Romans without them."

"We may die either way—because of them," Bran said with a frown "Then I guess not much has changed after all. Caratacus or not, that tribe... Curses upon them."

"Don't curse them yet, Brother. We will need them to get us through to the end."

"At least we drew the Romans away from Mona. The druids—and Brenna—are safe," Bran said.

I swallowed hard then held my brother's gaze.

"Boudica," he whispered, reading the expression on my face.

"She may have survived."

Bran shook his head then pulled me close. He said nothing, but I could feel my brother's thoughts. If Brenna had perished, then there was only him and me left.

"She may have survived," I whispered again, reassuring both Bran and me.

Bran nodded. "Yes. She may have survived." Inhaling a deep, shuddering breath, my brother stepped back.

"Don't tell the others. Not yet."

"I understand. I will call my men. We will make haste."

"I will do the same," I said, then turned to go.

Pix and Arixus joined me.

"Boudica," Pix said, a warning tone in her voice.

"I know."

"May the gods protect us from the unending depths of Catuvellauni selfishness and pride," Arixus said.

"And if they cannot, let the Catuvellauni be the ones to choke on it," Pix replied.

I said nothing, only made my way forward, praying we had enough time.

CHAPTER 49

We marched to Verulamium, making our way to the ancient stronghold of the Catuvellauni.

"Have you ever been here before?" Sorcha asked me.

I nodded. "Twice, to speak to the governors of Britannia."

"Which governors?"

"Scapula... and Aulus Plautius."

Pix flicked her gaze toward me but said nothing.

"I remember Aulus Plautius. He had black hair, didn't he?"

"He did."

"I remember when he came to Venta. It is my first memory of ever hating a Roman."

I chuckled. "You threatened to stab him with the little wooden dagger Pix gave you."

"Too bad I didn't."

"Yer mother is the one who should have stabbed him. She had enough opportunity."

"I'll stab him in the next life, just to make you both happy," I replied.

"Stab him, push him from the roof of fort, I'm not picky," Pix told me with a laugh.

I winked at her.

When we drew close to Verulamium, Chieftain Adirix joined me.

"You will not know the place, Queen Boudica. The Romans have destroyed and defiled our ancient seat," he said, then the two of us rode to the peak of the hill that overlooked the city. "I am not sure there is anything left of my people here. It is all now Rome."

He was right. In the years since Scapula had gone, Verulamium had bulged in size, rivalling Camulo-dunum in both its vastness and its Romanization. Everywhere I looked, I saw Roman-style buildings and houses. There were temples, theaters, marketplaces, and a basilica. The Catuvellauni hillfort, of which I was once meant to be queen, looked like a poor cousin to the new city below.

Across the city, a bell rang.

The Roman road, known as Key Way by our people, was filled with Romans trying to flee the city to the northwest.

The others joined us.

Chieftain Adirix motioned to the druid who rode with him to sound the carnyx.

"As agreed, my forces will push up the main street to the fort," Chieftain Adirix said.

I nodded. "The Iceni and the Coritani will take the left flank, the Trinovantes will take the right. Our Coritani friends will patrol the road."

The echoing sound of the carnyx rang across the valley.

"Then may the gods go with you, Queen Boudica," Chieftain Adirix said, inclining his head to me.

"And you, Chieftain."

The carnyx rang once more, and the Catuvellauni gathered their forces, preparing to ride out.

Chieftain Lors shouted to his men to make ready.

When I turned Dice, I got a good view of the vast army behind us.

So many had come. So, so many.

"It's like all the trees in the forest have shifted form and risen to fight," Sorcha said, her gaze following mine.

"Then may they fight with the strength of Duir," I said, then nodded to Bran who sounded his warhorn.

Pix reined in beside Cai. "Remember, loot first, burn second."

At that, Cai laughed.

"Ye need to find me something nice today," she told him.

"Maybe a fine Roman gown? You can wear it and pose like the women on the Roman vases," he said, holding his hands delicately above his head.

Pix laughed. "Why waste time with a gown you can see through anyway?"

Cai winked at her. "My thoughts exactly."

Chieftain Adirix rallied his army, screaming and raising his sword.

"Sons of Tagos. Daughters of Bel," he screamed. "Let us take back our ancient home. Let us purge Rome from our lands. Look what they have done! Look what has become of our city. Is this what the Catuvellauni have been reduced to? This, *this*, is what Togodumnus fought and died to prevent. This is what Caratacus warned us would happen. Where are our kings? Where are our nobles? Rome has taken our people, chained them, defiled our priests and our gods. No more. No more! Today we come as the wrath of Taranis. Rise, children of Tagos, and take back our home! With me," he called.

And with that, the Catuvellauni poured into the city.

Bran sounded his horn once more.

"Northern Iceni! Greater Iceni," I called. "Advance! Left flank! Left flank! With us," I screamed, then we rode into Verulamium.

The Roman soldiers, I quickly realized, had all but

abandoned the city. Those who had been left behind to protect the temples and villas of wealthy Romans quickly perished as our massive army flooded the streets.

Seeking to reclaim what was taken from them, our warriors looted as they fought their way through the city. Those who had fled had left many fine goods made of silver and gold, rich textiles, jewels and more behind.

I touched nothing.

There was not a single thing I wanted from Rome. There was wealth enough in Iceni lands.

Keeping to horseback, we pushed our way through the massive city. Those Romans who had stayed behind resisted mightily, as if they were fighting for their own lands. How could they believe such a thing? Because Rome had promised them land in a country that was not their own? The Roman lie had seeped into the very fabric of our world, tainting it from the root.

As I worked my way through the city, shield in one hand, spear in the other, I fought off the Romans who had foolishly thought they could take Dice from me.

One scrappy young Roman rushed from a narrow alleyway and grabbed Dice's reins, pulling the horse.

But Dice had been well-trained. Wild though he was, he was Druda's offspring and a horse of the Iceni people. I held on tight as Dice reared, yanking the reins from the man's hand, then crushing him under his hooves.

When the man tried to get away, he was met with a barrage of arrows.

I turned to see Sorcha with her bow in her hand.

"You'll need to loot the fletcher's stall for more arrows," I called to her.

"I already have," she said, gesturing to the full quivers hanging from her saddle.

I chuckled.

We pushed farther into the city. Turning a corner, I found myself standing face-to-face with a dozen people holding shovels, trowels, and other equipment. From their dress and looks, their complexion far darker than my own, I knew them to be slaves taken far from their homes by the Romans.

I signaled to Sorcha to lower her bow.

"Follow the road northwest if you seek Rome. If you seek freedom, go east," I said, pointing. "If you seek vengeance, come with us."

At that, they looked at one another then nodded. "We are with you."

Sorcha reached onto her belt, removing her second sword, and tossed it to the man who had spoken. "Then come with us," she told him, then we pushed forward.

It took much of the day, but finally, we rejoined the Catuvellauni who had taken their fort once more. The

Romans had left soldiers behind to defend it, but those men had perished. In a way, I pitied the men. Their leaders had failed them. Surely, Paulinus now knew he had not left enough men to defend the city. He had known they would die.

By leaving them there, he was buying time for his troops to arrive to reinforce him. A sacrifice of men in Verulamium meant nothing. I dismounted, leaving Dice with some Iceni soldiers, then made my way into the fort. As I did so, I bent to look at one of the men who lay dead there. I went from one man to the next.

"What is it?" Sorcha asked me.

"They are Catuvellauni themselves," I said, gesturing to the markings on one man's face, and another man's hands. "Conscripted soldiers."

"Conscripted?"

"Captured. Forced to fight or maybe taken as young men in the early years of the raid and turned Roman. Look at their armor."

"It's practically falling apart."

"Paulinus didn't keep his best warriors here. He threw Catuvellauni conscripts in front of their own people to die. And die, they have..." I said, then frowned. "Come on," I told my daughter, then we wound our way up the steps of the fort.

I knew where I would find the chieftain.

In the same room where Aulus and I had once dined,

I found Chieftain Adirix and the other leaders of the Catuvellauni cheering and drinking. Two young women in Roman garb were being pushed between them, the men groping the girls.

"Enough of that," I said firmly, banging my spear on the floor.

"Ah, Boudica," Chieftain Adirix said, but when his gaze flicked to Sorcha, seeing the haunted look on her face, he gestured for the men to let the girls go.

"Get them out of here," I told Sorcha who went to the girls and led them away.

"I am glad to see your fort recovered, but we must press on. There is no time to linger."

"Not even for a glass or two of Roman wine?" he asked, pouring me a cup.

From the smell in the room, the stains on their tunics, and the swaggering condition of the other chieftains, I could see that they had started celebrating before I got there.

I shook my head. "No. Not even for that. The Roman part of the city is burning. We must withdraw now and regroup."

A moment later, someone approached me from behind. I turned to see Tavish there.

"Boudica," he said. "The Trinovantes have completed their sweep. We are ready to call for the army to muster," he said then paused, a strange expression on his face. "What is that..." he said then leaned forward, breathing deeply.

"Musk and stubbornness," I replied in an annoyed tone.

"Let the men rest here tonight," Chieftain Adirix said, then began coughing. "Your army will be tired. Your men will need rest," he added, then started coughing harder. "You would be... You would be..." he said again and again, trying to get the words out, but his words were interjected by hard coughs.

Soon, the other chieftains gathered there also began hacking.

Rushing across the room, Tavish lifted one of the one decanters and sniffed it.

"Boudica," he said, aghast, then rushed forward, knocking the cup from Adirix's hand. "Did you drink?" he asked me in a rush. "Boudica, did you drink?"

I shook my head.

One of Adirix's men fell, then another, and another. Soon, the men began to spasm.

I rushed to Chieftain Adirix. He was holding his throat. His face had turned purple. His eyes were bulging. "Adirix," I said, trying to untie his laces on his jerkin so he could catch his breath. "Adirix, breathe. Breathe." But the man could not catch his breath. Panicked, I turned to Tavish who was trying to help another man. "Tavish. Tavish, what do I do?"

Adirix's body began jerking wildly.

I tried to hold him still so he didn't hurt himself, but there was nothing to be done.

"Adirix," Druid Dagda, the Catuvellauni's chief druid, shouted, rushing to join me. "What has happened?"

"Nightshade," Tavish replied. "The wine was poisoned."

Below me, Adirix grew still. Finally, he exhaled deeply and then grew limp.

My knees shaking, I rose.

All around me, the Catuvellauni chieftains and nobles, the last leaders of their people, died.

Pix and Bran entered the room behind us.

"In Epona's name," Bran exclaimed. "What the… They're dead. They're all dead. All their leaders…"

I shook my head. "The Romans knew. They knew we would take the fort and enjoy the spoils. They knew."

"Ye did not drink, did ye, Boudica," Pix said, terror in her voice.

I shook my head. "No. I was trying to get them to leave."

"Druid Dagda," I said gently, going to the aged man. "Wise One…"

"My people are gone," he said, looking around the room. "This is the end of us."

"No. Your people are outside. Thousands of them.

Thousands. And right now, they need you. They need you to lead them. We must leave. Now. We must meet the general. We need you to lead the Catuvellauni."

"I must stay with the chieftain, see to their funeral rites. I cannot leave them in such a state."

"Druid Dagda," Tavish told him. "Your people trust you. You must tell them what has happened here."

"We will arrange their bodies and cover them," I said. "But we must not delay a moment longer. Every second we stand here, Rome grows stronger. Already, we have lost our advantage because of Chieftain Adirix's will."

"The gods punished his greed..." the druid said, staring at the dead man. "The gods punished him for putting his wants before the people."

"We must go. Now. While we still have a chance," I said.

"I..."

"We will help you," Tavish said, then gestured to us to help collect the bodies. "We will lay them there. You can order a small warband to stay behind to build the pyres. But we need you now. There is no one else the army will trust. You must tell them what has happened here."

"Yes," the druid said, aching misery in his voice. "Yes."

priests. But they have not taken our hearts, our spirit. We are bruised, but we are not broken. We must rise, like the Morrigu herself, and be reborn. We cannot be what we once were. Tribes separated, bickering, warring with one another. That life, that world, does not serve us. We must build anew, even if it is on the ashes on our forefathers and those we have loved and lost. We are not broken. And we can still recover the beating heart of our lands. It doesn't reside in our ancient halls, or in our royal families, but in our people. In the very blood in our veins. That—that is what matters. That is who you are. We know ourselves as Northern Iceni, Greater Iceni, Trinovantes, Atrebates, Coritani, Cantiaci, Catuvellauni, and many more. But we are *all* the children of our gods. We are *all* the children of the oaks, of the stones, of the greenwood. Today, now, we must also be children of ash and iron.

"Rome has not been defeated.

"Camulodunum, Londinium, and Verulamium are reborn, but Rome has not yet been defeated. We are not yet free. And unless we fight on, we will *never* be free."

I turned and looked back at the fort on the hill. "So, I honor the dead. I honor the Catuvellauni loses, but if you want your freedom, we must march on. You must follow me! Rome waits for us. Don't permit her to grow too comfortable in our fields and forests. We must strike now! Quickly. And take back what is ours. Are you with me?"

At that, the crowd screamed in assent. The sound of it rolled like thunder across the fields.

"Are you with me?" I called again.

Again, they screamed, lifting their fists in the air, brandishing their swords.

"Then let's ride out! Death to Rome!"

"Death to Rome!"

At that, I turned and prepared to make ready.

"Ye always did have a big mouth," Pix told me.

"I've heard that makes me a good kisser."

At that, Pix laughed. "I don't disagree with that, Strawberry Queen."

I cocked an eyebrow at Pix, looking at the odd fur-trimmed metal helmet on her head. "Where did you get *that*?"

"My handsome boy looted it for me."

"It's ugly."

"That be a matter of opinion. Now, ride on, Morrigu. We will follow."

With the Roman structures in Verulamium burning behind us, we set off down Key Way...toward destiny.

CHAPTER 50

With riders ahead of us to try to gauge where Paulinus had gone, we marched our massive army onward until we found a suitable field to stop for a few hours of rest.

I had barely slept an hour when the first of the riders returned with news.

"Queen Boudica," the young Trinovantes man greeted Lors and me. "We've found him. The governor is camped in a field half a day's ride along Key Way. I grabbed one of their slaves and made him talk. Paulinus has been settled there since retreating from Verulamium. One of the legions, part of the Valeria Victrix, just joined him."

"And his men from Mona? The Gemina? Have they arrived?"

The rider nodded. "Yes, Queen Boudica. Just before I reached them."

"Banshees be cursed. I told Adirix..." I said, cursing the dead man. "Had he ridden on as I had said, he would still be alive and we'd have kept our advantage."

"How many men?" Lors asked. "How big is their army?"

"They have gathered what auxiliaries they could, conscripted soldiers, even some of our own people paid to fight with the Romans. There are ten, at most fifteen, thousand."

I turned and looked at Lors, both of us blinking in surprise.

"So few? Are you certain?" I asked the boy.

"Positive. I saw them myself. We are ten-to-one against their forces."

"We should move out at first light, before they have more time to draw reinforcements. Let the men rest a few hours more," Lors said with a smile. "It is done, Boudica. We will have our lands again."

While the odds were so much to our advantage, something within me hesitated.

"We must remember that half our soldiers are dressed to work the fields, many wielding knives and scythes meant for farming not fighting. We must go cautiously against their forces, who are outfitted to fight and trained for the same. You say he is encamped in a field?"

The boy nodded.

"If we split the army, get part of our forces behind him, we can crush him in the middle," I said. "What is at his back?"

"I… I did not really look. Forest, I think, my queen."

I nodded.

"We'll send two fresh scouts on fast horses. If we can split our men and surround the Romans, we'll have him," I said.

"I'll see to it," Lors replied, then quickly departed.

I looked out across the encampment.

Ten thousand men.

Everything was on our side. There was no way we could lose.

But if so, why did my stomach ache with so much dread?

JUST BEFORE DAYBREAK, I had a boy sound a horn, calling the army to muster.

I joined Sorcha, Artur, and Olwen, all of whom were preparing for the battle.

"I want you with me and Pix in the chariot," I told Sorcha, who immediately frowned.

"Why?" Sorcha asked. "I've heard the odds just like everyone else. I'll be surprised if I can even get close," she said with a laugh. "They'll all be dead before I get there."

But I didn't laugh. The feeling of trepidation that had taken hold of me had not let go, and I didn't understand why. "We won't chance it. Our people are good fighters, but the Romans are trained soldiers. A shepherd spends his days with the flock. Roman soldiers spend their days preparing for battle."

"She's right," Artur told Sorcha.

Sorcha gave him a playful scowl, but Olwen looked pensive.

"What is it?" I asked her.

She frowned then shook her head.

"Don't be worried, Sister," Sorcha reassured her. "It will be done by moonrise."

Olwen did not look so certain.

I pulled the ties on Sorcha's jerkin, tightening it.

"Can't breathe," she said.

"Don't complain. It will keep your body protected," I told her.

When I was done, I retied the laces on Artur's right gauntlet.

Artur watched me as I worked. Finally, he asked, "What is it, Boudica?"

I paused and looked up at him, the boy now a foot taller than myself. "I don't know."

Artur frowned then nodded.

Vian was already mounted and waiting with us. I joined her, Bran, Tavish, Arixus, Pix, and the others.

"I will ride with you to the front," Vian told me. "I want to see what you are up against. I hope it is as simple as it seems."

I reached for her hand, glad to know that I wasn't the only one who saw the danger here. A lack of caution had already killed the Catuvellauni.

We set off once more, marching down Key Way to meet Paulinus.

We had traveled for two hours when the first of the riders we'd sent to watch the Romans returned.

"Honored ones," the rider said, joining us. He lifted his hands to the druids. "The Romans have begun to pull back."

"Pull back?" Bran asked.

The boy nodded. "They have taken a defensive position with the forest at their backs," he said. "There are narrow slopes to each side of the army. They are rocky and densely wooded."

"Can we get behind them? Is there a way?" I asked.

"There is a ravine," the boy told us, gesturing with

his hands. "It's uphill from the field. The hills are on each side of the ravine. They're too steep to climb. The forest behind the Romans is dense with brush."

"Can we get around them? Push through the forest—dense or not—from behind?"

The rider considered. "If part of the army follows the River Anker then circles around, it is possible."

"I can go," Bran offered. "I will take the Northern Iceni. We can time the attack, begin at sundown. He will not expect us to attack from the rear. We can use the forest to hide our advance."

"For what purpose?" Lors asked. "Boudica, we are ten-to-one. We must take them head-on while their numbers are still weak. Adirix pushed us into a mess. We could have mopped up the governor and his cavalry yesterday. But now that we are here, we should not delay. We cannot give the governor more time to bring in further reinforcements. We must strike while we have the numbers."

Lors was not wrong. We had the numbers, and further delay *would* cost us.

"Governor Paulinus has the advantage of high ground," Vian said. "And you will not be able to easily attack his flanks."

"To wait for Bran to make it to the pass is not without risk," Tavish said. "If another legion joins, even with our vaster numbers, that is a problem. The Romans are well armored and seasoned fighters. There are some amongst us who have never seen battle."

"The druid is right. The general has legionnaires, cavalry, infantry... And I saw mounted horsemen, the Batavians, amongst their numbers," the rider told us.

I looked back at the army.

In the crowd, I spotted a boy perhaps no more than twelve or thirteen. He was wearing an oversized jerkin and a wool cap. His shield looked as though he'd made it from the lid of a barrel. He carried a long spear. Too long for the length of his body. How many of our people were armored similarly? If another ten thousand Romans came from the south, or if they were reinforced from the north, it wouldn't matter if we outnumbered them.

"Boudica?" Bran asked.

"We'll ride on. The delay is too risky," I said.

At that, the others nodded.

"Good," Lors said. "Let's have it done by nightfall."

I nodded, but my heart was torn.

Arixus reined in beside me. "All things are as the gods will, Boudica."

"Then why do I feel like I just made a decision that might cost us our lives?"

"Destiny is already set. We will either die or be free. No word from your lips will change that."

"Do you believe that? That it is all set and we are merely players in some great game?"

"Of course." Arixus smiled. "But we play anyway. That's the gift of life."

WORD WENT THROUGH OUR RANKS. Soon. We would meet soon. I directed the mounted riders to move to the flanks of our infantry, guarding our sides. Those driving light chariots came forward to the front of the army.

Leaving Bran, I rode down the line, my patchwork cape fluttering in the breeze, until I found the healers and women with supplies at the very back. I made my way to Olwen, who was riding alongside Bec and Rue.

I scanned for Melusine but didn't find her.

Olwen gave me a worried half-smile.

"Olwen," I said, reaching for her hand, which I squeezed. "We are approaching the army now. It will not be long. Stay back and at Bec's side."

She nodded, but I could see the worry in her eyes.

"It will be all right. We outnumber them mightily. Just stay to the back with the others."

"We'll be all right," Bec reassured me, but I heard the tremor of worry in her own voice.

"Save me one of Cidna's burned biscuits. I will have it to celebrate."

Bec smiled. "Be safe, Princess."

"And you, Priestess."

I held Olwen's gaze. Her eyes were teary with fear. "Olwen," I said. "I will be all right. No matter what happens, stay beside Bec."

She nodded.

"May the Great Mother watch over you, Queen Boudica," Rue told me.

"And you, my friend."

With that, I leaned in, set my hand on Olwen's head then kissed her cheek. "Olwen, no matter what happens, I will find you. I promise," I whispered to her.

Giving her one last, loving look, I made my way forward once more.

"May Epona ride with you, Queen Boudica!"

"May Taranis bless you, Queen Boudica!"

"Andraste's blessings upon you, Queen Boudica!

As I rode the line, the warriors called out to me.

I lifted my hand in thanks, then made my way back to the front. When I arrived, I discovered a rider.

"Boudica," Bran said. "They are just over the knoll and in the valley. They are making ready."

"Then we will do the same. Come."

We moved our great force from Key Way and into the field across from the waiting Roman army.

When I saw how few they were, I gasped.

"Suppose they're pissing their little skirts?" Pix asked with a laugh.

Vian reined in beside me. "Boudica, we have the numbers but he has all the advantages. He has the high ground, and you cannot penetrate him at the sides due to the slope of the trees."

"Suggestions?"

"Chariots with archers and javelins first. They will form a shield wall. Use your range weapons to kill the men behind the shields before they advance."

"Call for them," I told Artur who turned his horse and hurried down the line.

"Give me Dice," Pix said. "I will ready the chariot."

I dismounted then handed off my horse.

Arixus joined me.

Across the field, I could see Governor Paulinus on his horse. He was rallying his men, getting them into position.

"You suppose if I challenge him to single combat, he'd agree?" I asked.

The druid chuckled lightly. "As our ancestors did. Victory with far less bloodshed."

"The Roman doesn't care about his people. They are tools to him."

"And he will use them to every advantage. Vian is right. Get your riders in early and try to break their line.

Watch for his own javelin throwers. Once they begin throwing, the chariots must withdraw. We must do what we can to keep them on the open field, not get pushed together. Our people are good with the bow and spear, and our swords are longer than theirs. We need space. The Roman sword is better in tight quarters where it is hard to use a spear or bow. Don't get bunched up."

I looked toward the back, seeing the wagons pulling in to one side of the field, leaving the path to the road and the river beyond clear.

We stood in silence, watching as the Romans made ready. Their armor glimmered in the sunlight. Paulinus's strong voice carried on the wind. On it, I heard the confidence of a man who never lost. My gaze went to the Batavian riders, known for their cruelty and strength.

"Arixus…"

"Courage, Boudica. Courage. All the way to the end."

A SHORT WHILE LATER, Pix returned with the chariot. Sorcha passed Ember to her friend Aden, the saddler's son from Venta. I saw her with the boy, forcing him to take the mount. He had resisted her attempts but eventually relented. Pix passed Nightshade on to another Iceni fighter without a horse.

Our warriors had spread wide across the field, chariots at the front, cavalry in place. We were so many. So very many.

Across the field, the Roman sounded his horn, bringing his men to muster.

I gestured to one of the brothers of Condatis to sound the carnyx.

The druid stepped forward and lifted the tall instrument. The voice of the horse-headed horn, its tongue wagging, sounded all across the field. Soon, other druids came forward, all of them sounding the carnyx. The voice of the horns echoed in the ravine behind Paulinus. The sound made my skin rise in gooseflesh.

Scanning the line, I finally spotted Tavish. He, too, was sounding a carnyx, but he did so at the front of the Coritani. There, at his side, fully armed and wearing a torc around her neck, was Melusine. The banner of the Coritani flew above her head. *Queen* Melusine stood before the Coritani like the Morrigu herself, three lines of blue paint trailing down the side of her face.

Down the line, Bran and Bellicus came before the Northern Iceni. Lynet and the others were close behind him.

Pix, who had also painted her face, took my arm and

turned me toward her. Dabbing the blue woad in her hand, she began marking my forehead.

"'Tis the triskele," she told me. "Birth. Life. Death. It just be one cycle repeating again and again. I be at your side today, Boudica, as I be always. May ye remember, this is not the only life we get. If ye end up with a Roman javelin in yer belly, just remember that both that handsome young man from the muddy bog and your Strawberry King be waiting for ye, along with that sour brother of yours and all the like. Death 'tis nothing to fear."

"Very inspiring," I told her wryly. "You're supposed to urge me to be ready to fight, not ready to die."

At that, Pix laughed. "'Tis always good to be ready for both."

"Says the woman who managed to live since the time of Caesar."

"Ye see, no one can catch me. Especially not now that I have this fine helmet," she said, knocking on the metal dome. "Stay at my side, and they will not catch ye either."

I laughed but then held her gaze. "Pix... May Andraste watch over you."

"And ye," she told me, then grabbed me by the shoulders and gave me a good shake. "Now, let's kill some Romans."

I grinned at her.

"Boudica," Arixus said, stepping toward me with a black hare in his hands. "Let the gods speak."

"Where did ye find that? I haven't seen such a creature since I was with the fey," Pix said.

"Then you already know the answer, don't you?" he replied with a smirk then turned to me. "Go before the people," Arixus told me.

Slipping into the chariot, Pix, Sorcha, Arixus and I rode to the front of the army. There, Arixus and Sorcha stepped out.

Our horns sounded once more, then grew quiet.

Across the field, I heard Paulinus haranguing his soldiers.

"Now is the time for zeal. Now is the time for daring…" his voice carried on the wind.

"My people!" I called in a loud voice. "Children of the gods. Let your ancestors hear your voices. Speak, Greater Iceni!" I called.

At that, the Greater Iceni screamed, Sorcha along with them.

"Speak, Trinovantes!"

At that, Chieftain Lors and all his men shouted loudly.

"Speak, Northern Iceni!"

Bran, Bellicus, Cai, Lynet, and all the others lifted their voices.

"Speak, Coritani!"

Melusine lifted her sword and screamed, her people along with her.

"Speak, Catuvellauni!"

The warriors' voices rose into the air.

"And all you Cantiaci, Atrebates, and those displaced from your homes, speak!"

The sound of our collective voices rang across the field, echoing in the valley. The cries reverberated off the sides of the mountains, echoing all around Paulinus's men.

"Today, we have come to fight, not just for our gods, but for our families, our people, ourselves, and the very land under our feet. We are all children of the green-wood. The eagle has come to our lands, knowing nothing of our sacred stones, trees, pools, or the names of our gods. They know nothing of the little people of the hollow hills. They know nothing of the fey things in our forests. They know nothing of this land. And yet, they have come to take from us all that we hold precious. All that is sacred. All that is beyond their comprehension.

"But I say, no more.

"No more.

"Today, we will strike the chains off our gods. We will reclaim what is ours.

"May the gods, the ancestors, and all the wild things of our world be with us. For today, we fight with them.

We will take back this land. And with it, we will strike the eagle from the sky.

"Who is with me? Who is here to fight for this land?"

At that, the army screamed, their voices echoing.

Arixus stepped forward. "Queen Boudica, daughter of the Northern Iceni, Great Andraste speaks! She sends her messenger to show you the path to victory," he said, handing me the hare. "Show us the way, Andraste. Show us the path to victory!"

I lifted the hare above my head so all could see the black creature, a sacred symbol of the dark goddess and lady of battles.

Turning, I set the creature on the ground. As I did so, I whispered, "Show me the way to freedom, dark lady Andraste."

The moment I set the hare loose, it took off like a bolt toward the Romans.

I smiled at Arixus, but the druid's eyes were on the hare. On his face, I saw a strange expression.

I turned back to the army. "Andraste has spoken! Freedom lies on the other side of Roman blood! Prepare to march. Toward freedom!"

Pix and Sorcha slipped into the chariot with me while Arixus hurried to mount his horse once more.

Once we were in the chariot, I gestured to Pix to ride the line.

On the other side of the field, Paulinus did the same.

My spear in my hand, we made a pass in front of the army.

As we did so, their leaders called them to form up.

"Coritani, make ready!" Melusine shouted.

As I rode past my brother, I met Bran's gaze.

For a single moment we shared of our thoughts, feelings, hopes, and fears.

And then Bran turned to the Northern Iceni. "Northern Iceni, make ready!"

And onward I rode down the line, reaching the front of the army once more.

I paused a moment, inhaling deeply.

I closed my eyes.

Andraste, be with me.

And then, I lifted my spear. "Now!"

At that, Pix snapped the reins on the chariot and the charioteers rushed forward.

As we raced across the field, the Romans called out, and the infantry began to shift position, moving forward, forming a shield wall. The cavalry protected the left and right flanks.

"You see that?" I asked Pix.

"Aye, Strawberry Queen. Just as Vian said," she said, then gestured for me to take the reins.

Switching places with Pix, I took Dice's reins then raced across the bumpy field just as we had practiced a thousand times.

"Mind the distance, Boudica. Mind the distance," Pix told me then turned to Sorcha. "Get ready."

Racing forward until we were within range, I turned the chariot.

Pix began hurling javelins, Sorcha sending a barrage of arrows onto the Romans.

Working so systematically, the Romans lifted their shields to cover the assault. One line of men at the front had their shields forward to face oncoming blows. The row behind raised their shields to make a canopy overhead.

While I heard some cries from the Romans, we were hardly making a dent.

Working in line, our charioteers raced across the field, shooting arrows, and sending javelins toward the Roman army.

Again and again, we made our passes.

While the Romans resisted, their men did begin to fall.

It was fascinating and horrifying to watch as when one man died, another stepped forward to take his place in the shield wall. The resulting effect was that it appeared like the Romans had taken no losses.

"Like ants in a line," Sorcha said. "They just keep coming."

"Talk less, shoot more," Pix told her.

We made another two passes, then Pix said, "Almost out, Boudica."

"Same," Sorcha added.

"Sound for the chariots to retreat," Pix told me, then took my spot.

Pulling my horn from my belt, I sounded the horn, and we turned, rushing away from the field.

"They didn't move," Sorcha said in astonishment. "They simply didn't move. I…"

As we rode past the line, I signaled to Bran.

My brother rode to the front of the great army, sounding his horn.

As soon as we were clear, the massive army would push in, and we charioteers would reinforce the flanks alongside the cavalry as we went for the Batavians. As I drove to take my place, I was surprised when I caught a glimpse of the wagons at the edge of the field behind us. Before, they had been only to the south end of the field. Now, the wagons stretched along the entire back wall behind our army.

"Pix," I said, worry in my voice.

"I see them. Ye think we should—"

But then Bran sounded his horn.

With a deafening scream, the army advanced.

There was no time.

No time.

Frowning, I turned the chariot and made ready to advance once more.

What happened then became a total blur. The great army pushed forward toward the Romans. The sheer force of them would be enough to break the Roman line. But the charge was uphill. Governor Paulinus held his advantage.

One of the Roman officers barked a command, and then I saw javelins shooting across the skyline from the Roman army into ours.

They had waited to use their range weapons on the infantry.

"What the..." Sorcha said, watching the javelins streak across the sky into the thronging crowd of warriors. The sound of men's death screams echoed above the fray.

"Chariots be too fast, even for the best aim. They waited until they had a target they could hit," Pix said.

Again and again, the Romans barraged the army.

"Bran should pull them back. They should pull back until they run out of javelins," I said, looking anxiously toward the front.

"Ye can just as easily pull back the ocean, now," Pix replied.

I frowned hard and watched.

The Romans had not advanced.

"They aren't moving forward. They're holding the

line," Sorcha said as she eyed the pass. "The landscape narrows around the Romans. Our army will have to converge to break their shield wall."

Meaning, that the power of our surge—on top of the uphill battle—would be reduced.

"Bran..." I whispered, looking back.

Racing into position on the flank, we watched as Romans barraged the warriors with javelins and arrows. Finally, our people began to reach the top of the hill, drawing in close to the Romans. The surge was enough. They would break the line.

But then, a Roman trumpet sounded. Sending out short blasts, the Romans began to push forward. Shields in front of them, they began to press downhill, but their formation shifted...

"Like an arrow," I said with a gasp.

Paulinus had organized his men into a stiffly fortified V-shape. The Roman soldiers pushed downhill, into our own army who had, in the push uphill toward the narrow defile, bunched up at the center.

A moment later, a Roman horn sounded again, and the cavalry at the flanks began to push forward in time with the infantry.

"Get ye ready," Pix said. "There," she told me, gesturing for me to engage a secondary wedge, led by the cavalry, on the flank. Paulinus's warriors moved with purpose and symmetry which was both brilliant and horrible to behold.

We raced into the fray.

"Keep distance when ye engage, Sorcha. Those short swords will kill ye at close range. Keep distance," Pix warned my daughter.

The battle around us became a blur.

Working hard to keep to the edge of the field and use the chariot to our advantage, Pix and Sorcha took turns bounding off the chariot to fight, mainly using their spears, then rejoining once more.

Over and over again, we raced forward, battled and won, then retreated.

But around us…

The screams of my people became deafening as the Roman wedge drove the army back.

Soon, we too found ourselves bunched as our warriors began to get pushed backward.

"Boudica, ye must pull back," Pix told me. "We cannot get caught in the crowd or we'll be tossed from the chariot."

Hurrying toward the back of the army, we did what we could to prevent the Roman infantry, including conscripted warriors, from edging in on our people.

I looked across the field, my eyes searching for any sign of Bran, Bellicus, Tavish, Arixus, or any of the others.

Finally, I spotted Bran in the fray. Somehow, he had lost Foster in the fighting and both he and Bellicus were on foot. Not far from him, I spotted the brothers of Condatis battling hard, but the Romans pushed forward —shields before them, stabbing with their shorter swords, cutting a brutal path into my army.

I was about to draw Pix's attention to the others when one of the Batavian riders, his face painted red and white, screamed then rode toward us, a spear in one hand, a small axe in the other. Pix and Sorcha lifted their shields to protect us from the attack, but I could see in his eyes that we weren't the target. It was Dice.

"No," I said, then screamed, "Hold on." Yanking on the reins, I turned the horse just in time.

The spear narrowly missed Dice, but instead, it hit the rigging of the chariot. Something snapped loose, and the chariot flipped.

There was a strange moment when everything seemed to slow. I felt myself fly through the air then hit the ground hard. I rolled, feeling a searing pain in my shoulder and then my gut, then landed on my aching back. It took me a moment to catch my breath. After the confusion passed, I looked to see what had happened.

I had been tossed from the chariot. Pix and Sorcha had held on and were now crawling from the wreckage.

The rider turned, pulled his sword, and rushed toward them.

"No!" I screamed.

Racing forward, I picked up my spear from the ground where it had fallen. Remembering everything Gaheris had taught me, I gripped the spear hard, aimed, then threw with all my strength.

It hit the rider squarely in the chest.

The force knocked him from his horse.

The moment I saw my daughter safe, my head cleared, and again, I felt terrible pains in my body. I looked down to see blood pouring down my hip. I lifted my tunic and jerkin enough to see a deep cut there. Confused, I looked and saw the rider's axe lying on the ground nearby. His weapon had grazed me, but the cut still looked deep. I looked at my shoulder. A sharp piece of wood from the chariot had broken off and impaled me.

Nausea washed over me when I saw the wood there.

I took a deep breath, gripped the piece hard, then pulled it from my body.

For a moment, my head grew dizzy, and black spots swam before my eyes.

"Boudica…

"Boudica…

"Queen of oak…

"Queen of stone…

"Queen of the greenwood… Come to us.

"Boudica…"

"No," I whispered, my voice shaking. "No."

I opened my eyes, dug into my vest, and pulled out a bundle of dressing, then pressed it against my wound on my stomach. It was bad. I tightened the bottom laces on my jerkin to hold it in place.

"Boudica," Pix said, coming to me. "Ye have blood on ye."

"Cuts from the chariot. I'll be all right. Let's go," I said, then we rushed off to rejoin Sorcha.

When we finally were able to regroup, we looked back and saw a horrifying sight.

Despite our numbers, the Romans had used their position to their advantage. Our whole army was bunched together, smashed against one another as they retreated.

"The Romans are cutting through them like water," Pix said, aghast.

"Mother," Sorcha said, looking behind us, panic in her voice. "The wagons. If they get pushed into the wagons, they'll be trapped, and they'll all be killed."

"The Romans won't want to cross the Anker. Their armor won't let them get across easily. We can retreat across the river and regroup," I said. "Come on. Let's get the wagons out of the way then call for a retreat."

I rushed across the field to Dice, freeing him from the harness, then slipped onto him bareback, Sorcha sliding up behind me.

Pix grabbed the reins of the Batavian's horse, and we rode off toward the wagons.

"Get these wagons out of here," I started screaming at the women and children who had set up camp there. No doubt, they had thought the battle would be over quickly, our victory decisive. Some had already started fires for cooking. "Get them out of the way. Retreat across the river. Move these wagons! Now!"

"Move the wagons! Move the wagons!" Pix screamed as she raced down the line.

We raced past the line of civilians, calling for them to get out of the way. While the Iceni had only brought healers, the Trinovantes had brought whole families, complete with a barnyard's worth of animals for feasting, and their spoils from the cities we had looted. These families had come to watch Rome's fall. If they didn't move in time, they would serve as a barrier against which Rome would beat our army to death.

"Move! Move these wagons! Get out of here," I called as we passed.

"Mother," Sorcha said worriedly. "Your shoulder. And there is blood dripping down your leg."

"Just cuts from the chariot," I told her dismissively, then called to Pix. "Pix, the Iceni!"

Racing along the back, I kept one eye on the army being pushed toward me and another on the slowly moving wagons. The people pulled up camp as quickly as possible and some of the wagons were already rolling out of the way. But in other areas, I was astonished to see that several people had already erected tents, had fires burning and meat cooking. Barrels of stolen ale had been set out in what they had anticipated to be a victory feast.

"Break camp! Quickly! Get out of the way. Move these animals and cross the river!" I shouted at the people. "You are in the way. Retreat from here—but move these wagons!!"

Pix and I rushed forward to the Iceni, who were already readying themselves to move out of the path of the retreating army.

Rushing forward, I spotted Bec and Olwen working hurriedly to get the wagons underway. The moment we reached them, Sorcha slipped from Dice and ran to her sister.

"Olwen," Sorcha told her in a rush. "We… we must retreat. Come with us."

I could see in Sorcha's eyes that she knew the same truth that was slowly, painfully dawning on me.

We were dying.

We were dying.

"Bec," I called to my sister-in-law.

"Everyone, get the wagons moved now," Bec commanded. "I have them, Boudica. We will retreat south to Verulamium."

Rue working quickly with her, the Northern and Greater Iceni followed Bec's call and began moving out.

"Wagons, fall back to Verulamium! Fall back," Bec yelled.

When Olwen moved to go with Bec, Sorcha stopped her. "No. Ride with Pix," she said, then hurried Olwen onto Pix's horse before returning to me.

Then, I heard a chorus of screams coming from the northern end of the line. There was a loud clashing and the sound of men and women screaming in agony.

"Advance! Advance!" I heard Paulinus call.

"The Trinovantes," Pix said, looking behind us.

We watched in horror as the Trinovantes army was forced into the wagons. They had started to move, but it was too late. The Romans were rushing them, slaughtering every man, woman, and child.

"Go, Bec. Go!" I screamed at her. "Get out of here."

My head swooned, and for a moment, I swayed.

"Mother," Sorcha said worriedly.

Bec and Rue rode out then, driving the wagon quickly away.

"Bran. Where is Bran? Melusine? Tavish?" I said, looking frantically for them.

By the gods, the Romans had us.

How?

How?

We scanned the army. In the distance, I spotted

Tavish and Melusine. They were on one horse, the pair of them working their way across the field, dodging arrows and javelins as they went.

I looked toward the Northern Iceni.

So many dead.

So many of our warriors lay dead on the field.

And so few Romans.

How had this happened?

We were so many.

"There! There is Bran," Sorcha said, pointing. "Aye, gods," she then cried out. "Bellicus."

Not far from where my brother fought, I saw the lifeless form of Bellicus on the ground. Bran, enraged, raced across the field, sword in hand, Cai along with him.

He was rushing Paulinus.

Seeing Bran and Cai coming for him, Paulinus jumped from his horse. Another Roman soldier moved to protect the general and soon, a fray between the four of them began.

I watched in horror as Cai stabbed and slashed but was quickly beaten by the legionnaire, who thrust his sword into Cai's gut.

"No," Pix said, then moved to go forward.

Olwen set her hand on Pix's reins, stopping her.

My brother and the governor battled, their swords ringing across the field. In Bran's moves, I saw all our father's teachings, Caturix's, and those who had come before. But it was not enough.

When the general raised his sword to strike, Bran took his opportunity to hit the general in the weak spot in the armpit.

But the general's move had been a feint.

A dagger in his hand, he stabbed my brother in the stomach.

"Bran!" I screamed.

Bran dropped to his knees.

The governor yanked his dagger free and then swung his sword.

I looked away.

I didn't want to see.

Down the line, someone called for retreat.

Arixus.

The druid struggled to get the army out of the field, waving them toward the narrow gap created by Bec's retreat. The opening she had made was enough to get some of the army out of Rome's way.

"To the river! To the river!" Arixus called. "Retreat to the—" but the druid's words were cut short when an arrow pierced his throat.

He swayed in his saddle.

In that single moment, his gaze found mine.

The druid met my gaze, then touched his forehead,

gesturing to the triskele symbol painted on my brow, then fell from his saddle.

"No! Arixus!"

Out of the jumble of people, Lynet suddenly appeared. Blood was splattered across her face. "Boudica, we are defeated," she said. "We must fall back."

"Retreat, Iceni! Trinovantes, Catuvellauni, retreat! Retreat!" I screamed.

Lynet swayed on her feet.

Slipping from the saddle, I hurried to her. "Come. Get on Dice. We must flee this place."

"No," she whispered. "No, Boudica. I am already dead," she said, then gestured to her tunic on which I saw a blossoming pool of blood. "Fly, Boudica. Fly from here. We are finished. My sister. Get to my sister," she said, then pulled Gaheris's dagger from her belt and pressed it into my hands. "Take it."

"Lynet, no."

"Take it, Boudica. Get north to Skye. The dagger will be your key. We are dead, Boudica. The Romans will finish the Iceni. Get your children north. Now, go," she said, pushing me back.

Pulling her sword, she screamed and rushed back into the fray.

Leaving her, I slipped onto Dice once more. I stared at the unbelievable sight before me.

Our army had been defeated.

Not defeated.

Decimated.

Those who had survived were now fleeing toward the river. But how many? Two dozen, three?

"Boudica," Pix said. "We must go!"

"Artur... Where is Artur? Vian?" I looked all around. "Artur!"

"There, there," Sorcha said. "By the river. He's helping people cross."

I nodded to Pix, and we set off, racing away from the battlefield. When we finally got to the river, we hurried to Artur and Vian.

"Artur, come now," Pix told him. "We need to go."

"But we have to help," Artur said, confused. "We can regroup the army on the other side of the river and—"

"Artur, there is no army to regroup. Everyone is dead, and the Romans are still advancing," I said, panic in my voice. More than anything, I cared about my people. The horror unfolding was more than my heart and mind could bear. But there was nothing to be done. At that moment, I had a straightforward duty left—to try to save my children. I had to try to save my children.

"They're about to swamp us," Pix said. "We need to flee."

Vian stepped away a moment and stared at the scene

unfolding behind us. She turned to Artur. "Artur, they're right. We have to go. Now."

"But…" Artur said, looking back.

Around us, a ragtag group of warriors, many of whom were bleeding, struggled to escape. Along with them were many women, children, and elderly who had come in the wagons.

My gaze turned toward the road on which Rue and Bec had ridden. Aye gods, Bran was dead. Bellicus was dead. The Northern Iceni were finished. When they were done here, Rome would ride on Oak Throne, Venta, Frog's Hollow, Holk Fort…everywhere. They were all doomed. *We* were all doomed.

"Aden," Sorcha said in alarm, then ran to meet Ember, who came racing toward her. When Ember finally joined us, the boy slipped from the saddle. He was already dead, a bloody wound in his stomach. "Aye, gods. No!" Sorcha wailed, grabbing the collar of his shirt.

Olwen tugged on my arm and gestured to Dice.

"Let's go. We have to go," I said, then motioned to the others.

"Here. Here, take the Batavian horse," I told Vian and Artur. "Pix, get on Dice. We must ride north. Sorcha, up on Ember now. Olwen will ride behind you. Now. All of you. Move."

"North… Boudica, to where?" Vian asked.

I slid onto Dice, wincing in pain when I did so. I gasped, my head feeling dizzy again, then steadied myself. "We must get to Skye."

"Across Brigantes land?" Artur said, aghast. "Boudica, Cartimandua will…"

"Artur, we may be dead either way. Lynet gave us our only chance. We have to try."

With that, we turned and made our way toward the river.

Dice and Ember entered the water without hesitation.

Suddenly worried, I looked back at Vian and Artur.

Artur coaxed the horse gently. Finally, he submitted to going across. The water grew deep as we passed, but the horses swam on. When we finally got to the other side, I looked back to see the Romans had broken through the wagons and were now finishing what survivors they found.

"This way," Pix called, then we turned and raced off, Dice running at a hard gallop away from the scene, the others following.

I held on to Pix, pressing my cheek against her back. I willed my head to be still and the pain in my gut to quiet. When we stopped, I would clean the wounds. When we stopped, I would bandage myself up properly.

But not until we stopped.

"Pix," I whispered to her. "Ride on. Ride on as far as he can take us."

My friend said nothing, merely spurred the horse forward, away from the slaughter behind us.

I closed my eyes.

When I did so, Dôn's last words to me came to mind once more.

She knew any rebellion would fail.

She tried to warn me.

The eagle would not leave this island any time soon.

"Aye, gods," I whispered, tears streaming down my cheeks.

"Don't curse them yet," Pix told me. "Pray to Brigantia and the Cailleach, Boudica, because if ye would see your children safe, ye need to get through Brigantes territory first."

CHAPTER 51

We rode through the rest of the day and into the night, finally stopping when we reached a dense glade far away from any farm or settlement. There was a small stream nearby. When we dismounted, Pix took the horses for water while the others sat and stared.

Morfran, who had been following us, settled on a tree branch overhead.

Artur opened his ration pouch and handed some food to the girls. Sorcha, Vian, and Olwen ate absently. Once they had finished the meager food, they passed around the water pouch.

Not daring to light a fire, I worked in the moonlight to inspect my wound. Vian gasped when I finally undid the laces on my jerkin and rolled up my tunic.

"Boudica, you are injured!"

"I just need to clean it," I said, touching the tender wound. Even in the darkness, I could see it needed stitches. "I'll be all right."

"Mother, what happened?" Sorcha asked, coming to help.

"The chariot accident. I think... I think the rider's axe grazed me. And a hunk of the chariot went into my shoulder," I said, wincing as I poured water over my wound.

"Let me," Sorcha said, helping me clean my wounds. Artur patched my shoulder, but when Vian inspected the wound on my stomach, she frowned.

"I don't like the looks of it," Vian told me.

"Can't see anything in the dark," I replied. "And we have no salves or anything else with us. It probably needs stitches. Let's bind it for now. I will watch for healing herbs as we ride tomorrow."

Vian frowned heavily. I could see she wanted to scold me but held her tongue.

The look was enough.

"Here, let me," Artur told me, dressing the wound and wrapping clean linen around my waist.

As he worked, my head grew dizzy.

Olwen chewed her lip nervously, her brow furrowing.

"I'll be all right," I reassured her.

Olwen made the symbol for blackthorn, the symbol

of the Cailleach—and the Brigantes.

I nodded. "Yes, when we reach the Brigantes lands, maybe we can find help. Everyone should sleep," I said drowsily. "We should set off again in a few hours."

No one objected. Instead, in a state of shock and despair, they simply did what they could to find a comfortable tree to lean against.

Sorcha and Olwen huddled together in the crook of an oak.

"Cold?" Artur asked Vian who nodded.

He gestured for her to lean against him, then covered them both with his cape.

When Pix returned, she lay down on the ground beside me.

"I'll sleep with one eye open," she told me.

"Do you really think anyone is looking for us?"

"No. I think they be toasting their gods."

A soft wind blew through the trees, revealing the starry sky above.

"Bran is dead," I whispered. "And Bellicus. Lynet and Arixus too."

"Aye. I saw."

"I sent Bec and Rue to Verulamium where they will surely be killed."

"Boudica…"

"Melusine and Tavish… I have no idea what has become of them."

"They got around the Romans and rode into the valley behind them, fleeing into the forest."

"Then may great Cernunnos watch over them, and may Elen lead them far away from here. Oh, Pix. All those we left behind in Venta," I said, then began to weep. "Mara, Brita, Ronat, Betha, all the servants at the roundhouse, everyone in Oak Throne, I—"

"Sleep now, Boudica. If ye lay there reciting names, ye will never rest, and we need ye for what comes next."

I closed my eyes and reached out for Pix's hand. "To the end," I whispered.

"To the end, Strawberry Queen," she replied.

WE WOKE a few hours later and set off once more.

Pix was unusually quiet as we prepared to continue north.

"Are we in Coritani lands yet?" Sorcha asked.

"Hard to say," Vian replied. "But we should be very close. If we ride throughout the day at a good pace, we will pass through Coritani lands and into Brigantes territory by nightfall."

As I prepared Dice to ride out, I had to steady myself. My head felt light, and my stomach ached. And, oddly, I was sweating profusely, though I didn't feel fevered. When Pix joined me to mount Dice, she looked me over then frowned.

"Ye all right?" she asked.

"I will be. Let's just go."

"Ye need to freshen up that wound."

"When we stop next. The Romans will be on the move. We need to get some distance between us and them. If we can reach Brigantes land by night, I think we should push on, passing through in darkness. We'll be easier to miss."

Pix merely nodded then linked her hands together to boost me up onto Dice. Grabbing a handful of mane, she did the same. But I saw her wince when she did so.

"Pix?"

"Pulled something in the fighting. 'Tis barking like a dog. It will come right soon enough."

Once the others were ready, we set off once more, weaving our way through the forest and fields. We avoided settlements as best we could, keeping to the greenwood. But when we emerged from one forest late in the day, we found ourselves on a Roman road once more.

"Banshees be cursed," I grumbled.

"No. Wait..." Sorcha said, looking down the road. "There," she said, pointing. "That wagon. They are just farmers. I'll concoct a good lie. Olwen and I will go. No one will suspect anything of us."

"Sorcha," I said, meaning to stop her, but it was too late. She removed her sword, tossing it to Artur, then the girls trotted off. "Too trusting. Too rash."

"Nay, Strawberry Queen. She is as determined to get us to safety as ye."

Vian eyed the road. "There is a Roman road along the western coast of Brigantes territory. It isn't finished yet, but it will stretch all the way north to the Caledonian Confederacy. This must be it."

Hidden in the trees, I watched as my daughters spoke to the people in the wagon. From this distance, I could see it was an old man and woman. I closed my eyes.

Brigantia, mother of the Brigantes people, you do not know me, but I pray from one mother to another to keep my daughters safe. Help me find a way through your lands. Help me get them to safety. Ancient Cailleach, dark lady, protect us. Night has fallen on my people. Help us reach safety.

I felt a sharp pinch on my side, and nausea washed over me.

Please, Cailleach, help me get them safe before I can do nothing more for them.

After a moment, Sorcha guided Ember back down the road, turning at the trees to rejoin us.

"We are in Brigantes territory. There is a pass across

the Pennies mountains to the Brigantes seat a few miles north. I told them we set out from southern Brigantes lands, seeking to join the holy women of Brigantia. There is a shrine, they told me, a day's ride north, not far from the coast, at the edge of the Carvetti territory. Mother, if we can get there, the priestesses can see to your wounds."

"Perhaps the priestesses will help us get to Skye," Vian said.

Sorcha looked at me. "Mother, you are white as snow. We must get you to a healer."

"Vian be right. If there be any in Brigantes land who might help, it be the holy people," Pix said.

"The old farmer and his wife—they are chicken merchants—they said to follow the coast until we see the twin mountains in the distance, then watch for the standing stones to guide the way."

"May the gods be thanked," I said. "Let's go."

Leaving the Roman road, we made our way west until we found one of the old paths not yet spoiled by the Romans. We worked our way north. As the day progressed, my head began to ache. And that ill feeling in my stomach made me wince with every bump. Feeling cold, I pressed my cheek against Pix's back.

"You're so warm," I told her.

"Nay, Strawberry Queen. You're cold. And dripping like ice in spring."

"Mother," Sorcha said worriedly.

I had difficulty opening my eyes, so I simply replied, "I'm all right. Ride on. Let's get to the holy sisters."

My mind drifted then. I looked out at the sea to the west, watching the dark blue waters. A selkie jumped the waves, leaping and spinning. She paused and waved to me. Giggling, I waved back.

"What ye see?" Pix asked.

"A selkie. You see her?"

"Nay," Pix said worriedly. "Watch ye now, Boudica. You are slipping into the in-between realm. They will tempt ye, if they can. That's how they got old Pix."

Closing my eyes once more, I held on to Pix.

"Your skin is hot," I mumbled again.

"Nay," she replied, but this time, I thought I heard a lie in her voice.

When I opened my eyes again, we had turned from the sea and were in the forest. We had stopped before a standing stone.

Morfran sat perched on the top of the stone.

"Olwen," Sorcha said sounding worried. "Go slower. Olwen… Mother," Sorcha said, pleadingly. "Mother, we need you. She and Prasutagus were the only ones who understood Olwen well. Mother."

"Sorcha?" I whispered.

Olwen came to me then and began signing the Ogham, pointing inland.

I watched my daughter as if I were looking through Roman glass. She seemed cloudy and far away. I narrowed my gaze, trying to focus. "Olwen says to go west. Follow the stones to the mother... To Brigantia..." I said, then closed my eyes.

I felt Dice turn as we made our way into the forest.

"Boudica...

"Boudica..."

I looked up into the trees, spotting the red-capped piskies there. Sitting on the branches like birds, they watched me.

"Boudica. We see you, queen of oak. Why are you so far from Oak Throne?" one of the piskies, a button-nosed girl with bright green eyes and long, blonde braids asked me.

"Oak Throne is gone," I whispered in reply. "It is all gone. I failed to protect the oaks, the stones, the people. I failed them all..."

"Nay, don't speak of it, Boudica," Pix told me.

"Oh, Boudica," the piskie girl said with a laugh. *"You don't know what you've done. Others will come to protect us. But you... You have inflicted a wound to the eagle that will never heal. If you had not struck, they would have stayed a thousand years, and we would be no more. Don't you see? You saved us."*

"She's not that bright, is she?" one of the piskie boys, a

brown-haired creature wearing an acorn cap for a hat, said.

"Nay. But she was the best option we had," the girl replied.

"Fun to play with, though," the boy replied, then grabbed an acorn, took aim, and lobbed it at me.

The moment the acorn struck my forehead, my body felt heavy and my grip on Pix loosened. I could feel myself falling, but could do nothing to stop it.

Then, everything went dark.

CHAPTER 52

Wat happened next came in a patchwork of images. I remembered being on the ground, Pix examining me, a worried expression on her face. Olwen cooled my forehead with wet clothes while Sorcha looked about for herbs, cursing herself aloud for not paying more attention when I tried to teach her.

I opened my eyes just a crack.

Standing in the glade of aspen trees nearby, I saw the Seelie prince.

"*How now, Queen Boudica of the Iceni?*"

"I am queen of nothing, now," I whispered.

"Don't try to talk," Vian told me. "You're burning with fever. We need to get her to the priestesses."

"Lash her against me," Artur said. "We can ride more quickly."

"Queen of Nothing, that wound of yours is souring."

"It doesn't matter. I just need to get my children to Skye."

"We'll get there," Vian assured me.

"Nay, Vian. She's talking to the greenwood now," Pix said.

"I can take them," the Seelie prince offered. *"They will be very happy in my realm. You, too, can join me. You would be very happy in my lands under the forever sunshine."*

"No," I whispered.

"Do not listen to their charms, Strawberry Queen," Pix told me then called aloud, "I don't see ye, but I feel ye here. 'Tis not the time and place for ye. Leave her in peace."

The seelie prince laughed. *"Clever as a fox. As always, clever as a fox,"* he said, then faded.

"Clever as a fox," I repeated, then everything went dark once more.

"HURRY. BRING HER INSIDE," a stranger said.

Hands held my arms and legs, moving me quickly into a house. The heat of the fire felt so good, so warm.

"Sorcha? Olwen?" I whispered.

"We're here," Sorcha called back to me. "We're here, Mother. We're all here and safe. The priestesses will see to you now."

I looked up, seeing a white-haired woman looking down at me.

"You are in the Grove of Brigantia," she told me. "You are wounded. We will care for you now. Rest easy. You and your people are safe."

"The Romans..." I whispered.

The woman huffed a bitter laugh. "No Romans will come here."

"Rome goes everywhere, like an illness poisoning the streams, the rivers. I am burning from it now," I said drowsily.

The old woman set her hand on my forehead and smiled gently at me. "Rest easy. Just rest."

At that, Sorcha's voice faded, and I heard two women speaking to one another. Their voices were faint, but I caught small snippets of their conversation as they spoke of fresh dressings, unguents, and salves. I could feel them working quickly to clean the wounds, but there was worry in the voice of the elder of the pair.

"The axe wound," the woman said. "It still bleeds."

"Yes," the elder priestess said.

"And the puncture. It is so red and angry," the younger said. "And the smell..."

"There was wood still inside the wound. The injury has spoiled."

"Then she…"

"The poison is in her blood now."

At that, the younger of the pair grew quiet for a long time then finally asked, "Wise Mother, is she who I think she is?"

"Yes."

"Then we must send for her…"

"I already have."

"Who?" I whispered.

"Rest now, Queen Boudica. You are safe here. I have given you something to numb the pain. You will feel like you are dreaming for a time. We will take you now to the arms of the Cailleach. She will decide if you live or die," the priestess told me. "Have them prepare the mound."

"Yes, High Priestess."

When I next became lucid, the priestesses were leading me through a dark forest toward the mound. They held their torches aloft, lighting the path. For a moment, I thought I was in the Grove of Andraste. But it wasn't so. I was somewhere in a dense forest. The white-haired priestess holding on to me, I was able to walk, but the pain in my side made me gasp in agony. When I held my side, blood squelched from between my fingers.

In that single moment, as the pain wracked me, I knew a terrible truth.

I was dying.

WHEN I OPENED my eyes again, I found myself in a strange place. Everything was dark, lit only by torch-light. I was confused at first, but the scent of the place gave it away. I was in a mound. I lay on a stone altar. I could smell the pungent aromas of healing herbs used during rituals…for the dead and dying. I was lying on a stone bed covered in clean linens. Everything around me was so hazy, and my head spun. I shuddered hard, then blinked, trying to clear my vision.

"Mother," Sorcha said, hurrying to my side, Olwen right behind her.

Sorcha, her eyes red from crying, took my hand.

Olwen bent over me, cradling my head, hugging me gently.

I could feel her tears on my cheeks.

I looked behind the girls to see Artur and Vian standing there. I could see from their faces something had gone terribly wrong.

"What's happened? Who is hurt?" I whispered.

At that, Sorcha wept.

A voice from the other side of my bed answered.

"Your wounds have soured without proper care, Boudica. Your blood is poisoned, and your heart will soon stop. My priestesses have done everything they can to ease your pain, but there is nothing else to be done."

I turned to look, finding Queen Cartimandua standing beside me.

I gasped lightly. "Cartimandua…" I whispered, tears coming to my eyes as I recalled how the Brigantes queen had given Caratacus to Rome. "Oh, please. Please. My children. Please, do not betray them to Rome. They must get to Skye. Please. Oh, please… Not as you did to Caratacus."

At that, Cartimandua smiled oddly, as if there was some pain behind the expression, then took my hand. "I gave Caratacus what he deserved," she told me. "If I remember right, he had the blood of the Northern Iceni on his hands. So, you will understand me," she said.

"Yes," I whispered. "Yes."

"Skye?"

I nodded. "They must get to the sacred isle. Will you help them? Please? My children…and Vian and Pix. Please. I beg you, as a mother, please help them. They are all I have left. I must see them safe, but I cannot carry on. Aye, Andraste. Why now? Oh, please, Cartimandua, please help them. The Romans will hunt them, and they have already suffered so much. Please, Cartimandua..."

Cartimandua looked from me to Sorcha and Olwen. An odd expression crossed her face, like a shadow of heartbreaking misery. Her eyes grew glossy with unshed tears. She blinked once, a single tear slipping down her cheek. She wiped it away and then turned back to me. "I will get them there. You have my word."

"May the Great Mother bless you. Aye, gods," I moaned. "Pix, do you hear? Cartimandua will help. Pix?"

Sorcha began to sob.

I looked from her to Olwen, who shook her head, tears sliding down her face.

I turned to Vian and Artur. "Where is Pix?" I asked them.

Artur frowned and then looked at Vian.

"She was injured, Boudica. She didn't tell us. She said she was just trying to get you safe," Vian said.

"Where is she?"

"She is *barely* with us," Vian replied, choking back her tears.

I turned to the High Priestess. "Please, bring her here. Please, she must be with me."

"She will die if we move her," the woman replied.

"She will die all the same. They want to be together. I

will carry her," Artur told the priestess. "Please, honored one, let them be together in their last moments."

At that, the woman nodded then gestured to another of the priestesses. The girl and Artur disappeared.

I swallowed hard then reached for my belt, the dagger still hanging thereon. "Sorcha," I whispered, gesturing for her to come to me. "Sorcha…" When I tried to remove the dagger, my strength failed me.

"Let me help," Sorcha said, choking back her tears. Moving carefully, she unbelted Gaheris's dagger.

"Take this to Skye. Tell them Lynet gave it to us. This will gain you entrance to the shadowy one's keep. Cien… Lynet's sister is Cien. Speak to her. Tell her who you are and how you came to be there. Tell her what happened to her sister. Aye, Sorcha," I whispered, tears slipping down my cheeks. "You will never be queen, but you will be safe."

"Mother," she whispered, wrapping her arms around me.

When she let me go, Olwen came next, setting her hand on my cheek.

"My special girl. The gods made you the way you are for a purpose. Seek it out. On Skye, you may find the answers that have alluded you. I wish you peace, my sweet girl. I wish you peace."

Weeping, Olwen kissed me on my forehead and then let me go.

Vian came forward next, bending to set a kiss on my cheek. "Thank you, Boudica, for seeing in me what others did not. It was a golden life. I will take the chance you gave me and build on it. I promise you."

"Vian..."

She kissed my hand and then let me go.

A short while later, Artur appeared, carrying Pix.

"Set me down, boy," she told him. "Set me down."

Artur did as Pix asked.

She came to me, weeping as she looked at me.

"You are still wearing that ugly helmet," I told her, touching her cheek. But the blood on my fingers marred her pretty features.

Laughing and weeping, she pulled it off, her long, pale blonde hair falling all around her face, then lay her head on my chest.

"You're a liar," I told her.

"My job is to protect ye. I failed, but I thought I could get the children safe. I told them to cut my throat and leave me with ye, but they tell me I'll be dead soon enough."

"Aye, Pix," I said, stroking her head.

I turned then to Artur. "Artur," I said, gesturing for him to come closer.

Weeping, he joined me. "Mother..." he said in a

shaky voice. In his tone, I heard the little boy fate had given me as a son.

Pulling the heavy torc from my neck, I gave it to him. "There is gold enough here to buy you some future, whatever shape you seek. Artur, you are not alone in this world. Never think that. You have Vian and your sisters. Do not forget that you are not alone."

He wept, then nodded, taking the torc from me.

"Come now," the white-haired priestess told them. "Let us leave them in silence. The Cailleach will see to them now."

My daughters, Vian, Artur, and all the priestesses departed.

Cartimandua was the last to leave the mound.

"May the Cailleach watch over you both," she told us somberly. "And bring you all together again in the next life. You have my word, Boudica. Go to the Other-world in peace," she said then left me and Pix alone.

Pix reached out and touched the faded triskele on my forehead. "I still see the shadow of it there," she whispered.

I took Pix's hand, holding it tightly. "Pix."

"Boudica," she whispered. "It is growing dark."

"Yes."

"Ye remember when Brenna played for us?" she said, then lay down beside me.

"I do," I said, my voice catching as I thought of my sister.

"I saw my mother. She called to me… When she did, I heard me name."

"Pix… What is your name?"

"'Tis Aife… I be Aife. Can ye believe that? I am Aife. Now ye will know what to call me in the next life," she said, then grew silent. After a long time, she whispered, "I will sleep now, Strawberry Queen."

"Yes," I whispered. "Me too."

"I will find ye in the next life if ye will have me."

"You'd better be mad, or I won't know you," I said with a soft laugh.

"No better way to be."

"I love you," I whispered to her.

"I love ye too," she said, then grew still and silent.

Just before the world went dark, I heard waves breaking on a shore. I felt the sunlight on my face and smelled the salty air of the Wash.

"*Come, Boudica,*" Gaheris whispered. "*I've been waiting for you.*"

EPILOGUE

Sorcha speaks…

S word in one hand, dagger in the other, I tried to steady my stance as the rope bridge swung dangerously from side to side. I glanced down, seeing the raging ocean between the boards under my feet. One false step…

"You'll never win a battle that way, Princess," my opponent taunted me.

I looked up at Emer. She had pulled her curly black hair back into a knot behind her head. A simple sword in her hand, she smirked at me as she positioned her feet at the outer edges of the boards and joggled them back and forth, making the bridge shake.

"I hardly expect to be fighting my enemies while dangling over the sea," I retorted, more amused than annoyed.

"How do you know? There is no saying where the winds will blow you next. If you want to be worthy of that dagger in your hand, you'll learn how to use it in the place it was forged. Now, come at me—if you dare."

As she knew it would, Emer's goading had done the trick. I focused, quickly scanning the boards for their strong points—and noting the wider gaps and weaknesses—then rushed forward. Bounding from board to board with as light a step as possible, I made my way to my enemy.

Emer looked pleased but also taken off guard. She quickly raised her sword to block me, and the clash began. Well aware that going backward on the swinging bridge of death—as I had nicknamed it—would be virtually impossible, I fought vigorously, pushing Emer back.

"Ah, there is the firebrand we all know and love," Emer said with a laugh, retreating toward the second tower. We were almost there when a horn sounded. Emer paused, then turned to look.

The horn sounded again, and this time, I saw a crow fly toward the courtyard.

"Ship," she said, then grinned at me. "Wonder who that could be."

I felt a stirring in my heart, and my cheeks flushed red. Not wanting Emer to see, I shrugged. "Who cares? They are here to see Lady Niamh or Cien anyway. Let's continue."

Emer laughed. "You can't fool me, Firebrand. Come on. Let's go see."

I huffed a sigh, annoyed that she could see through me so well, then we made our way back across the bridge to the fortress.

By the time we finally wound our way across the bridges and towers of Dunscaith, the ship's occupants had debarked. They made their way down the dock to meet with Niamh, Lady of Skye. A dense fog occluded my view, but then the sun shone through just enough to reveal…

"Artur!" I called.

Rushing ahead, I made my way down the steps toward the party. I crossed the courtyard where the other warrior maidens were practicing drills with spears. Another group was working at archery. As I hurried to meet Artur, I spotted the other figure behind him.

"Artur *and* King Cináed of the Carnonacea," Emer said in sing-song. "Wonder who he's here to see."

"Lady Niamh, of course," I retorted, although my heart beat harder. "Artur!"

After bowing to Lady Niamh, I waved to my brother,

who hurried to me.

Artur lifted me off my feet, pulling me into a hug. "Ah, Sister," he said, holding me. "How glad I am to see you."

"And you. It's been far too long," I agreed.

Artur set me down.

I searched his face. "All well?"

"Well enough. Come," he said, then lowered his voice. "He has talked of nothing but you the entire voyage. Try to pretend you aren't in love with him. It will unnerve him, so you have the advantage."

"Artur," I said, punching his shoulder playfully.

"Ouch. Where is Olwen?"

"She went with the priestesses to the sea cave. She will be back soon."

"Artur!" a voice called.

Vian emerged from the castle, a bundle of scrolls tucked under her arm.

Since we'd arrived, Lady Niamh and Vian had grown very close, the Lady of Skye quickly realizing how brilliant our dear friend was. Lynet's dagger may have gained us entry to the island, but since then, we had all found a way to be of use to Niamh, earning our places here; Olwen with the priestesses, Vian serving the lady, Artur providing counsel to the king, and me training in the ancient ways of Scáthach.

I was determined to be a warrior maiden of the Isle

of Skye.

But more than that found me.

I just wasn't sure if I was ready to accept all the rest yet.

Joining Lady Niamh and King Cináed, I turned to the king. "King Cináed," I said, inclining my head to him and trying not to be taken in at once by his handsome features. But how could I resist those sky-blue eyes and wavy black hair? Fierce as he may be, there was softness underneath that rough exterior. On Beltane two years ago, I had pried it out of him. Since then, nothing had been the same between us.

"Princess Sorcha," he replied politely.

Niamh laughed lightly, seemingly amused at our formality, then gestured to the king. "My king, please, come inside."

As we passed Emer, she bowed to Cináed.

"Maiden," he said politely.

When she stood again, she winked at me.

I rolled my eyes at her.

We entered the ancient keep, adjourning to the small banquet room. Swords, shields, spears, and daggers decorated the place. Warriors had come to Skye to learn the ancient arts for as long as anyone could remember. But what many did not know was that deep magic dwelled here, magic that had called to Olwen since our first day on the island.

Niamh, Cináed, Artur, Vian, and I took our seats.

Servants poured us ales and set the table with fish, fruits, cheeses, and bread.

"King Cináed," Niamh began. "I trust your voyage here was without difficulty."

He nodded. "Indeed, we encountered no issues. I wanted to see you before the passage to Skye becomes too difficult."

"You are always welcome here," Niamh told him.

"Were it not for the crows, we could not find our way at all," Artur said, referring to the birds who served as guides through the mist, leading travelers to Skye.

Skye was not called the Isle of Mists for nothing. The ancient citadel was shrouded in an unearthly bank of fog that rarely lifted. Only those with ties to the island, or those who made their way here by the will of the gods, could find the path.

We had Queen Cartimandua to thank for helping us find our way here the first time. True to her word, the Brigantes queen had sent us by ship to Skye five years earlier. Without her help, we never would have found our way.

Cartimandua had been faithful to her promise to Mother.

She had gotten us to safety and didn't betray us afterward.

No one had come looking for us here.

"That is the way of things," Niamh said simply. "Come, let us eat and talk of simple things before you tell us the hard news you are not yet ready to say."

She gestured to the meal placed before us.

I sipped my wine and listened as Cináed and Artur shared a comical encounter with a Carnonache chieftain who'd gone mad and thought he was a kelpie. The druids had little luck capturing the poor man, so Artur and Cináed had devised a trap for the chieftain who'd sent them on a chase that lasted a night and day.

They had just reached the end of their tale when Cien and Olwen arrived.

Olwen gasped when she saw Artur, then rushed to him, just as I had done.

Cináed rose when the pair entered.

The king bowed to Cien. When Olwen and Artur parted, he greeted my sister as well. "Priestess Olwen, I greet you in Epona's name," he told her, raising his hands to his forehead in a gesture of respect.

Olwen bowed to him.

Both Cien's and Olwen's faces were marked with woad. The sea cave, a sacred space on the island, was one of many holy sites around Skye.

While there was no more Mona, the sacred island destroyed after the rebellion, the old gods still lived on Skye.

The night continued with pleasant conversation, but eventually, Niamh prodded the king.

"Now, tell me why you have come," Nimah told the king.

"The eagle flies north. The other Caledonian tribes would join together to ensure the Romans do not pass Brigantia's lands."

Niamh nodded slowly. "They have asked for your help."

Cináed nodded.

"Would you have Cien read the signs, or do you ask my opinion?" Niamh asked him, lifting her mug of ale to hide her smirk.

The Lady of Skye was good at making people answer their own questions. She was able to make you hear the answer in your own heart. That was why her words always rang true. All thought her wise, including me, but I had discovered her trick.

"I seek your counsel, lady," Cináed replied.

"Hmm," she mused. "You have given this much thought, I think. What would you do, Cináed?"

"Those seated at this table have all shared what they have seen, what Roman friendship cost them. While it has served Cartimandua, we can see the price she has paid as the Romans crawl about her country. We will not have that in the north."

"No."

"Rome is overstretched. The wound Queen Boudica dealt them has never healed. While there is none left to resist them in the south, in the north, we remain strong. It is my belief that if we join with the other Caledonian tribes and push back, we can remain free of Rome's yoke," Cináed said.

"Then it must be so. What do you think, Artur?"

"My parents bargained for freedom and lost. I would not advise those I care about bargain again."

Niamh turned to Cien. "You were in the caves today. Any message from the gods?"

Cien gestured to Olwen. "It is to Olwen that they spoke."

"Priestess? Did they speak to you of Rome?" Niamh asked Olwen.

My sister shook her head.

"Of what did they speak?" the lady asked.

Olwen paused, then looked at me. She smiled lightly.

My brow furrowed. "Of me?"

Olwen nodded.

"Hmm," Niamh mused once more, then turned back to the king. "The answer seems plain enough, I think."

"We will join with the others and resist," the king said.

"You will," Niamh agreed. "Very well, Cináed. Rest here tonight and depart in the morning. I suspect we will not see you again until spring. It is a very long time to go without the presence of the ones we hold dear. I will have my people prepare rooms for you and Artur. But now, Vian, Cien, and I have matters to discuss. I will leave you. Retire whenever you are ready," she told the king, then departed, taking the others with her.

"Olwen," Artur said, reaching for my sister's hand, "are you well?"

Olwen nodded, then gestured for Artur to come with her, the pair leaving the hall.

Cináed looked at me. "We are left to our own devices, Princess."

"Want to get into some mischief?"

"Always."

"Then, follow me," I told him, gesturing for the king to come with me.

Leading Cináed, we wound our way up a narrow passage, circling higher and higher until we reached the top of the first tower of Dunscaith. We then crossed the bridge to the second tower and onward to the rope bridge leading to the ruins of the third tower.

"Have you brought me up here to kill me, Sorcha?" he asked with a laugh.

"No, but watch your step all the same. The fifth, seventh, and eleventh boards are weak."

"And how have you learned that?"

"The hard way. My wrist is only now healed. It is a long fall."

"Sorcha," he said, aghast. "You fell? From here?"

I merely laughed. "I rolled, more like. Doesn't hurt much anymore."

The king merely laughed.

Moving carefully, both of us giggling when the bridge swayed, we made our way to the final tower. Crawling up the stairs of the ruin, we reached the top. Finally, we had a view above the bank of fog that occluded the island. Overhead, bright stars shone silver on a deep blue sky.

"Ah," Cináed breathed, looking up. "Beautiful."

"It is the only place on this island where you can see the stars... almost," I said, thinking of the sacred well of stars, but I had no business speaking of the holy place.

Standing there, we gazed overhead, watching stars fall across the skyline. The beauty of it was breathtaking.

When I turned to Cináed, expecting to find him looking upward, I found him staring at me.

"Cináed?"

"Come back with me, Sorcha. Come back with me and be my bride."

"I..." I began, my heart fluttering at the thought. In truth, the idea of spending another winter on Skye without him made something within me ache. "But I am training to be a warrior maiden of Skye."

"I know. Instead, I ask you to be the queen of the Carnonacae," he asked, taking my hand. "If you want to say no," he said, then paused, mastering the quiver in his voice, "I will understand. Rome is not gone. And they are coming for the north. The war you fled, the war your mother died for, isn't over. I can understand if you don't want to face such a world again, but, Sorcha, I cannot imagine my future without you."

Moved by forces I didn't understand, I grabbed the king and kissed him hard.

When I finally let go, Cináed chuckled and then touched my chin. "Shall I take that as a yes, Firebrand?"

"Is there another way to take it?"

He chuckled. "Then you'll leave with me in the morning?"

"I need to speak to Olwen but..." I said, then paused, remembering the look she had given me. "Olwen already knows."

"Then come, Sorcha, Princess of the Greater Iceni, the firebrand who has seared her name on my heart. Let's go and make ready."

"For?"

"A life of love, happiness, and death to Rome."

"That sounds like the perfect life for me."

"Sorcha...

"Sorcha...

"Queen of the Carnonacae...

"Queen of fire...

"Long may you reign."

BEFORE BOUDICA CAME TO POWER, the first recorded queen in ancient England reigned. Journey back to the days before the second Roman invasion and dive into the gripping saga of Queen Cartimandua of the Brigantes in *The Blackthorn Queen*.

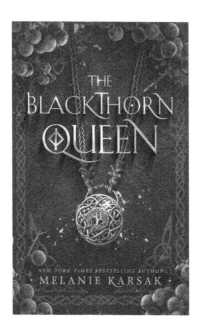

THANK YOU

With special thanks to Becky Stephens and Lindsay Galloway for their work on this series

Thank you to Gladys Gonzales Atwell for her support

Thank you to the Damonza team of the lovely covers

Thank you to Julie Cornell, a.k.a. MommaWolf, for naming Ember

Thank you to the members of my Facebook group, the Clockpunk Reading Room, for all of their support

Thank you to the MoonTree Readers crew and Jesikah Sundin, Alisha Klapheke, Elle Madison, and Robin D. Mahle for their support

Thank you to my ARC team for their hard work on this series

And, as always, thank you for my family for their tireless support

GET YOUR BONUS BOOK

Thank you for reading *The Celtic Rebels Series*. As a special thank you, I invite you to join my newsletter and receive *The Celtic Rebels Series Bonus Scenes and Shorts* collection for FREE.

Find me on Bookfunnel to get your bonus book here: https://BookHip.com/JJTVGTC

ABOUT THE AUTHOR

New York Times and *USA Today* bestselling author Melanie Karsak is the author of *The Celtic Blood Series, The Road to Valhalla Series, The Celtic Rebels Series, Steampunk Red Riding Hood, Steampunk Fairy Tales* and many more works of fiction. The author currently lives in Florida with her husband and two children.

amazon.com / author / melaniekarsak
facebook.com / authormelaniekarsak
instagram.com / karsakmelanie
pinterest.com / melaniekarsak
bookbub.com / authors / melanie-karsak
youtube.com / @authormelaniekarsak

ALSO BY MELANIE KARSAK

Shield-Maiden: Gambit of Blood

Shield-Maiden: Gambit of Shadows

Shield-Maiden: Gambit of Swords

THE HARVESTING SERIES:

The Harvesting

Midway

The Shadow Aspect

Witch Wood

The Torn World

STEAMPUNK FAIRY TALES:

Curiouser and Curiouser: Steampunk Alice in Wonderland

Ice and Embers: Steampunk Snow Queen

Beauty and Beastly: Steampunk Beauty and the Beast

Golden Braids and Dragon Blades: Steampunk Rapunzel

STEAMPUNK RED RIDING HOOD:

Wolves and Daggers

Alphas and Airships

Peppermint and Pentacles

Bitches and Brawlers

Howls and Hallows

Lycans and Legends

THE AIRSHIP RACING CHRONICLES:

Chasing the Star Garden

Chasing the Green Fairy

Chasing Christmas Past

THE CHANCELLOR FAIRY TALES:

The Glass Mermaid

The Cupcake Witch

The Fairy Godfather

The Vintage Medium

The Book Witch

Find these books and more on Amazon!

YOU MAY ALSO LIKE

Ready to dive into new worlds? I invite you to ancient Scotland to meet Gruoch, a follower of the dark Celtic goddesses, who is best remembered by the moniker Lady Macbeth. Then, let's meet Hervor, a legendary shield-maiden in ancient Scandinavia. Like the *Celtic Rebels* series, these series dive into mystical, pre-Christian worlds while following the lives of a strong, heroic women.

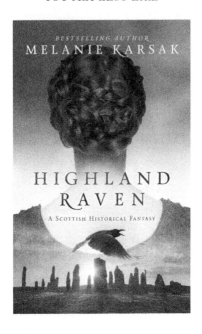

DESTINED TO BECOME QUEEN OF SCOTLAND.
BOUND BY BLOOD TO THE CELTIC GODS.

Scotland, 1026

Descendant of the line of MacAlpin, Gruoch should have been born into a life of ease. But fate is fickle. Her father's untimely death, rumored to have been plotted by King Malcolm, leaves her future uncertain and stained by the prophecy that she will avenge her family line.

Escaping to one of the last strongholds of the old Celtic

gods, Gruoch becomes an adept in arcane craft. Her encounters with the otherworld, however, suggest that magic runs stronger in Scotland than she ever imagined.

Haunted by dreams of a raven-haired man she's never met, Gruoch soon feels her fate is not her own. She is duty-bound to wed a powerful lord, if not the Prince himself; however, she's not sure she can stop her heart when she meets Banquo, a gallant highlander and druid.

Fans of **Outlander** and the **Mists of Avalon** will relish this sweeping Scottish Historical Fantasy that tells the tale of Gruoch, a woman struggling to escape her fate without blood on her hands. Dive into this thrilling historical scottish fantasy romance by *New York Times* best-selling author Melanie Karsak.

READ THE CELTIC BLOOD SERIES ON AMAZON

In addition to my **Celtic Blood** series, you will also enjoy my **Road to Valhalla** series, which chronicles the life of the shield-maiden Hervor:

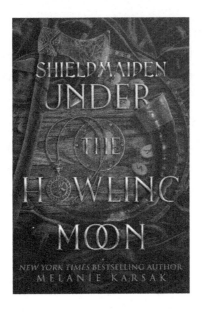

Chosen by Odin. Destined for Valhalla.

IN MY DREAMS, ODIN WHISPERS TO ME.
HE TELLS ME I'M DESTINED TO WIELD A LEGENDARY SWORD.
HE TELLS ME MY ROAD WILL BRING ME TO VALHALLA.

But when I wake, I'm only Hervor. Fatherless. Unloved. Unwanted. Jarl Bjartmar, my grandfather, calls me cursed. My mother, her memories stolen by the gods, has forgotten me. Everyone tells me I should have been left to the wolves, but no one will tell me why.

None but Eydis, a thrall with völva magic, believes I'm

meant for a greater destiny. Yet who can believe a devotee of Loki?

When the king and his son arrive for the holy blót, the runes begin to fall in my favor. A way forward may lie in the handsome Viking set on winning my heart, but only if I unravel the mystery hanging over me first.

Fans of *Vikings, The Last Kingdom,* and *The Mists of Avalon* will relish *Shield Maiden: Under the Howling Moon.* This sweeping Viking Historical Fantasy retells the Norse *Hervarar Saga,* depicting the life of the shield-maiden Hervor, the inspiration for J. R. R. Tolkien's Éowyn.

READ THE ROAD TO VALHALLA SERIES ON AMAZON